ILKA CHASE, author of 1942's unchallenged best seller, *Past Imperfect*, gives her fictional characters the same penetrating, witty once-over to which she subjected her acquaintances in her autobiography. Gay, clever, and honest, IN BED WE CRY is filled with refreshing observations and peopled with characters as glamorous and unpredictable as the cosmetic industry about which they revolve. Miss Chase's trenchant insight into what makes people tick and her ability to give them the tangible quality of a mink coat or a pink marble bathroom will attract readers to her fiction as irresistibly as they did to her non-fiction.

Devon Elliott was a success by all standards—professionally, socially and personally. She pushed her beauty business from a struggling start in a Greenwich Village loft into a fabulously profitable enterprise with a place in the cosmetic sun beside Arden and Rubinstein. She conducted an equally successful personal life with a rare combination of realism and affection, never able to completely divorce it from business. Jasper, her lover, was retained as her business manager when their affair ran cold, because he was competent. Tim, her husband, a brilliant scientist, was wooed from serious research to take over the management of her laboratories.

Though Tim never more than tolerated his part in their huge income and success, their marriage was happy and congenial. Under the impact of war, however, his growing detachment from the business became evident to Devon, and with a chill she saw it penetrate their personal life. When all her ingenuity failed to divert his driving desire to return to true research, she sought compensation—through a new lover and a new project for Devonshire House.

IN BED WE CRY is filled with the undercurrents of a world at war, but its primary concern is with the froth, which it dispels gaily, warmly, and with a slight touch of malice.

IN BED WE CRY

BOOKS BY *Ilka Chase*

IN BED WE CRY · PAST IMPERFECT

Ilka Chase

IN BED WE CRY

GARDEN CITY, N.Y.   1944

DOUBLEDAY, DORAN & COMPANY, INC.

To

Ken McCormick

Demon editor and belligerent believer
that fictional characters got rights, see,
same as anybody else—
this book is dedicated
with profound affection

In bed we laugh, in bed we cry;
And, born in bed, in bed we die.
The near approach a bed may show
Of human bliss to human woe.

ISAAC DE BENSERADE—1612–1691.

IN BED WE CRY

PART ONE

It was a bitter january evening in the year of disgrace, 1941. The storm that had risen two days before in eastern Montana swept across the spreading plains of North Dakota and Minnesota, roared and racketed over the Great Lakes, whipping them to foaming fury, howled its way to the coast of Maine, and doubled back on its tracks through northern New York, sending wild, sleet-ridden tatters down the Hudson Valley to veer across the city, deluging the bucolic stretches of the Bronx and lashing unmercifully the disconsolate reaches of Manhattan's most Central Park. Beating with furious bluster down a drenched and cowed Fifth Avenue, it spent itself at last against the Chinese green door of that exquisite and flourishing cosmetic firm, Devonshire House, Incorporated.

It lacked a few minutes to six, and Fred the doorman, a mountainous figure enveloped in dripping rubber, having just dispatched a car bearing one of the more fragile Devonshire clients, was pondering the force of feminine vanity that would drive a woman forth on such a night, when the green door opened again. Again a whiff of perfumed air ballooned like thin silk into the outer darkness, and Fred moved bulkily to extend his umbrella over the third successive batch of streamlined minks emerging into the storm. The unwieldy old umbrella worked overtime. Fred never remembered any Devonshire patron owning one. They used limousines instead.

As the mink-bearer scuttled beside him across the pavement to her waiting Cadillac, Fred glanced at the freshly serviced face under the swooping felt brim. He could see only the curve of the cheek, but it was Mrs. Carl Leland Potter, all right, and that babe was nudging fifty if a day and had been heard coyly to admit to thirty-eight. You certainly had to hand it to the Devonshire House treatments; the old gal looked pretty good, though according to Peters, her chauffeur and Fred's buddy, she had had a job done on her face in Europe far more drastic than Devonshire's creams and electric currents.

Fred recalled this nugget as he convoyed his brig across the pavement. He winked at Peters with his off eye, and saw her snugly berthed in the gray plush interior of the Cadillac. "Good night, Mrs. Potter. I guess tonight's making up to us for all the good weather we've been having so far."

"I guess you're right, Fred. Good night. Oh, here." Mrs. Potter dove into the depths of her brown suède bag and surfaced with a quarter. As she handed it to him, she reminded Fred of a seal's flipper, brown bag, brown gloves, brown furry arm. "Thank you very much, madam. Good night."

He closed the door of the car. On the posts and in the rippling reflections in the wet black pavements, the traffic lights switched from red to green; the stalled cars with rivulets of rain streaking over their sleek surfaces moved forward, their windshield wipers whispering frantically. As he watched the Cadillac slip into line, Fred became aware of the shouted invectives of a couple of hack drivers; there was a blast from the cop's whistle, a clot of cars broke and separated, and Devon Elliott's long black Lincoln Continental nosed up to the curb. The chauffeur slid along the seat and lowered the window. "Greetings, chum," he remarked to Fred, who peered in at him. "How's chances for the boss's coming out in the next hour and a half?"

Fred liked Owens all right, but he also envied him a little; there *he* was, rooted to his spot of pavement in front of the door all day, whereas Owens sashayed around town, drove out to the country, and frequently helped at the house when there were parties. It made for a richer life. Fred's greeting in consequence was a little cool. "What's it to you?" he asked.

"It's to me that I got a ticket for the fights, see, and I'd like to get there before the decision."

Fred couldn't resist a minor baiting. "How do you know you'll get off tonight? Like as not they'll go to the opera or something." But Owens was assured. "Not a chanct—the boss says so. 'If you want to make any plans for tonight, Owens,' she says, 'we won't be wantin' you after you pick us up at the salon.'"

Fred inquired whether their employer had said just when she'd be leaving.

"I ain't in her confidence, pal," replied the chauffeur. "I'm a menial, same as you. Her Majesty issues them blanket orders—'Be at the shop at six, Owens,'—but that don't mean she's going to leave then. I can damn well wear out my tail from six this evening till six in the morning if Her Ladyship don't get the steam up."

Owens' tone was more affable than his words. Devon Elliott was a not inconsiderate employer, and she paid well, but her capacity for work was enormous, and it never occurred to her that others did not share her enthusiasm. The sullen looks which her ardor sometimes evoked in members of her staff, she put down to stomach trouble. She herself had the digestion of a horse, but for reasons which no one had ever fathomed, she assumed that most people suffered from ulcers. "Poor Minerva," she would remark to her husband, referring to the manager of the salon, "she looked very glum this evening. I'm afraid it's her old trouble, unreliable stomach." It was not so much that Minerva's stomach was unreliable as that it was empty. Having lunched on broth and a salad of restrained calories at noon, by eight P.M. the pangs of famine would have assailed her, but often as not her boss would still be wrestling happily with new formulas, plans for a salon in a Midwestern city, or a scheme along the line of the Beauty Mill.

The Beauty Mill had been suggested to Miss Elliott by the editor of *Vogue*. It had occurred to the editor that, photographically, it would make a compelling feature, aesthetic nudity skillfully combined with a wholesome health routine. The client went through the green door at ten A.M., and she emerged at five, feeling like a new man. Furthermore, her chances of snaring him were good, for she had experienced the Works: oil treatment, hair styling, permanent, manicure, body massage, exercise, facial, high colonic, herb luncheon, and mental life; the Viennese psychiatrist on "The Submissive Approach to Feminine Allure." The Beauty Mill reaped rich rewards, and Miss Elliott daily blessed the journalistic mind which had suggested it.

Another plan not divorced from the profit motif was, it so happened, at the very moment occupying the attention of one of the most successful businesswomen in America, a woman whom the Mesdames Arden and Rubinstein would cheerfully have seen swinging from the nearest yardarm.

In her office on the seventh floor of Devonshire House, Devon Elliott sat in conference with Jasper Doolittle, vice president and general manager of the business; Tim Wainwright, her husband who was also the head of her laboratory; and Bruce Moreley of the advertising firm of Moreley, Todd & Delaney.

Conference was perhaps a formal word for their gatherings, which were frequently rowdy, vituperative, and totally relaxed, with, in this instance, vituperation leading by a length as the argument thundered on.

"Well, damn it all, Tim," Devon was saying, and her sea-colored eyes with their dark tangled lashes flashed angrily, "why isn't a line of inexpensive preparations advertised on the air a good idea? You just don't want to go to the trouble it might entail in the laboratory, that's all."

Her husband was sitting on a round leather poof in front of the fire, and Devon sat at his feet, her long, slender legs stretched out in front of her, her shoes off, as he massaged her neck. She had twisted under his hands the better to face him with her accusation, and he gave her neck a firm but expert wrench as he twisted her back again. "That isn't true, and you know it," he said shortly. "I've never shirked my work, but there are eight or ten reasons why I think this is a bum plan, and one of them, as Jasper will tell you, is your present contracts." Tim had a lean intelligent face, with vigorous slanting eyebrows that went off at tangents at the outer corners, and brown hair that stood up in a belligerent crew cut. Though they argued mightily, Devon considered him the most attractive human being she had ever met. She was also devoted to Jasper, who was tall, stooped, and in his early fifties. She sometimes referred to him as Gray Eminence, and the name suited him. He had gray hair, gray eyes, and gray clothes, and a great deal of gray matter in his skull. Her devotion was momentarily in abeyance, however, as he seemed to be siding with Tim. It was not a deliberate alliance, but unfortunately the facts sustained her husband's argument.

"It's true, Devon," Jasper said mildly. "We have those contracts with all our current buyers, the specialty shops all over the country as well as the drugstores. You know perfectly well we can't undersell them."

"But that's just the point," she said impatiently. "We wouldn't be underselling them on the lines they now carry. The cheap preparations that Moreley and I are talking about would be a whole new business, but you and Tim can't seem to grasp that simple fundamental."

Jasper and Tim looked at each other over Devon's head, and Tim shrugged. She was right, though the proposed plan might have struck a disinterested observer as a shade on the sharp side. Forthright in her personal relationships, Devon was rarely troubled by scruples in her business dealings. Let a scruple raise its head, she could easily stare it out of countenance; certainly, in this particular instance, was the scheme not charitable in its very essence? The advantages of Devonshire House preparations brought to women of the lower income brackets.

Moreley voiced her thoughts. "I consider Miss Elliott's idea is splendid, weally wevolutionawy," he cried, his *r*'s more than ever scrambled in his enthusiasm.

It is not only love and hate that are akin; dislike and expediency may also go hand in hand, and Devon frequently found to her annoyance that Moreley was her strongest ally. Physically she deemed him distasteful, and indeed he was an unlikely-looking product to have been spewed forth by the brash world of advertising. Soft and pudgy and in his forties, he had fat little hands which he waved like fins, and pale protruding eyes that reminded Devon of oysters, but he had an unfailing instinct for copy to catch the feminine imagination, and his advertisements were potent magnets for drawing cash from the pockets of women from sixteen to the final gasp. It irked him to be thwarted by the Grim Reaper, whom he considered a usurper of trade, and he had once had an idea for a special line of cosmetics to be worked out in collaboration with the Undertakers' Association. "When you gaze for the last time upon your loved ones, let it be the glow of life you will remember through the years." This macabre little suggestion had been hooted down by Devon and Jasper, but Moreley was a die-hard, and hope still fluttered in his breast.

He was at present opening a large black portfolio. "I have here some schemes for tie-ups between our magazine advertising and our pwojected wadio pwogwam which are vewy intewesting and forceful." Jasper said nothing, but Moreley suspected antagonism, or at least apathy, towards his pet idea. "I don't think, Mr. Doolittle, you wealize the scope of wadio," he said urgently.

"I realize its scope, Moreley; I'm just wondering if at this time we ought to appropriate that much money."

"Well, I don't see," said Devon, "that radio advertising must necessarily be so fabulously expensive. It's proportionate, after all— the number of sales you make as against your outlay." She was almost as averse to the spending of large sums of money as Queen Elizabeth had been, but when convinced, as in this instance, that the chances for large returns were weighted in her favor, she was a cool-headed gambler, not afraid to back her own judgment against opposition from Tim and Jasper; for Tim had again entered the lists.

"There's another obstacle, madam, that seems to leave you untouched, but there's quite a war on in Europe. It's going to be tougher and tougher to get supplies from over there, and before very long they'll be cracking down on the home product too, don't kid yourself."

"Nonsense, Tim, you're always harping on that. Even if you're right and we're in the war eventually, essential businesses will still have to continue."

Tim hooted derisively. "There's realistic thinking for you, by God: steel, oil, and lipsticks."

"And why not?" she demanded. "The cosmetic industry employs thousands and thousands of people, and besides they're always talking about how vital it is to keep up the birth rate in wartime. Well, believe me, it would drop like a plummet if all the women in the country had to go around with shiny noses and pale lips and wrinkled old hides."

"They seem to have done all right in the old days," Tim observed tartly, "before they ever heard of pore cream and turtles' hormones."

"They did not," shouted his wife. "In the old days every country in the world had little teeny populations, and that's why; the women were such sights."

Jasper in his long-accustomed role of mediator cleared his throat judicially. "They also had a high mortality rate, but my reluctance to have us take on a radio program, which you may recall we were talking about, is only partially due to a possible shortage of supplies, but Tim's got something there; not that I think the war is on our doorstep the way you do, Tim, though things are likely to get tougher. My point is, is radio ever our dish? We do a mass business, but it's a class mass business, so to speak. I don't know that it would be worth our while to try to win the Lady Esther and the Rinso users even if we could."

Devon's was a simple mind. "Why not? They have money, haven't they?"

"Have they enough to reimburse us?" asked Jasper. "Don't forget, radio time comes high."

"But think of the wuwal distwicts we would weach," put in Moreley, "the farmers' wives, the seamstwesses in little villages. With the Devonshire House name we can do a vast mail-order business in an inexpensive line."

"Maybe," put in Tim. "But you start giving them preparations at a quarter the price they've been paying, and the customers are going to wonder if you haven't been getting away with murder all these years."

If Moreley could have hurled it, Tim would have been felled by his glance. "I don't see why," Devon argued. "It's just as if I owned the Colony Restaurant and Childs'. You don't expect the Colony cachet at Childs' rates, even if you know that they both pay the same price for the raw food in the wholesale market. Surroundings count for something."

"You mean those hats?" asked Jasper. He was not a Colony man, and it galled him when Devon occasionally jockeyed him into taking her there for lunch.

"I was thinking primarily of the chef, Mr. Doolittle," she replied coldly. "Actually, we'd be going the restaurants one better, as in our case both the rich and the poor clientele would have the same chef."

"I'm not much on parables," said Tim, "but I gather I'm to take the bow."

"I gather so, old boy," said Jasper. "You're the head of the laboratory. You'd be turning out the stuff."

"Radio advertising would work like a charm," said Devon briskly. "And even if the mass women are a little hesitant at first about sending for the preparations, either because they think they're expensive or they're afraid they're too grand, they'll certainly be willing to spend ten cents for the booklet."

This pamphlet, "Beauty in Your Own Hands," was Moreley's treasure. He had already made up a dummy, firm in his belief that Devon would win her argument for the inexpensive line, and the booklet, illustrated in color, described its glories, each word a gem set with loving care. Devon had seen it and believed its impact would be irresistible. "And once they read it," she continued enthusiastically, "they'll have to have the products. Just think of the vistas it opens up! We'll become a sort of super Sears, Roebuck, beauty purveyors to even the most lowly." Her eyes shone with missionary zeal, and a halo seemed to settle about her artificially burnished head.

Tim, still engaged in his osteopathic endeavors, gave her a sharp poke in the shoulder blades. "Isn't this concern for the lower classes fairly recent, St. Cecilia?"

"No, it's not, it's absolutely sincere. You'll see. In the metropolitan centers we'll be a triple threat: the booklet, the products, and our operators too. It's only natural that when the rural women come to town they'll want a few treatments too."

"You've got it all doped out, haven't you?" Tim spoke with lazy amusement. "They may need fertilizer and gingham aprons or a barrel of flour far more, but, by golly, the money's going to go for cosmetics or you'll know the reason why."

Devon considered the remark irrelevant. "I presume they have the wits to supply themselves with the fundamentals," she said shortly. "And it's not my business to roam the Kansas plains to check up on them."

Jasper glanced at Tim curiously. He was not sold on Devon's idea himself, but he wondered what was causing her husband's reaction. After all Tim was in this business too; why shouldn't he want to see it prosper? He said nothing, however, having learned over a period of years that little went on in the firm that did not eventually land on his doorstep.

Though acute, Devon's annoyance with Tim was never long-lived, and she turned to him now with a mocking grin. "If I could get any co-operation from you tycoons, I still think we could make a go of this. How about it, Comrade Stalin? Even if you don't like the idea, will you admit it may be feasible and never mind the social issues?"

But Tim was not to be won by blandishments. "No, Devon," he said, and his voice was unfriendly. "I don't like any part of the idea in the first place, and in the second place I think it's an unnecessary financial risk."

Devon felt as though a cold finger had touched her heart. Tim had been funny recently; there was an irritability in his manner he never used to have. She was about to speak when Moreley intervened, a stanch oar to her rescue. "I can't agwee, Mr. Wainwight," he cried. "I'm convinced the financial wisk is negligible and the idea sound."

Tim turned on him. "I don't wonder," he said shortly. "To begin with, it isn't your money, and furthermore, you've no idea of the laboratory work it would involve."

Moreley flushed. "Well, the money is scarcely a personal issue, Tim," remarked Jasper quietly, "and I imagine Moreley feels that with our established reputation and an enormous untapped consumer group, we stand a chance of cleaning up."

"Natuwally I do." Moreley had the air of a miffed pouter pigeon. Devon almost smiled, but she knew the value of the little man and did not want to offend him. Besides, she was worried by Tim's sharp discord and wished she knew what he was driving at.

"Naturally that's what he meant, Tim," she said. "Anyway, since when has work become such a stumbling block for you?"

Tim lost his temper. "It isn't the work. I've never been stumped by work, and you know it. It's this constant cooking up of a false market that I object to."

His wife's swift irritation matched his own. "That's outrageous. It isn't false, it's helpful. We're trying to serve a larger number of people. If you're so interested in the deserving poor and the laboring man, I should think you'd want them to have a few of life's necessities."

Tim guffawed. "A jar of extra-rich nourishing cream is certainly a Pennsylvania miner's most pressing need!"

"It might well be his wife's," retorted Devon. "And furthermore, she's the one who'd think so."

"Exactly." Moreley had received a sharp setback, but he was a doughty warrior, quick to re-enter the fray. "And it could be delivered to her at a pwice she could afford. Of course the customers would have to be conditioned to a diffewent packaging, something much simpler. Packaging is vewy costly."

"So is advertising," and Jasper rolled a bleak eye on the copy writer.

"We wouldn't be cooking up anything, Tim, or gypping the customers either." Devon felt her point was just. "What the buyer gets will be pure, but after all some ingredients do cost more than others. We couldn't afford to give the inexpensive line the really precious stuff."

Tim looked skeptical. "You mean the Rare Eastern Oils from the factory in East Canarsie?" This particular gibe was directed primarily at Moreley and that campaign in which he had splashed the national periodicals with bogus Persian miniatures of dark-eyed beauties garnering oils and unguents which were supposed to be the base of Devonshire House preparations. Moreley caught the implication, but he looked at Tim blandly. "I think you will find, Mr. Wainwright, that the figures showed an appweciable jump diwectly twaceable to our Owiental campaign." Devon couldn't resist a chuckle; that was one up for Moreley. Devonshire House, like its competitors, was successful because it satisfactorily supplied an enormous demand, but Tim was right in that it also created a demand where there wasn't one; wasn't, that is, until the wily merchandiser by the power of suggestion persuaded the customer that she couldn't possibly manage without the newly devised product.

Devon was peculiarly adept at thinking up things that women didn't know they desperately needed, but as soon as Moreley's copy pointed it out to them, they too were appalled by their lack and hurried to rectify it. Why shouldn't they? thought Devon. After all, nothing she sold was harmful; quite the contrary, and the customers were invariably pleased and she made money. What was wrong with that?

Her great strength lay in the fact that she never bluffed herself. About the cosmetic industry she was indeed candid to a degree that Moreley found distressing. He had been pained when he had once heard her observe to Jennie Moore, the well-known actress and her greatest friend, "Baby, you'll reach old age even using my face cream, but it will take you a longer time to get there, you'll be prettier when you do, and you'll have a hell of a good time on the way." Such talk gave Moreley the shivers, and he had to concentrate very hard to get back to that plane where creams and powders were soft yet impenetrable barriers against Time's onslaughts and no eye grew dimmer than at seventeen. Crepy throat afflicted him more tragically than it did its feminine victims. He preferred to think not only of Jennie but of all Elliott clients as perpetually youthful goddesses, walking testaments to the magic of Devonshire House preparations, in striking contrast to the withered devotees of the opposition. It was hard to maintain this trance with Devon noisily planting both feet on solid ground. He couldn't forget the day when, in white heat, he had tossed a copy of *Consumers' Union* on her desk. "It's outwageous," he had cried. "Even those Communists have to admit our ingwedients are pure, but they say we make two and three and four hundwed pewsent pwofit. They imply we mulct the public!"

Devon looked at him. "Of course we do, Moreley," she said cheerfully. "All cosmetic profit is based to large extent on public gullibility. That's why we're honor bound to give them the best of everything. They get about one quarter of what they pay for in solid goods; the rest is watered stock, but there's this to be said: it's watered with hope. They half believe that balderdash which is your copy, and their belief encourages them. What if it does come high? They get their money's worth in anticipation. Besides," she tapped the pamphlet on her desk, "this little sheet is printed for public consumption. Don't you think it's significant of what the public wants if, in spite of reading it, they continue to buy Devonshire House cosmetics? Why, they're so crazy about our kind of business that they even patronize Rubinstein and Arden." And she chuckled with delight to think by how much she led this profitable field.

Concentrating now on the radio program which she hoped might set her even farther ahead, Devon's thoughts turned again to her friend Jennie Moore. There would be the very name to insure a wide listening public. "Hey," she said, "I have a suggestion. Tim, even you may think this is a good idea. If we do decide on a program, what about starring Jennie? And Nicky maybe; Nicky should be perfect for that kind of thing. We could build up a terrific show and one that would be bound to draw business. How does it strike you?"

"Well," said Tim, "since you ask me, I would take it easy. I appreciate your loyalty to your friends, but if you're hell-bent on this I suggest that Moreley get in touch with some of those radio producing firms and have them line up a batch of actors. They may feel that your own special buddies don't have mass appeal."

"Tim's right, Devon," said Jasper. "You launch a cheap line, it may take cheap, or shall we say popular, talent to put it over. That'll be quite a switch, and you may not care for it. Don't forget that our stock in trade has always been taste, luxury, elegance."

"And service," she said dryly. "We do do some good, you know, gentlemen. Tim here is full of the common people, and he's right, the age of aristocracy is dying. Well, let's hop on the band wagon. After all, it doesn't much matter what class has the money—they still have faces, and I assume feminine beauty counts for something even among the proletariat."

"Twue," said Moreley, feeling strongly that here was a woman who recognized a fact when she saw one.

"About the program, I'm willing to consider anybody you like," Devon continued, "but you can't say that Jennie Moore hasn't got mass appeal. My God, she tours even more than Cornell, and look at the business she does all over the country. People know her, all right."

"Pwesupposing we have that kind of a pwogwam, I think we might well consider Miss Moore, Miss Elliott, but though I admire him twemendously myself, I feel Mr. Van Alston is pwehaps a little special for the masses." Nicky Van Alston was a brilliant young English revue artist, who three years before had made an overnight sensation on Broadway by his portrayal of a drab little postman who described, in a patter song, the contents, touching, humorous, and bromidic, of the letters he carried. His comedy was sly and considered; he amused Devon more than any man she had ever known, and she didn't propose to hear an unenthusiastic word against him.

"He can't be as special as all that, Moreley. After all, he's a big hit in pictures."

But Moreley had moral courage. "Only in chawacter parts, and not so many of those. Besides, Miss Elliott, one of my ideas was that you would appear on the pwogwam yourself. I had envisioned you on the air, telling the women of Amewica how to be beautiful."

"Me? Why, for heaven's sake, Moreley?" Devon was surprised and a little flattered. "Do you think they'd listen?"

"Why not?" Tim asked. "You're one of the best-known women in the country."

"Well, but I'm not an actress."

"You're better. You're an authority on beauty. Why are they interested in actresses, anyway? Because they think they're glamorous, successful creatures with dozens of lovers. They yearn to imitate them, but they don't know how to go about it. The actresses guard their beauty secrets jealously; but look at you—you're every woman's well-wisher."

Tim's voice was cold and ironic. Devon was at a loss to understand him and didn't know how to parry his sarcasm. "Well, but why not?" she asked helplessly. "That's my business."

"Candid girl, now we're getting someplace. Generosity is the best policy, folks. Here we have one of the few women in the world who is kind to her own sex."

Her bewilderment grew. The attack seemed so uncalled-for. "Look, what is this anyway? Quite aside from my business, there are plenty of women I like. Are you disappointed that I'm not a green-eyed monster?"

"On the contrary, my pearl, you are unique. Far from being jealous of other women's good looks, you thrive on them. You're a fairy godmother, and the airy reaches of the radio are all you need to work your magic. Civilization may be reeling, but here is the beauty business sounding the clarion call to American womanhood. Ladies, you've got the world by the tail. It's a sick, rotten world, but it's yours. Paint your faces, girls, paint them so bright that the boys won't notice the outer darkness. You'll be boosting morale, and we'll be making a tidy profit. Use our products and you will be beautiful. If you have soft hands, your husband will call you up from the office after three years of marriage, but why wear yourself out with housework? Fame and fortune await the fair of face. Chuck old Joe and get to Hollywood. You too can be divorced in the head-lines!"

There was something so hard and bitter and mocking in Tim's voice that the others were shocked into silence. Devon felt quite cold inside in a queer state of suspended apprehension.

She thought, *Dear God, what is happening to Tim? These crazy, mean, sarcastic moods, they're becoming worse and worse, and they're getting more frequent. Something is happening that I don't understand, and why must he behave this way now, in front of the others?*

Aloud she said in a voice she tried to make easy, "Well, Tim, I don't think we're such charlatans, but the radio is probably not a good idea for me personally, in any event. Whether a woman whose business is beauty should ever face her public is a ticklish question. They expect you to be Helen of Troy."

"If I may say so, Miss Elliott, I consider you wemarkably attwactive," said Moreley stiffly. Devon laughed.

"Loyal Moreley! It's my noble spirit shining through." She got to her feet and went to kneel on the couch so she could look at herself in the painted mirror that hung above it. "I've always hated my square jaw, but I remember my grandmother telling me when I was a child that I'd be glad of it someday. 'It'll hold your dewlaps up,' she used to say. 'Lot more practical than those namby-pamby oval faces.'" And she traced her jaw line with her finger.

Tim rose restlessly and crossed to Devon's desk where Moreley had laid his portfolio; he leafed indifferently through the sheets of sample layouts. Devon followed his reflection in the mirror. "That's one good thing about radio, though," she said lightly. "If you're coony about keeping your pictures out of the papers, you can spare the listeners quite a blow."

Jasper was apparently unaware of Tim's outburst. "We haven't bought the time yet," he observed mildly. "And we haven't heard from the boss whether he thinks the laboratory could supply an increased demand, if we are a riotous success."

Dear tactful Jasper, thought Devon, *here he comes, trotting with the oilcan.*

Tim's flare-up had spent itself; he shrugged his shoulders. "I'm sure I don't know," he said listlessly.

"You're not very co-operative, pet." Devon's tone was offhand, but the atmosphere was taut. Tim looked at her for the first time.

"I'm sorry, Devon," he said, "but I really don't. The number of pots of goo manufactured per day doesn't strike me as a particularly vital statistic."

Moreley rose. "Pwehaps we should let the matter west tempowa-wily until we see what sort of a pwogwam the pwoducers have in mind." He was willing to make that much concession to the crisis, but he didn't propose to have his dream permanently sidetracked because of somebody's temperament. He applied the thumbscrews ever so gently just by way of reminder: "I understand that Wubin-stein is considewing a most ambitious wadio campaign."

Jasper looked up. "I thought the fact that Arden withdrew hers convinced Rubinstein that radio was no medium for the cosmetic industry."

Moreley had worked his way through the sleeves of his overcoat; he now folded his yellow scarf neatly across his chest and pro-ceeded to button himself in. "Quite the contwawy, she feels that her competitor's lack of success clearly indicates that the field is hers. Good night, all." He gathered up his portfolio and was gone.

Devon turned wearily to Tim. "May I ask what the hell that little exhibition was for? And what do you mean, you don't know about the capacity of the laboratory?"

"It may surprise you, Devon, and you too, Jasper, but there are a lot of things about the factory recently that I don't know, and I don't know them because I don't give a damn!"

"Tim!" Devon was as shocked as if he had slapped her face.

"Look here, Tim," said Jasper quietly, "if you're jammed up about something, why don't you and Devon have a talk, and if there's anything wrong we might all get together afterwards."

Devon looked at him gratefully. "You know Mr. Wainwright," she said. "He's the moody type."

As he spoke Jasper had pulled his watch chain from his trouser pocket and swung it gently so that it spiraled around his finger, the bunch of keys at the end making a soft little clinking sound. It was an old habit and, watching him, though she was upset about Tim, an unconscious smile flitted across Devon's face. She probably saw that watch chain a dozen times a day and thought nothing of it, but this evening for no reason her memory played her a sudden trick.

She thought of a long-ago Christmas Eve, now buried under the snows of eleven winters. She was twenty-four and the business was newly launched. The fact that though small and personal it was already solid was due largely to Jasper, who had been with her since the beginning.

With a little help from him and a small legacy left her by her father she had been able to buy a modest private business whose owner wanted to retire. The owner was an ancient Frenchwoman, enormously fat with snow-white hair piled like a wedding cake on top of her head and the skin of a baby. She had two basic formulas, a mud pack and a lubricating oil, and she swore that the baby skin was the result of faithful application. After some experimenting, Devon decided that they were no doubt beneficial, but that the old girl's flower-petal epidermis was chiefly attributable to the grace of God and a one-hundred-per-cent-perfect alimentary system.

☆ ☆ ☆

In the beginning, to save money, Devon and the preparations were housed together in a ramshackle loft affair in Greenwich Village that was part kitchen, part laboratory, and part living quarters. She had got hold of a good chemist and continued to sell to the private clients of the French ancient, adding a lotion here and a powder there and branching out in a modest way by placing her products on consignment with neighborhood druggists and the Woman's Exchange. Deliveries were by bus and subway, and in the future she was to take more pride in her first truck than in her first Picasso.

All went well till the day when Jasper returned from a trip to Chicago with the triumphant announcement that Marshall Field's buyer would take the line and hoped Miss Elliott intended supplementing it. Miss Elliott turned quite pale, as she, the chemist, and an adolescent assistant with adenoids already had their hands full, and although the prospect of beautifying Chicago womanhood was a dazzling one, the prospect of raising the wherewithal with which to manufacture was a stumper. Since Jasper, without batting an eye, had assured his client that their production capacity was more than ample to supply every need, brisk and immediate financial aid was vital if the nascent enterprise was not to founder.

It was here that he had shown his mettle. Within six weeks backers had not only been rounded up but separated from their cash, a junior factory had been opened, and the first tentative and hopeful plans for a New York salon discussed. The great pioneers in the field of feminine beauty, Harriet Hubbard Ayer, Elizabeth Arden, Helena Rubinstein, were both her models and her spurs, and Devon, a youthful opportunist with imagination and unbounded energy, had, with Jasper's co-operation, cultivated that field so assiduously that in the last three years the volume of her business far outstripped them.

In the beginning the relationship between Miss Elliott and Mr. Doolittle had been on a purely commercial basis and she almost never saw him out of the office.

Devon had her beaux—not many, for not many wanted this strange girl who was continually experimenting with some new-fangled diet to see what it would do to her skin, who preferred spending her nights dabbling in laboratories, and her days discussing outlets for her baby wholesale trade, to indulging in normal activities like dancing and football games. Men liked her, but they were leery of her. She was fun, but not much good at listening to their plans and ambitions, being too occupied with her own. Also she was making more money at twenty-five than they were likely to be earning at thirty-five, and while not exactly conceited, she was articulate about her achievements. But though she was not a gingham girl, no bucolic youth would ever spend long, inarticulate evenings sitting with her on the kitchen steps; she was young, attractive, and far from frosty in her reactions. The results were normal; men frequently made advances to which she frequently succumbed with grace and good humor. These affairs were as a rule short-lived; either she was determined to spur her young men on to heights they had no desire to attain and her proddings fatigued them, or she grew absent-minded and went off, leaving them high and dry while she joined battle with some business problem. At least she always told herself firmly that it was business, and in a sense this was true, for after all Jasper was business, but her concern for Jasper was bedecked with more bows and pink bouquets than is customary in a strictly business relationship. She knew she disturbed him, and the knowledge made her joyful; it was like champagne bubbles bursting softly in her heart with a delightful tickle. It was a charming sensation, but it didn't seem to progress.

Jasper was close to her, but he said little, for he was a grave man with a motherly wife who drank a good deal and two small sons, and they all lived in Nutley, New Jersey. But though Devon was stymied by his silence, he was urgently aware of this thin coltish girl, who worked longer hours than any man he had ever known, and who was so busy studying the science of cosmetics that her mouth was innocent of lipstick and her nose often shiny. Their relationship was satisfactory as far as it went, but the distance was short. In musing about Jasper she knew she was on his mind, but was it love or lust? *I suspect the beast in him is a splendid creature,* she thought, *but I pine for true love too.* She pined for quite a time, and Jasper was not enlightening, yet in a curious way he sustained her. She was such an integral part of him that he could afford to wait; being a gourmet in such matters, he savored anticipation almost as much as fulfillment. Also anticipation was less riddled with pitfalls.

Devon suspected that he was not unaware of her affairs, but they caused him little concern. He was like a man leisurely making his way through undergrowth, pushing it aside automatically while he kept his eyes on a distant goal. It sometimes disconcerted her that her young men were nothing to him, not even obstructions. But at last, when Jasper wanted it that way, it happened. Why then, why not sooner or later, she never knew, but this evening, eleven years afterwards, staring at the swinging watch chain, she remembered the night he had reached his goal.

They had been going over the books alone in her little office; that was when they still had the place on Fiftieth Street. Even since she was a child, Devon could understand figures, and they were meat and drink to Jasper, but that night he seemed to have lost his appetite, at least for his habitual diet. He had been a hungry man, though—my word, what a hungry man he had been—when he had found her mouth, when he had lifted her onto the couch.

That was a soft evening in September. The smell of Indian summer drifted through the open window and hung suspended in the room. They heard the drowsy cooing of the pigeons settling themselves for the night under the eaves of the cathedral. Far off, a motor horn sounded.

That Christmas she had given him the watch and chain. He had worn it religiously for a while, and then he sneaked back to his wrist watch. Devon waited politely for about three weeks, thinking perhaps it was being regulated and expecting it to reappear. When it didn't, she finally asked him about it, and when he said lamely that it was too grand to wear all the time and that a wrist watch was somehow so convenient, hell popped. There were tears and recriminations and a few Elizabethan oaths Devon had picked up from her father, who had been a professor of languages at Williams.

Jasper had been angry; cold and testy by turns. He had informed her that she was unreasonable and sensitive to a point of idiocy, but he put back the watch and chain, and they were now as much a part of him as his gray clothes and his gray hair and his dear gray eyes. He had been her lover for four years. He had been her friend for eleven. Her dear friend and a rock in business. Not that they didn't differ. Their arguments were epic, but they knew and loved their business and they rarely made a wrong decision. They had become comrades.

She sometimes thought how complex and basically healthy was the human mind that it could so throw off the past, that life flowed on unimpeded by retarding memories. Months would go by, she and Jasper would be together daily in close contact, bound by the same concerns, yet it would occur to neither that they had lain in each other's arms. It was a natural phenomenon and it interested her, and then of course there was Tim. Tim, who was her heart's darling, and who was behaving now in this strange way, so restless and sarcastic and just generally gritty.

She and Tim had been married for seven years. The first five years were exultant; the last two had been—well, probably that's what happened to marriage. Not that she didn't still love Tim, but a curious change seemed to have come over him, and deep in her heart she recognized the reason and was afraid. Tim's old training and his ancient desire that she thought had been quenched were beginning to reassert themselves. She had no proof as yet, but she knew him, and though for years her egotism and vitality were such that she had overridden his scruples and her own fears, she had succeeded in obliterating neither.

When she had first met him, Tim was on his way to becoming one of the most remarkable of the younger men engaged in scientific research. At that time he was engrossed in the pursuit of a cure for third-degree burns; he dreamed of discovering an agent which might re-create destroyed cells in order to form new tissue. If he succeeded it was of course the key to the cure of countless diseases of the blood as well. It was a fairy-tale wish, but so were hundreds of other achievements in that field, and science was the wand to make the wish come true. This lean, aggressive young man worked with a sort of ferocious ardor among his test tubes and slides and formulas, seeking the solution. Then Devon happened to him. There were men upon whom she made small impression, but where she did register she ceased to be merely a person and became an event. Tim, pulling himself together after the impact, had laughed a little shakily and said to her, "Honey, as far as I'm concerned, you're the year of the big wind," and indeed that is how he had felt.

Devon was not a conventionally pretty girl, but she was decorative, with extraordinary eyes and lovely legs and teeth, the same thirty-two she had acquired when she was six, and she exerted a strong sexual attraction. She had a magnetic personality and a gay ironic humor in piquant contrast to her hardheaded, hard-hitting business methods.

By the time she encountered Tim her affair with Jasper had settled into a jog trot, and Tim and she became lovers the first night they met. Contrary to all warnings, predictions, and jeremiads of the moralists, Tim proposed to her in bed three mornings later, and they were married the following week. Devon would have married him that very day, but she had nothing to wear.

It was shortly after the wedding that the innocent corruption began to ferment. Tim had only a tiny salary from the laboratory where he was working; Devon was already on her way to wealth. As far as she was concerned, they had nothing to worry about; there was lots of money in the bank; what did it matter how it got there or whose it was? But Tim had a burning pride and a sense of scruple his bride was never to achieve. To him it was a keen humiliation that he was not only not able to support a wife but had further to live off her bounty. Because she sensed this, Devon, out of love, out of longing to spare him, and out of a brilliant flash of business insight, persuaded Tim to take over the job of running the Devonshire House laboratories, assuring him out of her own sincere belief that he would still have time for his own work. His deepest instinct, his ambition, his common sense, revolted against the idea. His passionate love for his wife, the realization of what it would mean to him financially, and an unexpected desire to accept the challenge, to prove that in a practical if shallow world he could hold his own, led him to assume the job.

From the point of view of the cosmetic business it proved a brilliant coup. There was little that Tim didn't know about the human skin, and he evolved certain formulas and treatments that brought results over which Devon could gloat with triumph. His powers of concentration were tremendous, and because he was subconsciously resentful he threw himself heart and soul into his work that he might prove to Devon his gratitude for this remunerative opportunity. Though in the nature of the business setup he could never attain an income to match his wife's, with his salary, out of which he bought stock in the firm, he achieved a very respectable income which he could fairly consider his own.

For the first few years all went well. They were deeply in love, they worked hard, they lived if with great comfort at least without ostentation, and they gathered about them a coterie of devoted and amusing friends.

If Tim felt a certain void in his life he stifled it out of loyalty to Devon and because of a mental honesty whereby he had seen quite clearly and accepted without reservation the change in his existence the move was bound to bring. The deep hurting thing was that he had lost and knew he had lost the respect of his colleagues in the world of serious scientific research. They found it hard to understand how a man of his caliber could relinquish the vitally important goal which many of them felt was almost within his grasp. To such men the cosmetic industry was a joke at best, charlatanism at worst.

And Tim, who had at first believed he could continue his own work on the side, had ruefully to admit that his new life held no margin. It was filled to the brim with Devon and her business and his love for her. And gradually, little by little, his burning ambition faded, receding into the background as new interests crowded his world.

Curiously enough the first crack in the armor of deliberate indifference in which he had encased himself was caused by a not very large and certainly blameless domestic step. Devon wanted a new house. As soon after their marriage as Tim had started earning his fine Devonshire House salary, they moved into a pleasant but conventional apartment on which he paid the rent. He also paid the wages of their two servants and the household bills. If Devon wanted costly furniture or fabulous furs or her walls hung with modern masters, which she did, she could buy them. Tim had no objections, and if he had had, he would have thought it impertinent to voice them, but he was adamant in his insistence that the roof over their heads and their normal human needs should be supplied by him. In another man Devon would have considered this attitude no more than what one might legitimately expect; in Tim whom she adored it became an enchanting quality, and she got quite dewy-eyed thinking of his honor and integrity.

This happy state of wifely submission lasted for nearly five years, when she was one day unfortunately seized with the idea of buying some East River property she had seen, tearing down the two houses that stood there and building from scratch. She broached the plan to Tim, who at first tried hard to dissuade her. For one thing he genuinely liked their old apartment, but his more pressing argument was that he was able to afford it. "Look here, Devon," he said on the night when she told him she had spent all afternoon in conference with Henry Barlow, her lawyer, Jasper, and the real-estate people, and that they thought it an excellent investment, "perhaps it is if you have the money to swing it, and I don't deny that you have; but I haven't, and I don't relish the idea of a load I'd have to hock my soul to carry."

His spouse cried out in protest: "But my darling, it wouldn't be up to you to carry it. The whole deal will be amortized, or whatever it is they do, by Devonshire House, Inc. It's a perfectly sound business transaction and one that will help the firm."

Tim had grown a little acid. "How? Do you propose housing the operators there? Or perhaps Jasper and Mollie and the kids are to move in from Nutley and bunk with us. And don't forget a small sunny suite for Minerva." Though she supervised the salon admirably, neither of them cared much for poor Minerva.

"You will pardon me," said Devon stiffly, "but I don't think that's very funny."

"It's not supposed to be funny, and don't kid yourself with all this talk about how it would be such an asset to the firm. Cut it any way you like, you're building a house for you and me to live in, but I can't feel right in it because I can't pay the rent."

Devon's patience, never very sturdy, snapped. "Good God, Tim, what does that matter? Suppose the money is in my name, what of it? I wouldn't have anything like as much without you. You're one of the finest chemists in this country. Our products have met with fabulous success because of what you've been able to achieve. Why, due to you, eight times out of ten those miracles Moreley spouts about in his advertising copy actually happen. You're a blooming genius, darling," and her eyes were bright with loyalty, flecked with irritation.

Tim colored, but he said steadily, "That's nice of you, Devon, but genius doesn't come very high. I know I've helped the firm, but so would any other good man, and Moreley and Jasper and you yourself are every bit as responsible for your seven-and-a-half-million-dollar-a-year turnover as I am. More, actually; in our business shrewd merchandising is three fourths of the battle. I'm sorry if I sound like a prig, but, damn it, I can't help it, I think a man ought to support his wife."

Devon looked at him a moment, frankly puzzled. "But you do, darling."

Tim smiled, but his smile was sardonic. "I do have the satisfaction of paying the rent and the waitress, and even that dethroned empress who honors us with her presence in the kitchen acknowledges the master on the first of the month, and though these are not very grand achievements, I should like to cling to them. In some small measure they compensate me for the minks and Matisses with which you provide yourself."

"But, Tim, why should you care about the mink things? It's nonsense, I don't think you do really."

Tim laughed a little shamefacedly. "Well, I don't, I suppose, but someday I'd like the satisfaction of giving you something you couldn't buy yourself. That would make it a real treat."

Devon kissed him tenderly. "My angel, stop. You give me all I want in the world. I don't know what you're talking about." She knew quite well. What funny creatures men were! When Tim had first known her she had had a magnificent mink coat, and it was not until she had one day remarked that she thought she might turn it in on a sable wrap if Jaeckel's would give her any kind of allowance that Tim had let fall a comment by which she suddenly realized that he had thought all along that it was the gift of a former lover. "And I'll be damned," she had subsequently observed to Jennie Moore, "if he didn't seem a little less unhappy about the

lover idea than he was about my being able to afford it myself."
They had been sitting in Jennie's dressing room at the time while
Jennie made up for the evening performance, and as she spat on
her Devonshire House mascara, she said sagely, "But, darling, that's
only natural. After all, he might someday be able to compete with
a lover, but how can he compete with the cosmetic industry?"

Tim fought determinedly against the new house, but in the end
he capitulated, as he had known from the start he would. Besides, Devon had a way of gently nibbling his ear in the middle of
a violent argument, which took his mind off the point at issue, and
once the apartment began to fill with blueprints he got interested
against his will and made several remarkably helpful suggestions.
The architect treated Mr. Wainwright with the greatest respect,
and Devon convinced herself that Tim's recurrent moods of restless-
ness ever since they had been living in the East River house were
largely her imagination.

For two weeks before they moved in Tim had been away on a
business trip, so the completed splendor broke upon him unexpectedly.

The house was very beautiful, but the core, the focal point of
luxury, was the bath-dressing room, and she had planned it as a
little girl. For several years in her childhood she had spent her summer and Christmas holidays with her grandmother who lived in
Vermont, and as the flies buzzed or the winter winds whistled
around the outhouse the young sybarite vowed to herself that she
would someday achieve functional luxury that would have set the
Romans back on their heels. She had fulfilled her oath. The bathroom was a miracle of coral, blue, and jade green, with a tub of
flush-pink marble. There was also an open fireplace and a small
concealed refrigerator for keeping cold her lotions and the
Guinness Stout which Tim liked at bedtime.

Devon considered she had planned soundly; she and Tim each
had their own bedroom and frequently did their actual sleeping
apart. Tim was forever swishing the covers about and yawning
loudly and was frightfully disturbing, but when you were brushing
your teeth and taking a bath was the very time you wanted to be
sociable, so the dressing room was large, lovely, and designed for

two. Mirrored closets, glass-enclosed shower, a couple of low over-stuffed slipper chairs in coral satin, two washbasins, and a telephone.

When she first brought Tim to the threshold he emitted a long, low whistle and stood staring like a man who can't believe his senses. Devon giggled nervously. "It's terrific, isn't it, darling, but awfully practical?"

Her husband's eyes searched the magnificence. "Where's the can?"

"That's the best part. Look," and with the air of a magician whipping out the rabbit, she flung open a mirrored door. It was in a small closet of its own. The closet was lined with a rare Chinese paper, and the East River flowed past the window, but the object itself was gleaming white and unadorned.

Tim grinned. "How did Dickie come to let you have anything as plebeian as that?" Dickie Masters was their decorator, and Tim had some difficulty keeping a straight face when he was about. Devon had called him to task about it on several occasions. "Tim, you're very bad. I agree with you that some of the boys adopt pansyism because they think it's smart or something, but poor Dickie obviously can't help it. He's so fragile he must have been like that in the cocoon."

"Too damn bad he ever came out," Tim had muttered. "Why do they have to flutter and float in that silly way?"

"That's how butterflies get around, dear," said his wife reasonably. She would have felt like Madame Fabre if she had ever heard of Monsieur. She didn't admit to Tim that she had fought Dickie tooth and nail on this particular item. His willowy soul had yearned for a *chaise percée* of Louis XV cane or something draped in candy-striped satin, and Devon had felt like a pioneer woman as she stormed at him, but she won her point. "My God!" she had cried in disgust. "Candy-striped satin indeed! I never heard of such chi-chi. I don't plan to hold a levee on the damned thing!"

She closed the mirrored door, and Tim resumed his tour of inspection, moving like a cat in new quarters. Devon waited on tenterhooks, underscoring points of interest. "Isn't the fireplace sweet? I like it built up off the floor, don't you? And Tim, look at that chandelier, how beautiful, Venetian glass with those exquisite carnations, and isn't the pink marble something? It's really spectacular."

Tim said little but continued opening closet doors and turning the water off and on in the gold swan taps. "Well, say something, can't you?" Devon fumed. He looked thoughtfully at the exquisitely painted mirrors, at the softly falling curtains, the thick rug, the extravagant basins and tub, and the twinkling crystal bottles; then he turned to his wife with a curious expression, affection, bewilderment—and could it be a shade of anxiety?—all mixed up. "Is this what you want?"

"Of course. I adore it. Don't you like it, Tim?"

"Give me time, honey," he said. "Don't forget you're talking to a boy from Iowa."

Devon was half amused, half annoyed. "Don't forget I know a thing or two about Mother Earth myself, baby. I drew the first designs for this bathroom on the margins of the Sears, Roebuck catalogue in Grandma's privy when I was twelve. Damn it all, it *is* terrific!" A sudden large tear splashed down her nose.

Mr. Wainwright, belatedly stirred to gentlemanly reactions, took her in his arms and gave her a resounding kiss. "Tootsie, my only quarrel is with your vocabulary. The word terrific is a paltry term, in no way commensurate with this Oriental splendor. The jernt is catastrophic in its grandeur. You just wait—we'll be shooting deer in the living room."

"Why?"

"It's a cinch no human soul will go in there once they get a load of this. But wasn't it terribly . . . I mean it must have . . ."

Devon, uneasily aware of what he was thinking, hastened to head him off. "As a matter of fact, this is an economy."

"We're stinting, I suppose."

"Well, in a way. We've saved space and money. Instead of having to have two bathrooms and two dressing rooms and a little sitting room up here for us, they're all rolled into one."

In the end Tim succumbed enough to the fleshpots to design a contraption whereby he could read the Sunday papers in the tub while Devon sat at his side in one of the satin slipper chairs, sipping her breakfast tea and feeding him coffee cake. To Tim's way of thinking she always managed to look her best on Sunday mornings, which added to the holiday spirit. Nature had given her dark hair, but what with her profession and her temperament Tim was never sure just what he might find on his pillow. "Oh God, again?" he would moan when confronted with the constantly varying hues. Devon would unscramble her fabulous lashes, open her eyes wide, and smile. "But darling, I must test our dyes, mustn't I? I owe it to my clients."

☆   ☆   ☆

They had had a good life and now a strange and disturbing force had come between them. A holocaust was sweeping the world, and instead of binding them closer together it had seemed to Devon in recent months as though the crust of the earth on which they stood was breaking into pieces and separating them from each other.

Tim was resentful and unkind, lashing out at her and the business in a bitter, angry way. More than once he had made such a scene as had just occurred in the office, but though Devon had been disturbed and hurt she had never been as angry as she was now. It was humiliating to both of them to have him behave in this way in front of Jasper and Moreley. Why couldn't he have waited until they left the salon? She turned to him and said shortly, "Well, there seems no more to be gained by sticking around here. Shall we leave?"

"Right," said Tim. "Let's go home." Devon sat down and put on her shoes in silence, while he got their coats from the closet. Jasper started for his own office. "Will you be in in the morning?" he asked.

Devon looked up. "Of course."

"Good. I want to talk to you about a sales-promotion plan through the Midwest. Good night, Devon." His voice was gentle.

"Dear Jasper, good night. Let's go home, Tim. I told Anna we'd be in for dinner, and I have some reports Jasper wants me to look over." She crossed to the dying fire and drew the screen.

"Where's Hilda?" Tim was referring to Devon's secretary.

"I let her go. Put out the lights, will you?" Tim pressed the switch, and the pretty, fragrant room was plunged in darkness. They made their way in silence along the corridor to the elevator. It was after seven, and Devon's floor was deserted. The operators were all gone, and the cleaning women wouldn't be in till later. The elevator stopped at the fifth floor to pick up Minerva. Devon and Tim saw her with some surprise. "You're holding the fort pretty late, aren't you, Miss Ritchie?" he asked.

Minerva's silent reply was *And how!* Aloud she said with her bright headmistress smile, "Oh no, Mr. Wainwright. Inventory night, you know."

Devon forced an interest she didn't feel. "Of course, I'd forgotten. By the way, Hilda left the statement on my desk, but I didn't look at it, how did we do today?"

"Things were a bit slow, but then we must expect that with the storm, mustn't we? Such contrary weather." Devon half expected Minerva to click her tongue in disapproval, like a nurse whose little charge is not behaving very well for Mummy's company and who will get a brisk dose of What For once the nursery door has closed.

Though she was angry, puzzled, and haunted by a strange small fear, Devon could not resist a glance at Tim. There was an answering glint in his eye, and the same thought must have struck him, for as he followed Minerva and her out of the elevator, he murmured in her ear, "We're not our usual sunny self today, are we?"

Under the circumstances Devon considered the remark two-edged. "We certainly are not," she answered coldly.

They passed through the small and elegant lobby with its carvings, pictures, and illuminated show cases of perfume bottles, flowers, wisps of lingerie, and costume jewelry. As Tim opened the door on the foul night Fred sprang to attention. "It's pretty bad, Miss Elliott. You want I should get you your galoshes? Owens' got them in the car."

"Never mind, Fred. I guess I can weather the trek across the sidewalk."

Fred bulwarked her as best he could, holding onto her elbow with one hand and managing the big unwieldy umbrella with the other. Tim turned up his coat collar, pulled down his hat, and plunged after them. Inside the car it was warm and snug. "It's good Fred has the constitution of an ox," he observed as Owens pulled away from the curb, "or he'd be a goner if we get much of this weather. I don't see why he sticks around so late on a night like this anyway."

"Apparently his job doesn't bore him." Devon's voice was edged with sarcasm. "Besides he's got on overshoes, his winter uniform, and a rubber tent for an overcoat."

"No smallest item escapes the madam's attention."

"I have an eye for detail." The silence between them grew and thickened, till the car was packed tight with it. As they drew up to the house on the river, Owens tapped on the glass separating him from the tonneau. Tim leaned forward and lowered the window. "What is it, Owens?"

"Are you or Mrs. Wainwright going out again tonight, Mr. Wainwright?"

Tim turned back to Devon. "Are we?"

"I certainly don't plan to." She addressed the chauffeur. "If Mr. Wainwright doesn't want you, you can go, Owens. I told you that this morning." Her tone was sharp, and without waiting for him she flung open the car door, hurried across the pavement to the house, and pushed violently on the doorbell.

Tim followed her and was about to insert his key in the lock when Fairweather opened the door. Fairweather was their butler, and engaging him had been a major event in their lives. His references were so glowing that Devon was convinced he had written them himself, but she felt that if he had that much imagination he would be apt to encourage the good life in his new surroundings. He was obviously a devotee of the grand manner.

She was afraid of butlers but considered the aversion doubtless Freudian and one which would be overcome only by embracing her neurosis. She supposed it would have to be a figurative embrace even if he were attractive, because of the taboos. Taboos were interesting though confusing, and with the exception of an occasional fictional heroine few seemed to have truck with their butlers; yet a good butler filled an urgent need and was not easy to find, God knows.

When she had broken the news of this newest acquisition to Tim they were in the famous bathroom dressing for a dinner party. He was emerging from the shower, and she sat at her dressing table tastefully attired in cobweb pants, painting on her mouth. " . . . so as you said you'd be willing to try one, dear, I've gone ahead and engaged this fellow."

"What's he like?"

"Well," Devon was working with meticulous stroke on the lower left-hand corner, "he's fearfully correct, he's obviously seen a lot of drawing-room comedies and knows just how butlers should behave. It's going to be very humiliating if we don't play our parts as well."

Tim was sawing away at his shoulder blades with a vast Turkish towel and grim determination. "We'll show him," he said stoutly. "Watch me make with the epigrams. I'll put that tony bastard in his place. What's his name?"

Devon had shifted to the upper right lip, but though the job was ticklish her pause was deliberate. "Fairweather."

Tim let out a yell: "What?"

"I'm sorry, dear," she said with unaccustomed meekness.

"What is he, a nance?"

"Of course not!"

"Well, I'm goddamned if I'll go around truckling to any son of a bitch by the name of Fairweather."

"You're not supposed to truckle, you're the master. You must be gracious yet firm, like a man accustomed to the best since infancy."

Tim dove into his towel, to emerge almost instantly. "Fairweather would stick in my craw. What's the matter with his first name? We don't call Anna Mrs. Kendallbarker, we call her Anna, and we call Owens Owens and not O'Malley. Why can't we call him whatever his name is?"

"You can if you want to, dear." Devon had finished her mouth, and a provocative job it was; another man might have found it inspirational, but the words that dropped from it curdled her husband's blood. "His first name is Windermere."

"What!"

"I'm sorry, darling."

Mr. Wainwright looked at her with haggard eyes; he was a man beaten and betrayed. Each hair flared wet, rigid and outraged, from his skull. "Very well," he croaked hoarsely. "If the die is cast, I will abide by it, but I'm giving you fair warning—I am also giving you Fairweather, incidentally—and one chirp out of him about anything, but about anything whatsoever, like suggesting scotch if I want rye, and I boot him out so fast he won't know what hit him."

"You rarely want rye; besides, that is a grossly unfair attitude and one lacking in humanity. After all, the poor man can't help his name."

"All I want to know is, how did he ever get it?"

"I assume," said Devon with dignity, "that his mother gave it to him. She was probably literary."

This had happened about a year ago, and Fairweather had molded himself into their lives. As far as Tim was concerned, he was still an incredible character, but more human than he had expected, and certainly efficient, and though Devon had never been moved to literal embrace, metaphorically speaking she clung to him like a limpet.

As he opened the door to her now, it was a relief to see his familiar face, square and ruddy in the soft light of the hall.

"I'm dead, Fairweather. Bring us some drinks in the library, will you?"

"Certainly, madam. Would you like cocktails or highballs, and shall I bring something to go with them?"

"I'll take daiquiris and a pearl-handled revolver. Any messages?"

"No, madam, but Mr. Van Alston dropped by about five o'clock. He said he was in the neighborhood and just rang the doorbell automatically. I think he was pumping me for a cup of tea."

Tim said gravely, "I hope, Fairweather, you upheld the tradition of the house and refreshed the wayfarer."

"Well, no, sir, I didn't. He had Miss Flora with him, and if you will excuse me, Mrs. Wainwright, Miss Flora's condition struck me as so imminent, I was afraid of little ones in the front hall. I urged him on his way, but I suggested he ring you this evening, since you are going to be home."

Devon said absently, "Under the circumstances, Fairweather, I do think you might refer to her as Mrs. Flora," and dropping her fur coat into his outstretched arms, she brushed past him into the library.

"That new case of scotch you ordered came this afternoon, Mr. Wainwright. Shall I bring you some of that?"

Tim followed Devon with his eyes. He was aware that the battle was about to be joined. The battle was of his own making and by his own desire, yet he had small stomach for it and felt the need of an ally. "Yes, bring in a bottle," he said, adding as an afterthought, "You might keep the case handy too," and he started for the library, fingering his tie as he went. *God*, he thought, *I feel like a bashful suitor, and wouldn't I give my shirt if I were! This reversal is tough going.*

In the library Devon was lighting the fire. A fire always cheered her, and she felt that tonight they were going to need all the solace they could get. She knew that at last she was up against something she had for months refused to acknowledge. In some strange, unaccountable way Tim was slipping from her. There was no specific thing she could point to; it was more an attitude. She smiled wryly to herself. When she was a child in school there had been complaints about her Attitude. Her marks were not poor, but her Attitude had been considered supercilious. Well, Tim was not supercilious; that was the last thing on earth he was, but there was something—non-cooperative, that was what he had been.

Tonight's flare-up in the office was only a more violent outcropping of a mood that had been culminating for months, but although she found his indifference to her plans for expansion and his scathing disparagement of the clientele disconcerting, it was the disjointed status of their personal relationship that profoundly disturbed her. Even their lovemaking did not unite them as it used to. They were complementary and successful lovers, but Devon felt that recently there was a spare, almost academic quality in their union. The technique remained unimpaired but the music had ceased, the ineffable illusion had faded.

Tim was restless; and then there were the little incidents. They used to delight in making plans: the way they would remodel the Long Island farm, trips they would take; their schemes were endless, but now Tim, while not saying point-blank that he wasn't going to do something, would slip out of the frame of their future, smooth as quicksilver. There was nothing furtive about it, nothing sly; how it happened Devon couldn't say, but they would just be talking about something else.

Even the near future, even something as near as the spring party which they had given every year since their marriage. They generally planned it for late February, and only last week Devon had remarked that it was time they started going over the lists of guests and deciding on what sort of entertainment they would have, and Tim had spoken impatiently and said, "Oh my God, Devon, let's not bother about that right now. In times like these, why not give it a rest?" And she had asked rather resentfully if he didn't want the party, and after a moment he had said, "Look, darling, it's your party. If you want to give it, go ahead, why should I try to stop you? You're the one who does all the work anyhow, you and Hilda and poor old Minerva with her determined good humor," and then he had laughed and gone out of the room. Certainly he had not been very forbidding, and yet, Devon couldn't tell why, a panicky feeling had swept over her. It was fantastic, but it was as if . . . well, as if Tim didn't plan to be there.

These memories thronged her mind as she lighted the fire, and because she was uncertain and fearful her mood fluctuated wildly; but she had faced difficult situations before in her life, and she was too shrewd an opponent to be caught completely off guard by even her dearest enemy.

Getting out of the car and coming into the house had broken the tension a little, so when Tim joined her in the library her temper though fractious was under tight rein. "This chimney still smokes, Tim. I do wish you'd talk to the man about it."

"I know, it's a nuisance. I'll call him in the morning." Good, she thought. At least he wasn't planning to leave tonight. Tim pulled a crumpled pack of cigarettes from his pocket and held it out to her. "Smoke?"

"No, thanks." He lighted one himself and inhaled deeply, blowing the smoke out in three controlled and perfect rings.

"My, my, what steady nerves we have!" she observed lightly.

"We lead a clean, upright, wholesome life," said Tim in such a perfect imitation of Minerva's tone that Devon laughed in spite of herself.

Fairweather came into the room with a tray laden with the cocktail shaker, whisky and soda, and a plate of appetizers. Tim shoved aside a long row of overlapping magazines so he could set it down on the coffee table in front of the couch. Devon, though suspecting they knew everything that went on, subscribed superficially to the convention of Not in Front of the Servants; accordingly she remarked to Tim, "I wonder what Jasper's idea is for promoting sales through the Middle West. Has he said anything to you about it?"

"Not a peep. Don't bother, Fairweather, I'll pour out the drinks."

"Very good, sir. Shall I tell Anna to delay dinner a little, Mrs. Wainwright?"

If you are anticipating a scene, my good man, thought Devon, *you're probably right.* Aloud she said, "Yes, just for a bit. We don't want to rush our drinks."

Fairweather withdrew. Tim handed her a brimming glass. It was ice-cold to her fingers, of palest yellow-green, with minute scraps of mint floating on top.

"I must say Fairweather is the dream boy for a daiquiri," she said, waiting for Tim to mix his highball. He grinned.

"Windermere holds the whip hand all right, but he deserves it. I think even Anna's a little in awe of him."

"Grinds her under his heel, I shouldn't wonder."

"Good job too. Mighty handy for the upper classes. Well, here's how."

"Skoal." They drank.

The silence that had been in the car with them started to bulge again, a monstrous, tangible growth, but this time Tim pierced it before it overwhelmed them. "All right, go ahead, say it. I suppose you think I behaved badly in the office."

The tight rein snapped. "You're damn right, I think you behaved badly. And so did Jasper, and so did Moreley. Aside from everything else, whatever bone you may feel called on to pick with me, what earthly right have you got to talk to Moreley the way you did? I know you don't like him, but he's remarkably able, and he has one admirable quality, he understands his job."

Tim's grip on his highball glass tightened, so that his knuckles showed white. "We'll go into that job business in just a minute, and as for what I said to him about the money, I was quite right. The man has absolutely no sense of proportion. If you listened to him, every penny you took into the business would be thrown right out again on advertising."

Devon's eyes flashed. "To begin with, my dear Tim, you know very little about advertising and what it's worth, and in the second place, I'm not an intellectual pauper, though I realize I must be a trial to one of your rare scientific mentality. I am fully able to curb any of Moreley's more extravagant flights of fancy, and if I should weaken, Jasper's is a very steady hand on the helm."

Tim bowed sardonically. "Don't think, madam, that I don't appreciate your capabilities, or the fact that you and Mr. Doolittle are the supreme bosses of this business into which I had the infinite good fortune to be hired. But, ungrateful though it may sound, cooking up goo for women's faces is not the be-all and end-all of life. Anyway, not of my life."

Devon had finished her cocktail. She set her glass down with a sharp little click. "And that's another thing. That stupid smarty-pants crack you made in the office about the number of pots of goo not being a vital statistic—may I ask what's any more vital than knowing your own business?"

Tim turned on her, and his words were like little hammer blows. "I do know my own business, but my business isn't yours. Seven years ago I betrayed the most important laboratory job I ever tackled in my life, but thank God I'm getting it back again and I'm going to sweat over it until such time as I've found the answer, and if I ever do I'll have licked a problem that's really tough and one that plenty of other guys are beating their brains out trying to solve."

Devon was boiling mad, and her entire attention was riveted on him, so it would be impossible to say that her concentration deepened, but some sixth sense pricked up its ears to the possibility of a new cosmetic. "What is it?" she demanded angrily. "Anything we could use?"

"No, no," Tim shouted at her. "Good God, you're impossible to talk to! It hasn't anything to do with cosmetics. There's nothing at all in it for those dames you sell to, and even if there were they wouldn't give it a tumble, because it's honest and unromantic and they want to be bamboozled. What the hell else do they pay for?"

"They happen to pay for some very fine ingredients and some superb formulas made by a man who used to be tops in his job but who seems to have gone crazy. So help me God, Tim, I don't know what's the matter with you. What do you mean, my business isn't yours? Your attitude recently has been one long sneer. You haven't been yourself at home any more than in the office. Now, what is it? If you're sick of me or of the firm or of your part in it, say so, but don't work yourself up to these shocking exhibitions of meanness and sarcasm. I'm sick and damned tired of it."

"And I'm sick and damned tired too!"

"Well, what do you suggest we do?"

Tim's body seemed to sag, and he suddenly looked all in.

"I'm sorry, Devon. I've acted rottenly, and I know it. The real trouble is, I'm sick of myself."

Devon looked at him, and her anger subsided, but she still spoke grudgingly. "Well, I don't know what's got into you, but I wish you'd confine your outbursts to the home. Granny Moreley will have the news all over town."

"I'm not trying to alibi myself, but as a matter of fact, I don't think he will. He's a pompous old goat, and he doesn't like me any better than I like him, but he's loyal to you."

"What is it, Tim? You can't fool me. Something's been on your mind for a long time. What is it?"

Tim looked at her and held his breath and plunged. "Devon, I'm quitting the business." This, then, was what she had been waiting for. It was as if a tremendous hard, tight knot had suddenly dissolved, leaving thousands of loose ends. There was a long pause.

At last she said quietly, "Are you crazy?"

"I don't think so, but I'm getting out of Devonshire House."

Devon passed her hand over her eyes. "I'm sorry to appear stupid, Tim, but I don't understand."

"I'll try to make it as clear as I can," he said. "It goes back quite a way, but it's not very complicated. When we were first married and you offered me the job as head of your laboratory, it meant giving up my work that I'd devoted years of effort to. Well, I made up my mind to do it and gladly; don't think for one instant that I

regret it or that I reproach you. God knows because of your generosity I've had a wonderful life, and I've tried to do a good job for
both of us, but in a way, Devon, it's been professional suicide."

This was not easy to take, but when she respected her opponent
Devon was a stanch and gallant adversary. "I'm sorry you feel that
way about it, Tim," she said steadily. "But don't think I don't
appreciate your worth as a scientist."

"Thanks. I believe I am one—that's why I've got to leave Devonshire House. My coming to it was an indulgence I should never
have allowed myself, and now, my darling, the professional honeymoon is over. I've got to get back to my old job."

"But why just now, Tim? What's brought about this change of
heart?"

"I don't know—a hundred things—me—the way I feel, the
war . . ."

Devon could see that he was honestly trying to search his own
heart, or at least trying to find a way to make it clear to her.

"I've seen some of the old gang recently. That's influenced me
too, I suppose."

"But what is it you want to do particularly?"

"I want to take up where I left off . . . that research for the
treatment of burns, of all kinds of sick and destroyed blood cells.
And now with the war, with the thousands of wounded, there's a
tremendous opportunity for the healing of wounds without scars.
They've made big strides in the last seven years, Devon . . . the
use of blood plasma, the possible local application of proteins; the
protein business is hell and gone in the future actually, because
we know so little about them still, but I'm working on something
now. Possibly, just possibly, I'm on the road to the solution."

Tim was sitting forward on the edge of his chair, his blue eyes
shining, his long body tense. Even though it took him away from
her, this was the mood in which Devon loved him best. Part of her
pride in him was that he was an expert workman who knew what
he was talking about. She was swept up by his own eagerness. "But
this sounds wonderful, darling, only why on earth leave the
laboratory? Even if you haven't got your discovery complete, you
must have a pretty clear idea of it. We'll take out a patent. We'll get

together tomorrow, you and I and Jasper and Henry Barlow. Let him exercise those legal brains of his he's so smug about. He should be able to dope out a way to protect your process while it's in the making, and think what such an invention could do for the beauty business! While every other cosmetic firm in the country is dependent on some kind of foundation to cover scars or birthmarks, and none of them is really satisfactory, we'll be able to eliminate them because we'll attack the source. . . . I suppose for a while some surgery may still be necessary?"

Tim smiled at her eagerness, but he was dismayed by her lack of understanding. "Look, Devon, it's . . . this is altogether a different kind of thing. Our idea is that maybe in the misty future we may arrive at the elimination of surgery in certain instances. It's conceivable that through the use of proteins, intravenous feeding, and so on, the skin may effect a self-cure; but that's the very reason we're eager to devote our whole time to the job, it's so tremendous."

"Who's we?"

"We?"

"Yes. 'We may arrive,' and 'We're eager.' Who's that?"

"Oh. Well, primarily 'we' is Oscar Hogarth and I. You haven't met him, but he's by way of being a genius, screwy but a great fellow, a Czech scientist. I've had him with me a good deal; we've been sleuthing together on this protein business. What we're trying is a complicated damn thing and may be a flop, but we've done a lot of work and we're anxious to experiment further."

Devon looked at him curiously. "How long has this been going on?"

"The actual work? Seven or eight months, though the idea's been stewing in my mind for years."

"I see. And when do you do all this? You and Mr. Hogarth."

"In the lab. We work several hours a day."

She stared at him incredulously and then let out a howl. "What! On my time?"

Tim looked at her a moment, staggered. "But Devon . . ." Then he burst into helpless laughter. His wife was miffed.

"I don't see what's so funny about it. The laboratory's the heart of the business, and you've neglected it. This extramural research is all very well, but you should have done it on your own time. No wonder you didn't know whether expansion would be necessary or feasible. You weren't holding up your end."

Tim's laughter stopped, and he said seriously, "As a matter of fact, Devon, you're right. I'm not fair to you and I'm not fair to the firm. I know it, that's why I'm quitting."

"There's no necessity for that." Because she was alarmed her tone was sharp. "If you want to experiment, go ahead. All I'm saying is, don't neglect the lab. If extra help is needed, get it. Somebody else can take over for a while under your supervision. This invention—this discovery—may be the most revolutionary thing the beauty industry has ever seen. It'll make millions——"

"Devon——"

A false step. "All right, never mind the money, but think what it might mean to women; not only the comparative few who are scarred or burned, but this protein business may be the answer to all kinds of skin ailments." With characteristic optimism her imagination flew ahead. "Tim, supposing this were the fountain of youth, not water but food. Probably when we know enough about it and you've broken down all the component parts of the proteins and everything, we'll be able to replace the body's natural oils, to restore resiliency. No more wrinkles and crow's feet and puffy eyes and sagging chins—why, the American woman will be the most beautiful in the world, and eternally. Can you imagine Moreley? I can't wait to tell him."

Tim was growing desperate. "Listen to me for a minute. What you either can't or won't understand is this: I'm not interested in beautifying the American woman. I don't give a damn if their noses gleam like beacons and their lips are white as dust. I'm through, fed up with this rot about nourishing their flabby skins and searching out formulas that will shrink three chins into two. It's a colossal hoax and a shocking waste of time. For the most part they're vain, silly women, and no matter how you polish their shells, that silliness shines through."

Devon cocked an eye at him. "Cheer up, dear," she said dryly. "There's always a silver lining. Their silliness has kept you in considerable comfort for a number of years. Besides, think of the vast amount of employment they create."

"So does the opium trade."

"Oh, for God's sake, Tim, what are you? A crusader? And why pick on the beauty industry? I admit it's not all it's cracked up to be, but at least it's mildly beneficial. If you're so hell-bent on reformation why don't you attack something that's actually harmful, like cigarettes? What about those pictures they're always publishing of smokers' lungs looking like doom over Pittsburgh? Yet you personally contribute hundreds of dollars a year to the tobacco industry."

"That is true," said Tim. "But smoking at least has the dignity of a vice and everybody knows how bad it is for them, whereas our trade exploits the customers. Eternal youth is not in any little pot."

"So what? They love it. Oh, Tim, give us a break. I understand that what you're working on is a double-domed proposition with spectacles and a long black gown, but why shouldn't ordinary women profit by it?"

"I hope that eventually everybody who needs it will profit by it, but it has nothing to do with cosmetics." Devon looked depressed. "Oh, come on, things aren't as bad as all that." Tim chided her in the cozy tone peculiar to the blaster of hopes.

"Well, you can scarcely expect me to shout for joy when the finest chemist in the business, and my own husband to boot, announces that as far as he's concerned the setup is contemptible."

"I didn't say that."

"You implied it. I'm not taken in by my own advertising claims, Tim, but this industry has been bread and butter and champagne to us for quite a while, and regardless of your cracks, it makes millions of people happy, women because it improves their looks, and men because the women are pretty. I don't ask that you handle the poor old thing with velvet gloves, but I think a pair of common-sense mittens wouldn't be a bad idea."

Tim paced the room, his shoulders hunched a little forward. In one hand he held his highball glass; the other was thrust into his trouser pocket, rumpling up his buttoned coat in a gesture so characteristic that, though Devon noted it subconsciously, she was often to remember him in that pose. He came to a stop before her. "What I feel is this: we're living in desperate times. It seems to me it's up to everybody who can to try to combat them. To counterattack the destruction."

Devon, thinking of the loss to her laboratory, sighed. "I know what you say is true, Tim. This war is monstrous—but darling, must you save the world single-handed?"

Tim was scowling, not at her but from the concentration of his thought. "I must try. The politicians do their little best to destroy it. I feel it's up to the scientists and the gardeners and the states-men, all the people of good will, to hang on and restore it. And that means restoring the bodies that have been burned and broken and tortured just as much as it means restoring law and sanity."

"Yes sir." Devon was seated on the low couch, and Tim was standing near her. She marched two fingers up his trouser leg. "Here's a tortured body right at your feet and you're doing nothing about it. I'm tortured by famine."

But the Marines were on the way. Propelled by his intuition and as if on cue, Fairweather appeared. "I'm sorry to disturb you, madam, but dinner's been ready for some time and Anna is making a small scene. I believe there's a cheese soufflé."

Devon turned to Tim. "Shall we continue the slaughter at the table?" she asked politely.

Dinner was strained, and she felt like a supple rodent, twisting, turning, leaping, as she battled Tim with every wile at her com-mand, but it was no use. He would not change his decision about pulling out from the laboratory. It was after the coffee cups had been removed and they sat again by the library fire that she brought up the subject of Jasper's reaction. "He's sure to bring all the pressure he can to get you to stay on, Tim. None of us has ever had a contract, but for that very reason he's going to feel that you're honor bound to stick. Especially if we go ahead with the scheme to market cheaper cosmetics."

"Don't think I haven't thought about that, but if I'm going to leave, Devon—and believe me, I've got to—better I go now. There'll always be something—cheaper cosmetics or a revolutionary treatment or a fresh spring perfume. There are a thousand excuses for staying, and darling, I don't want to."

"I can't force you, Tim, of course, but who am I going to get? You're leaving me high and dry; you want the whole business to fail. . . ." The floodgates opened, and through her sobs she accused him. "Probably what you secretly want to do is to work for Rubinstein or Arden. How could you do this to me? I can just see the two of them—rocking with laughter. . . . I expect the whole business will go to smash. . . ."

He gathered her in his arms and pulled out his handkerchief. "I expect it won't. Baby darling, don't. Aren't you ashamed of yourself? Here you are, one of the most successful women in the country, the most intelligent and the prettiest when you don't have a large red nose, and you're blubbering like a booby."

The prototype of the American businesswoman drew out of his arms, dried her eyes, and blew loudly. "Well, God damn it to hell, why shouldn't I?" she demanded fiercely.

"That's my baby," Tim beamed approval. "That's my girl. Give 'em hell."

"It's you I'm giving the hell to. Who else can I get?"

Tim winked at her. "My darling wife, much as I appreciate the value you put on my services, the cold fact remains that I am not indispensable to the Devonshire House laboratories."

She stuffed his handkerchief back into his breast pocket. "I suppose you are to the protein business!"

He took her hand, turned it over, and kissed the palm. "I might be," he spoke quite seriously. "It's just possible that I'll be the boy who discovers the key to what we're looking for."

"I suppose that Czech genius will be working with you?"

"Yes, we're in this together, but if you'll relax a minute, you'll find that I'm not leaving you in the lurch. I think I've got hold of an excellent man to take my place. I'm anxious to have you meet him."

Devon was alarmed. "Tim, you haven't blabbed it all over town that you're leaving, have you?"

"No, dear. Within their limited capacity, my brain cells still function, but I've been watching this chap for some time. He's a top man, and from what I know of his situation, I think he'll be willing to take on the job."

"How much will he want?" Tim couldn't repress a smile. His bride might be in a burning building, but she would question the cost of the apparatus sent to the rescue.

"I don't think it will be out of line. As a matter of fact, you'll be saving money. He certainly won't expect my salary to start with."

That Tim would go off salary had not occurred to Devon, and it came as a little shock. "But you'll continue to draw money out of the firm, won't you?" she asked in surprise.

He looked at her quizzically. "Well . . . scarcely, Miss Elliott. You will forgive an ancient scruple, but I'm agin taking what I don't earn. I've got to see Jasper and Barlow tomorrow. If it's all right with all of you, I'd like to hold onto my stock which I've paid for outright, but I certainly won't draw a salary."

"Well, Jasper will be in a fury, that's all. He'll probably suggest that you stay on in an advisory capacity, at least. You could do that, couldn't you? Then you'd be entitled to a steady income."

"No, I couldn't, Devon. I don't want to be attached by any strings disguised as pretty ribbons."

Devon digested this for a few minutes. "How much will you make with these other people?" she asked at last.

"As the firm will consist of Hogarth and myself, the pickings will be lean to the point of attenuation, but that doesn't bother me too much. Even without a salary, with savings and dividends I'll be able to hold my end up here for a while and pay the rent for our own lab."

"Well, you can relax about the home front. The house belongs to both of us."

"But unfortunately, since the Civil War, domestic slaves have to be paid. There is also Uncle Sam's cut on the property."

Devon ignored these base considerations. "What about Mr. Hogarth's contribution to your common cause?"

"Financially Mr. Hogarth is finding the sledding tough, but his contribution is his mind, and as nobody but Mr. Rockefeller could pay for that anyway, he's working with me as a kind of dollar-a-year man."

"Sweet Tim. But you do pay the dollar, don't you?"

"And believe me, that's about all it is. But there's one fine exciting bit that I haven't told you."

"What?" Devon's eyes were bright. It was impossible for her to be angry with Tim for long, even if he behaved outrageously, as he was doing now. Though she considered his present action a grave default in line of duty, she was impressed by his idealism; and he was so straight, so able, and so beloved by her that whatever concerned him touched her imagination.

"Well, it looks as though Mr. Rockefeller knows a good thing when he sees one, and he may literally crash through with a salary for Oscar."

"Darling! You mean you boys are going to be working in Radio City? The Music Hall maybe?"

"No, my mental hazard. Not the Music Hall, the Institute."

"Oh."

"Yes. Fewer spangles but better test tubes. I think there might be a permanent berth for Oscar, though naturally I don't share in that."

Mrs. Wainwright's reception of this last was chilly. "It doesn't seem at all natural to me. That Czech may be good, but I know what you're capable of. Mr. Rockefeller can't be so hard to meet. After all, I'm rich and interested in research too. I'll have an interview with him, and I'll tell him——"

Tim grabbed her wrist. "Oh no, you won't! You leave Mr. Rockefeller and me alone. Anyhow, all this won't be for another six or eight weeks."

"Oh, good! Then you'll be able to get the new preparations under way before the other man takes over in the lab."

"Devon, I want to clear out next week."

"Oh, Tim! But the new fellow—what's his name, by the way?"

"Ullman. David Ullman."

"He won't know the ropes by then."

"I told you he was an expert, didn't I? I'll stick with him night and day for the next week, and believe me, he'll know what it's all about. He's a terrific worker, more dependable than your current fellow, and he's an amiable cuss too. The staff will like him."

Devon wasn't enthusiastic, but she was beginning to realize at last that she had no choice. "Well, if he's as good as you say, it may work, and after all, if there's any violent crisis, you'll be here. You can take time out from saving mankind to lend a hand, perhaps?"

This brought them to the rub. Tim realized he had given Devon a bad blow, and though he hoped it might have softened the impending second shock, he was none too sure. He was sitting beside her on the sofa. He laced his fingers and placed his thumb tips very carefully together. "Well, darling, no. That's one reason I want to be through at the office by next Thursday at the latest. It looks as though Oscar and I will be going down to Louisiana."

"Louisiana? Just what kind of research are you boys doing?"

"Honey, there isn't a Creole in a carload. That I guarantee. But there is one of the greatest laboratories in the world for an experiment we're about ready to make."

"You mean a hospital? An institute of technology?"

"No, the leper colony."

"Tim!" Devon was horror-struck.

"Now take it easy, baby; they don't go around with clappers any more, you know."

"But that dreadful disease, it's so infectious."

"That's just what it is not. It's much less infectious than tuberculosis. You'd have to live in close contact with a leper for a long time before you'd be likely to catch it, and anyway, many advanced cases lose their infectivity."

"Oh. Well, it still sounds awful and I don't see why it's necessary for you and Oscar Hogarth to go into a colony."

"I told you, we want to experiment with a new formula. It has to do with skin tissue and blood cells; there's a possibility that in those conditions we'll obtain the results we're looking for."

"How long would this jaunt last?"

"We've got to have a little time for observation. Possibly four or five weeks, but no longer."

"Well, I should hope not!"

Tim was grateful to her for taking it, if not with enthusiasm, which he could hardly have expected, at least without fireworks.

"You're swell, darling," he said. "You really are. It won't seem long, you'll see. You'll be launching the new line, and if you do decide on Moreley's radio program, you'll be up to your ears. You won't even miss me."

"I certainly will miss you. We've never been separated for so long. And what about our spring party? It'll be fine if you're not back for that."

"How much has that party cost us the last two or three years?"

"Oh, I don't remember offhand. Around twenty-five hundred—three thousand."

"That's what I thought. If you're still determined to give it, it's just as well that I won't be here. I'd be an awful blank this year, baby. I couldn't possibly afford to share it with you."

Devon looked at him with the detached air of an independently wealthy debutante contemplating an unreasonable parent. "What possible difference would that make? You're host in your own house, aren't you?"

Tim colored. "My idea of a host is one who pays the bills." Devon got up and walked restlessly about the room.

"Oh Lord, there you go again!" She straightened an ornament here, a book there. "You're always joking about me and my concern over money, but I don't fuss about it half as much as you do."

Tim uttered an irrefutable truth. "That's because you have it," he said. Devon wandered to a window and pushed aside the curtains. The sleet lashed across the panes, and the river a few yards away was invisible in the blackness. Set in the paved terrace, just outside the window, was a plane tree. It generally stood quiet and domestic, city-bound, but tonight, with its boughs tossing wildly in the storm, it reverted to the primeval forests. Rooted in modernity, it cried to its ancient heritage as it creaked and groaned in the wind. Inside, the fire had burned low, and the only sounds in the room were an occasional ember dropping softly and the ice for highballs settling in the silver bucket. Devon dropped the curtain and came back to him.

"Well," she said at last, "as long as you are making the break from the business, maybe it's better for you to be out of town for a while. There'll be enough gossip as it is, but at least this way I'll be able to say that you're doing vital research work for the Government."

Tim smiled. "That's a new touch, and the Government doesn't know about it yet, though naturally, if it turns out as we hope, it will be available for the wounded of all the Allied armies."

Devon stood with her hands resting on the mantelpiece, staring thoughtfully into the fire. "Is it the war that's made you do this, Tim, or would you have come to it anyway?"

"That's hard to say. The war has jogged me into it more quickly, but I rather think I'd have come to feel this way even without it. Though I suppose no one can ascribe to himself total credit, or total blame either, for that matter, for participating in any widespread movement. His participation may be good or bad, but we're so inevitably influenced by the time we live in that it's hard to judge honestly as to how much is our own impulse and how much we've absorbed from the air around us."

"The influence varies widely, wouldn't you say, or there'd be no wars?"

"That's my point; but even the completely ignorant and the amoral are swept along, willy-nilly. Obviously what they do about it is a matter of opportunity and temperament."

Devon smiled. "The trouble with you is you're a man of stature, Timothy."

"Sounds ominous."

"No, you're no stuffed shirt, but it isn't unadulterated bliss either, being married to a gent with a social conscience."

"It isn't so much my conscience, but I've got eyes in my head. Obviously, under the conditions that prevailed in the world, change was inevitable, but it needn't have been a bloody slaughter except for the greed and fear in Europe and the greed and pigheaded apathy over here."

"You're not very tolerant, Mr. Wainwright."

Tim stretched his long legs towards the fire, his hands deep in his pockets. "I don't believe much in tolerance," he said moodily. "These days it's just another name for sitting around and shirking your job while the right guys fight for their lives and ours with their backs to the wall."

There was a silence. Devon yawned. "Sleepy?" asked Tim absently.

"Kind of. Tim?"

"Uh-huh?"

"When will you leave for Louisiana?"

He turned to her; there was that alert, eager look again. "Oscar and I hope to get off a week from Friday."

"Why didn't you tell me about this sooner?"

"Darling, the idea of actually going south only jelled a couple of weeks ago, and I didn't want to say anything about leaving the laboratory until I was dead sure. Don't think the final decision wasn't a wrench for me too, and I certainly wasn't going to tell Jasper until I'd talked it over with you."

Because she had rarely been in a spot where she had to, Tim being forehanded in such matters and because she didn't believe in it on principle, Devon seldom asked him if he loved her; but tonight she felt a little bleak.

"Tim?"

"Madam?"

"Do you love me?"

"What do you think?"

"I'm not sure."

"Well, I'll tell you, if Mrs. Wainwright will come to bed with Mr. Wainwright, he will do his utmost to convince her of his good will."

It was not quite the answer she hoped for, but it was an extremely pleasant makeshift. Taking his hand, she pulled him up from the couch. "The invitation is accepted with pleasure and the merest modicum of maidenly reserve, but Mrs. Wainwright would suggest to Mr. Wainwright that he be mighty careful how he tosses that charm of manner around the Southland."

PART TWO

As DEVON MOVED ABOUT THE DRESSING ROOM she glanced occasionally at the telegram lying on the mirrored table among the jars and
bottles and powder puffs. It read:

STILL A LONG ROW TO HOE BUT REACTIONS DISTINCTLY ENCOURAGING.
HAVE SEEN NOTHING OF ANY CREOLES IF YOU EXCEPT THE SHRIMPS
BUT A NOT UNSHAPELY OCTOROON DOES OUR ROOMS AT HOTEL.
OSCAR RATHER SMITTEN BUT PERSONALLY IMMUNE HAVING AL-
LERGY TO MUSTACHES. PLANNING LEAVE END OF MONTH. LETTER EN
ROUTE. GOOD LUCK PARTY. ALL LOVE, TIM.

He had been gone a little over four weeks, and Devon was dressing for the party for which he wished her well. She had had moments when she missed him desperately: in the evenings, late at
night before she fell asleep, when she was dressing, and on Sundays. Sundays were awful. They were one of the few times when
she ever wished for children. *If I had a child,* she thought, *I could
take it to see its grandparents, if I had any parents. What a sorry
thing it is to be rootless!*

Never having had much family life, she seldom missed it, but
with Tim away a vague self-pity engulfed her on Sunday, and the
vision of a large family, after one discreet drink of sherry, sitting
down to chicken and mashed potatoes with a hole in the middle

filled with butter hovered vaguely before her like the balloon dreams of characters in a comic strip.

Devon had been an only child. The family had lived in a small village in northwest Massachusetts, and after her mother's death, when she was twelve years old, her father moved to Williamstown to teach at the college. He was a man of remarkable intellectual attainment and great personal charm, but after his wife's death he never met another woman he wanted to marry, and although as she grew older Devon came to suspect that the pretty and discreet ladies who occasionally fluttered into his orbit were after something a little more tangible than a marriage of true minds, any further wedding, as far as he was concerned, was in the sight of God only. Until she was fifteen and went to boarding school Devon lived with her father and a housekeeper in a small house on the college grounds, and was petted and spoiled and sometimes chastised by the professor of mathematics and his wife, who lived next door.

The Stevenses had had a daughter who had died in infancy. Devon was just the age she would have been when her father brought her to live in Williamstown. The childless couple had taken a great fancy to the new professor of Romance languages and to his skinny sprout with her long legs and dark curling lashes, who, in spite of her shyness and misery over her mother's death, had gradually come to love them with a passionate devotion. She called them Aunt Mom and Uncle Pop and wept copiously when she was packed off to school, where, because she was a professor's daughter, her indifferent marks pained her teachers far more than they did the professor.

At eighteen, her schooling finished if incomplete, Thomas Elliott sent her to Europe with Matthew and Matilda Stevens. The professor of mathematics was taking a sabbatical year, and because he and his wife had loving hearts and rude health, they returned in the wake of their young whirlwind with constitutions only slightly impaired and no indisposition that six months' rest and a nourishing diet couldn't cure.

At nineteen, considering she had loafed long enough, Devon quit the academic shade to conquer New York. Wishing to earn a living and blessed with no illusions about her personal beauty, but shrewdly aware that in the faces of others might lie a fortune for herself, she enrolled in a training school for beauty operators. Another man of his intellect might have wished a stratum slightly more elevated for his only daughter, but Thomas Elliott had faith in his offspring. He was certain that her boundless energy, her ability to think a problem through, and, in a pinch, her unwavering lack of scruple would carry her to the top of any business career she might select. Accordingly he gladly contributed towards her tuition and living expenses. In his wisdom he made the contribution small so that at his death, when Devon was twenty-three, his savings and investments formed the substantial part of the price she paid when she bought the small cosmetic business of old Madame Le Beau. She and her father had always held for each other sentiments of the most cordial friendship, but the more orthodox filial-parental relationship was lacking. They were two independent human beings, devoted to each other but self-sufficient. Her greatest regret was that he should have died before she had time to justify his belief in her, but it was a strong factor in her determination to succeed. Inherited from him was the unavowed conviction that the dead, if they chose to take the trouble, could perfectly well find out how those they left behind were faring. She had no intention of giving her parents the chance to glance through the pearly gates and raise supercilious eyebrows over their daughter's mediocre achievements.

When she met Jasper she realized that she had found the man who could help her gaily to thumb her nose at those quizzical shades. They had worked together through the years to such effect that the departed Elliotts could rest in peace, or if so inclined, give a triumphant toot upon their trumpets as they thought of their offspring's success.

Devon fully expected the current enterprise, the line of cheap cosmetics, to uphold her firm's high standards. Her time these days was completely taken up listening to auditions and making decisions on the packaging of Flower-Fresh, the name finally chosen for the new product. Devon had conducted a poll of their operators and salesgirls throughout the country, and Flower-Fresh had won by an overwhelming majority. "It's so dainty," the ladies cried, and

hough dainty was a word which caused her acute nausea, having
or her a mincing, prissy implication stemming from a violent child-
ood aversion to the Dorothy Dainty stories, she bowed to the
perators' vote, considering them representatives of the class she
oped to please.

"Actually," she had written to Tim, "I think we are lucky in
lower-Fresh, for it is a pretty name, light and jaunty. Thank God
hey didn't choose Highland Lassie or Dove Cote, which Moreley
lso suggested and fought for like a she-wolf. He would have been
lrunk with power."

As she dressed she smiled reminiscently at her reflection in the
riple mirror. She and Moreley and Jasper had had some brisk
attles, but the new preparations were now in the making and the
usiness future seemed full of promise.

Louise, Devon's maid, was standing ready with her evening dress,
nd as she slipped into it she thought warmly of Jasper and with
resignation of his wife, for to her surprise Mollie had accepted the
invitation to the dinner party. Devon was rather fond of Mollie—
she was so ample, placid, and good-natured, you couldn't help it;
but she was something of a trial socially, as in an unobtrusive way
she was generally three sheets to the wind. She never created any
trouble, but her large myopic eyes would glaze slightly, and pres-
ently she would be asleep. Outside of her immediate circle few
people knew of her weakness, for Mollie could usually receive her
own danger signals, and with a murmured excuse about a headache
she would retire. For Jasper's sake, Devon was relieved that they
were spending the night here in town with her, as it would certainly be easier for Fairweather to shepherd Mollie upstairs to bed
than for poor Jasper to bundle her into the car and drive to Nutley
with her mountainous bulk slumped beside him.

Louise finished fastening her mistress's dress. "It's lovely, Mrs.
Wainwright. Madame should wear that dress always. The color, it
is beautiful."

"Thank you, Louise." Devon looked at herself in the glass. The
dress was becoming, soft and clinging and a misty purple-blue. It
made her skin look very white, and she had darkened her hair
especially for the occasion. Fortunately the color scheme was a suc-

cess, for the nerves of Monsieur Emile, the hairdresser, had been badly frayed in the process, the owner of the salon not being the most reasonable of its clients. Had he missed by a millimeter Devon's wrath would have sent him scuttling to a sanitarium, a quivering wretch. As it was he was taut as piano wire at the end of the session, and two double martinis and a long, bracing talk with Gustave, his roommate, were necessary before he was himself again.

Devon took up a clip, a frosty affair of moonstones and diamonds, a joint contribution from Tim and Jasper two Christmases ago. The card had read, "Because we love you." As she fastened it onto her dress, she turned to her maid. "Louise, go in and see if you can't help Mrs. Doolittle, and if Mr. Doolittle's already gone down say I'll join him in a minute." As she sprayed her hair with perfume, she glanced at a piece of paper covered with erratic doodles, her seating plan for the dinner table. She was giving a party because she always gave one at this time of year, but with Tim away, and so much work at the salon a large affair had seemed a useless effort. This evening's gathering was merely a token entertainment, but one which Nicky Van Alston had at the last minute complicated.

They were to have been ten for dinner, but he had phoned to ask if he couldn't bring a friend. "God forbid, my rose, that I should have the bad taste to inflict an extra woman on you," he said, "but I have a cheery gent in tow, eager to serve at your shrine. He should appeal to your sporting instinct—he's a carnivorous wolf."

Devon had protested, "But Nicky, I can only seat ten at the table and it's all even."

Van Alston had given her short shrift. "Nonsense, we aren't coming to mate. Simply put eight at the big table and have a children's table set up beside it. You and Kurt and I will lord it from there and mess with our bland diet. Champagne and junket, I love it!"

"Nick, you're a nuisance. Who is this stranger and why should I entertain him?"

"His name is Kurt Fabri, purveyor of leather goods. He's one of the more worthless refugees, and it's his birthday."

"Will he settle for no cake?"

"Certainly not. He's only coming because he knows you have the best cook in New York. He expects—wait a minute—what?" This last was to someone at his end of the phone. Nick's voice came back to her again. "He's also asking for ice cream in the shape of chickens, but I'll beat him down on that. He'll settle for straight bricks or else."

"Nicholas, you are a fiend in a form which only careless syntax could classify as human, but I recognize a spot when I'm on it. Bring along your scion of the Old World. By the way, what make of refugee is he? I warn you I'm allergic to Czechs."

"That's because they're high-minded, but you'll love Kurt. He is the unadulterated product of the baser elements, Austrian and Rumanian—what?" There was more disturbance at the other end of the wire. Nicky relayed the results. "He says he also had an Italian great-grandfather, but he was the black sheep of the family—fought with Garibaldi."

"O.K. Who am I to turn down the grandeur that was Rome? Dinner is at eight, and as I hear the tumbrels rolling I'll settle for black tie."

She had hung up and spent the next few minutes creating the undecipherable diagrams which she now picked up from the dressing table and carried downstairs with her.

In the drawing room Jasper sat with a highball beside him, totting up figures on the back of an envelope. What Dickie Masters, her decorator, referred to as "the salon, my dear" was a very beautiful room of airy elegance, subtle colors, and pale old paneling, an admirable background for the modern French paintings which adorned it. But even with its fragile quality it was a room men liked, for the chairs and sofas were comfortable and the more impractical antiques ranged out of harm's way. Tonight it was fragrant with great crystal bowls of freesia and white narcissus.

As Devon stood for a moment in the doorway watching Jasper, her heart was touched. He looked a little tired under the lamplight, and his gray hair was getting thin. He inclined to sententiousness at times, but he was a basic darling; hard and shrewd and, some people said, a dirty fighter in a business deal, but that wasn't so. He was simply quick to see his advantage and quick to seize it, and what he had, he held. He was tough, but he wasn't tricky. When he was a young man, his business opponents had called him Poker Face, and indeed he had pulled some notable bluffs with a cold and steady nerve which they bitterly resented, as they could not achieve it themselves. In recent years he had become so successful that no bluff was necessary, but his cool, quiet manner of dealing with a situation, a holdover from his youthful necessity, seemed to hold a slightly ominous portent which alarmed his competitors. Devon was aware of this and highly approved.

She knew that the struggle for survival in the world in which she lived was a bitter one; the lucky breaks were few, and inefficiency didn't pay off. Sometimes when she considered the stamina and ability a man had to have to come out on top, she felt for him an admiration almost sexual in its intensity. The few women who were her friends she was profoundly devoted to, but for most women she felt a slight contempt. She considered women, on the whole, less pathetic than men, who seemed to her ill equipped for life's battles. Poor souls, they worked like beavers putting money in their pockets and got neuritis pulling it out again. Every minute there was something—dinner, taxis, newspapers, the rent, pinball machines. They wrestled with life insurance and debts, and struggled along on twenty-five dollars a week, trying to support a family, and measuring themselves, not against the giants and feeling a profound discontent, but against the other little men and saying to their wives, "Well, honey, we're not doing so badly." Spiritually, they were unsound, forever butchering and killing one another, or adventuring to far corners of the globe in the most flimsy contraptions and losing their lives for their pains. Under most circumstances a little money meant freedom to a woman, but to a man a little money was bondage. That's why, when a man really triumphed, Devon felt an intense excitement. It meant he was truly a master, and because she was a great worldly success herself and a profoundly feminine woman she had a deep need of domination, physical, financial, or intellectual.

She had first been drawn to Jasper because he had a cool, tough-fibered mind that appealed to her and a ruthless quality that insured success, but they had become lovers because the core of hardness within him was a challenge to her femininity. Jasper never asked her to marry him, and there was a time when marriage would have seemed the natural outcome of their relationship, but he never spoke of divorcing Mollie, though such a wife could only be a handicap to him. Devon during the period of her romantic attachment imagined him as profoundly unhappy, deliberately hardening himself against love out of loyalty to his domestic ties, but she finally came to realize that if Jasper had deliberately cultivated his hardness, he had done it so successfully that he was emotionally indifferent to the rest of mankind. If Mollie had died, he would not even have considered it a solution, because as far as he was concerned no problem existed. Married and a father, he lived his own life as completely as though he were a bachelor. The Doolittles rarely entertained at home, but if they did and Mollie was indisposed, he was a completely capable host. He frequently went to other people's parties without her, but if she accompanied him, when the time came that she had to be helped home—and almost invariably it came—he did it automatically and without resentment. He was an intelligent man and was capable of affection and desire, but love as an emotion that brought him pain or longing or the need to serve or even inconvenience, for that matter, he was never to know; and though seldom given to conjecture about the inner lives of others, it had occurred to Devon that it was perhaps this very attribute which aggravated poor Mollie's failing. The more indifferent Jasper was, the more she drank, and the more she drank, the more impervious he became. It was this flintlike quality which had eventually frozen Devon out of love. Also about that time she met Tim, and his vitality and quick, aggressive affection had obliterated the cool gray man, but Jasper and Devon had for each other a genuine fondness compounded of long association, mutual interests, a sense of humor which caromed off the same angle, and she supposed the subconscious memory of their physical union.

This evening, as she stood in the doorway watching him and waiting for her guests, she was touched and amused when she thought how much she had wanted to marry him, and how glad she was that she had married Tim instead, and how pleasantly things had worked out after all. Here was Jasper, close-woven in the fabric of her life and this very minute as much at ease as if he

were in his own house, and poor Mollie no stumbling block at all
She crossed to him and sat down on the arm of his chair. "What are
you figuring?"

"How much Flower-Fresh is going to set us back."

"Nonsense. It'll make our fortunes, and even with the initial expense you admit we're cushioned against loss."

"Well, I don't think we'll be left holding any bag," he admitted
grudgingly. Considering the masterly hedging he had done to protect them from such a contingency, Mr. Doolittle's remark was a
triumph of understatement, and Devon knew it.

"Then what are you beefing about?"

"My principles are at stake," said the vice-president righteously.

"You are a fraud, but I am devoted to you," said the president,
and she leaned against him and kissed his thinning gray hair.

"I know, I'm the sere type," he said absently and continued his
figuring.

"I like it."

Jasper grunted. "You missed your calling—you should have been
in the front row of the chorus, Donna."

Years ago he and Devon had thought they would like to learn
Italian; she was considering opening a salon in Rome, and they had
taken five lessons. She was willing to continue, but the professor
couldn't stand the strain. It was sometimes midnight before they
got around to him, and Devon was always wanting to work out
chemical formulas—"I must be able to instruct my Roman staff"—
which confused him. Also it had turned out that Jasper had not
much facility for languages, but he learned that *donna* meant lady
and he liked the way it sounded. As Devon was at the time the lady
occupying his heart, he gave it to her as a half-mocking pet name,
and somehow ever afterwards it had hung between them, a bright
forgotten bauble when the rest of the Christmas tree was dim. He
didn't use it much, only when he was in an affectionate mood or if
she had unexpectedly done something foolish in business, and the
three times she had had laryngitis; but whenever she heard it it
brought back the old feeling of the champagne bubbles in her heart,
only it was more mellow, as if the champagne had stilled to gold
sauterne.

She idly twisted a few of his waning locks about her finger. "We've been together a long time, Jasper. You are a lamb."

Jasper looked up suspiciously. "Whatever you want, save your cajolery till after dinner, when, according to tradition, I'll be in a better mood. I shall then relax, take out a Corona Corona, and you may wheedle me."

"There is nothing you can give me, Mr. Doolittle, but I am true as the North Star, and I love you very much."

Jasper looked at her gravely for a moment, and then he chuckled. "You are quite a lass, my Donna, but you have a weather vane for a heart."

"And you, my poor Jasper, have no heart at all. Furthermore, I will thank you not to malign me. I have always been absolutely true to Tim."

"And you are now only because there's no one else handy. The pickings, like my hair, are getting thin."

"That is not true. It's because I love him. But are you implying that crowds of men no longer fall at my feet?"

He looked her over with cool deliberation. "Any seeing you tonight are bound to fall right on their faces. That dress is an intentional conspiracy against man's better nature."

"Yours, I gather, is proof against it?"

"Not at all, but I am an aging suitor and must conserve my forces for a young doxy whom I currently covet." So saying, he bent and kissed the soft fullness of her breast, half revealed by her low-cut décolletage.

"Jasper, you're a beast, I'm happy to say," she murmured dreamily, and then suddenly sat bolt upright on the arm of the chair. "My God, it isn't anybody in the salon, is it? Jasper, you promised . . ." Three years before, there had been an unfortunate incident, when the salon buzzed with gossip, and when confronted by her, Jasper had admitted that his interest in one of the operators had perhaps passed the bounds of paternalism. Devon was intensely annoyed and had pointed out to him that it was difficult enough to maintain discipline, and that good operators didn't grow on trees, to which he had responded: "My complaint is that there should be as many good ones as there are." But he had willingly agreed to

the transfer of his inamorata to the Chicago salon, and when she
had married a salesman three months later, he had behaved very
handsomely in the matter of a wedding present. This time, however
his conscience was clear.

"As far as I am aware, our current operators could be made out
of wood and welded into tin breeches. The young lady to whom I
refer is a model in a neighboring emporium, Saks Fifth Avenue,
not to put too fine a point on it. She is not without allure, but her
taste in hair dye could be improved by Edward or Gene or who-
ever our wizard is."

"Emile. Is she in love with you?"

"As she is not without an eye to this world's goods, she says she
is. I forgot to tell you, she is putting her little brother through college."

Devon's left eyebrow rose in a quizzical arc. "What's her name?"

"I forgot to tell you, I'm a gentleman and can't mention it. Doris
La Verne."

"Really?"

"No, really it's O'Hoolihan. La Verne is for professional purposes."

"I see. Well, I hope you and Miss La Verne will be very happy."

"I see no stumbling block. She thinks I'm rich and that I wear
keen clothes."

Devon fingered his lapel. "As a matter of fact, this suit is darn
good-looking."

Mollie came into the room just in time to hear this last remark.
She would never be pretty, but there was a sweet and wholesome
air about her. She made you think far more of cookies than of gin,
but gin was her preference. From something in her manner as she
entered, Devon suspected she had delayed upstairs long enough to
fortify herself from a pocket flask. She was wearing a black satin
dress with a surplice bodice, and her soft brown hair was waved
straight back from her forehead a little too rigidly for Devon's taste.
She pinioned her.

"Mollie, who did your hair this afternoon? Emile?"

"No, dear, Mr. Paul."

"Well, it's too tight again. I told them you were always to have Emile."

"I know, Devon, but he was busy." Mollie's tone was conciliatory. "They wanted to tear him away from the head he was working on, but it didn't seem quite fair, and Mr. Paul was free and so eager."

Devon laughed. "You're hopeless. You let them walk all over you." Mollie always made her think of an enormous dormouse, soft and brown and gentle. The mouse turned large myopic eyes on her husband. "Do you think it's too tight, Jasper?"

"My dear, if you like it, it's all right with me."

Mollie smiled happily. "Don't pick on me, Devon."

"Darling, I won't. You're looking very handsome. I consider both the Doolittles models of sartorial splendor. I was just telling Jasper I liked his suit."

"It's his figure really," said Mollie, as nearly cross as she ever got. "I don't see why he can't grow a paunch like other men." And she lowered her ample self into the sofa.

Devon held up his arm and examined the buttonholes. "Where did you get it?"

"I broke the habit of a lifetime and went to a new tailor."

"Mercy, Jasper, you must be in love." His wife spoke with the matter-of-fact domesticity of one recognizing the familiar symptoms of a cold.

"At my age, one does not fall in love."

"Oh ho," mocked Devon, protecting Mollie. "At thy age, pet, is the very time, though I would assume that previous practice was necessary. In your case I would say this was unlikely, for you, Mr. D., are a chilly fish."

"Oh no, Devon," said Mollie placidly; the gin she had drunk enveloped her in a shining cloud, something like spun sugar, and through it Jasper's infidelities shimmered rather attractively. She was a woman whose husband had mistresses, and it made her feel in the swim, part of that sophisticated world which, closed away in Nutley, she sometimes felt she was missing, when the gleam wore off her gin-manufactured cloud, and a dull gray mood settled over her, and the pain began. "Jasper isn't a bit chilly—his heart just isn't in it," and she giggled, for she thought she was rather witty.

Devon felt a dull ache in her own heart. Poor, poor Mollie. "Well, anyway, Jasper," she said lightly, "regardless of your lack of emotion, I think you can hope for a few offers in your elegant suitings. You are a handsome figure, and I expect to see you written up in theater programs."

"It's nothing," said Jasper, but he was extremely pleased. He wore easy casual clothes, but he gave them considerable thought and liked them to be appreciated. "I'll take Tim to this new place if you like," he volunteered amiably.

"I'm sure he'll be green with envy when he sees you," said Devon courteously.

"By the way, what do you hear from Tim? When's he coming home?" asked Mollie.

"I had a telegram this evening. He's leaving Louisiana the end of the month."

"It'll seem curious, Tim not coming back to the plant," said Jasper thoughtfully.

"Yes, it will," agreed Devon. "On the other hand, his behavior was so curious before he broke with us, we're probably better off."

As she spoke, there came a disturbance in the hall, and Nicky's voice calling, "Hi, where are the intellectuals? Here comes the beauty and chivalry!" Devon moved to the door to welcome her guests. There was Nicky, lean and dapper, the thinness of his face accentuated by his enormous horn-rimmed spectacles, there was Jennie Moore, the actress, fair as a Botticelli angel, her strange hoarse voice, the stand-by of every impersonator in the country. Jennie was one of the most ravishing women of her day, but her very radiance was a liability. She had a numbing effect on most men, and as her beauty was bone-deep and indestructible, she had never learned the coquetry that was other women's bait. "Hello, my duck, my pretty duck," she cawed cheerfully as she entered the room. She kissed Devon, that is to say the two women laid their cheeks together in warm affection and respect for each other's make-ups, and went to greet Jasper, whom she knew well, and Mollie, whom she was struggling manfully to recall.

"Devon, how are you, darling?" It was Dick Hadley, the scenic artist. He was tall and sandy and possessed of shy, charming manners, a sensitive imagination, and a consuming passion for Jennie. He had been her lover for two years and still eyed her as hungrily as the first night he met her. Devon was devoted to him, but she wished for his sake that he might develop a thicker skin. He seemed to her a misfit in the theatrical world, for in his mania for perfection he suffered agonies every time he designed a production, and the chicaneries of managers were to him an ever-fresh and devastating shock. She greeted him with special warmth. "Dick, I am glad to see you. Jennie's told me about the Boston notices of the new show, and that they went to town on your sets. Isn't it wonderful?"

Dick smiled like a pleased child, but then his brow clouded quickly with worry. "Of course we can't tell about New York."

"Nonsense, when have you ever failed?" And she gave him an encouraging pat. Dick looked at her gratefully and went to join his Jennie.

"And this, Devon, is the birthday boy." Nicky gestured with a flourish to the man who had followed him in. She turned to welcome him.

"How do you do, and happy birthday. It's nice of you to spend it with us."

Kurt Fabri clicked his heels, bowed, and kissed the hand she extended to him. "It is you, Miss Elliott, who are most kind to ask me." He had a pronounced foreign accent, but he spoke distinctly.

Since he had put her to some inconvenience, Devon looked at him with interest. She saw a man above average height, rather heavy-set, with a smooth face, slightly Oriental in cast, a sensuous mouth, and clear hazel eyes. He was bald except for a close-cut fringe of brownish golden hair, and his bearing was militaristic, but when he smiled she quickly forgot her first fleeting impression of rigidity.

"I beg you to believe, Miss Elliott, I said nothing about chickens."

"Chickens?" she frowned in puzzlement.

"Yes, the ice cream. That is all a figment for Nicky's imagination. He is on my neck like the old man of the mountains."

Devon laughed. Nicky was delighted by his entry but spoke with perfect gravity. "What did I tell you? Isn't he a find? After the war politicians are going to make him roving chairman, so as to prevent any nonsense about a better understanding between nations."

Kurt turned on him. "Nicholas, you are not a friend. You bring me to Miss Elliott's house, and for this I am grateful, but it is to exploit me, like masses."

Nicky gave him a friendly cuff. "You're doing all right, kid. Come and confuse the others."

"Nick, introduce Mr. Fabri to Mollie and Jasper. You met Jennie Moore and Mr. Hadley as you came in, I think?"

Kurt's hazel eyes smiled into hers. "Before, even. Nicky and I are picking them up at Miss Moore's house and coming together in her car here." Their eyes held for a moment. Devon had a curious and not unpleasant sensation, as if someone had pressed a key and blue electric sparks had leaped between them. *Well, what do you know!* she thought with a quick glow. *Sparks, at my age.* But suddenly she felt bashful and was grateful when the arrival of Estelle and George Lowery turned her from him. She extended both hands in welcome to the newcomers. "Georgie darling, Estelle."

Estelle was Nicky Van Alston's sister. Her first husband, an Englishman, had died, leaving her with a small daughter, and three years ago she had married George Lowery. She met him when he was in London on business in the summer of '38, and wanted to persuade him to set up for himself there and spend the rest of his life in England, but when they at last realized that the conflagration was inevitable, George insisted on returning to America. He had been able to achieve nothing substantial in London and felt that with the country at war it was no time to start from scratch. Besides he was deeply devoted to his little stepdaughter and didn't relish the idea of a bomb dropping on her head. Estelle would have agreed eventually, but she was more quickly amenable to the idea of coming to New York because she would be near her brother, whom she adored.

As George had, on his return, resumed his old job in Wall Street, he naturally had unlimited leisure, but very little cash to spend therein, and it was soon obvious that if it was to be filled with something other than liquor and deep depression, he would have to be given the wherewithal. They were nearing the time when not only George's leisure but the family stomachs would be badly deflated, when Estelle, who had a graceful pen and something of Nicky's lighthearted slant on life, landed a job on the editorial staff of *Vogue*. Her first concern, after stocking the larder, was to buy George a workbench and tools. There was nothing he couldn't do with his hands, so for the first time in years he eagerly looked forward to three o'clock and the closing of the Stock Exchange, when he could hurry home to a carpentry job. They lived in a small ground-floor apartment that opened into a back yard, and there George had built a little shed where he and Cynthia, his stepdaughter, spent long, enraptured hours.

"It's his sand pile," said Estelle indulgently. "He has such a happy time." She was small and discreetly rounded, with crisply curling hair and the same clipped speech that was her brother's stock in trade. George looked and was an average man. His features were indistinguishable, but the over-all effect was pleasant, and although not fat, there was a general air of rotundity and twinkle.

"Hello, George, how's the master builder?" Jennie waved to him across the room. George went over to join her.

"Jennie, you *are* looking well. I see no reason for you to use the stuff, but that box I promised you for your make-up is almost done. It's going to be a neat job, if I do say so—little drawers and trays—all sorts of gadgets. I'm going to lacquer it too."

"You cheer me, my lad. I was beginning to think that by the time you got through with it, the only make-up I'd be needing would be embalming fluid."

Jasper, who was standing beside her, laughed. "You're a girl after Bruce Moreley's own heart, Jennie. He thinks the dead should glitter, courtesy of Devonshire House."

Nicky cleared his throat ostentatiously. "I don't like to complain, but frankly, if we were in a better environment, we would be drinking by now. Think of the happy patrons of Murphy's corner pub." *What a dear, intelligent boy he is*, thought Mollie.

Devon reprimanded him. "We are temporarily dry, Mr. Van Alston, because Fairweather, who is high-class British, as opposed to you strolling players, is waiting for two other guests."

"I see no reason for penalizing the prompt arrivals," he replied crisply. "We are all shy, restrained characters, and a wee nip would put us at our ease." As he spoke, a loud burst of laughter from the group at the other end of the room shattered this fiction. Devon looked up to find Kurt beside her.

"You are maligning our hostess, Nicholas. She is not a lady whose parties need icecrushers to getting going."

She smiled at him. "Thank you, Mr. Fabri. Still, there is something to be said for—— Ah, the oasis," and she gestured to the end of the room, where the paneling opened to reveal a small bar and Fairweather standing behind it. Mollie rose with surprising agility for one of her bulk and hastened towards him, and even those guests who had their backs turned seemed to be irresistibly drawn in that direction, like particles sucked into a vacuum cleaner. Only Kurt remained where he was. "Aren't you a drinking man, Mr. Fabri?" He looked at her again in that curiously penetrating way, and she seemed to sense again an inaudible crackle of sparks.

"It is very seldom that I take alcohol," he said quietly.

"But Nicky is right—surely an occasional icecrusher——"

He flushed. "I have said it wrong, yes?"

"You have said it very nicely. It is just that the orthodox version is icebreaker."

"But why must one always be breaking or crushing things? It seems a foolish way to feel gay. I am born feeling good, and when I meet a woman whom I have wanted long to know, how unwise to blunt the edge of such a pleasure."

"For one who is handicapped by the language, sir, you manage to say very pretty things."

"Not at all. If you ever allow me to know you better, you will be finding I say only these things I mean." He had a strange gravity of delivery which somehow took the flattery out of his remark and made it seem real. It was very nice, but . . .

"Why ever should you have wanted to know me?" she asked skeptically.

"Because you are like no other woman I ever hear of. You are making world-famous successes in business, and you are most feminine."

"That's very flattering of you, but surely in America, not uncommon. Lots of women do it. Take Miss Moore, for instance, or any of our well-known actresses."

"But this is totally different. Actresses are with us always, and their brains are not so noticeable."

Devon's eyebrows shot up in alarm. "Good heavens, are mine showing?"

"No, that is what is altogether agreeable. With you, one knows they are there, yet they are not aggressive. They are a hidden challenge. It makes it more adventurous."

Devon's eyes grew very large. She had devoted considerable time to the application of Egyptian Reverie, their newest mascara, and the result was potent. "Makes what more adventurous, Mr. Fabri?" So soft the voice, so ingenuous the air, that, as she expected, the hunter was piqued to further audacity.

"The pursuit, Miss Elliott."

"Of happiness, Mr. Fabri?"

"This is not necessary. The pursuit of knowledge is sometimes more engrossing."

Laughter and the clink of glasses came to them from the bar, but they stood in a little pool of silence. Kurt continued, "It is very strange, but sometimes long before acquaintance a personality appeals to one, he follows it like a bright flame."

"And if he gets burned?"

"That is the chance he takes."

"I see, occupational hazard."

"What is this?"

Good Lord, thought Devon, *why can't he let it pass? This must be what they mean by Teutonic thoroughness.* She struggled through an explanation. "Well—er—Nicky tells me that you, for instance, have a leather business. Is that right?"

"Yes, I am making and designing all sorts of articles, bags, cigarette cases, luggage. I have here in New York a workroom."

"I see. Well, I don't know anything about your business, but let us suppose you have to use very sharp tools; you may cut yourself, or if you ever have to melt any glue, you might burn yourself in the flame. These are the risks you incur doing your job."

"Thank you, I understand."

But Devon had warmed to her work. "Hunters of course take other chances. They may be shot by a companion who didn't know his gun was loaded, or it is possible that if their quarry is spirited it may turn and rend them."

"These examples are most interesting," said her guest politely. "These hazards are perhaps why so many men are content to hunt rabbits."

She examined him, her head a little on one side. "You, I gather, are not a rabbit fancier?"

"No," he said, and Devon thought to detect a certain shortness of tone, "I do not care for these meek preys, for what I believe is called fish-shooting in the barrel."

"*Monsieur est très sport,*" she murmured, when her attention was diverted by the arrival of the two tardy guests.

"Devon *darling,* I'm *so* sorry but it's your fault, you insisted I call for Claire and you know what an unpunctual bitch she is. Wait till you *see* the delirium she's got herself up in!" The speaker was Dickie Masters, the decorator, and he was exactly like a willow frond, curved and swaying and infinitely slim. Most of Devon's friends were sharply divided in their appraisal of Dickie; some condemning him outright as a creature offensive to all normal right-thinking citizens, others accrediting to him a kind of reptilian charm, and still a third group regarding him with incredulous but delighted eyes as he swayed across their orbit, creating, for them to live in, houses of the most exquisite taste and imagination. As Nicky was something like God, accepting all the earth's creatures with understanding, he was less condemnatory of poor Dickie than Devon's other male friends, saying only that he invariably reminded him of the curates of Mr. Rupert Brooke's "Grantchester," who trod "on lissom, clerical, printless toe." Seeing him come in now, Nick was the first to call a greeting. "Poor lad, come and sustain yourself with a wee nip of champagne."

Dickie looked with languishing eye at his hostess. "Darling, champagne? What heaven!"

"Of course, Dickie, it's a proper party. You don't think you'd be invited to anything but the best, do you?"

"Well, I can't be sure, I've been in some very odd places, dear. And who is this pilgrim?" Dickie had caught sight of Kurt, the only person in the room aside from Mollie Doolittle whom he didn't know. Devon introduced them. "Mr. Kurt Fabri, Mr. Masters."

Dickie looked at him with interest. "I say, are you the chap who's designing Cartier's new leather stuff?" and he drew from his pocket an original, extremely smart cigarette case. Kurt bowed.

Devon was delighted. "Why, Dickie, what a fortuitous compliment! But then, as you can see, Mr. Fabri, Mr. Masters is fashion's glass." She suspected a glint of mockery as Kurt murmured politely, "That I am realizing. This dark red dinner jacket is most novel, no?"

"It's positive drag, isn't it?" said Dickie good-humoredly. "But then I'm the chattel, the absolute chattel, of the tailor I've been going to for years. He adores dressing me—of course, he's a masochist, I never pay—but I put up with his tantrums, because his materials are sensational. I'm upholstering Fifi Vallambrosa's sofa entirely in his tweeds."

Claire Dangerfield, who had arrived with him, now joined them, having finished her belated toilette in Devon's powder room.

"Devon sweetie, I'm sorry we're late. Dickie, tweed is a revolting idea, so scratchy."

Dickie dismissed her objections with a white hand. "You're livid, pet, because you didn't think it up for Mary Mann. We all know that Fifi's sofa is a one-story riding academy. What more endurable than tweed for the sporting life?" And he wafted himself to the bar.

Claire looked after him with some irritation. "For such a thin pansy, Dickie has an awfully fat nature. He's all buttoned up in an impenetrable little coat of complacency. Any time you criticize an idea of his, he thinks it's because you're jealous. He ought to know that at McCormick's our very souls are upholstered in flowered chintz."

Kurt was standing with the slightly dazed expression of a man who not only doesn't know how to box, but doesn't understand the language his sparring partner is using. Devon's sense of hospitality smote her. Dickie and Claire were an odd pair, and no mistake, but while Dickie needed no explanation, Claire, under a rather trying exterior, was an engaging personality. Of course, her clothes were fantastic; tonight, her head was wrapped in a magenta jersey turban, she wore a navy blue wool sweater sparkling with sequins, Turkish trousers, platform-soled shoes, and ropes of pearls and gold beads twisted around her throat, but she had a piquant little monkey face and men found her amusing. They also had some vague idea of protecting her from herself, feeling that under her screwball goings on beat a tender woman's heart. The little creature had a heart all right, but it was rather like a New England field, soft and fertile in spots but thickly studded with rocks on which more than one way-farer had painfully stubbed a toe.

Devon, feeling that the decorating jargon was perhaps out of Kurt's line, sought to enlighten him. "Miss Dangerfield works at Mary Mann McCormick's, you know, the interior decorator, and of course Dickie's one too, so it distorts an otherwise beautiful friend-ship. I sometimes feel that the competitive system is basically un-sound, don't you?"

Claire cut in, "Even in a communistic Utopia, honey, there would be nothing beautiful in my feeling for Mr. Masters."

Kurt smiled at her. "But surely you are unjust, Miss Dangerfield. Probably Mr. Masters is so masculine he is thinking it is effeminate to go with women."

Claire tilted up her gamin's face. "I hope not, Mr. Fabri. Where attractive men are concerned the competition is tough enough," and she grinned at him with such engaging impudence that he felt warm all over. It was fortunate, as at that very moment a slight chill seemed to emanate from his hostess. Kurt was quick to sense Devon's resentment of Claire. Good, he thought, she was piqued; that meant she was interested, and a feeling of excitement quick-ened within him. He had been honest in telling Devon that he had wanted to meet her for a long time. He had seen her twice—once at an opening night and once at a large dinner given for Allied Relief —and there was something about the way she moved, the way her mouth curved when she smiled, that stimulated in him an erotic response. He had asked who she was, and when told she was Devon Elliott, one of the cleverest businesswomen in America and cer-tainly one of the richest, the information was a gage to his hunter's instinct. Her wealth for its own sake did not attract him, but the fact that she was capable of earning it piqued his imagination. To dominate such a woman was a challenge to the male ego. Kurt had singleness of purpose, a strong amoral sense, and was sunnily free from scruples about other people's marriage ties. Since his desire for Devon was genuine, the moment he felt her interest he turned with practiced deliberation to Claire. "The more I think of this Mr. Dickie Masters, the more I am being on his side. I would consider him a most desirable escort for the woman I cared about. The mind could be quite free from jealousy."

"Do you suffer much from jealousy?" asked Claire, all tender solicitude and dimples.

"I could not want a woman who was in love with someone else, so in that way I am lucky. I would not be jealous of the other man, but I would do my very best to see that she was not in love with him."

There he goes again, thought Devon, *sounding sincere and rather sweet where another man would sound foolish. And that Claire, cooing and smiling and making him think she thinks he's wonderful. She's mentally stabbing him to death or I miss my guess.* Aloud Devon spoke with the clear guileless tone of a little child: "You see, Claire, Mr. Fabri is part Turkish. I suppose Dickie makes him feel at home. Such a nostalgia you must have, Mr. Fabri, accustomed as you doubtless are to hordes of women surrounded by eunuchs."

"It is true, Miss Elliott," said Kurt gravely, "I am, how you might call individual walking melting pot, but I have no Turkish blood—Austrian, Jewish, Rumanian, and an Italian great-grandfather. There is also a family rumor that somebody was Armenian, but this I think is boasting."

"Oh? Still those Eastern customs are awfully fluid; they spread, don't you think?"

"Good Lord, Devon," said Claire, "with that hodge-podge, if he can regulate the customs at all, I think he's doing damn well!" And she looked at him with open admiration.

"Cocktails, madam?" It was Fairweather, who arrived with a tray of brimming glasses. Claire was being a nuisance; still she was a guest, and Devon supposed some sort of courtesy was due her.

"Drink, dear?" she asked crisply. Claire helped herself to an old-fashioned while her hostess turned a thousand-watt smile on their bone of contention. "As you're a customs official, Mr. Fabri, surely you'll break down and indulge in an early American one?"

Kurt reached for champagne. "I thank you, though in this house artificial stimulus would seem totally unnecessary."

Long afterwards, Devon was to remember that party as an emotional shuttle, a curious mixture of gaiety and venom, challenge and riposte recalled through a haze of champagne. One moment she would see him down the room engrossed in conversation with someone else, and the next, she would turn to find Kurt at her side.

"You are very attentive, Mr. Fabri."

"It is not to be attentive only. I am afraid it is the moth and the magnet."

And her own voice, "Why are you afraid? Magnets don't burn." She drank a good deal, and the party went on around her, weaving like a ballet, shimmering like a dream. Bits of conversation floated in her memory; there was Jennie telling everyone about her friends, the Hamiltons: " . . . and so as Joe's show had just closed and he was out of a job anyway, he thought he might as well go to Canada and try the R.C.A.F., and Beth has taken a little house to be near him." And Estelle Lowery, "Whatever for? I thought Joe was a fag." And Jennie, "So he is, dear, but Beth is a camp follower."

And the argument about Biblical quotations, and her own surprise to find George Lowery a modest authority on Holy Writ, saying firmly, "It has nothing to do with the New Testament. It's in Genesis. 'And God saw every thing that he had made and behold, it was very good,'" and Jasper, who had been holding forth on the Roosevelt administration, replying tartly that He was easily pleased.

She remembered dinner, and how when they reached the dessert, and there was ice cream, not in the shape of chickens, but heaped with great black cherries and flaming with brandy, Kurt had said it was his most sumptuous birthday, but when Fairweather brought in the cake ablaze with candles, he had said nothing, but he had stared at it enchanted, and later he had risen to propose a toast, saying, "Since I am a little boy, no such lovely thing has happened to me.

I drink to my hostess who has thought to renew my childhood, to remind me of my country in the happy days. Never, never can I forget her graceful thought." Devon's eyes were wet, partly because she was remembering Tim's birthdays, and partly because of the champagne and her dear kindhearted civilized friends, and this poor, poor homeless refugee, who had found asylum on these democratic shores.

"It would have been truer hospitality if I had made the cake with my own hands," she cried, yearning to give of herself in this great world conflict, but cutting through her effulgence, cool as a knife blade, came Nicky's voice, "As one who came face to face with the only egg you ever fried, my blossom, I would say that our Balkan cousin was shot with luck."

"Fancy," murmured Mollie. "It's so rare one meets a Balk."

She remembered Claire Dangerfield's emotional crisis, which the ladies had faced alone when they retired, leaving the gentlemen to their brandy and cigars. It had come about because Claire had been bickering with Dickie on decoration all through dinner, and Devon had asked why on earth she hadn't wanted Gil Emery, her standard beau, to be invited. "It would have been so peaceful, darling, and you wouldn't have had that thorn in your flesh." She was feeling amiably disposed towards Claire. There was no doubt about it, all through dinner Kurt had concentrated on her, Devon, in the most delightful way. He was not aggressive; there was nothing of the professional European charmer in his manner, but he had an amusing trick of paying compliments with the greatest gravity, and he took a childlike enjoyment in his food and in Nicky's quips; but Devon, who was not a specialist in the great mother heart, noted with satisfaction that there was nothing childlike about his hands, or the set of his shoulders, or the way he looked at her. Not that it was of any importance, and certainly with Tim and his whims, and the business, she had her hands full, and neither the time nor the inclination for extramural activities; still, the fillip of frank admiration was not unpleasant, and as Kurt had been attentive to her first in her own house, she felt she had staked a claim, ephemeral perhaps, but still, she had been piqued by Claire's interference. The claim was no more than a mirage, of course, and only for the evening, but she preferred to be the sole squatter. Nicky's idea of a table for three had turned out very well; she had, so to speak, clinched the deal, and she could dismiss Kurt temporarily and concentrate on Claire's involvements.

"Have you and Gil had a fight?"

"Well, I'll tell you, it's sort of complicated." The five women were upstairs, Devon and Claire in the bedroom, and Mollie, Jennie, and Estelle repairing their make-up in the dressing room. Louise had just finished passing after-dinner coffee.

"Shall I bring up liqueurs, madame?"

"Never mind, Louise, we'll have them downstairs." The maid withdrew, and Devon turned eagerly to Claire.

"Come on, tell me," she said, lowering her voice so as not to be overheard by the others in the dressing room. Claire looked like a naughty child.

"Well, you see, it's this way. There has been kind of a thing between Gil and me for some time."

Devon's expression was a comic mixture of disbelief and amusement. "Darling, they do claim there's nothing between you, which makes for a far happier situation, I'm sure."

Claire accepted this with complacency. "Yes, well, that's partly the trouble. A barrier has arisen."

"You mean . . . " Devon spoke with mock melodramatic intensity.

"Yes, I think I'm changing my mind, you see——" She stopped short as Mollie entered from the dressing room, carrying her coffee cup. Mollie's gaze wavered towards them, and she hiccupped abruptly. "Schuse me," she murmured, with a benign smile. Hiccup. "Coffee very hot."

Devon prodded Claire. "Go on"; then, seeing her glance towards Mollie, she murmured almost inaudibly, "Don't worry, she won't understand. Sit down over there, Mollie darling," she said loudly, and cordially waved the bemused lady to a satin-covered rocking chair some distance from the bed where they were sitting. She turned again to Claire.

"Have you met anyone else?" she asked, sincerely hoping Claire had. If Tim was going to be buried in proteins, it would be nice to have Kurt as a personal extra man, and Claire, when not hog-tied, had a predatory eye, and Kurt had been amused by her.

"Yes, I have," said Claire. "And the trouble is, I suspect I'm about to care for him. I recognize my own fatal symptoms. He seems to me kind of lonely. That's bad. Of course he has an encumbrance shaped like a wife, but he still seems to me lonely."

"Well, these things happen," said Mollie unexpectedly, and relapsed into her chair, where she continued dreamily to conduct the slow movement from Dvorak's New World Symphony with her coffee spoon. The melody had been running through her head all evening. "I'm very musical, dear," she said, to no one in particular.

Jennie and Estelle, in the dressing room, gazed at themselves searchingly in the mirror and, considering they had achieved the pinnacle of pulchritude, joined the coterie in the bedroom. In the soft light, her white shoulders gleaming through the fragile black lace scarf she wore, Jennie was indeed breath-taking. Devon looked at her with professional admiration. "You're a beautiful creature, Jen. I think I'll have you stuffed and put in our window." Jennie chortled, "Darling, I'd scare away the customers."

Estelle watched the couple on the bed with bright, birdlike eyes. "What are you two dishing?" she asked, in her fresh English voice. "You look as thick as thieves."

"Claire has a new beau."

Claire made a strange, muttering sound. To the surprise of the others, she looked far from content over this normally refreshing situation.

"I don't see that a new beau is anything to worry about," Jennie said reasonably.

"Well, I should think not." Devon's tone held warm encouragement.

"That's all very well," said Claire, a little annoyed by so much good will. "But I have, as you might say, overstepped the mark."

"With the newy?" Estelle's eyes were bright with interest.

"No, Estelle, with Gil, old tried-and-truey."

"But darling, you did that long ago." Estelle spoke with simple candor.

Claire considered her good nature was being pushed too far. "No, no, no, you don't understand," she said impatiently.

Estelle was a little hurt. "Well, of course, if it's a secret, Jennie and I can always leave."

"Nonsense," Devon said crisply, "Claire knows perfectly well we're not a bunch of blabber-mouths. Go *on*, Claire." The late-comers to the confidence, if a little hazy as to what it was all about, still gave Claire their unstinting attention. Though caution bade her keep her counsel, she could not resist this sweet adulation. "Well . . . we've been together a long time, and I am terribly fond of Gil—considering my first two husbands, he really is a lamb—but he hasn't any money and is full of scruples, so, wanting to break the deadlock, about five weeks ago I asked him to marry me."

Jennie turned the full force of her approval on her friend. Her beautiful eyes glowed with fervor. "Darling, how wonderful! That's the most courageous womanly gesture I ever heard of. Did he accept?"

Devon was contemptuous of such doubt. "Of course he accepted, Jennie. Look at all the others, why wouldn't Gil?"

"The others asked me," said Claire coldly. "But anyhow he did accept." Undeniably her manner was glummer than the recognized bridal standard. "He accepted, children, and there is my problem. What with this newer interest superseding the old, I am in an extremely delicate position. What I want to know, Mr. Anthony, is this: If I don't marry him, am I a cad?" There was a silence while the ladies pondered this nice point of etiquette.

"Well, one thing is clear," said Devon finally. "You must get the ring back."

"And your letters, darling," croaked Jennie. "My God, when I think of the after-clap of the written word! A bloody illiterate, that's the thing to be."

"Well, I am practically," confessed Claire. "I loathe writing letters, and besides if a man doesn't love me enough to stay with me, what's the use of pumping oxygen into his deflating emotions when he's away?"

The discussion swayed back and forth, the preponderance of opinion holding that Claire should hang onto Gil, certainly until the newy got his divorce and came panting up with ring and preacher.

The shifting pattern of the party wove through Devon's memory. The women had flowed downstairs to the drawing room, all except Mollie, who once she was near her bed could not resist it. Devon had helped her to her room and sent Louise to undress her.

She remembered later on someone asking about the puppy she and Tim were to get from Miss Flora's litter and that when George Lowery had asked Kurt if he had a dog, Kurt replied that he didn't care for them and George had looked at him suspiciously and remarked to her later that he was probably a Nazi, and though she considered it ridiculous prejudice, she found that her own liking for him chilled just a little.

Nicky had described the arrival of Miss Flora's offspring with considerable gusto, his eyes peering out owlishly from behind his horn rims. It had been a long haul, he said, and naturally he didn't like to leave a lady in distress, but the only nourishment the house provided was three Saltines and a bottle of scotch. "Well, children, it was share and share alike through the long night watch, and finally at four-fifteen in the morning I fell on my nose drunk as a skunk just as the litter arrived."

Dickie chortled, "My dears, can't you see them swarming?"

"Then you're a better man than I am, laddie," said Nicky. "Because even with a bottle of scotch under my belt, the most I could see was one."

"Oh no!"

"Oh yes. One minute rat." And he rolled the *r* in such a way and bit off the *t* so sharply that poor Miss Flora's effort seemed like sabotage.

"And who has it now?" asked Claire with interest.

"God."

"Oh, what a waste of time!" Dick Hadley's voice held real sympathy. "Poor Miss Flora must have been grief-stricken."

"On the contrary, she was delighted," said Nicky. "That girl is not the maternal type. She obviously felt that a wee one would frighten the boys away. I think she ate him," he added in a matter-of-fact voice.

"Poor Nick," said his sister. "You'll have to wait till Cynthia grows up to learn the art of being a grandfather."

"That's one thing about my spouse," said Jennie, "you'd certainly never think it, but he's wonderful with dogs. He and dogs are just like that," and she crossed her fingers, indicating the proximity. "He started a kennel once—the bills crippled me."

Kurt, overhearing this, experienced some surprise. On the way to Jennie's house earlier in the evening, Nick had implied that Miss Moore's escort was naturally her devoted lover, so the casual reference to a husband was unexpected. "I did not know you are married, Miss Moore," he said politely.

"Yes indeed," replied Jennie affably. "My husband's an agent and he's drunk." And she lifted her ninth glass of champagne in cheery salute. It was these candid and, he could not but consider, unfeeling admissions on his Jennie's part which caused torment to Dick's sensitive soul. Kurt who, owing to his European optimism, automatically assumed that if a woman was not deformed she had a lover and frequently a husband, was perfectly willing to drop the matter; but Dick, though he writhed with embarrassment and misery, felt goaded into explanation. "You see, Miss Moore's husband is not very strong."

"I see," said Kurt gravely, but Dick, already raw on the subject, sensed a further implication. "He . . . he frequently has to have treatments."

This Jennie gladly corroborated. "You bet. D.T.'s," and she shook her lovely head in lament.

"I am sorry," said Kurt, feeling that this English phrase was inadequate, but that in German, Rumanian, or Swahili the reply could have been no different.

"Oh, I don't mind," and Jennie turned upon him the smile that was box-office bait from New York to San Francisco, and which caused poor Dick's heart to miss a beat every time she flashed it. "You see, I was so used to paying him ten per cent anyhow that I automatically kept it up after we separated." She drank a little more champagne. "Ten per cent is just," she said, mouthing the words with care, "but Ollie—that's my husband, Oliver Newcomb—claims it's not enough, because drinking is pretty much his career, and with the new liquor taxes, his overhead has shot 'way up."

Kurt, beginning to feel like a man fighting his way through taffy, could only murmur that he considered her allowance ample. She turned towards him, and in a moment or two her great violet eyes came into focus. "You do? That's wonderful. Dick thinks I'm all wrong."

Dick spoke desperately. "No, darling, I only think you're wrong because you're too generous. The blighter shouldn't have anything. God, when I think of the way he treated you!"

"That's right, I forgot. He beat me, Mr. Fabri," and the deep tones were husky with tears.

"He did? When?" Dick's voice was tense. He had thought to have the full category of Newcomb's ignominies—he was listing them for a divorce; but, low as the fellow was, Dick had been unaware of physical violence. If he had beat Jennie, not only was it terrible, but she must have been with him recently, and she had sworn to Dick that she had not seen her husband for two months. As of that date, there had been no beatings. "When did he lay hands on you, Jennie?"

Jennie knit her beautiful brows in a titanic effort at recollection; then she giggled. "Really, darling, what a thing to ask me in front of all these people!"

The party had come to an end finally, but not until Nicky had played dozens of songs recalled from his English music-hall days, and Estelle, who had an unexpected talent for mimicry almost as sharp as her brother's, had regaled them with an imitation of the *Vogue* editorial staff in conference. Dickie Masters had done a swift and lethal caricature of Kurt ogling Devon while Tim sat in the midst of pencil strokes representing sugar cane, with his arm around a billowing black mammy. In awkward childish printing Dickie had captioned it *"Monsieur se console."* When she saw it Devon was torn between indignation and laughter, an effect Dickie frequently produced, but it was too late to lose her temper, for the artist had thoughtfully laid it on her pillow, and she didn't find it till she went up to bed.

Kurt had been most charming and appreciative in making his

farewells, and he and Nick had been the last to leave. "May I call you, Miss Elliott?"

"Of course. Perhaps you'll come and dine another time?"

"It would be making me the greatest happiness. I thank you." He kissed her hand and clicked his heels and bowed, and looked rather strangely at Jasper, who stood behind her in the doorway as she saw Nicky and Kurt out.

"I don't care for that guy," said Jasper when they went back to the drawing room to put out the lights. "Too damn much heel clicking."

"Do you think he *is* a heel?" Devon asked. She was standing by one of the soft-shaded lamps, pensively pushing the switch in and out.

"Shouldn't wonder," replied Jasper with the Yankee's distrust of a foreigner. "He probably realizes it subconsciously—all that clicking is a manifestation. Come on, make up your mind about that light and let's go up."

"Do you want me to come in with you to see if Mollie's all right?"

"Don't bother, she'll be dead to the world."

Devon sighed. She hated to go to bed after a party, but it looked as though she was driven to the last ditch, when she suddenly thought of a detour.

"I know what, let's go out to the kitchen."

"Good Lord, you're not hungry, are you?" Jasper was incredulous, because at one o'clock Fairweather had served a small cold buffet and a smoking tureen of hot gumbo.

"N—no, not exactly," said his spiritual colleague. "But I like to raid the icebox."

Jasper had had trouble with her appetite for years, so he was resigned. "O.K., I guess I can down a glass of milk."

"Force yourself, dear. It's lovely for your calcium."

They had gone into the gleaming kitchen, which was what Anna, the cook, referred to as "Real moderne, thank the goodness," and unearthed from the icebox a few remaining remnants of the saddle of lamb. As they stood contentedly munching—it turned out that Jasper was able to take a little solid nourishment as well—the sharp peal of the telephone made them jump.

Devon looked at him. "Who in the world——"

"That would be your boy friend, the member from Alt Wien."

"Humph," said the lady. "Kind of aggressive, ain't he? It probably isn't at all, though," she added, throwing a few grains of wheat to the gods as she went to the pantry phone. "Hello?"

"Hello," Kurt's voice came over the wire. "It is being most thoughtless, I know, to call so late, but I have just dropped Nick and am in a phone booth." There was a slight pause. Devon could think of no rejoinder, and besides, she was embarrassed by Jasper's unblinking gaze.

"Well—er—have fun," she said lamely.

"Please, I am thanking you for the most lovely evening I spend since I am in America."

"Aren't you nice! I was delighted to have you."

There was another pause. She liked him, but she wished he'd hang up.

"I have not awakened you, no?"

"Not at all." Devon spoke quickly, happy to find a conversational straw to cling to. "Mr. Doolittle and I are just going to bed." Which was how Jasper came to splutter, showering his dinner jacket with milk, and how Mr. Fabri received an impression which, while accurate, was seven years too late.

PART THREE

THE DAY AFTER THE PARTY Devon came home from the salon to find an enormous box of spring flowers from Kurt. His card was enclosed, but there was no personal message written on it. She automatically passed her thumb over the name—it was engraved—and stood for a moment flipping it back and forth between her fingers and gazing down at the flowers. The frail, subtle fragrance of narcissus, tulips, and white lilacs filled the room, and it occurred to her in one corner of her mind that Spring Freshet might prove a popular name for a cologne. The rest of her thoughts were centered on Kurt. It seemed even to herself that any judgment of character based on one evening's acquaintance, especially one champagne-englamored, was bound to be premature, but she felt the tug of a strong current between them, and he was the first man since she had known Tim who had so caught her interest. As she was no longer eighteen and had a husband to whom she was devoted, she did not in fancy leap through the proposal, the bridal night, and the graduation of her firstborn, a telescopic feat which had been her custom when, as a young girl, she met any young man who did not evince positive distaste at the sight of her. The idea of further meetings with Kurt, however, was distinctly pleasurable.

He had for her a potent appeal; but was it, she wondered, based merely on novelty and the jujitsu antics he performed with the English language? She didn't believe so, because he had a kind of dignity too, and politically he was sympathetic. *That's another funny thing,* she thought; *how much more involved love is now than in the old days!* Then one's young man only had to have sex appeal, a "cute line," and as much money as possible, and somehow politics never occurred to anybody, as naturally all right-thinking people above the Mason-Dixon line were Republicans and the politics of the South were easily explained by the climate. But the New Order had changed all that, although not all refugee Europeans were automatically desirable. Recent arrivals especially were so hell-bent on charming rich American women and trying to show up American men as poor lovers that their overzealousness made them ridiculous, but Kurt's charm was natural and unforced and his manners were polite, yet without that too high gloss affected by some men which is as offensive as too bright polish on their fingernails.

As his flowers and the thought of the note of thanks she would write him put her in an extremely good humor, she deliberately tossed a little salt on the foam. *He is probably an Armenian louse from 'way back in his grandmother's time,* she reminded herself, *all the while behaving in what the French refer to as a manner "très correcte."* That was one of the things that had sickened and disgusted her when France fell. The Germans had indulged in unprovoked aggression, they had slaughtered, robbed, raped, and hoodwinked a people, but because they clicked their heels and passed farcical laws legalizing their rapine it was said of them that they were *"très corrects."* From the little news that had come out of the country, she had learned that the Nazis had taken over the Devonshire House Paris salon, forced the safes, stolen the formulas, and were running the business for their own profit. This little swindle seemed to her so monstrously incorrect that she was bitterly resentful and, when she met Kurt, sympathetically inclined toward those who had been so victimized. Anyway, supposing he was nothing more than an amiable scoundrel, as Jasper seemed to think, it might be amusing—a couple of luncheons, tea in the drawing room before the lamps were lit or the curtains drawn, the river flowing past the window, and they two sitting in the twilight; what harm? . . . and the man had an extraordinarily male quality.

But the next day came the letter from Tim, and any thoughts of dalliance were swept away in the emotional turmoil it evoked.

Each morning when she rang Louise would bring up the breakfast tray and the mail. Devon's awakenings were pleasanter than most, as all bills were sent to her office; but of course, aside from personal letters, she got the usual amount of pleas, sales announcements, and advertisements. Nothing more annoyed her, because it was so wasteful, than to receive duplicate ads, one addressed to Mrs. Timothy Wainwright and one to Miss Devon Elliott, and she had forced her own mailing department, through considerable travail, to eliminate any possible repetition.

Today the breakfast tray looked unusually gay as Louise set it on her knees, the pretty flowered china splashed with sunshine, Fairweather's morning rose brightly blooming, and a fat batch of mail. As she lifted it from the left-hand pocket, the *Times* and the *Herald Tribune* neatly balanced the opposite basket, Tim's letter in its air-mail envelope lay first on the pile. His letters were grand, funny and affectionate, so she opened it eagerly.

DEVON DEAREST:

Things here have been pretty much the same since I last wrote. We've been continuing with the experiments and have unearthed, I think, some pretty exciting stuff which I will tell you about in as much detail as will be any fun when I see you. Did you know that we were participants in some of the Mardi Gras festivities? We cravenly took time out from bettering the lot of mankind and went down to New Orleans for three or four days. Baby, don't ever let anyone give you that baloney about Southerners being a lackadaisical lot. Each frail magnolia blossom turns out to be U.S. Steel for endurance. Some kind of shindig was held in our honor, and the bourbon rose over the levees. I want to tell you-all it was mighty fine, and I never did hear such fiddlin' or see such dancin'. Being in a somewhat sated state, I did not indulge in the dancing, but Oscar displayed unknown talents and, not content with the more normal forms of jive, improvised as he went along, leaping to heights which would have crowded Nijinsky. It was a couple of days before I thought it wise to bring him into contact with a test tube. A man can get a nasty cut from a shaky hand.

And now, my darling, with this brief exposé of the quaint native customs, I come to the real reason for this letter. I have thought about what I am going to tell you as sanely and realistically as I could. At first it never occurred to me to say it to you in any way but face to face, but now it seems to me kinder and more reasonable to write it to you first and to discuss it with you when I get back, and you will have had time to think it over.

Point-blank, this is it: when I return to New York from this trip, I do not want to come back to the house to live. No, I am not crazy, and I am not in love with anyone else. I love you, and I never expect to love any other woman, but my life has changed. It is hard to say it and not sound heavy, but I am engrossed heart and soul in this research work. It is possible that I may have to do a good deal of my work out of New York, even should the Rockefeller Institute appointment come through for Oscar, and when I am living in the city I will not have the money to contribute to running the house; and though I often tease you about your acquisitive instinct, it is because you are, with those you love, the most generous of women that I cannot face a setup whereby you support me. Please try to understand this, darling, and do not think I am going off half-cocked. I have lain awake night after night trying to work it out differently, and I always come to the same conclusion: in order to do my job and have any self-respect, I have got to stand on my own feet, and I have got to stand alone.

When I come back, I'll stop for a while at the club till I am able to get the laboratory running and see how the land lies. If we handle this with tact and discretion, I do not think we need fear unpleasant publicity. Besides, if I know my girl, she has never given ground to any reporter. I will, of course, wire you the exact date and time of arrival, and in the meanwhile know that, even if it doesn't sound that way, my love for you is unfailing.

TIM.

Devon put down the letter and sat for a long while, propped against the pillows, staring into space, while the jasmine tea grew cold and the fluffy, piping-hot muffins sagged unhappily. Tim wasn't coming back to her. For a time her mind was empty. The river flowed past the window, sparkling in the morning sunshine, the top branches of the terrace tree tapped a gentle greeting on the panes, and she was aware of them, but of no reaction from Tim's letter. It was as though she had had a spinal anesthetic; she was conscious, but no message went from her nerves or heart to her brain. She looked again at what he had written, and though her eyes were dry, the letters began to blur. Through the closed door of the dressing room she heard the soft roar of water rushing into the tub, and the homely sound somehow broke the numbness. Tim wasn't coming back. Curiously enough, she believed him when he said he loved her. For the last seven years he had given her too much proof of it for her to doubt him now; but it was for that very reason that she suddenly felt a terrible tightening in her heart. If their love for each other, which was great, still couldn't keep him with her, then the last and strongest bolt was already shot. She hadn't a fighting chance. This new interest was so all-engrossing that he didn't even want to live in the same house with her. *Dear God*, she thought, *if only it were another woman! That's easy; a clever wife can combat her, but when a man is claimed by an abstraction, what can you do? Women pall, but science is eternal.* She thought of Mollie. As long as Jasper would stay with her, there was nothing—no indifference, no neglect, no infidelity—that she would not put up with, because deep in her heart was the knowledge that the day would come when he would be too old or too tired or too bored to want to go out again. He would stay at home, he would be hers. But science! Long after a man was through with women, he could putter with test tubes and formulas. Even Tim's interests would never again center on her, let alone the loss of his person. And he wasn't a man one outgrew. He was fresh and stimulating; he was fun to be with, and he had no annoying mannerisms; he didn't keep clearing his throat or touching people when he talked to them, or use the same clichés over and over again in conversation. They still held hands at the theater, and they frequently kissed in taxis, they fought tooth and nail, and felt immensely refreshed and often made love afterwards. Tim was splendid about fights; he never adopted that sanctimonious attitude typical of many men, who couldn't hold their own in a battle, and who therefore piously declared, "I will not fight with you, my dear. I refuse to stay here and be party to a scene," and then walked out. Tim never walked out, he never . . . oh, didn't he though? What about the letter? There was walkout with a vengeance.

Devon read it again but the words had not changed. *Unfortunately, my girl,* she thought, *you have been given the all-time,*

*super-de-luxe, star-spangled brushoff, and there doesn't seem much
you can do right now but grit your teeth and take it. This, I suppose, is the way it feels to be blitzed*—only it wasn't so hard to sur-
vive a blitz, because you would be bolstered by rage, but an aching
heart was not a fortifying agent, a sense of inferiority did not stiffen
the spine.

But wait a minute! Supposing one could win by guile and finesse
what couldn't be attained by force, what then? What about those
ads, "Never underestimate the power of a woman"? What about
them indeed? What about her own ads? Good God, not only was
Tim breaking her heart, he was disrupting her business. Why, sales
would take a nose dive. That would be a fine thing—all that palaver
of Moreley's about how to hold a man with Devonshire House
cosmetics, "Enmesh him in fragrance," "Lips cherry ripe and irresistible," "Soft romantic hands." Soft romantic hands, and the cold
shoulder! A slender, delicately rounded figure, and the boot in the
behind! Why, she'd be the laughingstock of the industry. Miss
Know-It-All, the greatest authority on feminine allure in America,
can't hold her own husband. Tim's action was incredible, it was
outrageous. As the drums of war began to beat, the stifling sensation
she was experiencing somewhat abated.

She rang violently for Louise to come and take the tray. The little
maid came in smiling. "I see by the envelope it is a letter from
Monsieur. He amuses himself well, madame? He is coming home
soon, yes?"

Oh my Lord, the servants, thought Devon. "Handle this with
tact and discretion," the letter said; that was fine talk, but how were
you to inform your servants tactfully and discreetly that your husband was walking out? "The master has given the mistress the boot,
Fairweather." "Indeed, madam? Another woman perhaps?" "No,
Fairweather, he just finds me such an unattractive old bag he can't
bear to live in the same house with me." That would be a revealing
glimpse of high life, all right, all right. What it lacked in tact and
discretion it made up in candor. Playing for time, she simply said to
the maid, "Mr. Wainwright seems to be enjoying himself, Louise.
He ought to be home in about ten days now."

Louise grinned broadly. "I am so glad. It is so quiet around here with Monsieur away. He is gay always, he makes fun."

Tim was popular with servants, and Louise adored him. He abused her outrageously, accused her of training moths to eat holes in his suits so she could give them to the corner policeman, called her a parsimonious French peasant when she darned his socks so exquisitely and so long that she eventually replaced the original wool halfway up the leg, and sent her shrieking and giggling from the room in delicious turmoil by popping out from the bath with nothing but a small towel wrapped around his middle. Thinking of these gay goings on, Devon suddenly felt tears welling in her eyes, and on a trumped-up excuse hastily sent Louise from the room. She couldn't bear her unhappiness alone, so she called Jennie on the phone. It was early for Jennie, who even when she wasn't playing seldom rose before eleven, but Devon's need was great. The hoarse voice, even more befrogged by sleep, was, however, warmly sympathetic when Devon told her that she had received a letter from Tim which left her absolutely groggy, and would Jennie come and lunch with her in her office at the salon. "Of course I will, my darling," she murmured. "And whatever it is, don't let it get you down. Just remember that the man doesn't live who's worth a woman's little finger." It was stiffening talk and advice of which poor Jennie herself stood frequently in need.

Devon, eager to get to the office to speak to Jasper, hurried through her morning toilet, but emotion temporarily overcame her in the bathtub, and Louise, coming in to scrub her mistress' back, found her sitting in mute misery, her hair screwed in a knot, her face smeared with cream, and the tears pouring down her cheeks.

Arrived at the salon, she dropped her wraps, brushed past poor Hilda who was waiting with the morning mail and a sheaf of business problems, went into Jasper's office, and banged the door. Jasper glanced up from his desk and, seeing her, sensed that a blow had fallen.

"What's the matter?"

"Tim is leaving me."

He looked at her a long time. "It's that research business, I suppose." Devon nodded. The lump in her throat made speech impossible.

"I was afraid of that," said Jasper slowly. Devon went to the window and stood staring down on Fifth Avenue, fighting back the tears. "I'm sorry, Devon, terribly, terribly sorry." She faced him abruptly.

"You see, Jasper, that's just it, it's so damn final. It never occurred to you it might be another woman, and of course it isn't, but this thing licks me. When a husband is having an outside affair, there's that long period of shilly-shally and indecision, force of habit and weakness and what not; a wife holds all sorts of trump cards, but how am I to compete with some bugs and proteins? I should think I'd have qualities which they haven't, but apparently not, or anyway not enough to matter. Here, this letter came this morning." She fished it out of her bag and handed it to him. Jasper read it carefully and laid it on his desk. He leaned back in his chair, drew out his watch chain and twirled it slowly in the air, his keys making the soft familiar clinking sound.

"It's the axe, wouldn't you say?" asked Devon.

"He sounds sort of final, I must admit." Jasper stared into space a few minutes, then he caught his keys and put them back in his pocket. "It's funny how Tim's become so conscious of the money situation."

"Of course his attitude has a certain gaunt integrity, I suppose," she said bleakly, "but it puts me in a hell of a position, and I can't think that it's going to help business."

"Well, I wouldn't worry about that," said Jasper. "To begin with, it hasn't happened yet, and in the second place we're far more conscious of these things than the general public."

"It will happen though, Pollyanna, and let's not kid ourselves. You know Tim as well as I do, and as far as the general public goes, they soon will be conscious of it. It's inevitable, I suppose, that we'll be treated to the tasteful comments of the columnists, what with their heart toddies and Renova——" She stopped, struck by a sudden thought. "Jasper, you don't think Tim wants a divorce, do you?"

Jasper looked through the letter deliberately. "He doesn't say anything about it."

"I know, but maybe he's waiting till he gets home to break the news."

"No," said Jasper thoughtfully, "I would doubt that very much. Even high-handed people don't divorce without a good deal of cogitation, and somehow that isn't Tim's style. Besides, what would he gain by it?"

"I'm sure I don't know, but then I don't understand him at all any more," she spoke distractedly.

Jasper, realizing she was wrought up, spoke soothingly. "Look, Devon, don't torment yourself this way. You're imagining a thousand things that have probably never occurred to Tim. When he gets home you may even be able to talk him out of this idea of living away from you. My guess is that he's all on fire about the potentialities of his treatment, burning with the convert's zeal, and figures he's some sort of a monk, dedicating himself to it to the exclusion of everything else, including you. But people don't stay at fever pitch, you know. Tim's a reasonable man, and it is perfectly possible to have a life divided between your job, your home, and your outside interests. Look at Mollie and me."

"I don't want to be like Mollie and you, Jasper. I'd hate that setup. It—it seems to me lacking in dignity and responsibility, and God knows it's lacking in happiness."

"Well, my dear, I don't suppose any of us has a great deal of happiness, but I'm sorry you think me undignified, although I don't think I neglect my responsibilities."

"Oh, you pay the bills, of course, why not? You're a rich man."

"On the other hand, I am fond of my sons, and I don't get a divorce, though there are plenty of men who, in my shoes, might consider they had ample grounds."

"And what about Mollie's grounds?"

Jasper shrugged. "My infidelities apparently do not bother her. She knows I'll never let her down."

"Stout fella. Noble, like all the rest of your sex."

Jasper looked genuinely unhappy. He baffled Devon at times like this. To her way of thinking, he frequently behaved selfishly, yet was hurt when she told him so, but though she considered that he put up with his home life not out of a sense of duty but because it was a matter of complete indifference to him, he did put up with it, and by so doing he made the existence of a poor lost soul endurable and he created some kind of a pretense of domesticity for his two sons. She still felt gritty, but she made a grudging overture of truce. "Oh, forget it, what the hell, I suppose we're all the same, but your sex has certainly established a priority on alibis. Hand me Mr. Wainwright's prose masterpiece, will you?"

Jasper gave her Tim's letter. "I'd relax if I were you. He'll be home in about a week, and you can come to grips then."

"It'll be a pretty sight, I don't doubt. You'll help me, Jasper, won't you?"

"Always, my dear, you know that." She started towards the door. "Do you want to have lunch?" he asked. "I'm willing to suffer for the cause and take you to the Colony."

"No, thanks. Jennie's coming in. I thought we'd have something sent up from downstairs." As part of the Devonshire House regime, Beauty from the Inside Out, Devon about two years ago had installed a small restaurant on the ground floor of the building. It was called the Swedish Room, because of the décor, not the food, and was presided over by a large sullen genius who had the ability so to prepare and arrange health-giving fruits, vegetables, and salads that even plump epicureans from the suburbs were glad to shave off the poundage by lunching there daily, staving off malnutrition at teatime with a Luxuro Ice Cream Cake at Schrafft's.

Jasper himself when busy frequently had a tray sent up, but he was not a devotee of nature's way to health. He sighed now as he said to Devon, "Well, I suppose those herbs are the thing, but I'm damned if I can see why an occasional omelette or a piece of beef would destroy my corpuscles."

"You should ask for it."

"I have, but all Hedwig ever sends me is a bowl of grass and a little note saying meat and eggs are not part of the health regime. I don't know how the customers stand it."

"We thrive, but then women are more stalwart than men." She started for her own office.

"Say, Devon——"

"What?"

"If I were you I wouldn't say much to Jennie about this. I know she's devoted to you, but she'll blab it to Dick, and the first thing you know it'll be all over Broadway, and then it *will* be in the columns. Keep your own counsel a little."

"I know you're right, Jasper. I will." She looked very sweet and sincere as she stood there, planning in her mind each last fulsome detail she intended pouring out to Jennie. Just as she was going through the door, Jasper stopped her.

"Herr Fabri been on the phone recently?"

"No," she said coldly, "but he sent me some beautiful flowers, and I wrote him a charming note of thanks. He should have gotten it this morning."

"You'll doubtless be hearing from him."

"It's a matter of complete indifference to me whether I hear from the Herr or not," she replied with dignity. "And your implication that he will divert my mind from Tim is about as subtle as a shillelagh," and she retired to her own office.

It was Devon's good fortune that she was able so to immerse herself in work that personal problems were promptly forgotten, and although this particular blow was too outsize to be completely ignored, it was lunchtime before she realized that the morning had flown by. For one thing, there had been the allotment of the prize money that all cosmetic firms paid to salesgirls in stores throughout the country to push their own preparations ahead of their rivals'. It was so customary as not even to be considered unethical, and though actually these cash prizes, since they were paid by all firms, had the effect of canceling each other out, each organization was chary of being the first to abolish them for fear of the edge it would give the competitor.

There had also been the conference with Moreley and the two script writers about the radio program they were readying, and when the authors had departed, Moreley, bulging with pride, brought forth the pamphlet that was to be enclosed in every box of Flower-Fresh preparations. Though Tim guffawed coarsely at Moreley's literary style and Jasper read it in pained silence and with the picklepuss aspect of one who needs to get on the alkaline side, Devon secretly reveled in it. Cosmetic and medicinal literature, even the legends that came in a package of dog food, it made no difference, such printed matter fascinated her, and she pored happily over Moreley's effusions. "I am delighted that Flower-Fwesh is an actuality, Miss Elliott," he said, clapping together his little finlike hands. "Think of the service to the Amewican woman. Evewy woman should look her best so as to lead her life to the fullest. Womance is a woman's wight."

"It is, Moreley, but not even Devonshire House is infallible," and an intruding memory made her tone bitter. Moreley, as always if it was implied that the firm was not the alpha and omega of life, looked like one who has had aspersions cast upon his ancestry, but he went away happy when Devon warmly lauded his pamphlet and told him he was the only one of the organization who understood her goal. "Mr. Doolittle thinks only of money, Moreley," she said with a sad sweet smile, "but you and I go deeper, we cherish beauty."

"Oh, we do, we do, Miss Elliott, chewish is the vewy word," he murmured fervently and departed, tingling and exalted.

Jennie arrived a few minutes after one, her shining hair upswept under a forward-tilting black hat, her lovely face aglow with sympathy. "How are you, baby?" Her soft croak was very soothing to Devon's shattered nerves. She was about to open the floodgates when Hilda arrived bearing a tray, followed by Miss Hedwig, who ran the Swedish Room, balancing another.

As Jasper had complained, Miss Hedwig specialized in fruits and vegetables, cleansing, strength-building, non-fattening foods, but nothing to stick to the ribs. She and the secretary set the trays down on the desk. "You will enjoy this today, Miss Elliott," said Hedwig heartily. "It cleanses the whole digestive tract. The juices will work beneficially upon the colon too," and she retired with as near a beam of satisfaction as her square face could muster.

Jennie and Devon drew up their chairs, and Hilda lifted the silver covers. A few genteel and melancholy vegetables stared up at them. Devon picked up her fork. "Spare-looking mess, isn't it?" she observed.

"Well, darling, vegetables are always rather gloomy, don't you think?" Jennie's voice quavered with depression.

"Hilda, is this the kind of stuff we're serving downstairs?"

"Yes, it is, Miss Elliott. The salad bowls are even more popular, but I know you always like something hot for lunch, so I thought the vegetable plate was the better choice."

"We must be losing money hand over fist, aren't we?"

"Oh no, Miss Elliott," said Hilda earnestly. "The room is always crowded."

Devon bit into a parsnip. "I don't believe it," she said flatly. "Let me see last week's statement."

Hilda opened the large closet where the unaesthetic metal files were kept out of sight and handed her employer the statement. Devon glanced at the figures. "My God, women *are* crazy. We netted $268 in that little hole, serving only lunch and afternoon tea and juices."

Jennie speared a carrot. "It would be wonderful if we could use some of those profits for something to eat," she said wistfully. Devon picked up the gauntlet.

"Why don't we? After all, we might be allergic to this stuff." She turned to her secretary. "Hilda, go over to Madison Avenue to Hamburger Heaven and bring us back two big burgundy hamburgers apiece. How would you like that, Jen?"

"It would be wonderful, darling." Jennie's voice was a reverent whisper, and a limpid radiance shone from the violet eyes, reminiscent of the more emaciated saints of Renaissance paintings, who, with visible beams emanating from their pupils, faint in ecstasy as the clouds part, disclosing God the Father, cloaked in angels.

Hilda hurried into her hat and coat, but just as she was about to leave, an uneasy fear assailed her boss. "Oh—Hilda, be as fleet as you can, but maybe you'd better bring the hamburgers back in one of our own boxes or something. If any client saw you, she might not understand it, and I shouldn't like to hurt Miss Hedwig's feelings." Hedwig was a tartar and, though Devon would not admit it, the only member of her staff of whom she stood in awe. She also held Miss Hedwig in profound respect. If the woman could make health food show a profit, she had wizard's blood in her veins.

Hilda returned on wingèd feet, bearing not only the hamburgers but two mammoth slices of apple pie, the day's special, and while munching industriously—"After a while, grief always gives me an appetite, though when I got the letter this morning, I couldn't even swallow my tea," Devon had said—the two women discussed the situation. Devon, because she loved Tim, was crushed. Jennie, because she loved Devon, was outraged. She held her half-eaten hamburger in one hand and the letter in the other. "The thing that gets me down," she said, "is the ungratefulness of the man, not to mention the gall. My God, you're his wife, you behave like a goddess, and he coolly observes that he's not coming back to live with you. Who is he, not to live with you if you want him? Who could he ever get better, I'd like to know?"

"Oh, it isn't that, Jennie. Not that Tim doesn't like women and a lot of women seem to find him irresistible. . . . Remember Judith Evans?"

"And the time she pretended to faint out at the farm, and Tim had to carry her upstairs and sit with her because she was hysterical? Do I not!"

Devon could afford to laugh; that had been a long time ago. "And I admit it always strikes me that Claire is a dash more palsy-walsy than the relationship calls for, but those things don't bother me. Tim kids around, but he can be awfully final when he wants to stop playing. No, this is something else again."

"Well, I expect you're right," Jennie conceded. "But proteins and research! Granted that he wants to devote himself heart and soul to it, he's got to sleep, hasn't he? Why can't he sleep at home?"

Devon shrugged. "You read the letter. He says he can't afford it."

"Oh, my foot!" Miss Moore was more emphatic than elegant. "Men give me a pain. When he came to work in the laboratory, to all intents and purposes, you paid his salary, didn't you? But that didn't stop his loving you then and marrying you."

"No, it didn't, but of course there was a difference. It was a completely impersonal setup. He was paid by the firm, and he was certainly earning his salary. This business now seems to me silly, but I can see his point. This way he feels I'd be supporting him, giving him money out of my own pocket."

"Well, if you ask me," said Jennie, and Devon couldn't help but feel she was hitting the nail on the head, "it's pride far more than proteins that's making him run out on you."

"But what are you going to do?" Devon asked. "Men *are* proud. Look at Dick, you and he have been together for two years, and he's sick with love of you, but does he ask you to marry him?"

Jennie looked unhappy. "No," she said hesitantly, "but of course I haven't got my divorce yet."

But Devon in her own wretchedness didn't spare her friend. "What difference does that make? He could ask you and you could both be making plans, but you're a wealthy woman. He'd probably think it was bad enough if you'd inherited your money, but because you have to work hard to get it, he thinks it's inviolable. Dick overlooks the fact that you love the theater, that you'd be lost without it, and because he has pride and traditions or some damn thing he thinks he's not worthy."

There was a silence in the office while Devon paced the floor, and Jennie read Tim's letter again as though she hoped some new or hidden aspect might be revealed. She did seem to find one small straw and looked up. "Of course, Devon, there's nothing terribly final about what he says. If his love is so unfailing, it isn't likely he's going to want a divorce, and once he's discovered that dreary little vitamin or whatever it is he's after, he'll probably come panting home."

Devon stopped her pacing. "Do you think so?" She looked so hopeful that Jennie, who had only thrown out the idea as a wavering antenna, caught fire.

"Of course, darling. This is probably—what's that thing people go through?—a phase. He's probably having a phase. He's got to work terribly hard, your life *is* sort of distracting, and how can you tell? Maybe in the long run it's better he do it. He'll get it out of his system quicker, and if you don't try to stop him he'll be grateful to you for having been co-operative."

Devon had been so looking forward to Tim's return and his letter had been such a blow that she had leaped to the assumption that the separation must necessarily be forever. Why would he have hurt her so much if it wasn't final? But if Jennie was right, then, though the going would be tough, the end was in sight. "Oh God,

Jennie, I hope you're right," she said fervently. "I won't mind the gossip or even the loneliness too much if it's only temporary. I'll pretend he's off to the wars and I'll be lucky, because at least he won't be in danger. Unless of course a test tube explodes."

Jennie's entrancing smile broke for the first time that day. "And he's such a good chemist, darling, that's not likely. He's due back in about a week?"

"Just about. His telegram the other day said the end of the month."

"All right then, the thing for us to do is to map a campaign." Watching Jennie, Devon could see the wheels racing. "Now I imagine Tim will come home all primed for a tussle. The thing is not to give it to him. If you're acquiescent, it's going to take the wind out of his sails. Don't forget he probably fancies himself as quite a fellow, you know, pitting principle against love,—'when Duty whispers low, Thou must'—I've played those scenes a thousand times."

Jennie seemed to have the situation so well in hand that Devon was impressed. "In the theater?" she asked respectfully.

"Sure. Jessie Bonstelle's stock company. We did it every week. Say, that gives me an idea."

"What?" Devon felt helpless but eager. Unfortunately, Jennie's enthusiasm died.

"No, it might not work. It is kind of old-fashioned."

"Well, tell it anyway. I'm not in a very choosy position."

"Jealousy."

Devon looked blank. "Jealousy?"

"You've heard of it, dear. The green-eyed monster. Another man."

There was a slight pause. "Oh," said Devon softly. "Oh, I see what you mean," and her eyes shone with a thoughtful gleam.

"Of course I can't guarantee it." Jennie spoke like an honest doctor with an untried prescription. "Tim may suspect that you've only cooked something up, or it could be that in his present mood, even if he believes it, he'd be indifferent, but there are heaps and heaps of cases where jealousy has worked. Now—who do you know?"

"Well, I'm kind of limited. If it's to be convincing, it can't be Nicky or Jasper or anybody like that. Tim would laugh in my face."

"What about that fellow from the other night?" Devon smiled, but she didn't catch Jennie's eye.

"Kurt Fabri?"

"None other."

"I can't guarantee anything either, but I think I may be hearing from Mr. Fabri." She told Jennie about the flowers and her thank-you note. Jennie was satisfied.

"That looks very good," she said approvingly. "You needn't be obvious about it, but have the house full of his flowers when Tim comes to see you, even if you have to buy them yourself."

"Oh, I wouldn't mind doing that," said Devon candidly. "But the house is always so full of flowers anyway, he might not notice."

"Nonsense," Jennie spoke impatiently. "You must manage so that he does. Get something banal like American Beauties or a huge tree—mimosa or cherry or something. Nobody sends themselves a tree. He's bound to see it. Then, if you can wangle it, have Kurt phone you while Tim's there. If he won't, I will, but try to get him. There's nothing like a bona-fide phone call. I tell you, baby, I'm beginning to feel very good about this. If you can be calm and understanding, even sympathetic towards his idea, Tim might do a complete about-face."

"That I doubt," said Devon frankly. "But I'll say one thing, you've given my morale a terrific boost. And to be perfectly honest, I don't regard Mr. Fabri as any dose of salts. It would cause me no pain at all to give him a little of my valuable time."

From the lower depths, the ladies had shot with mercurial abandon to the heights. Life was no longer a walking shadow but leaping and full-bodied, and they themselves well able to cope with it. Jennie, her mission of mercy accomplished, was drawing on her gloves when Hilda entered in a flutter. "Miss Elliott, I'm sorry to interrupt you, I know you said you didn't want to be disturbed, but there have been a dozen calls, and now there's trouble on the sixth floor." The sixth floor was where the facial treatments were given, and trouble usually meant an outburst of temperament from the clientele.

"Who is it?" asked Devon briskly. Her spirits had risen, and she was not averse to combat.

"It's Mrs. Carl Leland Potter again." Hilda spoke with resignation. Mrs. Potter was one of the salon's trials; she was also one of its most fruitful sources of income.

"Good Lord," said Jennie, "I can't see what she's got to complain of. You keep her in such good condition that even in that flashlight photo at the Russian Relief party I could tell right away which was the bear and which was Mrs. Potter."

Devon laughed. "What's her beef this time, Hilda?"

"Clara's been giving her treatments for the past eighteen months, and now all of a sudden she thinks Clara's breaking down her tissues."

"Nonsense, Clara's one of the best operators we've got. I'll go down and work on the old girl myself and prove to her that she gives exactly the same treatment I do."

"Well," said Jennie in surprise, "I haven't known you to do that in a coon's age. What are you spoiling her for?"

Devon grinned. "I'm in a good humor; besides, her account with us runs about ten thousand dollars a year. For ten thousand, she should be spoiled." This was the kind of thing Thomas Elliott had in mind when, some fifteen years before, he paid his daughter's tuition at the operators' school.

☆　　　☆　　　☆

". . . *Tim will come home all primed for a tussle. The thing is not to give it to him.*" That's what Jennie had said. "*If you're acquiescent, it's going to take the wind out of his sails. . . . Tim might do a complete about-face.*"

It didn't seem to be working out quite that way. Tim was home, and they were in the midst of a long discussion, but his determination wasn't wavering. He and Oscar Hogarth had flown up from Louisiana. Tim had phoned her when they landed at La Guardia Field; he had then dropped his luggage at the club and come on to the house. The news had been broken to the servants more easily than she anticipated. Fairweather welcomed him at the door and asked with surprise where his bags were; on being told they were at the club, as that was where Tim was going to be living, he had after the briefest pause replied, "Indeed, sir?" and retired with the air of one who receives a most humdrum bit of news. Devon considered him a true gentleman and blessed him for his tact, which was more than she could do for her husband, who was making highly unpleasant noises:

". . . and so, you see, Devon, that's why it isn't feasible for me to live here in the house. It isn't a question of my not loving you, and it isn't that I'm not devoted to our friends, the Lowerys, Jennie . . ." It occurred to Devon to tell him how Jennie and Jasper had reacted to his letter, but she held her peace, suspecting that he would be shocked and angry if he knew she had shown it to anyone. Men were so funny about things like that. ". . . And you know how fond I am of Dick Hadley and Claire . . ."

"Especially Claire," said Devon cordially.

"Not *especially* Claire at all, but that's the very reason I've got to live by myself. Here we have a big house, servants, our lives are geared so that we can and do entertain. You do it charmingly, and naturally you enjoy it, but I haven't the time for it."

"You've always been a good host, Tim. Has that just been an act?"

"It's been so little an act that that's why I'm going. Call it weakness if you like, but I'm deliberately putting myself out of temptation's way so that nothing will interfere with my job."

"Why, Mr. Wainwright, you make me feel like Delilah. All I need is a candy-pink tunic and a wreath of roses on my head."

"If you're thinking of any of the Delilahs we've ever heard, you also need a good deal more heft." Tim looked at his wife appreciatively. She had a lovely body, and her exquisite simple clothes displayed it to advantage; yet looking at her he felt no desire for her or the life she represented. Jasper had guessed right; Tim was like a man who, after years of atheism, embraces not only Catholicism but the priesthood. He did not disapprove of a worldly existence, but for him it held no further interest. He continued amiably enough:

"Won't you see my point, darling? I can't very well stay here and say to you, 'Don't lead a normal social life, don't go to the theater and the opera and dinner parties,' but it so happens that personally I'm fed up with them. I never was much of a fan for such things, though having people here at home I did enjoy, but now more than ever that kind of activity, whether it's for social or business reasons, seems to me a terrible waste of time."

Devon was disgruntled and showed it. "Well, my Lord, if you have to concentrate to that extent, why don't you enter a monastery?"

Tim smiled and looked at her in a way that always brought a catch to her heart. "Because I'll want to see you and you're too disturbing for a monastery."

"Then I'm not a pariah?"

"Scarcely."

"Thanks awfully, dear boy." Her tone was mocking, but her heart was heavy. There was a pause. When Devon broke it she spoke carefully. She felt she could get through the sentence without crying if she laid no emphasis upon it. It was a little as though she were crossing a frail, swaying bridge; any undue stress and it would break through. "Tim, how long do you want this arrangement to last? Am I to think of it as a permanent separation, or is it only for the duration, so to speak?" There, she was safely over the chasm and on the other side.

Tim hesitated. It wasn't that he was confused; he simply had not thought beyond his current interest, which was his research work. The words "permanent separation" implied all sorts of complexities. Why did women have to be such extremists? A fellow had a job to do, it was naturally all-engrossing. It was too bad if after seven years you couldn't count on your own wife to understand these things. How were science and plasmas and proteins connected with love? They weren't, except in that circuitous jelly roll women called their minds. His reply was not the answer to her question, but the culmination of his own thoughts: "You, of all women, ought to be able to understand that, Devon."

Not having been on that particular train ride with him, the answer struck her as cryptic. "Understand what?"

Really, thought Tim, for an intelligent woman, she was exceptionally obtuse. "Why must you keep thinking of this as something final?" he said impatiently. "Believe me, there's nothing personal involved. You have your work and your interests, but so have I got a life of my own."

"And if I may say so, you don't seem any too well able to cope with it. I do work hard, yes, but it doesn't make me so selfish that I can't consider anybody else. I can hold down a job and love my husband and entertain my friends to boot; why should it be so difficult for you?" The minute she had said it, she wished she hadn't. That certainly wasn't handling the situation very cleverly. She knew that Jennie would never consider this "sympathetic" treatment. It could only put Tim's back up, and besides deep in her heart was the knowledge that he too could do all these things if he wanted to; he certainly always had. He was probably trying to save her feelings by blaming his inability to co-operate now on his work, when all the time the real reason was that he no longer loved her. How could she be such a fool as to say things that would force him to tell her so?

He was looking at her now with alien eyes. "It's true that you do a terrific job, Devon—no one can take that away from you—but it so happens that if you want to you can delegate a good part of your work. I can't, I'm a one-man factory, and as I told you before I went away, I don't dare take time out. Thousands of people are being hurt, burnt up and wounded; those of us who know how to help have got to work fast to alleviate such suffering as we can. That's the real, basic reason for an action which seems to you purely selfish. That and the fact that, if I did stay here, I'd have to live on your bounty, and I can't stick the idea."

Devon spoke with a kind of comic despair. "How is it possible for money to be such a nuisance? If we lived in California it would be community property and you'd be doing me a great favor by claiming half of it. Your ideas are so old-fashioned, Tim. In our world there are lots of wives who have more money than their husbands, and it works out all right. Look at Estelle and George—they have nothing comparable to our setup, but proportionately it's the same. Look at Jennie and Dick, for that matter."

"I notice that Dick isn't breaking his neck to marry Jennie, and probably for the very good reason that he can't support her."

"She can support herself. Good God, do you think that financial superiority in the male is the only basis for matrimony?"

"Certainly not," Tim's voice rose. "But I think it's a damn good beginning, and it's obvious from your theories that male mentality is still superior."

Devon's tone topped his: "You reason like a corkscrew. A husband has other responsibilities, and I'm not at all sure they aren't more important than money. What about loving and cherishing? What about affection and companionship and sex fulfillment and children, if you happen to have them? Those, I suppose, are mere bagatelles. Toss them overboard, boys, so long as the old man pays the butcher."

Tim opened his mouth to speak and shut it again. "Look," he said at last, "this isn't going to get us anywhere. As a matter of fact, I think women ought to work. I think every human being ought to, not only for economic reasons but because they're a damn sight happier. Why do you suppose so many of these wacky dames wear themselves out doing war relief? Because it's such a blessed change from their eternal bridge and shopping routine. Even when they're lousy at it, it's a kind of challenge and they enjoy it, and as long as it doesn't hurt anybody else, let 'em rip. But you notice it's their husbands who keep the office fires burning. With you and me it's different. I can't see you up every morning at seven-thirty, eight o'clock, going through the endless details of that work day after day, traipsing around the country three and four times a year to check up on the salons and the sales force, knocking yourself out with advertising campaigns, radio, and God knows what, while I do nothing to help."

Devon looked at him in bewilderment. "But Tim, I've worked that way for years, and you've seen me do it. Why all of a sudden is it so awful?"

"Because up until now I've been in there pitching too, and I think I've contributed to your success, but if I cease to do that, I can't continue to live off the profits you make."

"I suppose it doesn't matter how hard I work as long as you're not around to see me do it?"

"As long as I'm not around to live off you and watch you do it. There's a difference."

Devon looked at him coldly. "Did you ever win a hair-splitting contest as a boy?"

"No," said Tim angrily, "but I never lived off anybody either, and I don't relish the idea of loafing by the fire, holding up my little hands, and saying to you, 'Keep it pouring, dear.'"

Devon was so keyed up that at this ludicrous picture she burst into hysterical laughter. "Timothy, it's my weakness that I love you, but so help me, the Empire State Building could knock you in the eye and you wouldn't see it if you didn't choose to. When have you ever loafed? Certainly not in the years I've known you, and if you're sincere about this new program, you'll barely have time to brush your teeth. So where would the loafing come in? Another angle that seems to escape you is that I adore my work. Next to loving you, it's the greatest satisfaction I have in the world, and from the looks of things," she added pointedly, "it's the only satisfaction I'm going to get."

There was another pause. The two geysers, having momentarily spent themselves, fell to bubbling quietly underground. They were both taking stock of the situation. Tim was too honest not to know that what she said about matrimony made sense, but it didn't make any difference, and that's why, though he wouldn't live off her money, he was grateful that she had it. Had she been poor he could not have afforded to continue his research work; had she been idle even his sense of responsibility would have troubled him that she should be left alone. But matters had turned out very neatly. Not only was Devon a wealthy woman, she was a busy one; his conscience was clear.

She was thinking along other lines. She still had one more card to play. If reason couldn't sway him, jealousy might. What did he expect anyway? That he could wander off for as long as he liked on this wild-goose chase and return at his own good pleasure to find her faithfully waiting? Patient Griselda? Silently she defied him: *You are likely to find, my friend, that life doesn't work out quite as patly as that,* or so she hoped. Yet she definitely wanted to plant in his mind the idea of a return. It would be unwise to let Tim think she resented his action too much. It would give him an easy excuse for not coming back. "You were in such a huff, my darling, I naturally didn't think you'd want me again." It wouldn't be honest of him, for he would know better; but since when was love run according to Hoyle? Apropos of strategy, this would be the moment for Kurt to phone; it would strengthen her hand. She and Jennie had discussed the matter again and decided that even if not entirely satisfactory a synthetic call was better than no call at all. If Tim thought there was a mysterious suitor in the background it might pique his curiosity and arouse some uneasiness.

Actually, though he had phoned several times, Devon had seen Kurt only twice since the party, once at luncheon with Nicky and once when he had come for tea.

Tentatively to sound out his reactions she had touched lightly on her anticipated difficulty with Tim, but though he had listened politely he had withdrawn into a kind of impervious shell, causing Miss Elliott to conclude that his interest in her was not yet sufficient to warrant any heart-to-heart confidences. She had to admit to herself with amused admiration that he had been canny not to fall for this slightly spurious bid for sympathy.

Kurt had no wish to become involved in anyone else's marital complications, yet he did not doubt that her feeling of bewilderment over her husband's actions was genuine. It might not be too difficult to focus her attention on himself, and she seemed to him extremely desirable. Before he left her he said seriously, "You tell me you are being confronted with this problem in your life. That I cannot work out for you, but though I have met you only three times, there is nothing I would not do for you. What do you want? What can I get you?" They had looked at each other for a long moment, and then she had smiled, and there was something a little sad in her voice, though she said lightly, "Supposing I should want you?" Kurt said simply, "I am here," and then he had kissed her hand and gone away.

He had called her once since then, but the conversation had been bantering and brief. The restrained technique, she thought to herself. Well, even when a woman knows it to be deliberate, it will almost invariably win out. The wisdom of the practitioner is solidly grounded on the delights of anticipation. Still if she and Kurt *were* embarked on the eternal game, though wise to the technique of the three or four days' rush and the abrupt withdrawal, Devon considered his timing poor. With Tim arriving, it was the very moment to send flowers and hang on the telephone. It was true, as she had told Jennie, the house was always full of flowers anyway; they were her greatest extravagance, and she kept the greenhouses at the farm functioning the year round; but the home product was on the subtle side. This morning she had gone out and bought an enormous basket of American Beauty roses, and there they were on the stand in the bay window of the library, half strangled by a preposterous crimson satin bow, the sort of thing she would never in the world have ordered herself, but that a flashy type bent on conquest might well consider irresistible. However, if Tim noticed them, he made no comment. Perhaps he genuinely didn't care if she had a lover. They said people changed every seven years, and of course she and Tim had always had a great deal of independence. Owing to the exigencies of business, she was forever lunching and dining and talking with an endless stream of men. If Tim thought about the roses at all, he probably thought they were from the head of a department store wanting to carry the line, or from some advertising agency after the Devonshire House account, eager to squeeze out Moreley. Remembering the thirty-five dollars she had spent on them, she was intensely annoyed to realize that she might as well have thrown the money out the window for all the impression she was likely to make. Jennie was a darling, but not all her ideas were sound by any means. Besides, if there were any truth in that old saying, it was just about time . . .

"Tim?"

"Yes, dear?"

Oh God, how sweet he was! Even when he was walking out, there was a quick warm sympathy. He was a courteous man.

"Do you suppose there's any truth in the saying that we change every seven years?"

She expected that he might laugh, but he didn't. "I don't know," he said seriously. "It's possible, I suppose. Maybe our chemical reactions change, or maybe our enthusiasms are only able to span seven years, then we have to move on to something else."

"Toss off the past like that old glove."

"Not necessarily. It's probably not so much a case of tossing off as of adding something new."

"It doesn't seem to be working that way in our case, does it? You're a toss-and-run boy, but you don't have to be. I mean I'd be willing to be like the first layer of those ancient European churches —remember San Clemente in Rome? It's actually many churches built up through the centuries, but always on the same site. You could stay right here at home if you wanted to and pile the proteins on top of me."

Tim took both her hands and held them tight. "My little sweet, it's not like that at all."

"But it could be, Tim, it could be." Her lovely sea-colored eyes shone with earnestness. "Don't forget I know quite a lot about chemistry myself. Why couldn't I work with you? Look at the Curies!"

Tim chuckled. "Darling, to be any good at self-immolation, you have to have those persecution blues. I've always felt that Madame Curie discovered radium by way of avenging Poland—but you're far too blooming. Why, a Nazi general would take one look at you and hand over the village egg. You've got to be wizened to stick to the kind of dull, slogging job I'm undertaking."

"Well, of all the conceit! A person would think you had a corner on sensitivity. I'm a persecutee myself, for heaven's sake. What about the Paris house? I don't care if the Nazis have stolen it, I certainly consider myself the rightful owner and the director, but I don't even get the twenty-dollar gold piece. And what about my five French apartment buildings? If you've seen any rent checks since June 1940, you're holding out on me."

"I know, Devon, and it's maddening, but not quite on a par with what Poland and Czechoslovakia and Greece are having to endure."

"Why isn't it? The Germans have taken our money, haven't they? You're extremely inconsistent, Tim. One second you're full of piety and money isn't everything, and the next, it's so all-important that you can't continue to live in your own home with your own wife simply because she's richer than you are."

"You know something?" said Tim thoughtfully. "This separation may be a tonic we're needing more than we realize. We're thinking kind of far apart, Devon, we're . . . we're engrossed by different ideas. We don't even think of each other the way we used to."

"I see," said Devon sarcastically. "I suppose in my worldly pursuits I've neglected you?" Tim considered that she was being grand, like a small bitchy girl fighting with a little friend, and his risibilities were suddenly tickled.

"You sure have," he said with heartfelt agreement. "It's been years since you made up a cologne expressing my personality."

Her sails collapsed. "Why . . . why, Tim . . . why, darling——"

"Don't darling me," he continued coldly. If they were to have grandeur, he would take the lead. "When we first met, you told our whole love story to the world in cologne and perfume. What about that fall when we were lovers, what about that fine manly job you made up in the cork-covered bottle? Autumn Glory, you called it, and you launched it on my birthday."

"That's right, darling." Devon's face was quickly aglow as she followed the will-of-the-wisp of memory. "I meant it as a kind of tribute to you. You inspired it. It sold three and a half million bottles," she added reverently.

"My soap went over very well too," said Tim smugly.

"And look at Carillon, still selling."

"That was to celebrate our wedding day."

"Yes."

"And I want you to know," he said formally, "that I have always appreciated the very graceful compliment you paid me on our fifth anniversary."

"Felicity." Devon smiled in reminiscence. "I remember when I was searching for a name for it. Moreley had some awfully fancy ones, but I wanted to choose it myself, it had to be just right, then I thought of Felicity. It sounded good, but you know how often words betray me, forever meaning something quite different from what I think they mean, so I looked Felicity up in the dictionary and it was the very thing. 'A state of great and well-founded happiness; comfort and content.' Oh, Tim——"

They looked at each other, and the room was very quiet. The silence was shattered by the telephone. Devon was sitting near the desk and picked it up. "Hello?"

"Hello, duck, how are you doing? This is Kurt, remember?" It was Jennie's voice, gruffer than ever and very low. Devon was startled; she had forgotten their plan and was momentarily at a loss.

"Oh—oh yes, of course. How are you? Nice of you to phone."

"Is Tim there?"

"Yes, yes indeed." Devon gave what she hoped was a rippling laugh. It made Jennie feel slightly embarrassed, but she continued gamely.

"Good. What about the flowers?"

"Oh, those!" Devon's voice was scornful, and she shot a vicious look at the American Beauties.

"Hey, hey!" Jennie's near-whisper held alarm. "Be pleased, thank me, for God's sake." *Lord, I was a fool to get embroiled in this,* she thought to herself; *Devon can act about as well as my left foot.*

Devon was acting now, and her voice held the phony graciousness of the leading woman in a second-rate stock company: "Your roses are perfectly charming. I can't *tell* you how kind I think it was of you to think of me. . . . I *never* expected them."

"All right, all right, don't overdo it," cautioned Jennie. "Now just make some sort of dinner engagement and hang up, and for heaven's sake call me back as quickly as you can."

"What?" said Devon and stopped. Jennie sensed an attack of the blanks at the other end of the wire. It was the kind of thing that sometimes happened to inexperienced actors; she handed Devon the direct cue, "Will you dine with me Friday night?"

"No, I——"

"Say yes."

"I mean, yes, yes, I'd be delighted to dine Friday. Thank you. Good-by." Devon hung up with infinite relief. She was a bad liar and a worse actress, and this sort of thing made her nervous. It flashed through her mind that it was probably the way Tim felt when she insisted on smuggling things through the customs on their returns from Europe. She herself was exhilarated, but Tim had indigestion for forty-eight hours. She would never ask him to do it again, but at once she realized glumly that she might never be in a position to ask him. Tim had listened unconcerned to the conversation. He said nothing, but she felt impelled to explanation. "Someone who wants me to dine Friday," she said brightly.

"Anyone I know?" he asked politely.

"No," she said in a casual tone. "Just somebody Nick brought to the house one night while you were away. He sent those," and she waved languidly towards the gangster's choice filling the bay window.

Tim's eyes twinkled. "Either his intentions are dishonorable or Anna outdid herself with the dinner."

"They're not very imaginative, would you say?"

"Oh, I don't know." Tim looked at the flowers thoughtfully. "I think they show a good deal of imagination."

Devon's heart beat faster. What did he mean by that? It would certainly be humiliating if he guessed she was sending flowers to herself. She knew Tim. It would appeal to his sense of the ridiculous, and he would shout with laughter. She wouldn't be surprised if he possessed elements of greatness, but she felt there was a certain coarseness in his temperament, a hang-over doubtless from his Iowa boyhood, which was extremely disconcerting. She herself was country-bred, but in an academic atmosphere. It made a difference. She well remembered times when, hoping to impress or touch him, she had succeeded only in evoking laughter or succinct and pungent comment quite out of line with the respectful reaction she had anticipated. She hoped to heaven that he had not caught Jennie's voice through the receiver. That would be the last straw; but the chances were she was safe. Tim was no dissembler, he would have hooted right off. She hoped. Still his remark was disturbing.

"Why do you think the bushel basket imaginative?" she asked.

"I think your beau has a great deal of imagination if he imagines you would like it."

Ah well, that was better. And the nice thing was that Kurt was imaginative about the flowers he sent. He had seen that white blossoms were perfect for the drawing room and had sent the first fragile lilac. Generally men who weren't effeminate didn't have such sensibility. Generally men . . .

"What about that, Tim?"

"What about what?"

"Men. I suppose you won't object if I go out from time to time?"

"My darling, you have always been free and I have never for one instant doubted you. I know you too well to think that you would ever do anything you'd regret."

Coming from another man, that might mean that she would never love casually or unwisely; coming from Tim, who in spite of Iowa was sometimes more subtle than appeared on the surface, it could mean that she would never pass anything up on the grounds that we regret only what we have missed. She studied him for a minute. "Cryptic cuss, aren't you? Do you think I'd ever do anything you'd regret?"

"I hope you wouldn't. I hope you'll never stop loving me, Devon, but I can't force you to physical fidelity, if that's what you're talking about."

There was never any use beating about the bush with Tim. He instinctively knew what she was driving at, and it was frequently a great relief. She toyed briefly with the idea of staging a scene about Didn't He Care and Did He Want a Promiscuous Wife, and What Were *His* Intentions. It seemed the conventional move under the circumstances, but even as she framed the first sentence, she discarded it as unconvincing; besides, Tim was speaking.

"You've concentrated on me for a long time, darling. You could probably do with a few new beaux. Think what a pleasant change it's going to be."

"I've enjoyed you, Mr. Wainwright." What she really wanted to say was that his six weeks' absence had given her all the taste she wanted of what it was like for a woman to have to organize a social life for herself without a man in the house. It was especially difficult for her, as she was so busy. Half the time she'd come to six o'clock and realize she had no plans for the evening. When Tim was there, if there was no set engagement it didn't matter. He was her plan. They would drive out to the country of a warm spring evening: in the winter they could dine quietly at home before the fire,

or go to a movie or the theater, stop in someplace for a drink afterwards if they felt like it, and it was easy. Curiously enough, for a
woman alone, informality was the greatest problem. What Devon
thought of as the Set Pieces, dinner parties, a box at the opera, the
horse show, God forbid, were comparatively simple to arrange. You
put Hilda on the phone with a list and that was that, but Sunday
brunch for four or dinner for two was something else again. Dinner
for two, unless the two were lovers, was singularly unremunerative.
She wanted to explain this to Tim, but pride and a kind of gallantry which would not let her take advantage of his sympathy kept her
silent. On his side, it occurred to Mr. Wainwright that his position
was equivocal, to say the least. He was voluntarily leaving his wife
whom he loved; knowing her temperament, he could scarcely expect chastity, yet he supposed the decent thing was to hope for it;
it seemed to mean a great deal to the Hays office, and he understood that Orientals went quite mad if their wives peered over
the yashmak at any male under seventy-five, but somehow to him,
now, it didn't seem important. He was scarcely a gentleman if he
implied that she could not find a lover, but surely some code
would be affronted if he urged her to take one. Honest feeling
and established convention dovetailed so infrequently, yet he was
not unaware of the risk he ran. The thought of a lover did not
move him; the thought that she might cease to love him was excessively painful. Deciding that to face a problem squarely is often
to blunt its hurting edge, he deliberately pressed the point.

"Don't think I'm so complacent as not to realize that I'm taking
an awful chance, Devon. You may well stop loving me. I hope to
God you don't, but I couldn't blame you if you came to care less.
There are attractive guys in the world, and I say to myself, the girl
has taste, after all, look at her husband. You might fall in love with
someone else."

"Yes, I suppose I might," said Devon, and Tim thought there was
pain in her voice. "That's the sad thing about love, I think, we get
over it. I know it's possible to love several people in a lifetime. As a
matter of fact, I've never had much patience with those who say
they can only love once; I always feel they could do better if they'd
try, but I hate being put in this position where I have to try. I've

been very happy concentrating on you, Tim. If I do meet an attractive man, I might come to care for him, but I don't want to. I want to go on loving you."

"Please do. I'm likely to be around for a long time."

"This separation is mostly because of your job, isn't it, Tim?"

"It's entirely because of the job—and the economic setup."

"We've had no fight, have we, and we can see each other sometimes?"

"All you want, darling." But this Tim didn't mean. He said it so as not to hurt her now; but to see Devon often would nullify the step he was deliberately taking. Let him do his job first. What the future held, he neither knew nor cared.

PART FOUR

The announcer's voice, enthusiastic yet soothing, came through the loud-speaker, informing listeners that they had just been the guests of Devonshire House and cajoling them to listen in next week, when their host would again be that wise, witty, and observant man-about-town, Nicholas Van Alston, who would present the glamorous star, the first lady of the American theater, Miss Jennie Moore. "In the meantime, remember the thrilling new perfume sensation adored by every woman, irresistible to every man, that stimulating, tingling, fragrant cologne, Overture, spelled O-V-E-R-T-U-R-E. Get your bottle today, so that your own life story may be as dramatic, as gay, as exciting and as full of promise as the scent of Overture cologne, the great new Devonshire House preparation. This is Jack Hastings bidding you good night and fragrant dreams. This is the National Broadcasting Company."

Matilda Stevens switched off the radio and turned in her rocker as her husband Matthew entered the sitting room. Matilda was sixty-two and Matthew was sixty-six, and in forty years of married life they had come to bear a close resemblance to each other. Though Matilda was plump and Matthew was spare, though where Matilda's cheeks were round and pink as apples, Matthew's were furrowed as the Saint Bernard's, the same good humor shone from their blue eyes and the same expression of gentle mirth was likely to twist their softly curving lips.

Matthew had retired on pension from his professorship, but they still lived in Williamstown in a small and charming house on Main Street, and though the odor of freshly baked bread, the luscious smell of tomatoes, and the tart sweet fragrance of stewing fruit quite properly wafted from Matilda's kitchen window, when the breeze was right it unexpectedly blended with the more sophisticated odors of Carillon, Felicity, and currently the widely touted Overture.

As her husband entered, Matilda spoke with the girlish enthusiasm which was her most beguiling trait. "Matthew, you are careless. Devon's program is just over, and it was exceptionally good. That Mr. Van Alston is excellent, most amusing. I shall write Devon and tell her he ought to do their sales bits, he's far more persuasive than that young man at the end with all the refinement."

"I didn't mean to stay such a time, dear," said Matthew mildly, "but you know how long-winded Jeffers is on the telephone. Anyway it's probably just as well I missed the announcer. Those gentlemen are so mellifluous, they make me feel quite gross. Who's on next week?"

"Jennie Moore. Isn't it nice she and Devon are such friends? You remember *Seek Not Tomorrow*. We saw it last year when we were in New York."

"Certainly I remember it." Matthew's tone was a little testy. He considered there was something presumptuous in Matilda's refreshing him on anything connected with the theater. Matthew was an inveterate theatergoer during the two or three weeks a year they spent in New York, and he religiously read all published plays. His one serious grievance against Matilda was that she was not theater-minded, at least not in the right way, for she had one dreadful vice, an incomprehensible passion for moving-picture magazines. This morbid craving had come upon her late in life, and Matthew had Devon to thank for it.

When she had opened her first salon she naturally insisted on Matilda's visiting it when they came to New York on their annual trip, and there, under some horrendous contraption called a Drier, Matilda had been initiated into this scurrilous school of journalism. There the virus had entered her blood, and ever since, when she should have been reading the better novelists or challenging her imagination with the printed play, she would be following bright-eyed, through the column of a certain Mr. Cal York, the love life of the cinema queens. Matthew quite genuinely abhorred this obsession. He considered the theater a great and cultural institution. Pictures were fodder for the masses, to whom he was not sympathetically inclined.

Though it irked him immeasurably seeing these cheap sheets strewn about his house, he bore with them with what grace he could summon, reminding himself firmly that Matilda was on the whole tolerant of his weakness, which was certainly more costly than her own, the purchasing of small and inaccessible parcels of real estate. And of course it had to be admitted not all plays were masterpieces; the one Matilda had just mentioned was a case in point.

"*Seek Not Tomorrow* was poppycock," he said sharply.

Matilda's eyes twinkled. "What a weather vane you are! As I recall, you felt at the time it had a very special quality. You said the third act was most ingenious, and you went all by yourself to a matinee just two days after we'd seen it with Devon."

This tactless memory caught Matthew off guard, but he brazened it out. "It was poppycock with an unexpected twist."

Matilda chuckled. "An unexpected twist and the most ravishingly pretty woman since Lillian Russell."

"No, since Matilda Saltmarsh," and he bent and kissed his wife's soft white hair.

"Yes, I was pretty," she said complacently, "but Miss Moore is a beauty. Still, beauty isn't everything. That poor girl has a drunken husband whom she has to support, and while you certainly can't call Devon beautiful, except, of course, for her eyes, she's done remarkably well for herself. It just goes to show."

Matthew crossed to the window and stood looking out at the April evening and the softening tracery of the elm trees. Across the street, in front of one of the fraternity houses, a group of boys sprawled injudiciously on the still cold ground. They were singing softly in harmony Williams' loved song, "The Mountains":

"*The mountains, the mountains, we greet you with a song,
The echoes, rebounding their woodland heights along . . .*"

The refrain drifting into the room still had the power to touch Matthew's heart, evoking that melancholy common even to the young nostalgic for their fleeting youth.

> *"Will mingle with anthems that wind and forest sing,*
> *Till hill and valley gaily, gaily ring."*

The plaintive melody expired on the evening air. Matthew's thoughts returned to their conversation of earlier in the evening. "You know," he said moodily, "I don't much like this business about Devon's husband."

Matilda's knitting, a long white British seaman's sock, dropped into her lap. "Matthew, do you think that's the whole story, what she wrote in her last letter about Tim's doing research work for the Government?"

"Oh, I don't doubt that that part's true. He's a fine scientist. But his leaving home seems rather odd. I hope there isn't a woman in the woodpile. Devon's got a lot of pride—it would go hard with her."

"She's got a lot of heart too," said Matilda stoutly. "And I've always thought she was dearly in love with Tim."

She glanced across the room at a folding leather frame which held two photographs, one of Devon and one of Tim. "He's got a nice face," she said. "Lean like you, Matthew, and his eyebrows are splendid, the way they go shooting off."

Matthew too studied the photograph. "A little diabolic, wouldn't you say? I like his mouth, though. Firm. I doubt if Devon's wiles are always successful with that young man."

"Well, at least he's not conceited," said Matilda with satisfaction. "Any man who cuts his hair that way can't think much of himself."

Her husband threw back his head and laughed. "Matilda, after all these years in a college town, I should think you'd be converted to a crew cut."

"I will never be," said Matilda firmly. "Most men aren't so handsome that they can afford to play fast and loose with the little the good Lord gave them. I suppose when He took one look at Adam and realized what He'd done, He simply had to give women loving hearts to overcome the handicap."

"Well, anyway, Devon thinks a lot of her Timothy. Considering her temperament, I feel she has shown admirable restraint while keeping the world posted on their marital status in cologne and perfume. What's the one I like so much?"

"Felicity, but she launched that two years ago."

"Oh yes, on their wedding anniversary. I should think it might have been a slightly embarrassing tribute." Matthew's tone held gentle mockery, but he spoke with affection. They were devoted to Devon, who, after she had grown up and gone to New York to live, still kept in touch with them. They stopped with her on their yearly visit. She wrote them at fairly regular intervals, and she kept the little house in Williamstown afloat in perfumes and swamped in creams. It was a point of pride with her that the very first container of any new preparation to come out of the laboratory must be shipped immediately to Mrs. Matthew Stevens. On his small professorial salary the wife of the mathematics teacher had for years smelled more expensive than many of her movie glamor queens. The local minister's wife, who eschewed even lavender water, had been heard to remark that Matilda Stevens was rather fast, but Matilda reveled in her bottles and jars, and even Matthew was entertained when Devon reached some kind of a milestone and named a new product in celebration, and a large carton arrived at the house. Matthew himself used Felicity after shaving, and even before Devon started advertising Overture on the air an enormous flagon of it had arrived via parcel post. He was ruminating on the profitable way in which their foster child combined sentiment with business, when he was struck by a disquieting idea. "Matilda, what did you tell me the name of the newest cologne was?"

"Overture, dear. It's that big new bottle upstairs."

"M-m-m-m." Matthew glanced again at the two photographs. Matilda watched him. "Why do you ask?"

"Devon always had a pretty strong imagination," he said thoughtfully. "I'm wondering if Tim really did walk out on her."

"Good heavens, Matthew, you mean you think it's vice versa?"

"I'm not saying that," his tone was judicial. "But it occurs to me that Overture is a curious name for the end of a relationship."

"Oh dear." Matilda looked distressed. "You don't suppose it's she who's fallen in love with some other man and left Tim, do you? Oh, Matthew, that would be dreadful. He's just the right husband for her, and they don't grow on trees. She'd be making a great mistake."

"She didn't mention anybody in her last letter, did she?"

"No, but it isn't likely she'd tell us if she had a—well, a new beau, is it?"

Matthew smiled. His Matilda was an outspoken little body, but she had had in the past uneasy suspicions about Devon. There seemed almost no doubt that there was a period in there when she did have lovers, and though of course the fact that it was Devon who had them made Matilda realize that there could be nothing wicked about it, still it was a distressing tendency, and a word at which she jibbed. Matthew took the hurdle for her. "No, it isn't likely she'd tell us of a new lover. But we've generally known about them, at least the important ones. Remember Indian Summer?"

"Mercy, yes, but that came out years ago. You know, Matthew" —Matilda's eyes were round and her tone conciliatory as she broke the bad news—"I'm afraid Devon really did live with that Mr. Doolittle."

"I'm afraid so too, Matilda." Matthew's whisper was heavy with conspiracy, but little lights jigged in his eyes.

"I believe he was quite a nice man actually," she said.

The thought relieved her. After all, if the sinners were agreeable people, nicely brought up and quite clean, the moral lapse was less flagrant. Matthew grinned.

"I seem to recall that you took an awful scunner against him when he wouldn't divorce his wife."

"Naturally. That was when Devon wanted to marry him, but she got over it when she met Tim, so then it was all right, and he's been a great help to her in the business."

"Indian Summer." Matthew savored the sound. "A graceful way of announcing that her lover wasn't as young as he might have been. What was the first perfume Tim inspired?"

"Autumn Glory, but that had nothing to do with his age. That's when she met him."

"Oh yes, Autumn Glory. H-m-m-m-m-m-m. . . . Overture. . . .

H-m-m-m-m. . . . Well, I shall await with interest the next product from the Elliott laboratory."

Two men sat in a bar on First Avenue, drinking a scotch and a beer, smoking and talking intermittently. They were dissimilar but companionable, and they both looked a little tired. Oscar Hogarth, the great Czech scientist, was short and thick set, with vigorous pepper-and-salt hair and shrewd kindly eyes peering through thick lenses. He had a little cropped mustache and round cheeks, and he was puffing comfortably on an old bitten pipe. He watched Tim with sympathetic objectivity. His younger colleague had been distracted and out of sorts for the last two days, and Oscar was waiting for his suspicions to be confirmed. Tim crushed out his cigarette, caught his companion's eye, and his lean, sardonic face twisted into a grin.

"A man who knows where poison lies and who deliberately goes in search of it when he doesn't want it is a pain in the neck. Right?"

"Right," agreed Oscar amiably, his *r* richly rolling.

"I know and I go; therefore, through scientific deduction, I am a pain in the neck. Right?"

"Wrong," said Oscar. "This is the very curious thing with science. An enemy does a stupid thing: he is scientifically and per se condemnable; a friend commits the same blunder, and one sees only a rich humanity."

"You're quite a guy, Oscar."

"I am indebted to you, Tim," said Oscar gravely, but his eyes glinted behind his spectacles. "We serious men of science sometimes get so involved in abstractions and formulas that we forget the human element, but I have only to turn to you and there it is, functioning steadily like a dynamo, and I am brought down to earth again."

Tim took a swipe at him, almost upsetting his beer. Oscar seized it lovingly. "My person you may abuse; on my beer I do not permit of trespassing," and he drank deeply. As he set down his glass, Tim beckoned the waiter and ordered another round.

"Poison of course is a fairly strong word," Tim said, carefully tracing a red square on the tablecloth with the end of a burnt match.

"You have been recently with your Devon, yes." The remark was a statement rather than a question.

"Twice, but through no fault of my own," said Tim sternly. "There is a very screwy dame, Oscar. Hell of a businesswoman, but a loony. Two days ago I had to go to the house. There's a little safe in my bedroom; I've left a lot of papers and stuff in it, and I wanted to check on some reports I'd made before we went south. Well, I got there around two-thirty—three o'clock; it seemed a safe time, I've seldom known Devon to be at home then, but, by God, the other day she was. She was home, and what's more, she was about to clamber into bed."

Ah, thought Oscar, *here we come to it. He sees this woman whom he loves, and she is ill and the blood-cell industry is out the window; no wonder he is so distrait in the laboratory. That unfortunate rat who had curled right up and died when Tim gave him the wrong injection. Ah well—a sacrifice on the altar of science.* "Your wife's illness, it is serious, I hope not?" he asked with interest.

"I figured she wasn't feeling well, too," said Tim, "so I asked her if she was sick, and she looked at me through those lashes as if I were a moron and said, rather sharply I thought for an invalid, 'Don't be silly. I have a business appointment,' and then she propped a mirror on her knees and tied a pink bow in her hair."

"I would say your wife had great respect for your understanding, my boy."

Tim's hand struck the table. "She was on the level, by God. She did have a business appointment, and she'd thought up a little plot to make your head swim—a beaut. It seems she was expecting a fellow from the coast, one of those big movie make-up manufacturers; she and Doolittle are working on a deal to buy him out. Well, he had to talk to her today, but it so happens that both Jasper and Henry Barlow—that's the firm's lawyer—are out of town, but the madam doesn't want to be left holding the bag, so she receives him in bed with no rouge and a wan smile. She explains to me that they will discuss the matter and she will come to terms. In case, however, she wants to change her mind, she personally is not entirely sold on the coast tie-up; it's Doolittle's idea, but in case this guy thinks he has a deal and gets tough, she sics Barlow on him, who tells him that no matter what the agreement he can hardly expect to hold an ill woman to a commitment, and the whole thing's off. She's got witnesses all lined up too. Her secretary knows she was too ill to remain at the office; Louise—that's her maid—can see that she's wretched; and she adds brightly that my coming is a godsend, as in a pinch I too will be able to testify that she was home in bed in the middle of the afternoon, a most unusual occurrence. I try to explain about testimony between husbands and wives, but she says it's only that you can't testify against, and that's why gangsters are always marrying their molls, and that we are not yet so lacking in grace—those are her words—that a husband can't say a sympathetic thing about his helpmate in a courtroom, and she should think I would co-operate in a legitimate business transaction. And there in a nutshell, old boy, you have life in the paint factory, and damned glad I am to be rid of it."

Tim lifted his glass and drained the remaining half of his high-ball at a gulp. Oscar was shaking with silent laughter.

"She is a realist, your wife," he said at last when he could speak. "She too has the scientific approach," and he lifted his beer and toasted her with relish.

The story amused him, but what interested him was that Tim should tell it to him. Throughout their Louisiana trip he had been singularly reticent about Devon and his home life, and now, though they spent hours together daily, their conversations were confined to their work, and they rarely met outside. Oscar lived in Jamaica, Long Island, with his wife and nineteen-year-old daughter, and Tim was staying at his club until his plans became more definite. There was strong likelihood of his going down to Johns Hopkins to do some work. Away from the laboratory the two men saw little of each other, and Oscar was glad of this pleasant interlude. Though he had given small thought to it in their months of collaboration, he had in the last couple of days been forced to the conclusion that it was probably just as well Tim had left his wife. When he was separated from her he was able to engross himself completely in his work. The few times he had seen her, to Oscar's knowledge, only served to upset him.

"I suppose in one way I'm a heel," Tim continued, pulling industriously at his left ear lobe. "After all, I'm still involved in the business to some extent. Last week Devon called me up and asked me would I go to a stockholders' meeting. It was yesterday, so I went."

Oscar, for all his learning, was like a child about finance. "These are big gatherings, no?" he asked with naïve interest.

Tim smiled. "I believe they can be quite a clambake, but at Devonshire House it's more on the cozy side. My wife and Mr. Doolittle between them hold a tidy seventy per cent. Bruce Moreley, who handles the advertising, has a small interest, and so have I and so has the lawyer. The floating supply is small—traded in over the counter. It's not vital that I be there, and I can't imagine why Devon insisted that I show up, unless it's because she's looking damn well and wanted me to know it."

"This seems to me logic," said Oscar seriously.

"I will not give a dissertation, Oscar, but women are curious specimens. Part of their lives they spend telling you that you are the air they breathe and they can't live without you, and the rest of the time they devote to proving to you that they are infinitely more desirable, beautiful, and far happier with you away."

"I do not know whether it is good or bad, Tim, but I would deduce that your wife cares for you if it is important for her to have you see how she looks."

"Lord, Oscar, I want her to care if she isn't made unhappy by it, but I don't know." Tim was silent for a moment. "There's something kind of funny going on. I don't know," he said again, staring into his empty glass as though it were a crystal.

"You know many other things, Tim," said Oscar comfortably. "Myself, I do not consider women romantic and unpredictable creatures—far too much time is wasted while they and we pretend this is so—but they are only important in so much as they produce worthy things: children, comfort, precise experiments. In the field of art they are essentially second-rate, but they are of first-rate reflex value, because men love them and often take their color from them. You are a good man, Tim. For this reason, then, I want your wife to care if you want her to, but I tell you a man is better free of these things."

Tim gave him a mocking grin. "You're a fine one to talk, the most uxorious husband I know."

"I am devoted to my wife," said Oscar placidly, "because she is an excellent creature not consumed by ideas of competition. Also she devotes herself to my welfare so I can give all my time to my work. Also, we are so sure of each other that my mind is completely free. With you it is not thus."

"A funny thing happened at the office yesterday," said Tim. "While I was there they brought in some advertising layouts. It seems the world's about to be drenched in a new Devonshire House perfume."

"So?"

"Yeah. The name of it gave me pause."

"What is it?"

"Morning Song."

"This is very nice."

"Yeah. Nobody'd be likely to sing in the morning unless they were pretty happy, wouldn't you say? I mean—you'd have to be feeling pretty satisfied. Everything jake."

"That would seem obvious."

There was a long pause. "Yeah, that's what I thought."

The shutters were closed and the flowered chintz curtains drawn across the open windows, but the early morning sun of a clear July day shimmered through, permeating the bedroom with a soft, aqueous light. When it touched Devon's eyelids, she awoke reluctantly, but, too sleepy to reach for the eyeshade on the bedside table, she lay drowsily watching the patterns slipping across the ceiling and listening to the chirping of the birds. The barnyard was at some distance from the house, but the crowing of the cock was borne on the still air, and the barking of the farmer's dog. A flock of crows flew cawing overhead, and from below the terrace came the whir and clatter of the lawn mower. If she had spoken to the gardener once, she had spoken to him a hundred times, but it made no difference, he preferred cutting the grass in the wee hours and over the week end. Devon lost the battle with what grace she could muster and chose to assume that a dawn barbering had some salubrious effect obtainable at no other time, but she sleepily pondered the incongruity of seeking peace and quiet in the country when the banks of the East River were far more tranquil. Comparatively little traffic passed the town house, the rear windows overlooked the silently flowing river, and there was nothing to break the stillness but an occasional foghorn eerily moaning through the morning mist or sending its plaintive warning through the dark evening, and it was a sound she loved.

The sweet smell of the meadows and the flower garden abandoned under the sun drifted through the curtains, and she thought, *That's the feeling I have for Kurt, that's the way the heart feels when it's in love, like a flower full-blown and tremulous.* She turned and very gently kissed the naked shoulder of the man asleep in the bed beside her. Kurt lay on his right side with his back to her, and he slept so quietly that sometimes she thought he had ceased to breathe, and more than once her hand crept to his heart in alarm till she was reassured by its soft, rhythmic beat.

She glanced at the jeweled clock on the bedside table. It was not yet six; she would let him sleep a little longer before waking him and sending him back to his own room. That was what was so lovely about the time they spent in the country; they could be all night together, and no one was actually the wiser, regardless of what their suspicions might be. To be sure, they did not sleep quite so well; Devon especially had almost always found it impossible to relax totally with anyone else in the bed, but she was so much in love that it was sweeter to pass a restless night semiconscious of Kurt beside her than to lose him completely in oblivion. Anyway it was only an occasional night, when they were at the farm. In town it was impossible. She almost giggled when she thought of the expression on Louise's face were she to walk in with the breakfast tray and find Kurt in her mistress' bed. Of course Louise was no fool, and she probably guessed, but she could say nothing. That was certainly one up for the capitalist system; whatever he might know or suspect, a servant was not in position to catechize a master, but at that it was remarkable the trouble the master went to to keep him in ignorance.

Since her affair with Kurt, Devon had more than once thanked her stars that she didn't live in an apartment; what with elevator men and doormen, the thing was a nuisance. Some deep sense of prudery or caution had for a long time kept her from giving Kurt a key to the town house, but in the end she had done so because it was simpler for him to let himself in when he came to see her late at night than for her to keep a lookout, and it was obviously highly undesirable for him to ring and summon Fairweather. Of course if he called in the afternoon or came for dinner, he pealed with a will, and Devon wanly hoped that Fairweather merely thought that the madam had an attentive swain, which was surely justifiable when one thought of the heartless way in which she had been abandoned by her legal husband.

An attentive swain. . . . Well, Kurt was, she supposed, attentive; certainly he was intensely jealous. Jealous of what he referred to as his personal freedom. He was a remarkably independent lover, and his personal freedom loomed large in his scheme of things. As far as Devon could make out, it seemed to consist of always doing exactly what he wanted to do when he wanted to do it. In one way such behavior had an advantage; it was certainly honest, so that when he was with her Devon could be sure he was enjoying himself. The minute he ceased to enjoy himself or wanted to be elsewhere, he left her. It was as simple as that. Whether his action caused her unhappiness or inconvenience was a matter of complete indifference to him, and through considerable heartache and more than one harrowing scene she had learned the folly of asking him where he had been or with whom. She was not temperamentally possessive, but she was desperately in love and suffered agonies of jealousy when she thought of him with other women. It was, she believed, impossible for him to be with a woman and not to make love to her, but questioning angered him; he became cold and unkind, and his usually pleasant voice grew rasping. "These are my affairs," he said shortly. Devon's heart contracted.

"That I don't doubt," she replied cuttingly. "You seem to have a good many of us."

"Devon, this is very stupid. Why must I always be with another woman when I am not with you? You are having an absolute inferiority complex."

"Perhaps I have," she said, "but it is unkind of you to foster it." Kurt found her piteous, and therefore irritating. Also he usually was with another woman. He enjoyed it and saw no reason why he should be made to feel guilty. Just because you slept with a woman, why should she consider that she owned you body and soul, or that you intended to change your mode of living? Life could be so simple and enjoyable if women would only learn to take the good things as they came. They took them all right, but they were loath to let them go, and then too they harped so. Devon, for instance. "You see, dear," she had once said, "I always assume you are with another woman because I had a tough lesson to learn in the early days of our romance."

Ach Gott, we must go through this again, he thought, for he knew to what she referred. They had been lovers for about three weeks, when Devon one night came to his apartment. He was expecting her but not quite so soon. When he had got in he had found a message that Miss Madeline Valdane had phoned; the news had depressed him. Miss Valdane was a lady to whom he had been paying assiduous court, but alas, the dew had gone from the rose, though she, obtuse girl, was unaware of it. Still she had her points; among them three brothers extravagant in their use of leather goods, and while Kurt was in no sense a fortune seeker, why turn away business when a little *Küss die Hand,* which was after all not unpleasant, might clinch the deal? He had returned Miss Valdane's phone call while waiting for Devon, but the conversation had been more protracted than he bargained for. As was so often the case, the lady had been reproachful and censorious. *It is amazing,* he thought to himself, *how frequently these American girls mistake attention for intention.* She had railed at him and accused him of faltering in his suit. But Kurt had one advantage which he was quick to press. Miss Valdane herself was not unpopular, and Devon arrived at his door just in time to hear him say, "It is not so that I do not care. How often have I called you and you are not alone?" She stood for a moment dazed. Kurt's apartment was small and in a remodeled private house. Anyone standing in the little hall could easily overhear a telephone conversation. At first she didn't realize he was on the phone and thought someone was with him. She stood hesitating as to whether to ring or not, thinking that she had misunderstood him about the time, or that a caller had unexpectedly dropped in; then she caught the sense of the conversation. . . . "No, no, no, darling, you are foolish, of course it is not over, why should it be?" The protestation of steady ardor was made in a testy tone, but his words came as a shock to Devon. Kurt's suit had been so ardent, his desire for her and his delight in her so genuine, that though she assumed he had had countless affairs in the past, it did not occur to her that he would make love to another woman while their own love was still a joyous thing. Her pride suffered a terrible blow. She stood sick and trembling in the little hall. His voice receded, then came to her again, good-humored this time, gay: "So let us have no more farewells, yes?" And then an amused laugh.

Go away, go away, said her intelligence. *If this is how he is after only three weeks, what will it be like in a few months? . . . Stay, stay,* said her heart, as she rang the bell. She heard Kurt slam down the receiver, and he was at the door in an instant.

"Darling, come in," he said with a frank and happy smile. She looked at him coolly and walked past him into the room and over to the window, and stood staring down into the back yards. In the darkness she could see some sheets flapping on a clothesline, and thought to herself that the woman who left them there was a slipshod housekeeper.

"How are you, darling?" he asked. She was silent. "Aren't you going to take off your things?" Kurt's voice was cordial, but he was suddenly uneasy and didn't quite dare take her in his arms. If by any chance she had overheard him, it was going to be a damn nuisance. That Madeline, it wasn't the first time she had caused him trouble, and his Devon was a darling and tremendously exciting. Life had an exhilarating fillip since he met her, it was only that . . . Oh Lord, the complications.

She was thinking desperately, *Dear God, what is the wise thing to do? To pretend I heard nothing, I suppose; but why should he get away with this cheap two-timing? He has no real tenderness or sweetness, he doesn't love me at all. Maybe there's someone whom he does love, and I'm just an easy conquest. A lay. Charming word,* she thought, her mind curling away in disgust. *And he's right, that's what I'm here for, isn't it, except that I happen to be mad about him?*

Kurt was uncertain, but thought perhaps he was being foolish. After all, she might well not have heard anything, she might have come swiftly and rung the bell and been only conscious of his voice, and not have distinguished any words. She was very quiet, but perhaps she was simply in a bad mood. Anyway, it was far wiser not to raise the issue. Kurt considered that the man who gave himself away was inexcusably gauche, and he was rarely guilty of such a lapse. "Darling, please, turn around. I have waited for you for such a long time, and now I see only your back." Oh, the sweet sound of his voice, warm, cajoling, and full of promise. She murmured something indistinguishable. "Please, darling, I am impressed by the beautiful color of your new suit, like violets, and I observe that your sables are of rare vintage, but I would like to see that little face."

She turned her small face to him; her incredible eyelashes were spangled with tears, but her voice surprised herself, it was so steady. "Don't you think you had better call the lady back? It's very rude to hang up on anybody."

"What are you talking about?" said Kurt. "You are crazy." He often said that when she disagreed with him. He couldn't seem to think of many arguments.

"Not at all. She probably thinks you were cut off. I'll go in the bathroom and run the water very loud and you can have complete privacy."

Kurt honored her with a slight bow. "You are most thoughtful, but I do not have to call back anyone."

She stood there uncertainly, but her heart lifted. Perhaps there was nothing to it. After all, why shouldn't he have an affectionate friendship for someone? If he had had to reassure that other woman, didn't it prove that he probably hadn't called in a long time, maybe not since he'd met her, Devon? He was probably being pursued, poor devil. Of course if the other one was in love with him, Devon was sorry for her, but a change of heart was part of life; she'd have to be tough-fibered and accept it. That's how things were, and Devon herself would do well to relax. It was silly to let him know how much she cared. "Poor Kurt," she said, and her voice was light and mocking and infused with sadness, "he has such trouble with his women, the most complicated love life in town."

"This is not true. Why do you talk in this foolish way?" His slightly Oriental features were impassive, but his voice was cross, like a spoiled child's. Devon turned from him and addressed his reflection in the mirror over the mantelpiece, as she wiped a tiny particle of smeared lipstick from the corner of her mouth.

"I hope I don't intrude?"

"Intrude is when you are not wanted?"

"Yes."

"You do not intrude. All day I am looking forward with eagerness to this time when we will be together." And that was so; he had been. His ability to find brief happiness with almost any attractive woman largely accounted for his sunny charm. There were so many of them that he was perpetually in a good humor. Like other human beings he had his cares, mostly financial, but his pleasures were manifold. Devon was not exactly pretty perhaps, but she exerted over him a strong sexual attraction. There was something about the sheen of her skin and the way she walked that stirred him. Besides he had genuine respect for her ability, and she was of course famous. Kurt was not averse to the gentle prickle of star dust in his nostrils.

Devon was hurt and sad, angry and hopeful, the usual turmoil of emotion she experienced in his company. Rarely was her feeling for him unadulterated by conflicting sentiments. He still made no reference to the telephone conversation, and she was amazed by his obstinacy in blandly forgoing any explanation. It seemed to her callous and in a curious way shocking. "Have you Prussian blood too, Kurt?"

He looked blank. "No. Why do you ask?"

"You are so remarkably stubborn. You remind me of a cushion I once saw."

"A cushion?" Kurt had no idea what she was talking about, but he was on guard like a wary fencer.

"Yes. A friend of mine has it on the couch in her drawing room. It's a green cushion, and on it is written in white letters, 'Never complain, Never explain.' That's a maxim. A maxim is a thing they have in copybooks. I guess you wrote the book."

"Darling, come here a moment. Do not hurt yourself this way." He took her hand and led her to the sofa. She sat down, and he drew up a small chair and sat facing her. He sincerely didn't want her to be unhappy, and he considered her extremely foolish, deliberately to inflict pain on herself. For anyone to suffer from an act of his struck him as willful masochism. Owing to a virulent egotism, it was nearly impossible for him to be hurt by others, and he was therefore baffled and resentful when women accused him of authoring their miseries. Considering the amount of time and affection he lavished on them, he could only judge them ungrateful when they reviled him.

"You see, Kurt," Devon was struggling to sound self-possessed, "perhaps I seem unreasonable to you, but it makes me unhappy when I hear you saying to another woman that nothing is over, why should it be? I—I wouldn't expect you to give up any friendships on my account, but I would like to think I was your only love affair. It's more flattering somehow."

Kurt said nothing. He had been untrue to Devon in the three weeks since they had become lovers, but as he was neither a kind man nor a coward, he seldom lied. He was also lazy, and lying required considerable energy and a sort of mental bookkeeping which he found irksome. He neither admitted nor denied her implication but waited, his clear hazel eyes looking into hers as a doctor waits for a spasm, about which he can do nothing, to pass from a patient.

She knew then that she was lost, and his nearness had already cast a spell over her; her desire for him was so great that all her uncertainties and doubts were swept away in a flood of longing. But Kurt had his delicacy. She was shaken, and he felt it would be unwise to rush her. He knew, by instinct and through his body, subtleties his mind would never learn. "Do you want me to take you home?" he asked gently.

Her pride made one last desperate effort. "It's too bad this had to happen," she said, as one who says, *Things might have been different, but of course this changes everything.* "You see, it was so pleasant, and I—I was just beginning to care for you."

Kurt said nothing, but Devon didn't move. He was conscious of the subtle and disturbing fragrance which enveloped her. It was Overture, and desire stirred within him. He waited a few moments; then he leaned forward and very gently laid a kiss on the corner of her mouth. She pressed her face to his. He took her in his arms and drew her towards him. She sank to her knees and melted in tears against him.

That had been nearly four months ago, and the scene drifted through her memory as she lay drowsing beside him in the summer dawn. A hundred times it had been brought home to her how far wiser she would have been, how far less heartache she would have suffered, had she turned from his door when she overheard the conversation that night, and a hundred times she had been grateful that she hadn't. So much ecstasy, so much fun would have been lost. She recalled with wonder how she had come to love him in a brief space of time. She had been deeply unhappy over Tim's leaving her, and she was lonely, and Kurt was there. He was charming and he was dominant. Because of his Jewish blood he appealed to her imagination as a symbol of the persecuted; she felt for him tenderness and desire, and her love had sprung like a wild and flowering forest, rioting almost overnight through her heart. Sympathy for him, pity for all his kind had played a part, but she also respected his ability to land on his own feet. Within his limited sphere he had a shrewd business sense, which gratified her, and she applauded his tactics. Having little money, he still had that peculiar courage required to stand pat when the success or failure of a deal may alter a man's whole life.

Virtually unaided, Kurt had opened his small leather business, and he was building it into a going concern.

Although his Rumanian grandfather had amassed a fortune, his father had lost most of it contributing to the Dollfuss movement in a vain effort to save Austria, and Kurt had arrived in America nearly penniless. His secret ambition and not inconsiderable talent lay in the field of photography, but there the native competition was great and the return for a beginner microscopic, but as Kurt had an aversion to luring his rich friends into the plusher hotels where they would be fleeced that he might earn a small commission, seemingly the only employment open to upper-class refugees, he had borrowed a little money and opened the workroom where he designed and made leather goods.

In so doing he was turning a dilettante interest to practical advantage. His grandfather had owned a great export house in Braila, dealing in corn and wheat, and had bought a magnificent estate in Sinaia, where Kurt spent much of his childhood. The old man had a passion for horses and their equipment, and the sumptuousness of his carriages and harnesses was as famous in Vienna as in Rumania. His grandchild acquired from him the love and knowledge of leather which was to stand him in good stead in later years.

Devon appreciated the realistic attitude which enabled Kurt to work long hours designing and making up models of sports equipment, luggage, and accessories and submitting them to Fifth Avenue shops. Sometimes they accepted them and paid him, and sometimes they turned him down and later copied his ideas themselves, but little by little he was becoming established, respected as a talented designer and a man who would one day offer serious competition in the retail trade. Devon was even toying with the idea of backing him in business herself, but she was not convinced that he was yet ready to swing it, and a congenital antipathy to giving men expensive presents had so far prevented her. If you were married to them, that was a different matter. She would have bought Tim diamond mines had he wanted them, and she had once even thought of presenting Jasper with a small yacht—she was in a position to force the sale—but as he turned Robespierre-green at the sight of a dinghy, she abandoned the idea. Present-giving was a pleasure if the man was an integral part of your life, and it was something you could share, but Kurt was a light-o'-love. He had no emotional stamina. Though Devon adored him, she could never count on him. Because he said he would telephone did not necessarily mean he would, and though he was having a passionate love affair with her, it did not guarantee that she saw him every evening. It was true that would have been difficult; her life was too established, and she had no wish to embarrass Tim by rumor and gossip, but she had to admit to herself that Kurt was far more responsible for maintaining the outward convention than she. Had he been willing to accompany her, she would gladly have taken him everywhere, but this he refused to do. He said it was not so much that he hated parties as that he disliked being taken to them. "I do not like to go where I am not known and have not been invited," he said stiffly, and she had murmured, "Of course not, darling, it shows great delicacy, but people can hardly get to know you unless they meet you, can they?" To which he had replied that under such circumstances he preferred never to meet anybody. If in this he was mentally deficient, as Devon considered, he was also adamant. In further discussion it developed that what Kurt really liked about parties was going to them alone.

"Then I am free," he had explained. "I can come and go as I want and speak to whomever I like."

"But good Lord, Kurt, there are no strings attached. You are certainly free to speak to whomever you like even if I happen to be with you."

"No, you do not understand. That I would not do. If I am with you in a party, I consider that it would be unfair, beginning something with another woman, asking to see her again."

Devon looked at him quizzically. "It would not, however, be unfair to do it behind my back?"

"No, it is in no way harming you. My life away from you is not your concern. If this hurts you, I am sorry, but this is why it would be wrong for me to marry ever. I do not want to spend always my life with one woman, to have to come home always to her, and that she would have a right to be angry when I am not there."

Devon, who had occasionally considered the prospect of married life with Kurt, flared in indignation. "You can relax, my friend. If this little hint is thrown out to me, it's a waste of time. Marriage is only possible when there is maturity and a sense of responsibility on the part of both members."

"And you are thinking I am adolescent, yes?"

"You took the words from my mouth."

Kurt sighed. "Always these talks are leading us to disagreements. You do not understand how it is with a man. That's why people give cocktail parties; there it is not such fun maybe, but it is a kind of market place, a telephone exchange. You meet someone, you like her, you take her number, and it is when you call her and take her out away from the crowd that the pleasure begins. At least there is always the chance. When one marries, the doors are closed."

Devon was silent, remembering her extreme youth. She had worked harder than most young women and gone to fewer parties, but what Kurt said was to some extent true. Then there had been the sharp tingle of expectancy in every invitation. Perhaps this dinner, perhaps that cocktail party would be where she would meet Him. To be sure, in her own case it had not worked out so profitably. There had been a few transient Hims, spewed from the social whirlpool, but the lads who stood firm, Jasper and Tim, she had found far from the haunts of the anchovy and the olive, and an exquisite relief it was when she no longer had to search. Not that a new face wasn't refreshing—why should Kurt feel that the desire for novelty was peculiar to men?—but once a woman married, novelty was a side issue. The frill upon the lamb chop, so to speak. Pleasant but not vital. Deep inside she was glad when she no longer had to depend upon the parties. Deep inside, it seemed a man was sorry, although the majority fortunately found in their wives and families compensation which outweighed the joys of free-lancing. They accepted, perhaps with gentle melancholy, but they accepted the fact that they were responsible members of an adult society, and when you came right down to it, a man no longer in his first youth looked pretty silly bounding expectantly from cocktail bar to tea table, from picnic plate to ancient spode, flaring the air like a hound dog in the spring. Still she admired Kurt's candor; duplicity was not one of his faults, but she would have appreciated a graceful garment of illusion. It would have been nice of him to pretend that with her he felt differently. How heavenly if he could feel differently!

She looked at him for a long time. "Going someplace with a person you love never doubles the fun for you, does it, Kurt?" And he answered that it did not. "Whenever I dream of my ideal life," he said, "I dream of traveling, of making money, of owning a house even, but always I am alone."

Perhaps he was dreaming now, for he shifted his position, turning almost completely over in bed, but he did not waken. Devon lay watching him. His face was unlined and scarcely more impassive in sleep than it sometimes was in his waking hours, when he jealously refused to disclose his most prosaic activities. When Devon, planning a dinner party or some quite humble jaunt to the movies, would ask him if he was free on a certain evening, he had a way of saying abruptly, "No, I'm not," and that was all he would say. His refusal to give any further explanation infuriated her, and she accused him of boorishness. "Good God, Kurt, I don't expect you to confine your life to mine, but after all, we are lovers, though that doesn't seem to mean much to you. You want all the joy of a love affair, yet you insist on the total independence only possible when no human being gives a damn about you, or you about them."

"I am sorry that I am able to do nothing to please you." Kurt spoke a little wistfully and with no sarcasm.

Devon's wrath evaporated. "Don't worry, you do plenty to please me. It's your stubbornness I object to. Who the hell do you think you are, dear, royalty, that you never have to account for your actions?"

"This I cannot help. Since I am a child it is the same. When I was ten years old and went from the house, my father would say, 'Where are you going?' and I would tell him, 'Out,' but I could never say where."

Devon looked at him skeptically. "This Freudian divulgement would touch me more if you never disclosed your whereabouts, but I have noticed you are less repressed when it's a large dinner party or a session with businessmen. Why isn't it just as easy to say, 'I can't be with you Wednesday, darling, because I am taking Mary Snooks to the theater'? I wouldn't make a scene, I promise you."

Kurt laughed in good-humored derision. "And how well would you like me taking this Miss Snooks to the play?" he asked teasingly.

"I'd like it a damn sight better than coming smack up against a blank wall. And though you vaunt yourself on never lying, the idea that if I don't know you're untrue to me it's perfectly all right to be does not strike me as the soul of integrity."

"Why shouldn't I go out with other women?" he asked coldly.

"It isn't that you shouldn't, Kurt, it's——" She couldn't go on. She wanted to say, "I want you to love me so much that you won't want to go out with them," but her pride wouldn't let her. But Kurt was aroused now, and he considered her unfair.

"You make your own engagements when you like and with whom you like. Why shouldn't I?"

"Any engagements I make without you are for the most part business."

"And that is another thing," he said angrily. "In your business I have no part at all. It takes you completely away from me and is your only real interest in life. It is abnormal, not being like a woman."

"Why, that's the most idiotic——" began Devon, and stopped abruptly. Kurt's complaint had a familiar ring. Tim had never been jealous of her work; that he understood and was a part of; but the fact that she made so much money had proven a stumbling block for him too. Kurt did not speak of the money angle as such, but he also probably sensed in it a barrier. Men were wrong about that, but apparently it was the way they felt; they thought money made a woman independent. Of course materially, thank God, it did. But a wealthy woman was just as dependent on masculine affection and companionship as a poor one. More so, maybe, for she needed desperately to feel that she personally was desirable; but men didn't seem to think that counted.

In her own case her business was so much herself that the idea of anybody being jealous of it was ridiculous. It was as though he were jealous of her hands because they were a part of her. "But Kurt," she said lamely, "the business is me. Mine and Jasper's and Tim's. I've had it all my life. It is my life, or rather the shell of it. You're the lovely inner part. That's why you're so important to me, my darling. Without you I have no person in my life. I have only things."

She said this so sweetly that Kurt was somewhat mollified, but the fact that she was so capable and that if she did need help she turned to Jasper still rankled. Though in their relationship it was she who did the kissing and he who turned the cheek, within his limitations he was in love, and as her business was the most important thing in her life, his ego demanded that she confide in him just as other women turned to him with their important problems, their sex life, their servants, their clothes, and their husbands. Kurt spoke mockingly, but he meant what he said. "I am, I think, not so deeply important. You are saying nothing to me ever about business matters. These are her little secrets, yes?" And he took her by both arms and bent them back in a kind of playful sadism.

"Hey, ouch," she said, and broke free of him. She held his face in both her hands and kissed him on the tip of his nose. "Darling, the reason I don't talk business to you is because it is excessively dull and you would be bored."

"No, it is because you do not consider my mentality very good and you have no confidence."

"Darling," her voice was warm and throaty and full of love, but Kurt had spoken her very thoughts. Furthermore she was temperamentally closemouthed about her affairs, and though she was passionately in love with him, that seemed no reason for discussing the cosmetic industry. A lover was, well—a lover, not a business manager or a husband. Working women with outside men in their lives should have the wit to know where to draw the line. History and business were full of ladies who let men make fools of them against their better judgment. Catherine the Great, for instance. Fancy believing that cock-and-bull story of Potemkin's!

Not to take a lover if one had the opportunity and wanted him seemed to her a drastic course, but there were one or two women she could mention who would do well to follow it. Their daytime world was overbalanced by their nocturnal activities, and that was bad. Their minds had no fiber. A vulgar spirit disgusted her, but the idea of varied and transitory passion did not shock her, as she had never considered that there was anything cheap or censorable in the physical act of love. It was prostitution when it was done without love or joy or grace, but surely there was nothing immoral in a man and woman giving each other delight and satisfaction.

This was her honest creed, and it functioned perfectly from a rationalistic point of view, and in an emotional vacuum, but when she suspected her lover of giving delight and satisfaction to other women, it broke her heart. In calmer moments she thought to herself, *That's where people go wrong, believing that the same theory will hold good in love as well as out.* It was another land and the prevailing winds were different. The things that lovers really thought and felt about each other! Dear God, where had the legend arisen that love was a beneficent state? She thought, *A philanderer is a poor thing because no matter how many women may love him he is incapable of giving to any one of them delight and satisfaction whole and shining. Each one holds in her hand only glinting fragments ephemeral and spurious.*

She glanced again at the clock on the bedside table. Between reverie and dozing, over an hour had slipped by. This time she would have to wake Kurt. Louise and the other servants would soon be about, and one could never tell what early guest might be stirring. There was a houseful over the week end. Most of them could be counted on to lie decently in their beds till a Christian hour, but not George Lowery. George had been known to rise at six-thirty, and he *prowled* so. All she would need would be to have Kurt and him bump into each other. Kurt could hardly say he had been in her room borrowing an aspirin. George was unsophisticated, but he wasn't simple. She turned to her lover. He still slept in innocence, and it occurred to Devon with a kind of sardonic humor that while she had lain torn between love and heartache, the object of this concentration lay in blissful ignorance, replenishing his forces for another day of happy egotism. Men were certainly something, she thought, but it wasn't little boys. She kissed him lightly. "Darling . . ." There were murmurings from Kurt. "Wake up, my sweet, you must go back to your own room."

Kurt opened his eyes. "Good morning, my darling," he said and gathered her into his arms and kissed her hair and breathed deep. "You have the sweetest hair. Is that my perfume?"

As she smiled he felt her cheek move against his. "Yes, my honey love, Morning Song." They lay still for a few minutes, and then his hand wandered gently over her body. "Darling, please, it's after seven. You must go at once."

"At once," said Kurt. Twenty minutes later he left her.

☆   ☆   ☆

Though Devon had wakened early, it was nearly eleven before she put in an appearance downstairs. When Kurt had gone, she had fallen into a deep sleep for two hours, and appeared on the terrace fresh as a daisy, the golden tips of her short dark hair, Emile's newest fancy, glinting in the sunlight, wearing superbly tailored white sharkskin slacks, and prepared to battle for the Sunday papers.

It was very strange about Sunday papers; no matter how many sets you ordered, each complete unit comprising impartially the *Times, Herald Tribune, News, Mirror,* and *Journal-American,* someone else always had the war news and the dramatic and magazine sections, and you were left to munch on rusks: real estate and that fascinating part about automobiles. As Devon looked at her recumbent guests she saw at a glance that tradition still held. "Good morning," she said brightly, hoping to lure one of them from his prize, but she was setting her snare for wily birds. To be sure, Cynthia, the Lowerys' little girl who was spending the week end with them, jumped up from the hot flagstones where she was lying sprawled on her stomach blissfully engrossed in the funnies, and ran to hug her, and Kurt, naked except for a pair of figured Hawaiian shorts, sandals, dark glasses, and a coat of sun oil, came over and kissed her hand, but the *Times Weekly Review* and complete copies of the *News* and *Mirror* he kept clutched to his chest. Estelle was not around. George merely grunted by way of good morning. He was absorbed in Senator Pepper's latest speech, with which he agreed in toto. Nicky, with Miss Flora beside him, was stretched at ease in the rattan chaise longue, completely enveloped in an outsize blue toweling bathrobe, engrossed in the "Help Wanted" section. He peered at Devon over the top of his spectacles. "I say, people are in need of the most extraordinary services. Listen to this: 'Wanted, Boy to learn diamond-setting trade, must also be able to do light work in medical laboratory.' I can just picture the setup. Chap from the Kimberley diamond mines who's smuggled out a few Kaffirs who have concealed on their persons a flock of uncut gems."

"I don't get it," said Devon.

"Well, if we're to believe all we hear about where they conceal them, dear girl, I don't wonder this lad has got to be able to putter about a medical lab."

Devon gave his head a push. "Nicky, you dope."

"Milady never knows what brave men suffer that she may have her baubles," he murmured, his eyes running down the charmed columns as he probed the needs of the human race.

Devon, knowing when she was licked, sat down on the top step of the terrace beside Cynthia. The flagstone was hot even through her slacks, and she wondered how the child stood it: she was wearing nothing but a faded skimpy little bathing suit which she had outgrown. *Poor kid,* thought Devon, *I ought to give her some things. Estelle must have all she can do to keep the three of them going and take care of the house too.* The flagging really was hot. "Hey, Kurt, toss us some mats, will you?" Kurt got slowly to his feet, still reading the paper, and without looking at her tossed a couple of canvas cushions in their direction. "Here, dear," she said to the child. Cynthia was again flat on her stomach, lost in the funnies, which she read deliberately, whispering the words to herself, her small face stern with concentration. Devon lifted her by the seat of her bathing suit and slid the cushion under her. Cynthia never missed a beat but went rhythmically on with her reading. Devon looked at her objectively. "You should say 'Thank you,'" she observed.

"Thank you," said Cynthia. Watching her but seeing no spark of amusement light her face as she read, Devon wondered what intrigued her. "Are the funnies funny?" she asked.

"Wonderful," said Cynthia, finishing the Phantom without a smile and systematically turning the page to the Lone Ranger. A doll lay sprawled on the step beside her. As Devon picked it up, the china-blue eyes opened and stared at her blankly. She surveyed the lethargic group around her and looked back at the doll. "You seem as alert as the rest of my friends," she said to it coldly. Hearing her own addressed, Cynthia pushed back her dark curtain of hair and looked up.

"Her name is Annabelle," she said.

Devon suddenly smiled. "I'll bet she's ten years old."

Cynthia was surprised. "Why, yes. How did you know? Of course she's not really. Mummy gave her to me in the spring, but I pretend she's ten."

"Of course, it's the perfect age." She knew how old Annabelle was because she knew how old Cynthia was, and when she was a child her dolls had always been her own age. It was very satisfactory. In that way they were contemporaries, but by a magic arrangement one was also the parent as well and could scold them and pet them and put them to bed and generally wield the whip hand. Devon suddenly decided Cynthia was sweet, with her great dark eyes and skinny little brown body, and she made up her mind that she should have not only a new bathing suit but lots of other clothes as well. She hurried on, characteristically forming plans, ignoring the reactions of others. She would be able to persuade Estelle to let her help her—she was sure of that—and it would bring a safe and wholesome delight to herself, a pleasant change from the neurotic uncertainty of life with Mr. Fabri. Probably children were the answer. God knows one's own life ceased to hold much interest after a time, and for the first few years children might be very satisfying, before they started turning into vipers like the rest of the world.

She glanced at Kurt. He was capable of the most utter relaxation and lay now with his head thrown back and his eyes closed, basking like a lizard. Devon wondered where he was going to be tomorrow night. Not with her, she was sure of that, for he had said nothing of his plans. That was his way. They had agreed that he would drive her into town Monday morning, but he had not asked her if she was free or planning anything for them Monday night. She supposed that she would wait all the way in for him to say something about the evening, but in her heart she knew he would not.

She was aware of the folly of shadowing her present happiness with past and future remissness and made a deliberate effort to free her mind of her corroding thoughts. It was a day for happiness.

Why spoil the lovely flavor with bitter tincture? She was surrounded by friends, and the scene before her was enough to lift the heart. The house stood on a rise, and below the flagstone terrace, with its graceful balustrade and pots of tumbling fuchsia, the ground dropped away and lawn and flower gardens sloped gently down to the cove. A gentle breeze stirred the leaves of the great trees, and away to the left were the open meadows and the ridge on which stood the magnificent wineglass elms. They were the reason she had bought the place. She could never look enough at those lovely sentinels against the sky. The air was so pure that light seemed to rise from the earth, from the bone-white beach, from the glittering grass, and from Long Island Sound, sparkling like a million sapphires in the sunlight. Dozens of white sails flecked the water and drifted across the wooded hills of the jutting headlands as across a backdrop, in perpetual regatta.

She stretched luxuriously—how often had she told her clients to emulate the cat—and asked, "Who's for a swim?"

"Me, by God," and Nick tossed away the "Help Wanted" section. Miss Flora rose, also emulated the cat, and trotted over to Kurt, where she sniffed interestedly at his oil-smeared legs. Kurt squealed and drew them up like a woman seeing a mouse. *The guy is ridiculous*, thought Devon, and immediately felt better. George disengaged himself from the farsighted principles of Senator Pepper and shot a suspicious glance at Kurt. He had never cared for him from the first night he met him at Devon's dinner party and found that he did not like dogs. "Miss Flora won't bite you," he said coldly. George had toyed idly with the idea of sicking the FBI on him, but Kurt was obviously sincere in his appreciation of Roosevelt, and George was baffled. How could an out-and-out bounder—and what else were you going to call a man who didn't like animals and was stiff and self-conscious with children?—how could such a fellow have the perspicacity to side with the sane political party? George concluded that human nature was inconsistent, and there didn't seem much he could do about it. He thawed slightly towards Kurt. "I guess you aren't used to dogs," he said with more geniality than he had hitherto shown.

"They are my curse," said Kurt, and at the moment Devon almost sympathized with him. Miss Flora, finding the oil delicious, started licking him ecstatically and was bounding with joyful leaps and sharp barks in an attempt to reach his face. Kurt batted at her futilely. "Down, boy, girl, fiend, whatever you are," he shouted. "Nicholas, call off your hell's hound." Cynthia was jumping up and down in wild excitement, and George and Devon were laughing with loud, callous enjoyment, which increased in pitch as the farmer's Irish setter, attracted by the excitement, came streaming up the terrace steps, convoyed by Devon's three toy poodles.

"Come on, Miss Flora, hey, my girl, come on, my beauty." Nick was laughing so much that his entrance into the fray was half-hearted, but his blue toweling bathrobe swung behind him with a flourish as he tried to dodge the poodles, parry the setter, and reach his own spaniel. "That's the stuff, boys, give tongue," he shouted encouragingly, and the whole pack barked madly as Kurt thrashed amongst them with a folded newspaper.

"What is this?" he cried, his accent thickening in his excitement and distress. "There is a plot. I am like the honey pot to these wild beasts." Devon was doubled up with malicious enjoyment. For once his bland indifference, his easy self-control, was shattered. The three toy poodles, gray, black, and brown, leaped with the precision and grace of circus dogs, their lean little bodies close-trimmed, except for the outsize chaps on their front and rear legs showing to admirable advantage, their shaven ears with the tassels at the ends flying on the summer air. Estelle arrived in the midst of the hullabaloo to be informed by her daughter in ecstatic shrieks that all the dogs were jumping on Mr. Fabri.

"I say, Nick, you are shocking," she called laughingly to her brother. "I know perfectly well it was that awful Miss Flora who started it." Miss Flora, having achieved stage center and the undivided attention of the entire company, turned with sudden indifference and sat down by George, resting her head on his thigh and gazing soulfully into his eyes. The setter went sniffing after her, and the three poodles sat down and laughed, their pink tongues lolling out of their mouths, their eyes bright with further deviltry.

"Heigh ho," said Nick, returning to the chaise longue and gathering up his bathing cap, "I spent a quiet Sunday in the country once, but this isn't it. Come on, old boy," he added, addressing Kurt, "you need a bath." Kurt was trying to achieve an even surface by smearing his sun oil over the spots that had been licked clean in the attack.

"Ach, I am being the Pied Piper for dogs," he muttered, laughing in spite of himself. George felt quite warmed by this sudden humanity.

"Once you get accustomed to them, they're fine chaps," he said graciously. "But perhaps in your country you don't go in for them. Spend a little time with dogs, you get crazy about them."

"Thank you," said Kurt, "I have. I have even what you call served time. My grandfather had the largest kennels in Rumania."

"Oh," said George.

"Let's go." Nick was halfway down the terrace steps.

"Shall we walk or shall we take the car?" asked Kurt. The beach was about a quarter of a mile from the house, and he was not a man to waste his own energy when he could be propelled by gasoline.

Devon called after him, "For heaven's sake, walk. The novelty will do you good. It wouldn't hurt you to lose five pounds around the middle, either." This last she muttered to herself, but Estelle heard her and laughed.

Nicky turned back towards his little niece. "Come on, Miss Hopalong Hoptoad, how about a swim for you?" The child bounded after him. He boosted her up pickaback, and they disappeared around the corner of the terrace, the five dogs in exuberant attendance.

Devon, at last able to snare a paper, picked up the *Times* and turned to the Devonshire House advertisement. It was eye-catching and debonair and in Moreley's most lyric vein extolled the virtues of their two newest and greatest lines, Overture and Morning Song. Morning Song was a pat reference to her own emotions that very day. A contented little smile lighted her face as she remembered Kurt's early greeting and the enchanted hour in the night when with violence and subtlety he gave her rapture. In more objective moods she was, she supposed, lucky to have Kurt even part time. She wished her temperament would let her leave him at that. He was a man of many good qualities and a loyal friend where he did not love, but the woman who gave him her heart was in for a bad time.

Estelle came and sat down beside her and read the ad over her shoulder. "I'm glad you've got Chambray drawing for you," she said. "He's a good man."

Devon pulled her ear lobe, a trick she had acquired from Tim. "Yes, he is, but I'm going to bring out a new line in the fall, and I want to advertise it differently." Estelle, like the rest of Devon's friends, had been amused by the names of the recent products, and the source of inspiration was no secret, but she was worried by Devon's infatuation for Kurt. Unlike George, she didn't feel actively antagonistic to him, but she was devoted to Tim and didn't care for the turn things were taking.

"What are you going to call the new preparations?" she asked casually.

"I don't know yet," said Devon, "but for the magazine advertising I want to use photographs. Of course they're no good for newspapers—stock is too cheap—but I think we'll buy twelve pages in the glossy-paper magazines and run a knockout campaign."

"Have you got a good photographer?"

Kurt was professionally ambitious, and Devon's plan was to give him his first opportunity in the new campaign, but she wasn't yet ready to tell anybody about it. Even Jasper and Moreley didn't know. In answer to Estelle's question she said merely that she was watching the work of a new man who she considered had originality.

Ideas for naming the line seesawed in her mind. When Kurt was sweet and she was happy, exhilarating thoughts of Splendor, Crescendo, Rapturous Hour, exalted her imagination. When his implacable ego reduced her to misery, she was likely to think in terms of Winter Heart and Stink Pot.

The two women's conversation continued intermittently. George made an abortive attempt to persuade them to a game of badminton but finally departed to join the bathers.

When she and Estelle were alone on the terrace, Devon broached the subject of Cynthia. "Look, Estelle," she said, "I've been thinking. Cynthia's a sweet kid, but it can't be cheap to bring up a youngster, and you must have your hands full. Why don't you let me help out with her education and clothes and so on?"

Estelle hesitated before answering. Devon was a wealthy woman, and her proposal was tempting. Having to support three people in New York City and dress well herself on the salary she received from *Vogue* was not easy. But even under stress her loyalty to George never wavered. She naturally wished he had a job, but he was affectionate, sweet with Cynthia, and such an accomplished putterer that he was rarely moody or at a loose end. Away from the city George would be self-sufficient; his affinity lay with the earth and animals; and he was in the best sense a handy man. He understood a woodpile, and he was tolerant with ice cubes. Life in the country, so he and Estelle in their unblooded state fondly hoped, would be cheaper than town. She could swing the household with comparative ease and would take pride in doing it, but there was another reason why she hesitated. Many of those who knew her said that Devon was close-fisted, but personally Estelle found that rather like the legend of the Scotch. They were the butt of all the jokes about penny-pinching, and the most quixotic people on earth. So it was with Devon. She knew to the last mill what her income was and her every expenditure, but when she was moved to a charitable act, she did it in the grand manner, though George once remarked that her generosity sprang not so much from a kind heart as from her need to see things shipshape. This in itself was not reprehensible; the trouble was that they had to be the shape of Devon's ship, and this intensely personalized imprint Estelle found disturbing. Once she started to subsidize Cynthia, her preoccupation with the child would be such that she would unconsciously wean her away from her parents. Not deliberately, for Devon was no lady in the sense that her misdemeanors were unintentional, but she got swept up by her enthusiasms. Estelle's was an independent spirit, and though devoted to Devon, she did not relish herself in the role of poor relation to her own child.

At last she said simply, "Thank you, my dear. You're kind, but I can't accept the offer. I realize it would mean a great deal to Cynthia, but she might as well learn that until she's accomplished something herself there's nothing special about her, no reason for her

having things that don't come to her legitimately through George
and me."

Devon felt deflated but actually not surprised by this response.
She knew Estelle had spunk.

Estelle finally weakened to the extent of saying that if Devon
wanted to give Cynthia a new frock occasionally, or perhaps a bicy-
cle, she would be a great darling and they would all be grateful,
but that was as far as it must go.

Fairweather appeared to ask whether Devon knew how many
there would be for Sunday-night supper. "I'm not sure, Fairweather," she said. "We're eight in the house, and Mr. Doolittle's
dropping by this afternoon, he'll probably bring somebody, and he
may be staying, and Mr. Briskin's coming down . . . you'd better
prepare for about fourteen or so, as it's buffet, it doesn't matter."
Max Briskin was the composer for the revue Nicky was going to do
in the fall.

"Very good, madam."

"Has Anna got everything she needs, because Owens can probably find some place open in the village?"

"I imagine so, but I'll ask her."

"Oh, and Fairweather, we'll have tea about five."

"Yes, madam."

The rest of the morning and the early afternoon slipped by peace-
fully enough, but at five, when Fairweather appeared in majesty
bearing the great silver tea service, the place was a beehive of
activity. Max Briskin had arrived from town. He was a moon-faced
pudgy-fingered Jew, surprisingly young-looking when one considered that for the past twelve years his compositions had studded
every Hit Parade that strode across the nation. He had magnificent
teeth, curly brown hair, and he wore thick rimless spectacles. His
manner was breezy but beguiling, and when he sat caressing the
piano keys, his rotund figure stuffed into a plaid sports coat rhythmically rocking like a scow in a gentle swell, both he and his music
were irresistible. Beside him sat a thin dark nervous little man with
a self-effacing manner and a slight tic. He was Eddie Miller, the
most expert lyric writer in the business. He and Briskin had been
associated through their careers, and Max at the piano would play

a refrain and chorus and then he would say, "Sing, Eddie," and Eddie would give forth that thin little piping sound which song writers call their voices. The compositions had that haunting nostalgic quality germane to American popular music.

"*Sunshine for the weather man, but storm clouds in my heart,*"

piped Eddie. Nicky leaned over the piano and sang along with him, giving him substance.

"*My heart is sluiced with silver rain,*
 I feel the ancient pain
 Of those who love yet know that love will soon depart."

Devon glanced around for Kurt. He was standing talking to a strikingly pretty girl perched on the arm of a chair. Jasper had brought her over from the house where he was spending the week end without Mollie. She had long, silky blond hair, a slim figure, ripe red lips, and a dead face. You could tell at once she was a glamor girl. Her name was Babette Danforth, and she was from the profound South. She was talking about the effect hats had on her and her head. "Sugar, I never wear a hat, but never. I'm positively terrified of them."

Devon, strolling near, stood laughing down at her. "Oh come, we're living in troubled times. You must screw your courage to the sticking point." She was vague as to who said that first, but having heard Tim use the expression, she assumed it was probably his own, and it made her feel snugly entrenched to be able to flaunt a clever saying of her husband's in front of Kurt and this little ninny.

Kurt glanced at her quickly, and a look of suspicion crossed the glamor girl's face. She didn't know what Miss Elliott was talking about, but she recognized that Older Woman tone. The twin blue beacons of her eyes flashed back to Mr. Fabri. Foreigners were always so appreciative of American girls. Not, of course, that Mr. Doolittle wasn't as cute as an old geezer like him could be, and they did say so rich, but that Mr. Fabri was a mighty strong-lookin' man. From the way Miss Elliott had spoken to her, Babette guessed he must be her sweetie. Well, if you had to be in your thirties and up to your knees in the grave, Babette admitted Miss

Elliott did look kind of good, but my Lord, who wouldn't, smear
ing themselves with all that cream and stuff. She was probably mac
because Mr. Fabri certainly appeared far from bored; ladies' mil
linery was probably mighty interesting to him. "You know wha
happens to me when I get a hat on my head? I put a little old thing
on, an' I think, God A'mighty, what's gonna be? I'm just terrified
so I mostly never wear a hat," and she lifted the thick curtain of her
hair and let it slip over her wrist like a waterfall.

Devon, ashamed to let Kurt see she had so much as noticed that
he spoke to another woman, drifted over to the bridge table, where
Delphine Conway and Lieutenant Bramley sat playing Towie.
That is to say, they were waiting for the return of the third hand,
who had been called to the telephone.

Delphine was a woman in her early fifties. Socially secure, she
was the independently wealthy widow of a defunct financier. The
banker's relic, Tim called her with his usual irreverence for the
stodgy rich, and although she laughed at her too, Devon felt rather
sorry for her. Delphine was a fool, but she was not basically snob-
bish, and she was a kindhearted little soul. People were put off by
her petulance. She had lived a spoiled and idle life, and she had
a spoiled face. A tiny rosebud mouth pinched between pudgy
cheeks, a chin and neck flowing contiguously, and round babyish
eyes. She had almost no brows, and though Devon had read the
riot act to her, Delphine insisted on penciling in two startling arcs
of chocolate brown. Her hands were remarkable, little white par-
tridges loaded with rings. She had sloping Victorian shoulders, and
in spite of her wealth still wore almost exclusively the clothes she
had gotten in Paris in the summer of '39, because she said she
would just as leave go naked as wear what the New York shops
had to offer.

Her companion, Lieutenant Nigel Bramley, was what the French
were wont to refer to in the seventies as a young English milord.
The Earl of Dunkeld, Lord Bramley, had left his ancestral estates
for the British destroyer which had recently borne him to American
shores on a naval lend-lease commission. The lieutenant was tall
and good-looking, with a charming voice and English dentures. He
had an eye on the glamor girl, but this old tub at the table was after

all his hostess and remarkably kind. Besides, though he considered Mrs. Conway's other house guest, Nat Elkins, a fossil, he was a power in the American isolationist press and the kind of man the English were trying desperately to convert to an interventionist point of view.

In a few minutes Elkins returned. He was a heavy-set rugged-looking individual with a distinguished façade and no mind. He had been a beau of Delphine's for years, and though she remained skittish about conferring her hand and fortune upon him, he continued faithful in his suit. Devon had finally concluded that he had a genuine affection for the old girl, though her querulousness must often have irritated him. She pounced on him now as he returned to the bridge table. "Who was that called you on the phone, Nat?"

"Someone I had to talk to."

"Well, who?"

"No one you know, Delphine."

Kurt and Babette had gravitated near the table. She overheard Nat's rejoinder and giggled. "I know how you feel, Mr. Elkins. Aren't women just awful the way they try to pin a man down?" Mr. Elkins muttered and dealt a hand. Babette addressed the table at large. "Course they try to spy on each *other* too." Delphine considered the choice of the word spy unfortunate, and glanced coldly at Babette, her old baby's face puckered with dislike. The southern belle remained blandly unaware of her antagonism. "Why, down home it drives my mother crazy when I won't tell her who I've been talking to on the phone. She nags and nags, but I never say. I just can't bear having to account for every little move."

"How well you put it, Miss Danforth, and how I am agreeing with you." Kurt looked at Devon as he spoke, his eyes glinting with malice. The gaze she turned on him was level. In view of her emotions when he was indulging in Personal Freedom, she considered that her self-control was admirable.

Kurt watched with amusement the rapprochement between young Lieutenant Bramley and Miss Danforth, a charming girl, he thought, though it was impossible to understand what she said. Certainly Babette was doing what she could to promote Anglo-American amity; it would be a crime to let the lieutenant go to waste. He was keen-looking in his uniform, and with that cute accent and all. Besides, Mrs. Lowery had said he had a title. In vision Miss Danforth was already moving across the emerald turf of England with the butler murmuring "Tea is served, my lady," while dukes in white flannels festooned the lawn and Oxford and Cambridge bowed over her hand.

The Earl of Dunkeld, while it did not occur to him to install this pretty creature as the hostess of Portage, the family seat, was not blind to her gentle curves and admiring glances. She was a bit of all right, and no mistake. American women were really splendid, and he thought with a pleasurable glow of Nancy, the American woman aged twenty whom he was driving back to New York to spend the evening with. He had, as a matter of fact, several items on his mind: Nancy, Babette, and this discussion that had arisen with old Elkins. The Towie game had lapsed, and Elkins was holding forth on the Orient. It was, he maintained, impossible for Japan to attack America, and he was quoting figures and naval tonnage to prove it. Bramley listened respectfully, but as an officer of the largest navy in the world, which was still finding the sailing rough, he was inclined to skepticism. "You may be right, sir, but Hawaii is a long way from the mainland. Either you have to risk it or maintain a tremendous force for its defense. The Japs might well decide to close in on you there."

Elkins scoffed. "Not the remotest likelihood, my boy, not the remotest. Pearl Harbor is impregnable. They're not madmen. I tell you America's greatest contribution to this war is to stay out of it."

"How do you figure that?" George Lowery was straddling a chair, leaning over the back and puffing peaceably on his pipe. His tone was mild, but his glance was skeptical.

Elkins explained: "We can do far more with lend-lease, keeping the sea lanes to Britain open and the supplies flowing. Once in it, we'd be using the material for ourselves. Our game is to play for time until we're really prepared."

The piano came up forte.

> ". . . *storm clouds in my heart,*"

sang Nicky on the other side of the room.

"Here I do not agree," said Kurt firmly. "Any country prepares best under pressure when need is urgent, not when she is thinking there is no hurry."

"But you're asking us to do overnight what Germany with her great organization took seven years to do."

"No, no," said Kurt with conviction. "This is mythical. In America I am seeing much better organization than ever existed in Germany. It is their clever propaganda. The whole world thinks of them as invincible, and so they are wanting it, but I tell you over here all things are better and larger. Commerce, industry, railroads. America must realize this."

This was a side of Kurt that Devon liked. He did not indulge in that *Schwärmerei* for the Old World common to many refugees He had a realistic appreciation of the situation and no hesitation in acknowledging America's material superiority. It was actually one of the things that most appealed to him in his newly adopted country.

George scratched his head with the stem of his pipe. Men of Elkins' opinion frankly puzzled him. "But you see on any score we should be in the war," he protested. "There's nothing idealistic about it. For the democracies it's the old story of hanging together unless they want to hang separately."

"That's the way Tim sees it, George," Devon said eagerly. Whatever her feelings about their personal relationship, she was tremendously proud of Tim. He was one of the few men she knew who had unwavering convictions and acted upon them. Kurt felt an unexpected twinge in the general region of his heart and was suddenly angry. Why couldn't she leave her husband out of this? It was bad taste, to say the least.

Talk ranged back and forth about the war and the democratic way of life, Lord Bramley even tactlessly broaching the Negro problem in America, a topic evoked for him by Max Briskin's music. Max and Eddie had switched from torch ballads into a jive version of Harlem. One of the revue numbers was to be laid in a Harlem street, with Nicky in blackface playing a dapper blade. There was to be a rather daring political tinge in the script and lyrics, and the authors were feeling the virtuous satisfaction of the socially conscious, pleasantly spiced with anticipated royalties.

To the somewhat startled surprise of the visiting Englishman, when he hit the Mason-Dixon line the fair Babette tore into the home stretch, in pungent terms enlightening him on the capabilities, treatment, and social status of the nigger. "Daddy knows about such things, Lieutenant," she said firmly, noting a slight air of incredulity in Britain's flower, "and Daddy says our system's best."

Across the room Max was tickling the keys with infinite skill.

> *"I'm glad I ain't in Dixie,*
> *That sad, mad pixie land,"*

crooned Nicky.

To the concealed discomfiture of Miss Danforth, Lieutenant Bramley left shortly after her attempted but subtle engineering of a future date. He had to make town by seven o'clock, but he did ask if she was living in New York and if he might telephone her if he got back from Washington before returning to England. Though foiled, Miss Danforth smiled with dazzling warmth. "Why, of course you may, Lieutenant," she said cordially, again lifting her long hair and letting it slip like liquid gold over her wrist. "I certainly hope you do get back. That old Hitler's responsible for an awful lot of broken hearts." As he drowned in her blue eyes, Lord Bramley could not but feel that George III had been a distinct drip to let the colonies get away from him.

Jasper, overhearing Babette's blarney, remarked dryly that the local talent would do its utmost to patch up her wounds. His interest in this honey-chile, while not burning, might be said to be smoldering. After all, he had brought her here and was entitled to an occasional crumb.

Though they sat at the same small table at dinner, Kurt, Devon was gratified to see, treated Babette with no more than common courtesy. He was, she supposed, adhering to his code of not embarking on any new trails while in her company. He would not, in her house, ask this pretty girl for her telephone number, but he did lead the conversation in such a way that Babette knew quite well the location of his workroom and the hours when he was to be found there. *I suppose,* Devon thought with a malicious chuckle, *he hopes she'll call him up and ask him to a cocktail party. In that way he can eat his cake with a clear conscience.* The temptation to let him know when she saw through him was great, but she had learned early in her career that to do that with a man was to experience short-lived satisfaction and long-winded regret.

The party broke up early. Max and Eddie drove back to town, Mr. Elkins and Delphine returned to her house, and Jasper went home to his week-end hostess accompanied by Dixie's pride, who, since the youthful aristocrat had evaded her, suddenly remembered Mr. Doolittle's lovely money and treated him with the greatest sweetness. But Jasper's hazy dreams of future joys were bright bubbles destined to melt with the week end, Miss Danforth being a young lady urgently aware of the secular advantages of an ascetic gold band upon the third finger of the left hand.

The Lowerys, with Cynthia and Nick, were planning to make an early start for town the following morning, as Estelle wanted to get to the office not later than nine-thirty. Nick, in a spirit of co-operation, had offered himself to Devon and Kurt so as not to crowd the other car, but the suggestion had evoked a noticeable lack of enthusiasm.

Earlier in the evening, when they had found themselves alone together for a few minutes, Nick asked Devon casually if she would like to dine with him and maybe go to a movie Monday night, and she had said brightly, "Darling, I'd love to, but I have an awful feeling there's something on my calendar. Can I call you after I get to the office?" and Nick said gently, "Of course, duck," but there was a little ache in his heart for Devon, and he suspected that the only thing on her calendar was the hope that Kurt would be with her.

That night, when she went to bed, she read for a few minutes and then turned out the light and lay waiting in the dark for Kurt to come to her. She had left her door ajar so it wouldn't creak, but she hoped he realized it was a matter of indifference whether he came or not and that she could quite easily go to sleep without a good-night kiss and not feel a martyr about it. After all, they were an adult pair, and it was certainly not the first affair for either of them, and that was the fact. It was also the fact that she lay straining her ears, hoping for his footsteps. For a while she was very firm. *Good Lord, you've got a little pride, I hope,* and the self who hoped so spoke with laughing derision. *It's a funny thing,* said the other self, a party who could be just as clearheaded and sensible as the smug mentor, *a good-night kiss is an issue to me, whereas he, poor devil, doesn't even give it a thought. It has nothing to do with whether he loves me or not, I'm sure. It's temperamental. . . . Anyhow, why must it always be a question of pride? You love him, it's as simple as that, besides, maybe he tried to come and heard someone prowling around in the corridor, maybe he was reading and fell asleep, why this song and dance about it?*

The result of this straight-from-the-shoulder thinking was that Miss Elliott rose up from her lovely bed, a large gay affair airily canopied in ruffled and embroidered lawn caught back with candy-striped ribands, slipped into a diaphanous negligee, and went in search of her love, only to meet him head on in the darkened hallway. They collided with force and broke into suppressed hysterical laughter. He held her close, and she felt the warmth of his body through his thin silk robe and pajamas. He drew her into a recessed window through which the moonlight streamed, and they stood close together, looking out on the serene and balmy night. She fingered his pajama collar. "Darling, how wonderful. You do own a pair."

"Not really," whispered Kurt. "I rent them for swank over the week ends. Baby, I tried to come sooner, but it was George and Nicky, they were going downstairs again—Estelle, it seems, wanted a glass of milk."

"Poor darling," murmured Devon, "trapped like a rat." And she buried her face in his neck. Kurt lifted her head and rained a dozen little light kisses on her cheeks and eyelids. "Good night, my baby, sleep well." He released her. She turned and started cautiously towards her room, her hands extended before her in the darkness. She heard a hoarse whisper from Kurt and turned back.

"What did you say, dear?" Her own voice was a strong hiss.

"I said be careful not to fall."

"Oh, thanks for the advice. I'll watch out." Once safely back in bed, she gave a sigh of relief and then chuckled inwardly. "Of course he might have given himself the pain to tuck me in and render a few other courteous services, but I suppose nobody gets everything in this world," and she fell asleep and dreamed that she and Kurt were having an argument and that she was being frightfully witty, and she woke up laughing at her dream jokes at three o'clock in the morning.

Monday broke clear and hot, and the two cars, the Lincoln Continental, with Owens at the wheel, and Kurt's Plymouth convertible, with himself and Devon, swept out of the driveway within ten minutes of each other. All the way into town he was the most charming of companions. Even Queens Boulevard, a grim stretch calculated to dampen the brightest spirit, failed to blight him. He was affectionate, he had a trick while driving of cupping her chin in his right hand and drawing her near to him that he might kiss her cheek, he commented on the news in the morning papers with what Devon supposed was as much insight as anybody else was likely to show, and he talked to her with obvious respect for her opinion about a deal he was negotiating whereby he would design luggage and accessories for Mark Cross on a royalty basis. They also discussed his new apartment. Kurt, spurred by Devon, had decided he wanted to move, and she had offered to go through the winnowing-out process for him. She would begin the hunt this week. They spoke also of ideas for the photograph to be used in the advertisements for the new Devonshire House preparations. "The way I see it, Kurt, it ought to be something frightfully sexy but tasteful as all hell."

Kurt laughed. "It is the challenge, such an assignment. The two are not anonymous."

"Synonymous, darling."

"I did not say that?"

"Not quite."

"It is easier for me to imagine a composition for the photograph if you are deciding on a name for the perfume."

"I realize that." They drove in silence for a few minutes. Devon had had long discussions with David Ullman, the head of the laboratory since Tim's departure, about the quality of the scent she wanted the new preparations to have. "It must be a rather heavy scent, Ullman, warm and rich and languorous. Something with the spiciness of our old carnation odor, but nothing a person can put his finger on. But it has to be exciting too, so that you want more and more of it, only God help you if any sickening sweetness creeps in." To fulfill this tall and intangible order Ullman went to work with oils and musk and ambergris and after several false starts had finally told Devon last week that he believed today he would have the fragrance she was looking for.

"You see, Kurt, I'm hoping we've got a marvelous lush smell. I want something that'll make you think of the full flower and richness of love at the great moment. Culmination is really the word, but the customers won't know what it means."

Kurt chuckled. "If it is having the effect you hope for, they won't let you send it through the mails."

"There are two names I like, but I can't make up my mind."

"What are they?"

"Splendor and Crescendo."

"But they are not quite the same thing, no?"

"No, but they are both——" and Devon threw her arms wide, hitting Kurt in the nose and causing him to swerve madly, narrowly missing another car.

"Oh, darling," she was at once apologetic, "I'm so sorry, but you get the idea, don't you?"

"Clearly," said Kurt dryly.

"And I feel that's what the photograph should have, a radiance with somewhere a dark core."

"It must catch the eye, yes."

"It should catch the breath too."

"Yah," said Kurt, and his face lighted with interest.

All in all, an interesting, friendly, and pleasant trip, but as they neared the city and the wall of heat pushed towards them implacably, Devon's spirits wilted along with her fresh print frock. Kurt made no reference to the evening. It would be pleasant sitting on the terrace behind the house, watching the river slip by and sipping Fairweather's rum swizzles from tall frosted glasses. Tim and she . . . never mind about Tim; that was over and the way he wanted it. Kurt seldom touched alcohol, but the smoothness of the rum drink pleased him, and one night he had gone hog-wild and taken three. Like many Europeans he was firmly convinced that liquor did not affect him. Indeed, though he had never tested himself to the full, it is probable that he had a high boiling point, but for all that it turned out that Continental brains were made from the same tissue as American ones, and the fumes of alcohol penetrated them too. Devon liked Kurt when he was the least bit high. It melted the icy inhumanity he was capable of.

When the car stopped for the red lights the heat settled over them like a pall. Devon, who had not intended going back to the country till the end of the week, began to reconsider. If only Kurt would come along, it would be fun. They could leave around four-thirty and have a fine swim before dinner. "I think I may drive back tonight," she said.

"Why don't you?" said Kurt courteously. What a fool she was! She had known before the week end started that he was doing something else, as surely as if he had shouted it in her ear.

"I suppose you're tied up?" She had fought hard not to say it, but in her defeat she managed at least to salvage a tone of the utmost casualness.

"Yes," said Kurt, and he said nothing else.

"Well, I may take some people out with me, or if I get tied up at the salon I may not bother. After all, the house is air conditioned and perfectly comfortable." She hoped subtly to impress upon him that there were not many air-conditioned private houses in New York, and she doubted that the woman he was going to would be able to offer such comforts, but apparently he was as impervious to coolth as to love.

They came across the upper driveway of Queensboro Bridge in record time. There were hundreds of cars, but they poured swiftly and without interruption until they clogged in Fifty-seventh Street. There was small pleasure in sitting steaming, bumper to bumper, at the bottom of a stone canyon, but the curious alchemy of love transposed it into a sort of mangy garden spot, and Devon felt an oppression not caused by heat as she anticipated the moment when they would roll free and Kurt would deposit her at the door of the salon.

The thing that saddened her most was that with rare exceptions he felt absolutely no jealousy. The idea that when she was away from him she might meet another man whom she would come to care for either never occurred to him or, if it did, caused him no concern. "You must understand, darling," he had once said, "I have a philosophy about such things. If lovers fall in love with other people, there is nothing to be done about it, so why worry and be unhappy?" This was lofty, but, as far as she was concerned, where there was no jealousy there was no love.

They drew up at the brilliant green door of Devonshire House. Fred in his alpaca uniform—in her mind's eye Devon had envisaged something very smart, but one had to face facts, Fred was not the smart type—crossed the pavement to open the door of the car. Kurt took her hand and kissed it. "Good-by, my baby, thank you for a lovely week end. I'll call you."

"Good-by, Kurt, it was wonderful having you." She smiled charmingly, her eyes narrowing and gleaming behind her lashes. *That Spartan boy with the wolf at his vitals,* she thought. *I can quite see how he did it. People's insides may be experiencing the most grueling emotions and the face behaves with the greatest decorum. I'm sure I look quite normal.* She glanced at Fred for reassurance. Fred admired the boss, and it was written in his open honest countenance. He thought she looked swell under her wide white hat, in that coral-colored print.

When she entered the salon, the ground floor was empty except for the girl at the reception desk and a couple of operators idly gossiping. The bibelots and the artificial flowers bloomed unnoticed in their glass cases, and the closets holding the preparations were closed. A summer morning was a slack time, but the recently established refresher treatments had proved a great success, and the salon buzzed in the late afternoon with feminine shoppers boosting their morale before meeting their husbands at the five-fifteen, and with business girls in for a cleansing and a quick veneer before the evening safari.

In her office Hilda was waiting with the morning mail. Jasper was not in yet, and it occurred to Devon that men had very little stamina. "They're pawns of the weather, that's what," she observed to Hilda. The salon was pleasantly air conditioned, and it made her feel quite brisk. Hilda had opened most of the letters, but there was one from Tim still sealed and postmarked Baltimore. Devon's hand trembled just a little as she took it up. *What's the matter with me?* she thought in bewilderment. *I've been married to Tim for seven years, he leaves me, but I still love him. I meet another man and I'm mad about* him. *I've got a heart like a college prom. Each one I dance with seems the best of all.*

Tim's letter was short:

DARLING MADAM:

It was with mixed emotions that I received last month's statement, to which as a minority stockholder you seem generously to feel I am entitled. Trade, I observe, is brisk, and while as a capitalist I am pleased to see my interests in such competent hands, as a working man my ego is a bit deflated. Ullman is too damn good.

Why, Tim's crazy, thought Devon. *They're all his own formulas. Ullman has nothing to do with it.* She continued reading:

My own job, while highly satisfying to me, is undramatic in the telling, and would, I suppose, be a fearful grind if I weren't obsessed by its urgency. I'm negotiating now in the hope I'll be able to get into one of the services. I don't greatly care which, but I want to be in a position to carry on, and I feel I may be able to work to better advantage if I have some kind of Government alliance, which would be the case if I were with the Army or Navy. Of course it's no good to me unless I have complete freedom, and it may be that I'm trying to marry two antitheses, but in any event I'm getting all the dope I can.

Outside of this my news is slim. I'm living in small but inadequate quarters near Johns Hopkins, and I miss you and think of you. I also miss and think of Fairweather. Windermere polishes a mean boot and has a way with a pair of pants foreign to the local tailors. I pretend I am above such things, but I have a bulgy look about the knees which depresses me.

Take care of yourself, darling. I bought a bottle of Morning Song a while back. Quite invigorating. I gather you're highhearted and that life is hunky-dory. Please write to me. My love always.

Tim.

"I miss you and think of you," he had written. . . . *Dear Darling,* she thought. ". . . Life is hunky-dory." *Well, my lad, not necessarily. In fiction the love affair is idyllic, with a gleaming hero, tender and brave, the boy with the plumes, but in la vie it doesn't work out that way. I also note that "quite invigorating," Mr. Wainwright. This is, I suppose, the dig, but what can I expect? For that matter, love, what can you expect?*

Her thoughts ran on as she turned to her secretary. "Hilda, call the country. Fairweather's coming in in the station wagon, but I want to get him before he leaves." When the butler was on the phone, Devon went straight to the point: "Fairweather, you're going on a trip."

"We're just leaving now, madam. Anna's all ready."

"You're going farther than that, Fairweather. Mr. Wainwright's badly in need of you. I want you to go to Baltimore and look after him for a few days; get his clothes in order and organize his living a little. It sounds to me as though he were cooking on a gas ring."

Fairweather's soul revolted. "Oh, madam, surely not?"

"I wouldn't be surprised." In fancy Devon saw Tim bent over a sputtering gas jet, his emaciated form hung in rags, rather like the Moscow Art Players in *The Lower Depths*. "And take lots of shoe polish with you, Fairweather, and a flatiron and things. It's enemy territory."

"Er . . . yes, Mrs. Wainwright." Fairweather supposed his fears were groundless, yet could one be quite sure about the Indian situation? He had been in America eight years, but his beat had been confined to New York and Long Island and a three-weeks' holiday in the Berkshires. Ah well, a new experience might be exhilarating. "When do you want me to leave, madam?"

"I think you might as well get off this afternoon. I'm not planning to do any entertaining this week, so I won't need you. Call me when you get into town, and in the meantime I'll have Miss Boylston look up trains and get your tickets."

"Does Mr. Wainwright know I'm coming?"

"No, but I'll send a telegram when you leave. Then it'll be too late for him to raise any objections."

"Very good, madam."

Devon hung up and turned to Hilda. "Get him a ticket, Hilda, and take this telegram to Mr. Wainwright but don't send it till afternoon: 'Fairweather en route with serum. Neither of us can bear thought of you in baggy pants. Please keep him as long as you want him darling maybe he can induct local tailors into mysteries of Savile Row. Here we are very hot, hope you are getting better break. Love Devon.'"

She attended to her correspondence, but Tim's letter she saved to answer till she got home. She was in no mood to dictate her thoughts to Hilda.

There was a good deal of routine work connected with the whole-sale business to get through, and Moreley had sent over some advertising copy for her O.K., but at last her desk was clear and she settled down to a list of apartments submitted by a real-estate agent. After studying plans and descriptions she concluded that there were nine possibilities and that she might as well look at them today.

She told Hilda to postpone any appointments, and after having called Nick to say she had been mistaken about her engagement and was free and would be delighted to dine with him, she left the salon and started systematically through the list. The heat was overwhelming, and her temper grew short, but it never occurred to her to postpone the job till another day. Her energy was high, and besides she had the snooper's instinct. She secretly liked peering around other people's houses, though the preponderance of red silk lampshades dismayed her, and she was pained by the state of their closets. Her own closets were tremendous and miracles of order, with dresses and lingerie glass-encased like mushrooms *sous cloche,* and her shoes marching in precise rows along their slanting shelves.

She had looked at eleven places; the original nine had expanded, each proving unsuitable, and had about decided that although slaving for him might be one way to bind a man to you, the question was, was he worth it?—when she came upon the perfect quarters. The rooms were occupied, and though neither the furniture nor the tenant appealed to her, the proportions and the location did. There was also an English valet in the house, and Devon fancied the idea of Kurt in digs; a general atmosphere of Mayfair in the spring seemed to pervade the premises. When she found that the current occupant had a lease running till October and no intention of moving, she was temporarily nonplussed, torn between wishing to get her own way by paying him off, and experiencing reluctance, scissor-sharp, at the idea of parting with any money. In the end her desire outstripped her economic scruples, though not to the extent of rashness. By dint of concealing her identity and inventing an invalid brother who was coming down from Boston to undergo special treatments in New York—a grave hernia condition, poor chap—and had to have the apartment, she got the gullible male tenant, who had never experienced anything quite like her eyelashes and that haunting fragrance—Felicity—to agree to move, she to pay the moving men and the rent of his new apartment for two months after October first, provided it was less than what he was currently disbursing. The tenant sensed that he was a soul entangled and tried manfully to battle his way out, but Devon explained to him that by signing a year's lease in his new place, which would cost him less than he was now paying, they would let him live there rent-free till October first, and that with her assuming responsibility for the next two months, he would be on the cuff for four months, a saving he could never hope to effect by staying where he was. That he liked where he was, could afford it, and had no wish to change, she was able to conceal from him until he had signed the agreement. By the time he came to and realized that as of Wednesday morning he was a homeless waif, with no place to lay his head, the eloquent and smiling vision had vanished, leaving only a ghostly fragrance like the reverberation of a sound.

When she got home she called Kurt to tell him of her triumph. He was gratifyingly grateful for her efforts, and she was so flushed with success that she hung up before she realized she still had no idea where he was going to be that night.

Tit for tat was not Kurt's strong suit. Because she had done something to please him, it did not follow that he should do something to please her. However, he was without malice, and it worked the

other way too. When she tried to hurt him he bore no g
Who resents what he does not feel? Yet in a way Kurt found
self becoming more and more attached to her. Not to the exte
of physical fidelity; that he could never give to any woman, nor
could he understand wherein lay its desirability. On the contrary,
to concentrate on one woman to the exclusion of all others seemed
to him insensitive. Because one loved the lilac, must he ignore the
rose? But while Kurt was emotionally cold and self-sufficient, he
found considerable satisfaction in being with her. As long as these
insufferable outbursts of temperament over his personal freedom
didn't become frequent enough to be really irritating, she was an
agreeable companion, entertaining and easy to get along with. He
considered that she derived a certain satisfaction in playing the
role of martyr, but on the other hand she had no annoying mannerisms, and though successful her intelligence was not aggressive.
Marriage was a bad business, in no way compensating for the independence a man lost, but supposing it was not always necessary to
lose it? Devon knew him after all. She certainly must know that
being muttered over by a third person who joined them in matrimony didn't change two people's characters. If she would agree
to complete independence for them both, marriage might not be a
bad idea. She was deeply in love with him and probably not too
averse to the thought of divorce. Kurt would never marry for money
alone, but if he were affectionately inclined toward a woman and
sexually attracted to her the fact that she had great wealth was no
deterrent. Somewhat to his own surprise he was doing well in
his business, but it was never the kind of thing which could
bring big money, and with America about to get into the war—
for, in spite of what these people thought, she would soon be
swept in—the luxury trade would be finished. There was also another consideration: though he had taken out first papers, he was
not yet a citizen and might not be called, but you never could tell.
He would certainly not try to evade the draft; at thirty-eight, he
might even be too old; but married men were deferable, at least
temporarily.

Kurt began to feel a warm glow around his heart, and a sudden
desire to hear Devon's voice swept over him. He had been thinking

along these lines for some time now, and the nostalgic music of the Mexican singer to whom he was listening touched his emotions. It was two o'clock in the morning and he was at the St. Regis roof with Madeline Valdane and the Bill Farnsworths, old friends of hers whom he knew casually. He had asked Madeline to dine and go to the theater, but when he called for her she was only half dressed. Kurt offered his help so effectively that they missed dinner and arrived at the play in the middle of the second act, and were now having supper at the St. Regis with the Farnsworths, whom they had met when they came in.

As the last notes of the love song died away, Kurt excused himself from the table and went to call Devon. He felt quite safe in doing so. The first few times when he phoned late at night she used to ask him where he was, but then he had punished her by not calling for nights on end, so now she spoke quite nicely and seemed pleased to hear from him and never embarrassed him by prying. . . .

She was sound asleep when the discreet buzz of the private number wakened her. She reached for the receiver in the dark. "Hello."

"Hello, darling, you are sounding like a little sleepy kitten. Did I wake you?"

"It doesn't matter, lamb. I love to talk to you."

"Darling, tell me about my apartment. Where will I get my furniture and things?"

Devon laughed. He was sweet and funny, being so eager. "Wherever you want to, dear, we'll go shopping."

"Ach, this is a great trouble. I am better off in the furnished apartment I have, no? I have not even bed sheets of my own."

"You haven't even a bed of your own, my lad."

"Miss Elliott, you should not be mocking a poor refugee. Maybe this apartment idea is a mistake. Suppose I want to move or go away, what do I do with my property?"

"If you're planning any long jaunts you can do what other people do, put it in storage, or you can sublet, but a little domesticity won't do you any harm."

"This is what I am thinking too." Should he . . . ? No. Better wait a little longer yet, better be awfully sure before he said anything about marriage.

"Hurray," said Devon. "For once we're in agreement."

"No, this is not so. We often are. You have changed me very much."

Through the telephone she heard faintly the strains of a dance orchestra, so she knew he was in a night club. That didn't seem like much of a change, and it was improbable that he was there alone, though there were one or two places he sometimes dropped into on his way home. He had a couple of refugee friends in the night-club trade. It always seemed odd to her that a man who neither drank nor danced should so enjoy night life, but she assumed it was his early coffeehouse training in Vienna.

"Darling, maybe I should have a decorator, if it is not costing too much."

"Decorators are always costing too much, dear," said his love crisply. "But I could probably make some kind of a deal with Dickie Masters if you want me to."

"You do not think this is very dangerous? He might debauch me."

"That's one vice you probably don't have. Whom would you prefer?"

"I would prefer to have you do it, but this is taking too much of your time. Maybe Claire Dangerfield would help."

Devon laughed softly. "I'd thought we'd get around to Claire."

"Ach, you are a maicutule, a little stupid thing. I'm not thinking of her as a woman."

"That'll be an interesting challenge to her. I'll tell her." There was a pause, the loaded silence of the telephone.

"Are you there?" asked Kurt.

"Yes, darling, right here."

"You are funny. Why don't you say something?"

"I'm just sleepy, that's all."

Another pause. Kurt often made these pauses; they were because he was not at ease on the phone, but Devon was convinced they were because he wanted to make her ask when she was going to see him again. But she was just as stubborn as he. *You can rot, my fine friend, before I'll do that,* she thought. He had an alternate trick of saying, "When am I going to see you?" but if she said, "What about Wednesday night?" as often as not it would turn out he had an engagement, so she had learned to say blandly, "Whenever you want to, darling." If there was to be any bag-holding, it was man's work and let him do it. The pause became a little oppressive; finally Kurt spoke, "Am I seeing you tomorrow night?"

"If you want to and are free."

"I am quite free. I will call you in the morning and we can decide what we'll do. Can we look at the apartment maybe?"

"I think it would be easier if you could manage to take a little time off in the morning or the afternoon. The man's out all day."

"All right. I am having to see the Mark Cross people first thing in the morning, and later on I must show to Cartier's a design for another cigarette case they want from me. I will call you as soon as I am through."

"Do that, my darling. Good night. I love you."

"The same feeling is prevailing here. Good night, baby."

He hung up. Devon lay in the dark, the quiet tears slipping over her cheeks. Oh God, the weary game! Why couldn't two people love each other exclusively, and at the same time, and if it had to end, why couldn't it end for both at once? *I must be getting old,* she thought, *or perhaps Tim has spoiled me. This banter and technique is taking too much out of me, and dear Lord, the waste of time! I love Kurt to phone me at night, but if he does I can't go back to sleep, and I'm in fine shape to go to the office in the morning. Why have I no pride? Why do I put up with this cheap, humiliating now-and-then kind of love? The all-or-nothing people, those are the ones. They have integrity and common sense. But what are you going to do if the all-or-nothing doesn't come your way? Miss out on a lot of happiness through fear or pride? And besides, even the all-or-nothing is not to be counted on. That doesn't last, either: look at Tim.* Still, she thought, probably she was lucky. Think of all the lonely women in the world with no men at all— either because they weren't attractive, or because they lacked that damned technique, not to mention opportunity, or because their men had been killed in the war. She did have a husband, an absentee lord, to be sure, still she had him and she might get him back, and she had a lover whose iniquities served to occupy her thoughts completely what time he wasn't there in person. She reached under her pillow for her handkerchief and blew her nose. *It's a mug's game,* she thought, *and if I'm lucky, God's idea of luck and mine do not jibe.*

Kurt, once he was installed in his apartment, was delighted with it. Devon, mindful of the two autumn months when she was personally going to have to pay for the erstwhile occupant's new quarters (it had seemed wiser not to mention that little sleight-of-hand to Kurt), had decided he would have to fend for himself in his furnishings, but pressure of business and her sense of decoration got the better of her. Kurt could afford so little that it was more satisfying to her to select good stuff for him, lie about the cost, and pay the difference than to take the time to search out bargains. She lied because she wanted to save his pride, but even so she had to use discretion. Kurt had known beautiful furniture all through his childhood and youth, and it would never do to bring in a Chinese Chippendale break front and say she'd bought it at the Flea Market for twenty-two-fifty. For that reason she was glad that his taste ran towards modern design; she could more easily toss a handful of dust in his eyes.

She had turned over the fundamentals to Claire, and they spent considerable time in vociferous argument which they heartily enjoyed.

Kurt, more out of habit than desire, had tried Claire with his conventional opening gambits, but somewhat to her own surprise she turned him down cold and promptly developed for him an active dislike which was aggravated by the trouble he caused her. She considered that Devon catered to his whims to an unreasonable degree, making her change a color scheme or a piece of furniture just because Kurt didn't like it. "Listen," she would shout angrily, shoving and hauling the furniture into place in his apartment, "the guy's lucky he's not in a concentration camp. How dare he beef about the size of the writing desk, and what does he mean that that leopard cloth for the couch isn't manly? It's *rugged,* for Christ's sake."

"Well, I can't help it. He—— Ouch, damn!" Devon was driving a nail in the wall as she spoke and caught herself squarely on the thumb. "He says it reminds him of Theda Bara and he feels embarrassed."

"There are plenty of other things in his life that ought to embarrass him more than that," muttered Claire darkly. "This little jaunt down lover's lane is costing you plenty."

"Claire, if you ever tell him what these things are really worth, I'll kill you."

"Don't worry, but when I think of all those lucky dames who are kept by men——"

"Not so much any more, I don't think. Times are changing."

"And, baby, we're born in the wrong times. At no dinner party I ever went to did I find a hundred bucks and a diamond bracelet on my plate." As she spoke Claire drew a big square of material from a manila envelope. "Do you think His Lordship will actually settle for this natural-colored raw silk, or will that affect his psyche too?"

"He claims not. He says it's the very thing to go with those two leather chairs he's having made in his workroom."

The two chairs were the inadvertent cause of piling another small straw on the camel's back. The day they were delivered Kurt and Devon had a dinner engagement, and it was arranged that she would pick him up at his apartment so she could see them. Just as she was about to leave the house he called her. "My baby, will you do me a great favor?"

"Of course, darling. What is it?"

"Would you very much mind to stop by the workroom on your way here and pick up my mail? I have been in the factory all day and didn't want to go there out of my way. I would have been so late for you. I am hot and dirty and must take my bath."

"All right, darling. Scrub good. I'll be over in a little while."

It was after seven when Devon got to Kurt's workroom, but the faithful Hans, who was assistant, secretary, and general factotum, was still there and gave her a small pile of letters. As she drove uptown she scrutinized the envelopes carefully. They were all business letters except one from a man in Arizona and a square blue envelope addressed in a woman's handwriting, postmarked Red

Bank, New Jersey. Devon turned it over, but there was no return address on the back. She held it up to the light, but the paper was opaque. Her curiosity leaped like flame up a pine tree. Who was this one, and where had Kurt met her? Sometimes the envelope glue was poor quality, and if one tried ever so adroitly, he could succeed in unsticking . . . Not this time, though; the mucilage held, a faithful guardian. Devon wished for a kettle of boiling water. She had never done it, but steaming open letters was highly spoken of in detective novels, and she had sometimes been tempted to try it, but had been deterred by lack of a handy kettle and the fear of being found out. How did you seal the flap up again? With library paste, or was the stickum on the envelope still sufficient? She arrived at Kurt's house with the riddle unsolved. It seemed a little obvious to hand him the mail with the murmurous missive on top, so she slipped it in the middle of the pile. Kurt thanked her warmly and sat down to read, clad in his shorts, shirt, a tie and a pair of socks. "Darling, you don't mind, no? We will see who these are from."

"Not at all," said Devon, delighted to have her curiosity satisfied. The first letter was from the Metropolitan Life Insurance Company, bubbling with interesting statistics. The second was from a wholesale leather firm, stating that shipments of Morocco were delayed but that they hoped to make delivery within the fortnight. The third . . . Devon casually lighted a cigarette. Kurt glanced at the blue envelope and slipped it to the bottom of the pile. The fourth bewildered him. "It is from the Chemical Bank and Trust Company," he said. "Why are they telling me these secret things?"

"How do you mean?"

"I don't bank there. It is not my business how much money they have."

Devon took the letter from him. "They probably want your patronage, dear. They send you this to whet your appetite." The communication was a form letter gratuitously setting forth to the world at large the assets and liabilities of the renowned banking institution.

The fifth letter was from a Rumanian friend of Kurt's who had married a wealthy American woman and was finding life on a dude ranch wearing to his spirit, and in the sixth, the Diamond Horse-shoe reminded its patrons of the caliber high and hot of its entertainment.

Kurt rose. "Are you getting hungry, darling?"

"I could cope with a small steak."

"Me too. Where shall we eat?" He crossed the room as he spoke and threw the torn envelopes and letters into the scrap basket. The billet from Red Bank went into the desk drawer. Kurt finished dressing and, having decided on the Colony for dinner, they left the apartment. It was a long time before Devon was to find which lady used blue stationery and lived in Red Bank, and by the time she did, it was too late.

"Well, personally I am vewy glad we settled on Cwescendo. There's weal excitement in it," and Moreley looked with satisfaction at the layouts for the new advertising campaign. Their classic preparations were to be plugged, of course, but the emphasis lay on Crescendo, the new fragrance which had materialized in perfume, cologne, face powder, and bath oil. If it proved as successful as they hoped, the line would be enlarged to include creams and cosmetics.

Devon turned to Jasper. "Well, what do you think?" She was referring to the layouts, and specifically to those in which Kurt's pictures were used, for the advertisements varied; some of them were line drawings, some were in color, and four or five, including the opening gun, were photographs.

"I like them," said Jasper. "That Crescendo is quite something." The admission pained him, as he had been opposed to the idea of a commercial tie-up with Kurt. "I assume this chap is your lover," he had said to Devon, "but I see no reason for involving him in the business," and she had replied, "The involvement, as you call it, is for purely practical reasons. The photographs are effective. Besides, I seem to remember an instance where love and business worked out all right," but Jasper didn't rise to that one. He gave a grunt and merely said, "Take it easy," but that was before he had seen the pictures. When he did, he acknowledged that her judgment was sound. There was no doubt that the first one particularly was eye-compelling. Low on the plate in the foreground in deep shadow one could dimly discern two recumbent bodies close-embraced, melting into still deeper darkness. From them rose a radiance mounting in palpitating waves to the top of the picture, but what gave the photograph its effectiveness was the extraordinary quality of luminosity which Kurt had achieved. If a woman thought that through the perfume she might achieve the results implied in the photograph, it was a cinch that a bottle of Crescendo was in her home and her money in the Elliott till. Devon knew this and felt quite satisfied with her find in the photographic field.

On the whole she was pleased with life in the past few months. Though Tim was still away, and the war situation was worsening, it was hard to feel intense personal concern when her own existence was on a comparatively even keel. Business was good, and Kurt and she seemed to have struck a happy stride. He was working hard and apparently had conditioned himself to friendly procedure to the extent of frequently confiding to her his extramural activities. Not the more colorful ones, perhaps, but the truth was that if he tossed off the smallest scraps of information, she evinced very little further interest and had a disconcerting way of forgetting the vital statistics of his actions and whereabouts.

She and Jasper and Moreley were discussing the advertising campaign and also the arrangements they would have to make to do next week's broadcast from Boston, for Nicky Van Alston was playing there now in his new revue and the program had gone back on the air the first week in September. As Moreley propounded the mysteries of line charges, the phone rang and Hilda announced that Mr. Fabri was on the wire. Devon would have preferred taking the call from another office, but she didn't want Jasper and Moreley to know it. She stayed at her desk and picked up the receiver. "Kurt, hello, I was just going to call you." This wasn't so, but it sounded more businesslike. "Jasper and Moreley are keen about your photographs. They really compose awfully well in the layouts. I think you'll be delighted." She had intended saving the news for dinner that night and was going to take the proofs home to show him. It was a curious feeling, but she did not want Kurt in the office. He had been in the salon only twice since they had known each other, and both times she felt disloyal to Tim. It wasn't very logical; why was it all right to have Kurt at the house and not all right to have him in the office?—but that was the way she felt. He was pleased that his first commercial efforts should have met with approval. "Really?" he said when she told him. "Oh, this I am glad about, but darling, listen, something has happened."

"What is it?"

"About tonight."

There goes our dinner date, thought Devon, but she said, pleasantly enough, "What about it?"

"You know Hockmeier, who is frequently doing designs for me?"

"Yes."

"Well, he has asked me so many times please will I not dine with him and always I put it off, but last week I told him I would tonight if he could get free, because I didn't think he could, but now he has done this and he is terribly disappointed if I do not come."

She did not say that she too was disappointed; that kind of behavior was a nuisance, and besides it did no good. "I see," she said. "Well, do whatever you want to, of course. Would you like to bring him to the house perhaps?"

"No, darling, this is not good. You would not like him, and he would be embarrassed."

She had known his answer before she asked. Kurt never wanted to share his friends with her; he seemed to feel that nothing but mutual boredom could result. But even if he was right, what of it? Occasional boredom was part of life, but Kurt panicked at the thought of it. His philandering, and his embarrassment if two people whom he had brought together did not like each other were part of his insecurity.

"It's all right," she said lightly, "I don't mind. Call me when you can."

"You're not alone in your office, no?"

Devon laughed. "You guessed it, my lad."

"Darling, you are sweet. Hockmeier is nice, and I do not like to offend him. He wants to be just with me because we are friends, but I will call you later and we can plan for tomorrow, yes?"

"We'll see," said Devon. "Good-by," and she hung up. She was disappointed, but after all there was nothing very reprehensible in dinner with an old friend, male, and their own relationship had been bowling along so smoothly of late that it was due for a slight setback. She might have enjoyed sending a few well-chosen phrases winging along the wire, but the presence of Moreley, Jasper, and Hilda prevented her, so she attacked the problem of the Boston broadcast with determined energy. When the men left her she put in a call for Jennie, whom she had not seen for several days, to ask if she was free for dinner.

"Darling," croaked the lovely creature, "I certainly can be, but I've got to go to the theater afterward to look at an actor Mark wants for my new show. He's playing in *They Never Grow Old*. Have you seen it, or would you like to come?"

"I think that sounds fun," said Devon. "I'd love to see it."

"Where shall we have dinner?"

"I don't care. What about Voisin's? I haven't been there in ages." She and Kurt sometimes went there because the food was delicious and it was run by an Austrian. "Do you want to meet me there a little after seven?"

"Yes. No, wait a minute. I've been looking a ripe seventy this past week. If I can get a treatment late this afternoon, I'd rather come to the salon and pick you up afterwards."

Devon turned to Hilda. "Call the sixth floor and find out who's free around half past five or six. Miss Moore wants a facial." It developed that Miss Suzanne would be delighted to take Miss Moore. Miss Suzanne's delight was verbal, this appointment damn well bollixed up her date with her young man, but Miss Moore was a big star, and what were you going to do when the boss ordered a command performance?

Suzanne, however, even when disgruntled was apparently a miracle worker, for when Jennie came up to Devon's office after her treatment that evening her reported seventy years had dropped away and in her dark green woolen suit she looked like a flower embedded in moss.

As Owens drove the two women from the salon to the restaurant Devon told Jennie about Kurt breaking their engagement. "But I honestly can't complain about that," she added, laughing. "He's been a sweetheart recently, and as he had the grace to tell me why he was breaking it, I consider we've come a long way."

"I tell you," said Jennie, and her tone was positive, "the guy's going to ask you to marry him yet."

"You're dreaming," Devon said brusquely.

"I'll bet you. I'll bet you a thousand bucks."

"A thousand?" Devon was aghast. Jennie laughed. "What's the matter," she asked, "too steep for you?"

"Well, my Lord, Jennie, a thousand dollars, that's a lot of money."

"Exactly," said Jennie with relish. "I could use a thousand bucks, and I'm absolutely certain of what I say."

"That Kurt will propose to me?"

"Yes, m'am."

Devon was torn. The thought of a thousand-dollar loss was acutely painful, on the other hand supposing Jennie was right . . . suppose the miracle happened? "Done," she said. "But I warn you, you're out of pocket, my girl."

But Jennie was game. "O.K. Only no fair putting him off just so you won't have to pay me."

Devon laughed. "To tell you the truth," she said, looking rather like a naughty child caught in the act, "I don't know what I'd do if he did propose to me, except accept, I suppose. I'm mad in love with the man, yet I seem to belong to Tim. Figure that out if you can. Woman loves husband, has affair with other man, loves other man, still wild about husband. That makes a lot of sense, doesn't it? A psychoanalyst's field day."

"Did you ever think of going to one?" asked Jennie.

"A psychoanalyst?"

"Yes. I've sometimes thought I might," Jennie continued, "though I suppose in my family the logical candidate for the lads with the X-ray eyes is Ollie, that pickled quince I'm married to. Still, the idea of lolling around and telling your dreams sounds kind of luxurious, but who has the time?"

"Or the money? Believe me, baby, it's sounder to invest in face treatments. If you look like a million dollars, you don't need some high-priced stranger snooping around in your brains."

This analysis of the human psyche brought the two scientists to the door of Voisin's restaurant. Devon told Owens to get his dinner and to be back in time to take them to the theater. In two weeks Jennie was starting rehearsals in a new play, and the young actor they were going to see tonight was one the management hoped to filch from the rival producer and cast in an important part in the new production.

"I've never seen him," said Jennie, as they sat sipping cocktails, "but Mark thinks he's the hottest thing since Leslie Howard, so I promised to go. I hope Mark's right. With all the My Sweets tied up in the war, we're having an awful time getting the right man to play Damon."

Devon chuckled. Jennie always referred to English actors as the My Sweets. She said it was their one term of endearment, and two of the four words in their vocabulary, the other two being Old Boy. "It's remarkable," she said, "the mileage they travel and the money they make on those four syllables."

"Is *They Never Grow Old* doing any business?" Devon asked. Jennie made a fluttering gesture indicating so-so. "It's a funny thing about war plays," she said. "With all that drama running riot, you'd think the authors couldn't fail, but they can. I guess it's hard to be any more dramatic than the headlines. That's why I'm glad the war is only incidental in our show. I think we stand a better chance."

They discussed Nicky's new revue, which they had seen at the Boston opening, and were just polishing off their smoked salmon well seasoned with olive oil and freshly ground pepper, when Devon glanced up to see Kurt and his friend, Mr. Hockmeier, standing in the entrance to the restaurant, the wide archway opening off the little foyer. "Why, for heaven's sake," she said to Jennie, "look who's here." They waved, and the two men came over to the table. Kurt introduced his companion, but it struck Devon that his manner was a little stiff. "Do you boys want to be alone?" she asked, laughing, "or won't you join us? We won't be here long, we're going to the theater."

"You won't even have to pay the check," added Jennie encouragingly. "That's how we are, independent modern women."

"The pal type," said Devon.

Mr. Hockmeier bowed. "Thank you so much, but we are not alone." As he spoke two girls distinctly not the pal type appeared in the doorway and glanced hesitatingly about the room. By pooling their coats they could have started a silver-fox farm of no mean dimensions. One looked like Hedy Lamarr, but her hair was longer; the other was sleek, with an upswept coiffure and a great deal of blond pompadour topped by a cabbage rose. "Perhaps those are the ladies you are waiting for," said Jennie, and a thread of steel glinted through her husky voice. Mr. Hockmeier hurried to welcome them, but Kurt wavered for a moment at the table.

"Are they designers too?" asked Devon. Her tone was polite, but her eyes glinted wickedly.

"These are friends of my friend, Hockmeier," said Kurt formally.

"The friends of my friends are my friends," quoted Devon, and she added kindly, "Even if they're not designers, they're decorative. Occupational necessities, I'm sure, for inspirational purposes."

"What is this?" Kurt spoke with heavy banter, but his eyes were cold. "I have not said we would be alone."

Devon winked at Jennie. "Even if you didn't say it in so many words, that was the impression you conveyed, darling." Her voice was silky sweet and affected Kurt like the scratching of chalk on a blackboard.

"Excuse me," he said, bowing, "but Hockmeier will think me rude if I am not joining him."

"Hockmeier's feelings should be considered," said Devon gravely and extended her hand. Kurt kissed it and Jennie's also and joined his party at their table at the far side of the room. Devon watched him go. "He has nice manners, hasn't he?" she said. Jennie glanced at her, but her face was empty except for a slight social smile. Jennie took Devon's hand and held it tight.

"Darling, don't you care. Maybe the bastard is telling the truth for once. Maybe he didn't know anything about them. That pair looks to me just like the choice of a guy named Hockmeier, but of course Kurt's so obstinate, he'd rather die than explain."

Devon made a little sound of weary disgust. "He's a tough nut to crack and no mistake. For a man who's Rumanian and Austrian and Jewish and Lord knows what else, he's the most Prussian human being I've ever met."

"That's partly the trouble, I suppose," said Jennie. "Such a hodge-podge must make it impossible for him to know where he's at." She eyed him thoughtfully across the room and then shook her head with a little laugh. "Poor devil, he's an absolute *stew* of blood, isn't he? I wonder he doesn't give off sulphurous fumes when the weather's hot."

In the subsequent quarreling and the making up which followed this debacle, the customary acid aspersions were tossed, Devon remarking that the sportsmanship involved in deceiving those who loved you was negligible, as it was natural for them to believe what you told them, and Kurt stating that it was childish to think that two grown men would dine alone if the opportunity arose to be with two pretty girls, and even more childish to think that because they had dinner they were also having an affair.

By way of proving that she was a woman of spirit, Devon refused to see Kurt for a week. She would neither ask him to the house nor go to his apartment in spite of his repeated invitations, formal, bantering, or urgent, till at last he hit upon a way to break down her defenses.

With the failure of Nicky's Miss Flora to produce any offspring, Devon had given up the idea of cocker spaniels in her life and had become the chattel of three toy poodles: Trinket, Jot, and Tittle, the trio who had added to Kurt's discomfiture that summer Sunday in the country. She adored them and Kurt hated them. "Dogs are not nice," he said firmly. "They are licking things in the street and then you are letting them kiss you. This is unhealthy."

Devon would feel depressed by this; she would feel she was not fastidious and would put the offenders from her, but when she picked one of them up again, which she was forever doing, he would quickly turn his head and get in a good lick against her cheek, and she would think he was cute. This Kurt considered reprehensible, nor was he any better pleased when she told him he should be grateful that he wasn't Napoleon. "He was an emperor and went rampaging all over Europe, but he had to share his bed with Josephine *and* her little dog!"

"This is disgusting," said Kurt, adding angrily, "And it gives headaches." Where he had picked up this bit of lore Devon didn't know, but though she refused to banish the poodles she kept them out of his way as much as possible.

Actually his first antipathy towards them had cooled somewhat, but though he genuinely disliked the canine, his antagonism for this trio was intensified by jealousy. Besides, they were always sitting around, talking and laughing together, at his expense. When he was with Devon he resented any divided attention. However, he was finding life without her staler than he would have believed possible, so he hit upon a scheme to weasel his way back into her affections. With taste and humor he designed three extremely smart collars and leashes for his three antagonists: chartreuse leather for Trinket, who was gray, shocking pink for the black Jot, and azure for brown Tittle. He sent them into the enemy camp with a note, reading,

DEAR BOYS [Tittle was a female, but they were always referred to as the boys]:

I am sorry if I have hurt your feelings in the past or your mistress's feelings in the present. I think she is hypersensitive, but I love her very much, so if you are willing to be settling up old scores and will come to my apartment your first free evening with your mistress on the other end of these leashes, I shall be grateful and forgive you all the times you are jumping on me and licking me with such wet tongues.

Your new friend,
KURT FABRI.

Devon found the note and the peace offerings to the dogs when she got home one evening about half past five. At seven-thirty, so as not to seem too eager, the four of them were at Kurt's house.

PART FIVE

In october Devon started on a tour of the Devonshire House salons around the country. There were thirteen in all, but that was counting New York, Mexico City, and the one in Palm Beach, which wouldn't open till December. She planned to be gone about a month, and her itinerary led her through ten cities, starting in Boston and zigzagging across the country through Philadelphia, Washington, Cleveland, Detroit, Chicago, St. Louis, Dallas, San Francisco, and Los Angeles. Whether she went to Mexico City or not depended on Kurt. If he could get away and join her there for a little holiday, she would go; otherwise she would return to New York and make the trip in the spring.

"My angel, I do hate to leave you," she said to him the night before she left, "but here's my whole route and the hotels and everything, and write to me every minute and we'll telephone like mad." He had not asked her for the itinerary, and she pretended she hadn't noticed, though she would have been happy had her whereabouts been important to him. They used to be to Tim. Tim knew to the minute when she was arriving any place, and there was always a telegram waiting and sometimes flowers if it was a special day. She could never tell why it was special, but it might hit Tim that way, and a bouquet would be delivered to the hotel, and in the strange handwriting of the local florist would be the message,

"Because it's Tuesday and I love you," or "St. Louis is noted for the Cards who are stalwart characters, but I will feel safer if you fill your room with these instead," and there would be an enormous box of the tawny russet chrysanthemums she loved.

As she thought of these attentions she gazed at Kurt with cold speculation. "Are you thoughtful, my treasure?" she asked with a kind of icy objectivity which he found disconcerting.

"You should know by now," he said.

"Yes-ss," she said, and sat beside him and pushed his cheeks up with her two hands so that his already slanting eyes closed to narrow Chinese slits. "Treat me gently, you monster," she murmured with soft commination and suddenly bit his nose. "And write to me, see?"

"Do not do this," he cried, taking her by the wrists and pulling her hands away. "I do not care for these brutalities. It is you who are the masochist," and he held her wrists in such a grip that he stained the flesh, but she only laughed. "You are very funny," he added. "You want me to write and you say you do not like to leave me, but I am not allowed to take you to the station even."

"Oh well, darling, be reasonable, that I can't help. It's a business departure. To begin with, there wouldn't be room in the car. I'm taking my secretary and a maid, and then there's Jasper—Jasper always comes to see me off on these trips—and probably Moreley will be along, and maybe Henry Barlow."

"And who is this Mr. Barlow who is being so indispensable?"

"My lawyer, darling. He always has last-minute precautions to offer. You see, this isn't a tour of only the salons. I'll be seeing a lot of our biggest buyers—Marshall Field's, Neiman-Marcus in Dallas, Bullocks-Wilshire—a whole raft of them. Barlow lives in terror I'm going to make some fatal commitment. I can't imagine why. Even if I slipped on integrity, the commitment would be to our advantage."

Kurt was half laughing, but he was shocked. "But this is not honest."

"Sure it is. It's a catch-as-catch-can world, my friend. Perhaps I am tough in business, but these deals are impersonal—creams and lotions and real estate and freight rates and God knows what—but I have more respect for the human heart than some I know," and she gave him a long and insinuating kiss.

☆   ☆   ☆

Four days later, having finished her business in Boston and Philadelphia, Devon was in Washington for the opening of Jennie's new play, *The Mountain Top,* and Tim was with her.

He had come over from Baltimore, and with the post-mortem after the opening performance disposed of, Jennie and Dick Hadley, Tim and Devon sat in Jennie's suite over supper and drinks. They were in happy humor. The play had had an enthusiastic reception, the star had acted with beguiling skill and looked like an angel, though Dick still agonized over the lighting of the second act, and Devon had had a minor seizure about the color of eye shadow Jennie had unwittingly chosen, but all agreed that these flaws were not irreparable.

Mr. Hadley was sitting near Miss Moore, his plan having been to filch a couple of morsels from her plate; what with setting up the show he had not been to bed for two nights and was too tired to eat much, but though his fairy love tossed him a dazzling smile from time to time, she kept tight hold on her steak bone and asparagus hollandaise. Dick, frustrated, retired into his highball and thought with a pleasant glow what a hell of a fellow Tim was. Why Devon wanted to mess up her life with that Fabri was more than he could understand.

The conversation was easy, friendly and informal. They discussed the theater, the cosmetic industry—Devon had that day gone from cellar to attic of the Washington salon and had been gratified by the list of diplomatic names in the appointment book—and had swung to the war.

"Of course," she said happily, "if we do get in it, Washington will be a madhouse and the salon will boom. Wives of the big businessmen who'll come pouring in here will need all kinds of treatments to help them endure their husbands' headaches, and there'll probably be thousands of girl office workers too. The competition for men will be terrific. You know, I think I'll inaugurate a series of very cheap facials. They ought to go like hot cakes."

Tim grinned. His Devon was certainly the one for whom they had coined the line about "an ill wind that bloweth no man good." Even when she sat still, money dropped in her lap. Dick observed that should the United States enter the war men of his profession would be greatly in demand in the camouflage division, and perhaps he would be wise to apply for a commission now.

"I imagine the Government will really do a job on the coastal areas, don't you think, Dick?" asked Tim.

"They already have. It's almost impossible to spot the hangars of the big California plants. They've got them all rigged up with false fronts and silhouette villages on the roofs."

"How ingenious!" said Jennie. "Still, it must have occurred to the enemy to buy a map, don't you suppose?"

Dick sighed patiently. "That's not the point. If you're bombing from the sea or the air, it's tough to place your shots accurately if you're confused by shadows and forms, not to mention gunfire."

"They think of everything," murmured Jennie. Her tone was reverent, if a little muffled by steak.

"Tim, how would this be . . ." Devon sat on the edge of her chair, her eyes bright, an eager hand on his arm. "It's true about the Commandos smearing themselves with burnt cork and stuff for those raids, isn't it?"

"That's right."

"That's where *we* could help the war effort and maybe do thousands of dollars of business with the Government. We could manufacture camouflage make-up for the whole American Army! A white grease foundation for the boys in Greenland to melt into the snow, a wonderful sort of beige for deserts if we've got any men there, and something rich and green for tropical parts."

"That's a wonderful idea!" cried Jennie. "You could settle the whole thing while you're here in Washington, Devon. Why don't you see the President in the morning?"

Tim and Dick exchanged despairing glances. "It's just possible," Tim said, "that he has a previous engagement. Anyhow, until the Army issues complete changes of costume to go with the different make-ups, it wouldn't make much sense."

"What do you want to bet they will?" Devon's face was bright with the animation so typical of her when she was talking shop. "The whole thing could be very practical, with the make-up packaged in small containers, capsules, maybe." The others laughed, but less than a year later she was to be again in Washington, negotiating a government contract for just such an assignment.

It was shortly after two o'clock that Dick broke up the party by dropping asleep in his chair. Forty-eight hours of hanging and lighting the sets of *The Mountain Top* had exhausted him. Tim and Devon were all for going without waking him, but Jennie said truly enough he'd feel badly not to say good-by to Tim, who was leaving early in the morning. "Besides," she added, "it'll be a kindness. Think how uncomfortable he'd be, sleeping in his clothes." They shook him gently.

"I feel like a brute," said Devon. "I guess it's the way explorers feel, keeping each other awake in the snow. It's for their own good, but the sleep must be heavenly."

Dick rose groggily to his feet to bid them an affectionate farewell and promised Tim he'd come over to see him in Baltimore before the company went back to New York. When he and Devon had left, Dick turned to Jennie. "Did it strike you that Tim seemed awfully eager to have me come to Baltimore?"

"Yes, it did, rather," said Jennie as she started slowly undressing. Dick picked up the steak bone from her plate and gnawed on it as he stood leaning against the bedroom door.

"I think Tim's a lonely fellow. He's nuts about his job all right. Boy, his face lighted up when he talked about it, but I should think emotionally he'd be all tied up. That Devon-Fabri situation can't be easy to take. It's a funny thing about that Fabri guy. He doesn't seem to have had much education in the sense of going to college and all, like an American, yet he's intelligent; I enjoy talking to him, but I have the feeling Devon's under kind of a strain with him. With Tim, it's different—even when they're arguing their heads off, they're having a high old time."

"I'm not sure Kurt's so intelligent," said Jennie with a trace of belligerency. "He doesn't know a thing about the theater."

Dick smiled. "Of course, honey, that doesn't necessarily make him a dope."

"Well, he's a dope to treat Devon the way he does."

"Yes, I guess he does play around. Naturally it makes her unhappy, but she exaggerates it too, Jen, don't fool yourself. My Lord, if he did all she accuses him of, he'd be a cripple."

"Oh dear," said Jennie, as she picked up her nightgown, a frail wisp of pink foam, and slipped it over her head, "I do hope it works out all right. Tim's such a sweetheart. Look how gay he made the evening, and under the circumstances there might have been a good deal of tension. As you say, he can't not know about Kurt. Overture and Morning Song and the new one that's just coming out, Crescendo. What does Devon think he thinks?"

Dick laughed and tossed away the bone. "She ought to launch a side line and call it Give Away."

"Of course," added Jennie thoughtfully, "Tim's in no position to do much thinking. After all, *he* walked out on *her.*"

As she spoke, in a suite on the floor below the tension which had been submerged all evening was rising to the surface. Tim held in his hand a copy of *Vogue,* opened to a full-page Devonshire House ad. It was Kurt's Crescendo photograph. Tim tried to speak jokingly, but he was obviously angry. "Listen, Devon," he said, "I don't know what the hell goes on in your life; not that knowing your tendencies, I can't make a fairly shrewd guess, but are you reduced to printing this kind of stuff to get customers?"

Devon's voice was icy. "Just what do you mean by my tendencies?"

"That old business trick of blazoning your love life to the world. It never struck me as the best of taste, but I sometimes thought it was provocative, and God knows it was profitable, but this is going too far. Why not rent Macy's window at high noon?"

"Tim, you're revolting. That happens to be a magnificent photograph, and I resent your implication. I didn't pose for it, you know."

"Whose picture is it?"

Like many advertisements the photograph carried no credit, and Devon felt this was not the time to let him know it was Kurt's work. The picture was good, but she knew Tim would consider any business association with Kurt a bad error of judgment. As professionally she still very much wanted his good opinion, she answered casually, "Nobody well known. Chap brought his work into the office one day, and I was struck by his ability."

"Are you using any more of his stuff?"

"I may use three or four others. It's a big campaign, Tim, we've got to have variety, neither all photographs nor all drawings."

"Well, my advice is not to take any more of these without Jasper's and Moreley's O.K."

"I haven't," she said shortly. Tim closed the magazine and tossed it on the table.

They lapsed into a silence which Devon was the first to break. "It seems funny to be doing the tour of the salons and you not know where I'm going to be or anything."

Tim smiled. "I know the itinerary pretty well. You could tell me the dates and I'd drop you a line. I believe the U.S. mails are still going through."

"You write sweet letters, Tim."

"I like to keep in touch with my old friends."

"I believe you do. It was fun seeing Jennie and Dick, wasn't it?"

"God, yes." Tim spoke so sincerely that Devon was touched. "I haven't had such a grand evening since before I went to Louisiana." It was a charming compliment, whether deliberate or not. Before he went to Louisiana he had been with her.

"Are you happy, darling?"

Tim's tangent eyebrows shot up. "Who, me? I'm the original clam at high water."

"Oh. I mean, good. I suppose there are lots of interesting and intelligent women working at Johns Hopkins too?"

Tim watched her with an amused gleam. "Yes, there are."

"All of them frightfully interested in skin tissue, I expect."

"Well, I'll tell you, it's a funny thing about skin tissue; it doesn't seem to matter much what you experiment with during the day, but at night you're more particular. It so happens that two of the nicest tissues I've seen in months belong to you and Jennie. That's what I enjoyed so much about this evening, the scientific angle."

"I should have shot you years ago, Mr. Wainwright," said his wife, but she was lapped in warmth and comfort. Then the telephone rang. The warmth and comfort vanished.

"Shall I answer it?" asked Tim politely.

"Er . . . I'll take it." *This*, thought Devon, *is going to be great.* It was nearly three A.M. and scarcely likely that the call would be one of business. Her mind flashed back to that day when Tim had come home from Louisiana and she had prayed that Kurt would phone her. She was now temporarily praying he wouldn't. Times, she reflected as she picked up the receiver, had certainly changed. "Hello?"

"Hello," came Kurt's voice. "How is my baby?" His baby, if he wanted to know, was on the griddle. She was also mad; she had been away from New York for four days, and this was the first she had heard from him. In Boston it was she who called him. She had intended taking him to task for his cavalier manner, but the moment seemed inopportune. Since Tim was listening, it behooved her to be lighthearted, charming, noncommittal. A woman loved and sought after, the kind a husband was a fool to leave, there were so many others to claim her. On the other hand she didn't want Kurt to know that she was not alone.

"Hello," said Kurt again, this time with more emphasis. "What is the matter?"

"Nothing. I'm fine," said Devon brightly. "I know you'll be happy to hear that Jennie's show went over splendidly."

Kurt was unmoved by her enthusiasm. The theater was not his passion. "Darling, what am I caring for this silly play? I called to talk about you. Why have I had no letters? You promised to write." This was too much! She wanted to shout, "What about your writing to me, you heel? What have you been doing so important that you couldn't telephone?" but such humiliating betrayal in front of Tim was not to be thought of. Instead she answered with what she hoped was beguiling coquetry, "I know I did, but I've been so terribly busy, you've no idea. Do forgive me." Her conversation was usually generously sprinkled with "darlings" and "angels" and "lambs," so that their omission was noticeable. Kurt was obviously puzzled.

"You are so funny," he said. "Why are you angry?"

"I'm not at all. It's your imagination."

"No, this is not so. I know you. I know something is the matter. What is it? Are you alone?" he asked, suddenly suspicious.

She hesitated. If she said yes, her manner certainly required explanation. If she said no, further explanation at any time might be rather complicated. Kurt was unreasonable about Tim. She compromised. "You know these theatrical post-mortems." This she considered rather neat, it divulged nothing to either man. Kurt was ignorant of post-mortems, but he caught the general trend.

"Jennie and Dick are with you?"

She went on with her embroidery. "And producers and an author or two." The room was filling up.

"It is curious," said Kurt, "the party must have grown suddenly. I tried to get you two hours ago. I am in my bed since eleven."

"I'm terribly sorry, dear. We must still have been in the theater." She felt she could afford one "dear." Tim couldn't be suspicious of that, and it was by way of a small fish to Kurt.

"Will you call me back when you are alone?"

"Yes, of course."

"Good-by."

"Good-by."

Tim was gazing at her speculatively. "Do your friends usually call you at three in the morning?"

She smiled. "Do you object?"

"Not at all, but it can't do you any good, having your rest broken into. Once you're awake, it takes you forever to get back to sleep."

"I'm touched by your solicitude. You never used to be so thoughtful. You used to toss and turn and yawn out loud and run the shower at the most heathen hours." The sins were manifold, but the indictment was delivered without anger.

"I'm sorry, madam."

"I never minded."

Tim rose and stretched. "Well, if your swains will leave you alone, I will too. I guess we could both do with a little sleep."

"Don't worry about my swains. That call was only to find out how the play went." She was propelled to the lie through affection for Tim and because there were times when they just seemed to pop out willy-nilly. *It's probably nature's way,* she thought, *keeping women in practice for the times they need to lie.*

Tim's reactions were confused. He felt, not exactly resentment that his wife should be having a love affair—he had automatically assumed that such was the case when he heard the gossip about her and Fabri—but he was angry that she should have chosen such a man. Tim knew little about him, but that little was not to his liking. Yet there seemed nothing he could do. If a husband wouldn't live with his wife he was scarcely in a position to dictate her mode of behavior. Still, an adult woman ought to be able to protect herself in the clinches, at least to pick a lover a husband could respect. Surely he had the right to expect that. "Tell me something, will you?" he asked suddenly.

"Of course."

"Are you in love with this guy you're running around with?"

"Isn't that kind of a silly question, Tim? I don't expect you've been leading the life of a monk since we've been separated, but I consider that that side of your life is your own."

"Well, I . . . I just hope he's good enough for you, that's all."

"I'm sure, dear, that all husbands and wives wish that for each other, but I don't suppose they ever fully approve the choice. I can recall one or two of your indulgences who I felt were scarcely worthy."

"My indulgences were figments of your imagination."

"I suppose I dreamed up Judith Evans?"

Tim laughed in spite of himself. "You certainly did, and even had it been the truth, a man can fall for a little trollop and it doesn't make much difference, but you put that in reverse and it's bad news."

"You mean that it's degrading for a woman to love beneath her, so to speak, but it's all right for a man?"

"Well, that's a bum phrase, but I guess it about expresses it."

"Tim, I'm ashamed of you. I thought you could think straighter than that. If it's bad for one sex, it's bad for the other, but if a man can have an affair and be immune to love, let me assure you a woman can too."

There was a pause. "I see," said Tim.

Alas, no, my darling, you don't, thought Devon. *Mine is not a case in point. Unfortunately I happen to be madly in love, but my argument still holds.* Aloud she continued, "Men may not like to think so, but it's the truth, and that other poppycock is a myth they've invented for their own convenience."

"My little goon, you don't know what you're talking about."

"Oh, yes, I do, and if you want to know my opinion, I think that if there's any degrading involved, it's more degrading for a worthwhile man to have an affair with a cheap woman than vice versa. After all, a woman may do it out of expediency or courtesy or any one of a dozen reasons, but she can be passive. A man damn well has to want it if he's going to get to first base. Believe me, dear, very few men are ever raped!"

Tim spoke with some heat: "He doesn't necessarily have to want it with his mind or heart. That just happens to be the biological arrangement. You keep men away from women for any length of time and they'll seek sexual relief where they can find it, but that has no more to do with love than the Greeks eating garbage because they're ravenous has to do with the appreciation of food."

"I'm not talking about extreme situations, Tim, and you know it, though in passing I might say it's a good thing the ladies to whom you refer can't hear you. Some of them might not care for that garbage association, but in any event why shouldn't the same needs apply to women?"

"Physically they do, but emotionally women are different. Don't forget that most women don't want freedom from ties. Domesticity is their ambition."

"That's a kind of ready-made theory, isn't it? I thought you were a scientist."

"I'm also a husband, and I think I know a little something about——"

"About women, I suppose?"

"No, just about you and the kind of setup you need to be happy."

Devon looked at him. "You might have considered that eight months ago," she said quietly. "But I bet anything you like that with the growing economic independence of women, which will grow even faster because of the war, and with a wider knowledge of birth control you're going to find that they'll cease being ashamed of admitting their physical needs and they'll have the same mental attitude towards sex that men have."

"I don't say you're entirely wrong, Devon, but the basic reason for the sexual act does happen to be the procreation of the race, and because women bear the children, consciously or subconsciously they're more aware of that than men."

"That's a very interesting thing," she said chattily. "You're right as to the reason, of course, but it's remarkable how few people consider that when they have l'amour on their minds."

Tim grinned. "There's another aspect too which you've ignored, my freethinker, and that is the so-called *imponderabilia*. You can't wipe out the moral training of generations overnight."

But this was Devon's meat. "Baby, believe me, it was never so much morals as it was economics and the fear of pregnancy and its consequent social stigma that kept women on the straight-and-narrow."

Tim couldn't resist baiting her a little, but he was amused because secretly he thought there was a good deal in what she said. "Isn't that a pretty cynical viewpoint?"

"No, I think it's honest, but naturally it won't be popular. There'll be a lot of outraged denials, and I can already hear the thunder from the pulpits. After all in the old days they got a lot of credit for the local virginity, and it made them feel very good, but I see no reason to exempt the clergy from fact-facing any more than the rest of society."

"Well," said Tim, "even if you're right and women get to be free as air, you might tell your feminine friends that a little restraint has more appeal for the boys than the too generous offer."

"I'm sure it has," replied Devon. "Continence is a quality I myself much admire, especially in a man. It's hard to maintain any interest in a stallion. Men are quick to call women pushovers, but if some of those lads aren't pullovers, I'll eat my hat." She spoke with such feeling that Tim looked at her searchingly.

"You're not referring to me by any chance, are you?" he asked.

"Certainly not. You're a sentient human being whom I respect."

"Thanks." He spoke absently. Her remarks carried too much emphasis for him to believe that this was a philosophic summation impersonally arrived at; she must have a concrete example very much in mind. If it turned out to be Kurt Fabri and she was really in love with him, that was a fine kettle of fish, and Tim had himself to thank for precipitating it.

"Devon, I'm terribly sorry about all this."

"All what, Tim?"

"Oh . . . us . . . the separation . . . the money . . . that it had to be this way."

How strange, thought Devon; *perhaps Tim wants to come back, and I do love him . . . dearly . . . but I don't want to have to live with him now.* She was suddenly panicky at the thought of any obstruction between her and Kurt. "Oh, that's all right, Tim," she said kindly. "We're lucky really. We're able to do our work, we're free, and we're friends."

"Are we?"

"Is there anybody else in the world you'd sit up with till four in the morning arguing sex for women with? Is there? Lie to me, darling."

Tim looked at her with great affection. "No, there isn't, and that's no lie. And now, my pink, I'm leaving you. You're dead and so am I."

"But I don't go to Cleveland till tomorrow afternoon."

"But I've got to make an early break back to Baltimore."

"Well, why do you bother going to that other hotel, the Hay-Adams, or wherever you left your bag? You can sleep here and get a razor and a toothbrush in the morning. I've got two beds in there, and I'm only going to use one."

Tim burst out laughing. He knew that Devon was perfectly sincere and made the offer with no self-consciousness. "Do you know something?" he asked with warm good humor.

"What?"

"You are a fabulous dame. I will be in touch with you, madam, but I shall now leave you. Good night."

"I don't get the joke, but good night."

She had been alone for five minutes before it occurred to her that Tim might have considered her offer tasteless and that another woman might have been restrained by a nicer sensitivity from ever making it. When this thought struck her, she stared at herself incredulously. She was in front of the bathroom mirror at the time, removing her make-up. "Why, for God's sake," she said aloud, "the old goat!" She burst out laughing and straightway dispatched a telegram to Tim which was delivered to him the next morning as he was paying his bill at the Hay-Adams. It read:

DEAR GOAT, THERE WERE NO STRINGS ATTACHED TO LAST NIGHT'S OFFER. I AM A MEMBER OF THAT RESTRAINED CONTINGENT TO WHICH YOU REFERRED SO ADMIRINGLY. ACCEPT, DEAR SIR, A CHASTE SALUTE.

But that night, just as she slipped into sleep, a prickly thought had insinuated itself into her mind: maybe Tim was in love with somebody else, an antiseptic girl with tissue, and she made a little prayer, "No, God, please don't let that be. Let him have affairs and things but never love anybody but me. I'm able to love two at once, but he wouldn't be. And if he were, I'd hate it."

Cleveland, Detroit, Chicago. Surely in Chicago there would be a letter from Kurt; flowers too, maybe, since she was going to be there three or four days; but when Devon arrived at the Ambassador Hotel, though there was a stack of mail from the office, a report from Fairweather on the household—it was intact—and letters from Tim and Jennie, there was nothing from Kurt. Her heart was heavy in her breast. Why couldn't he write? He said he was a poor correspondent, but he was worse than that. He was destitute. Destitute of heart or fantasy, she thought, and untruthful, for though he was much more glib with his "I love you's" than he used to be, how could one love and not want to reach out to the loved one? Devon herself was no great hand with a pen, but love letters were a form of self-indulgence, they warmed the heart. For the space of time it took to write them, one was no longer alone. She could well understand laziness and reluctance when it came to other forms of correspondence, and she thanked heaven for secretaries to whom one could dictate, but it saddened her that Kurt should feel no need, find no comfort in writing to her. He either could not or would not understand the comfort of a letter in one's purse.

Devon lay in her bed at night and fumbled, a little gingerly, for it was work she was unaccustomed to, among the metaphysical reaches of the human spirit. What made people behave as they did? How was it possible that she and Tim, who loved each other so deeply, who understood each other so well, had drifted so far apart? How was it possible for her to love Kurt, feeling about him as she did, seeing him clearly for what he was? And on his side, why, when he was so often irritated, angry, indifferent to her, why did he always come back? They were like two stars in the same orbit, now close, now far, but moving always in relation to one another. It seemed to her that Kurt was her doom, in the sense that she was unable to free herself of him, yet she was doomed without dignity. The word doom had always somehow suggested a Greek tragedy, Homeric figures against a darkening sky. It had certainly not evoked a bald, slightly overweight gentleman with an Oriental face and a passion for marinated herring.

Yet that is how it had turned out, and her heart had been drawn from her breast and lighted on her sleeve. Why, why, why? She could not blame Kurt, he was as he was. *Isn't the lack rather in me,* she thought, *if, having known a man like Tim, I can still love him?* What kind of perversity pervaded the human spirit so that one well able to distinguish between the desirable and the unfitting, the good and evil, should hanker for the lesser man? Not that Kurt was evil, really. He was capable of generosity and gaiety and spontaneous charm, and he was a masterly lover. It was simply that he lacked humanity. *It's as though,* thought Devon, *he were a practically complete robot. Come one, come all, see our incomparable achievement: walks, talks, even thinks like a man! Only one tiny ingredient missing, folks, to make him live: compassion. All right, so I know that about him.*

Why should I expect that he will act in any way except that which is native to him? What is that French proverb? Ne cherchez pas, ne cherchez pas . . . well, anyway, it means 'Don't look for high noon at two o'clock.' And sound advice too, and why don't I take it?

These questions drummed through her mind, but the answer was not forthcoming in the Ambassador Hotel in Chicago.

Nor in St. Louis either, for that matter, though in St. Louis the argument for continuing the affair made a slight inroad. In the home of Tim's Cardinals, a letter from Kurt awaited her, a page and a half on small-sized air-mail stationery. Her heart began to pound when Hilda handed it to her with the rest of the mail, and she went into the bedroom and closed the door so she might be alone to read it. The writing started very small but sprawled out towards the end:

My DARLING:

You are scolding me for not writing to you, but what is there to write about? All the little things we talk about which are so important when you are with me seem frivolous set on paper. I do not like to bore you with what I am doing in the workroom, and otherwise nothing of interest happens to me.

Oh yes, Mr. Moreley did send me the proof of my second photograph which you are using for the ad, and I think it looks very well. I know you are telling him to do this, and it is very kind and thoughtful of you, and I am grateful. You are the sweetest person I know.

I hope you are having a pleasant trip. Do you know something? I miss you more than I like to admit to myself. Please write often, every day, and come home soon.

I love you.

KURT.

Devon dropped the letter in her lap with a smile, half tender, half rueful. Well, bits of it were quite cunning . . . that end part . . . but it was not what you might call meaty, scarcely something to have been on tenterhooks over for the past two weeks. *I guess what I want,* she mused, *is a cross between Horace Walpole and Don Juan. Oh well, even if he's not satisfactory, I suppose it's better to store up memories for your old age than to have nothing to look back on but a few good books and an emotional vacuum.*

Still, despite its meagerness, the letter gave her a lift, and she went through the salon like a whirlwind doing a complete job of reorganization; the Boston manager received a wire to come at once to St. Louis; St. Louis was sent back to New York for a jacking up, and Chicago departed for Boston, leaving the Windy City to sail under its own breeze for the next ten days. The ladies themselves were ignorant of the cause of these upheavals and vaguely resentful, but since the result was to boost the St. Louis profits by one per cent, Devon considered her maneuvers justified, though Jasper later questioned her sharply on all those railroad fares and living expenses for the managers.

Kurt's brief message elicited from her a long, affectionate, and informative reply, and gave further impetus to his thoughts on marriage, but letter-writing still remained for him an irksome task which he rarely performed.

In Dallas, Texas, she was carried along by the St. Louis momentum and by the fact that for the two days she was there she could barely crowd in a bath, so much business and Honoring were being done. She sent a wild telegram to Tim:

SO MANY FRUIT CUPS HAVE BEEN EATEN IN THIS TOWN IN MY HONOR IN THE LAST FORTY-EIGHT HOURS FEAR GRAVE OUTBREAK OF URTICARIA. HIVES TO YOU. NUTS TOO IF I DON'T HEAR FROM YOU PRETTY SOON. LOVE AND KISSES, DEVON.

It crossed a wire she received from Tim saying he was going to be in New York for a few days to consult some books and papers he had stored at the house, and would she mind if he stayed there. She replied at once that it had always been his home, and as long as he was in it he could blow out the candle that was burning in the window.

Reveling in the tactful and expert ministrations of Fairweather, whom he had not seen since Devon despatched him to Baltimore, Tim had to admit to himself that there was something to be said for the life of the rich. It probably stultified the brain, and it was a regrettable fact that in the long run luxury rotted the inner fabric, but boy, it was sure an enjoyable process.

Tim had just had a bath. The house boasted an elaborate water-softening installation, so that, after the liquid rocks he had become accustomed to, bathing at home was an indescribable delight. He had emptied the bath crystals from one of the great glass jars into the tub. It was Crescendo, and as the insinuating heady fragrance rose in the steam about him, he muttered to himself between clenched teeth, "The son of a bitch!" His sense of physical well-being was such, however, that his wrath faded with the vapor and he began leisurely getting into his clothes before going down to one of Anna's superlative dinners. Oscar and his wife were coming, and he looked forward with pleasure to a stimulating evening. The old girl was rather of the dumpling school, but she had the sense to keep quiet, and Oscar was a hell of an appealing guy. As he wandered around the dressing room, Tim remembered Fairweather's greeting on his arrival that morning. It had struck him as a shade on the cryptic side. He had said, "Welcome home, Mr. Wainwright. It's good to have you back, sir. You're needed here."

What the devil did that mean? Did Fairweather think Devon was lonely, or was he afraid she was not? What about that Fabri guy—did she have him at the house much? No man worthy of the name questioned servants about his wife, of course; the mere thought was distasteful; besides, he didn't give a damn, it was just that . . .

In his meanderings—Tim was a slow dresser; Devon had often thought it was the one thing he and Kurt had in common—he opened the mirrored doors of one of Devon's closets, the one in which she kept her negligees and dinner gowns. Tim remembered that the rods pulled out the way they do in shops. He pulled one of the chromium knobs, and there was a whispering sound as the soft garments swung forward to meet him. A subtle perfume rose from their folds, but it was a blend of Devonshire House products, and as such did not infuriate him. Tim was, unexpectedly, good about women's clothes, criticized them intelligently and appreciated them, and nearly always remembered them, and as he looked at the unfamiliar gowns and lifted the pliant velvets and wools and chiffons, a wave of sadness swept over him. *How many new dresses she has that I don't know about. How many new thoughts and emotions and experiences that I'm not sharing. I'm doing what I must, and I'm satisfied. It's just that . . . it's hard for women to realize that love can be in abeyance for a long time in a man's life and that, at best, it's secondary; work and ideals and war and sex, the first things first, and love must fit itself in as it may.* Someday perhaps he and Devon could work it out if it still seemed important, but now his job was tremendous and exciting, and he wanted no ties holding him back. If these new experiments developed as he hoped, he wanted to get to Europe. If what he had to offer was sound—and he'd stake his life on that—he wanted to see it in use in advance dressing stations on the battlefield. Time might mean everything; if the men could be treated at once, the chances for success were that much greater. There were tremendous potentialities, and he was only at the beginning, but if he was right, he would have opened the door to boundless possibilities.

He was still staring at the new clothes when a streak of color caught his eye. He lifted it out from behind the others and recognized an old friend. It was a dinner gown of dull powdery lavender, the color of faded violets, that Devon had had for several seasons but never discarded. It was Tim's favorite, and as he ran his hands over it now he remembered the feel of her body under it, warm and supple, and there was a sudden catch in his breath and he lifted the soft fabric and buried his face in its folds.

For a man to come back into a house where he had lived happily with his love was not, he decided, the wisest way to maintain a detached and scientific attitude, but what really drove him from the dressing room and downstairs to a double scotch was seeing the blue ribbons. He had opened the drawer of her dressing table to look for a nail file, and there they lay. Devon had a pair of little kid curlers on which she used to wind two short locks of hair which curled over her ears, and they had ribbons at the ends which tied into bows, because, she said, that made it gayer. But, seeing them, Tim felt decidedly un-gay. They evoked so vividly her piquant face, her sea-colored eyes with their dark lashes, and her soft curving mouth, that he slammed the drawer shut with a vicious bang.

While Tim was sentimentalizing in New York, Devon in San Francisco felt the cold stone of loneliness drop into her heart, and hurrying through her business, flew down to Los Angeles, a town for which epidermically she had very little use. San Francisco was damp and the women had good skins because of it, but what were you to do with the southern city—raw one minute and boiling hot the next, and everybody dying of pneumonia? Fortunately the salon did very well. It was located on Wilshire Boulevard, halfway between Los Angeles and Beverly Hills, and some of the deftest of the Devonshire House operators were employed there. Devon considered it only fair to give the feminine citizens a break. As she said, "The picture stars have every advantage and may even be beautiful to boot. The civilian women need the best they can get in order to compete."

The day she arrived Kurt phoned from New York to say he had made every effort but it was impossible for him to get away at this time, and why didn't she come home and they could go to Mexico City in the spring? In the back of his mind was the idea that by spring they might be married and it would be a very pleasant honeymoon. If things went well with his business and he could afford it, he would be delighted to pay for both; if not, well, Devon had so much money—she was, after all, a corporation—that one could not take it personally when her office ordered plane tickets, hotel reservations, etc.

She settled her business with the Mexico City salon by telephone, was honored at three dinners, two by the trade and one by the richest of the independent picture producers, wound up her affairs and landed at La Guardia Field a week from the day she had arrived in Los Angeles.

Kurt found himself remarkably glad to see her. There was a momentary dearth of fresh talent in his life, and it was comforting and stimulating to have her back. She had a sharp eye for detail and a pungency of phrase in describing her adventures which he found entertaining, and they were drawn close by mutual desire sharpened by the weeks of separation. In this felicitous atmosphere his heretofore diffused thoughts of marriage suddenly crystallized, and one evening shortly after her return he proposed to her.

They had had a simple dinner in the neighborhood and gone back to his shop afterwards, for Kurt was working on a new design for a small duffel bag and he wanted to have a drawing and a half-finished model ready for morning. She thought that his trade and his temperament were aptly wed, for he took a sensuous delight in his medium, in touching and working the supple skins, drawing them through his hands and gathering them into folds. Devon always enjoyed seeing him work; as he moved back and forth between his drawing board and the workbench she perched on a table and watched him contentedly. He looked awful, tired and a little grimy, and she felt at peace. Nobody else would be likely to want him in this condition. There were shadows under his eyes, his coat and tie were off and his shirt sleeves rolled up. The light from the hanging electric bulb glinted on the fine gold hairs along his arms, and she smiled faintly, for she knew how exquisitely soft they were to the touch. The room was very quiet except for an occasional gust of wind rattling the big windows and now and then a grunt from Kurt as he applied the adhesive glue to the skins. When they worked the leather for the real pouch it would all be stitched by hand, but Kurt wanted to see a model, so he was piecing together such scraps as he had in the studio.

It was cozy there, and she was happy to be with him, proud to feel that, out of all the women he knew, she was nearest him. *It's nice,* she reflected, *to be with the one you love in the important public moments, of course, but it's even nicer to be with him in the simple private times, like now. Come to think of it, when isn't it nice to be with the one you love?*

She looked around her approvingly. It was a good room, with the integrity of an honest workshop. Over in one corner stood his camera, covered with a black cloth, a couple of dozen plates stacked beside it. Tacked up on the walls were a few of his best pictures, and torn from a copy of *Vogue* was the full-page Crescendo ad. That was the one note of sex; the other photographs were severely functional: a still-life of leather tools, the green shade of the electric-light bulb and a T-square in improbable juxtaposition; luggage piled to resemble a skyscraper; and, somewhat unexpectedly, a bowl of eggs. The rest of the loft was devoted to stacks of hides, a few sample models, and the properties of his trade. Devon was carefully rolling a scrap of red morocco leather into a cornucopia when Kurt found words for the idea he had been nurturing all these months.

"You know what I am thinking, darling?"

"What, my lamb?"

He drew the tube of paste along the edge of a piece of leather, put it aside, carefully laid another piece of leather along the smeared border, pressed hard and plunged. "I am wondering if you would like to marry me."

Devon, who had imagined this situation some hundred-odd times but never like this, stared at him, let the cornucopia flap open, and said blankly, "What?"

"I am asking if you would like to marry me. I am making you a proposition."

She shook her head gently. "No," she said softly. "No, my darling, my guess would be this is the first time in your life you are not making a proposition."

Kurt looked a little puzzled. "It is not so when you ask someone to marry you?"

"That's called a proposal, my heart, but I understand that the word is new to you."

Kurt looked at her, an amused gleam in his eye. "You bitch," he said softly. "How dare you mock my first request for marriage in all my life!"

"Darling. Have you really never asked another woman to marry you?"

"Never. Once when I am seventeen in Sinaia, I thought I might have to ask my mother's maid, but it blew over." There was a silence. "You do not love me perhaps?" Suddenly it seemed desperately important that she should love him.

Devon slipped down from her perch and walked slowly to the corner of the big worktable. "Never fear, I love you all right, it's only——"

"Only what?"

"I thought you were so opposed to marriage. What about not wanting to come home to one woman, what about those cocktail parties where you get the new numbers?"

"I have changed."

"Kurt, Kurt——"

"Why not? Other people fall in love and change. I am in love too."

"Do you really love me enough to want to marry me?"

"My darling, I am asking you. I want to have you always. But you will let me out sometimes, won't you?"

His face wore a comic expression of mock alarm, but the thought was so typical of him that she burst out laughing. "Getting cold feet already?"

"No, you do not understand, it is silly to talk this way. All these things about numbers or seeing other women, you are wrong. That has nothing to do with two people loving each other and building marriage together."

"I see. The old marriage of convenience. . . . Well, it's the European viewpoint."

Kurt looked at her incredulously. "It is not nice to discuss these things at such a moment, but are you telling me that American men are not untrue to their wives?"

"Not at all. They are, I know that, but it's unusual to plan the infidelities during the proposal."

Kurt flushed. "This I am not doing, nor have I such thoughts, it is your sense of inferiority which makes you feel this, but we are adult people with outside interests. I hope you will want to marry me enough to get a divorce and do so, but we cannot go and live by ourselves in a little house in the woods."

"Why not? It sounds fine."

"Darling, please. This is for me a serious moment. I do not know whether I will be accepted or not." And he smiled, but there was something disarming and humble in his smile, and she was deeply touched.

"I do not know whether you will be, either," she said quietly, but her thoughts were in turmoil. The incredible had happened. Kurt had asked her to marry him. Surely, surely, that was proof of his love; yet would it change him? The leopard did not change his spots, but sometimes he did. She knew one or two instances where marriage had made a big difference. Men had stopped drinking too much, they had stopped chasing. She thought of one chap in particular, a friend of the Lowerys who had seemed an incurable philanderer but who had become a model of uxoriousness; would that happen to Kurt?

And then the thought of a divorce . . . what to say to Tim, how to say it? Maybe he wouldn't agree to it. The idea gave her a tiny unacknowledged sense of relief. She adored Kurt, but her instinct told her that to marry him would be folly; it would be an invitation to heartache and despair, yet God knows there was not much to be said for the present setup. That was heartache too, except that theoretically she was free to leave it. The other way she would be tied and helpless. And yet they had good times too; what grand times they had when Kurt was amusing and intelligent and affectionate! He had his good points all right, if only he could let other women alone. . . . What to say, what to do. . . .

She did not realize how long she had been silent. Kurt was speaking to her. "My darling, as you say, it is true I am new to these proposals, but I have read of such things. I believe the lady is usually giving the gentleman some answer. After all, it will soon be a year that we are together, for me the loveliest year; you know how I am, yet you have often told me you love me. I am in love with you. I think we could have a good life married." He came to her and put his arms around her and kissed her, and they stood for a few minutes embraced and cheek to cheek. They moved their faces together gently the way two horses do.

"I think we could too, my darling." She loved him, but her heart was heavy with the thought of Tim.

"You will ask your husband for a divorce?"

"I . . . yes, I'll speak to him."

"He has no cause for holding you. He is engrossed in his war experiments."

She felt a slight sense of irritation. "Still, dear, I am his wife. I have reason to believe Tim loves me very much."

"But he cannot expect no other man will want you." *What a charming thing for Kurt to say,* she thought, *and so true after all.*

"No, he certainly can't," she said righteously, but she wished she felt a little more convinced. "As a matter of fact, if he had gone away just because of the war, it would be wrong of me to leave Tim, but it isn't only that. His work is more important to him than I am." A piteous vision of a loving and neglected bride wavered before her.

"Perhaps, then," said Kurt, "he will be glad for a divorce. It will leave him freer."

This was a new view of the situation, and an unflattering one. She was anticipating opposition from Tim and even hoping for it. It would give her time to make up her mind, and if she decided definitely that she did want to marry Kurt, she felt sure that she could persuade Tim to let her go; but it had not occurred to her that he might want the divorce.

"You may be right," she said slowly, and added proudly, because she wished to vindicate Tim's leaving her and also to take a slight dig at Kurt for suggesting that he might want to, "He's doing some remarkable experiments. The government people are tremendously excited. They feel that Tim is making a magnificent contribution to the war effort." That this statement was something less than literal troubled her not at all. The Government might not be involved, but Tim was working for the good of mankind and had a puritan conscience about the war, something which could not be said for this foreigner who certainly ought to be more concerned than he was about serving the land which was giving him refuge.

"Then you will see, darling," said Kurt happily, "he may very well make no objection. You can go to Reno right away."

Devon mocked him. "Just think what a wonderful six weeks you can have while I'm out there."

"You see that is what you don't understand about me. I am never behaving any differently behind your back than when you are around." In a sense she felt this to be true; his infidelities were not curtailed by her presence. "Besides," he continued, "I will come out part of the time and be with you if you want me."

"Angel! Would you? I'd feel much less bleak."

"Of course."

"I suppose," she said, "there's bound to be a lot of publicity, and I can't imagine what Jasper's going to say."

"This is no business of his. Why do you even speak to him?"

"Darling, I wouldn't dream of not. You forget how close we are. Besides, now that I'm an engaged girl, I feel I should tell him about it. I want his blessing."

"And also, though you will never admit it, you are having an affair with him once."

"Nonsense. You've always thought that, and it's entirely your imagination."

"Oh no, it is not, my little liar. I am aware of this the first night Nicky brought me to your house. Believe me, I can tell. My Oriental blood senses these things."

"Well, your Oriental blood has curdled in this instance." She had no intention of bandying old love affairs. "But, by the way, that's something I've always meant to ask you. You remember after you left the house you telephoned me that first night?"

"Yes, I remember."

"Did you think I'd ask you to come back?" Kurt laughed. "Come on," she teased, "did you?"

"No, but I wanted to confirm my suspicions about you and Mr. Doolittle."

"But you knew he and Mollie were staying with me overnight. What did that prove?"

"Well, then I admit it. I thought you were extremely attractive and there was no harm in trying my luck."

"Were you in love with me?"

"No."

"Just curious, eh?"

"Yes."

"You louse."

He kissed her. "Darling, let us talk no more of these things, they are over. Soon we will be an old married couple."

Kurt felt quite content. His life would be passed in charming surroundings with a wife who was a delightful mistress as well as wealthy, and by exercising a little discretion he could continue his usual extramural activities. It was just possible he might not even want to . . . one became involved, and then women were more trouble than they were worth, and Devon had become very dear to him. If the war didn't upset everything, it might all work out even better than he had anticipated.

When she got home that night Devon sat down and wrote out

a check payable to Jennie Moore for the sum of one thousand dollars.

Tim, having concluded his business, had left New York a few days before Devon returned from the coast. When she reached the house she had found a note thanking her for the hospitality and saying that he expected to be back in town early in December and would telephone her. They were now nearing the end of November, so she decided to wait till Tim's return to ask him for the divorce.

Kurt was a little miffed by the delay, which she found flattering, at the same time considering him obtuse not to understand that this was a matter which could not be tossed off in a letter.

Tim arrived in New York on Friday, and that evening, having unexpectedly bumped into an old pal, celebrated the reunion with one of his rare nights on the town. He had in fact remarked to the old pal, "My boy, in this binge you are witnessing a hen's tooth," and, his customary sobriety once established, proceeded to get crocked. They covered "21," the Stork, El Morocco, Bill's Gay Nineties, and somewhere along the way merged with splendid womanhood; but the next day, as soon as he could lift his head, along about noon, Tim telephoned to Devon. She asked him if he would come to tea on Sunday, as there was something important she wanted to talk about. Tim said he would prefer to drop in about six or six-thirty for a cocktail, as he was taking a friend to a professional football game at the Polo Grounds, and though he wanted to see Devon, it would be a little awkward dropping the friend immediately afterwards like a hot potato. Mrs. Wainwright, however, proved obstinate. "I'm sorry, dear," she said firmly, "but I have an early dinner engagement and six-thirty or even six will be too late. Except that the matter I want to talk to you about is very personal, I would ask you to bring your friend."

"No," said Tim hastily, "I wouldn't do that. You two would have nothing in common."

"Not even you, dear?" she asked sweetly. There had been further tussle, ending in the customary compromise; Tim agreed to come for tea.

On Sunday afternoon he sat in the Polo Grounds with his companion, a by no means unappealing number with eyes wide and wondering under a chestnut bang, but Tim was experiencing a slight irritation heretofore lacking in their relationship, a mellow alliance of forty-eight hours established the night of the celebration. The usually receptive vessel at his side seemed to grasp neither the intricacies of professional football nor the reason why he had to call on his wife immediately the game was over. "I thought you and she were busted up?" she said loudly.

"As I have never mentioned the matter to you, Larraine, I see no reason for you to think anything about it one way or the other," he replied with dignity.

Miss Collins pondered this a moment. "Look," she said, "maybe I'm no Dorothy Thompson for brains, but isn't your wife Devon Elliott?"

"Yes," said Tim, and pointed enthusiastically to the field; he was hating this conversation. "Look at that Mel Hein. God, what a beautiful play!"

"What's so beautiful about it?" Larraine asked coldly.

Tim laughed. "If you'd let me explain the game to you, you'd really enjoy it."

"I doubt it, but if your wife is Devon Elliott, she's got some hot boy friend. I read about it in the columns. I think it said a refugee or something, so I don't see any reason for you to knock yourself out for her." Tim was silent. "I thought we were going to have dinner," continued his companion.

"I told you, Larraine," and there was an ominous note of patience in his voice, "I have to leave you after the game, but I'll pick you up for dinner later if you'd like me to." *And what's more, Toots,* he added to himself, *it's our farewell banquet.*

There was a roar from the crowd as the Giants completed a brilliant surprise pass, and Tim himself leaned forward with a yell. As the team went into a huddle, the whistle blew for the end of the first half, and a voice came over the loud-speaker asking if Mr. Ivan Annenberg, of the *Daily News,* would please call the paper. A few minutes later came another request: would Mr. Annenberg's chauffeur come at once to the parking lot, Mr. Annenberg wished to get to his office.

"Gee," observed Larraine, "what do you suppose it is? A big murder maybe?"

A few minutes later the loud-speaker called again; a message for Colonel Donovan, would he please go to the nearest telephone booth, Washington calling. As two or three other names were called out, it occurred to Tim there must be something in the wind. It was not uncommon for a doctor to be summoned away from the ball game, but it was strange that all these public figures should be called for. Two minutes later he knew the reason. Just below the box in which he and Larraine were sitting were the newspapermen photographing the game. A small crate beside them held the *Journal-American's* carrier pigeons, who when released flew back to the office with rolls of film clipped to their legs to make the early editions. One of the reporters Tim had been observing with some amusement. He was a thickset carrot-topped bundle of energy who had been engaged in violent altercation over one of the newspaper phones in front of him most of the afternoon. He suddenly banged down the receiver and turned to his companions, his broad face white with excitement. He spoke with such intensity that even above the noise of the crowd and the blaring of the loud-speaker Tim could hear him. "Holy Jesus, it's come. The Japs have bombed Pearl Harbor and Manila. We're at war."

So that was the way of it. The act so many knew to be inevitable; the act so many sincerely believed would never happen. Tim felt an urgent need to get to Devon at once, to talk it over with her. He grabbed Larraine's arm. "Come on, kid, we're getting out of here."

"Why? Honestly, Tim, you're screwy. One minute you're nuts about the game, and the next you'd think the place was on fire."

Tim's glance rested on her, but she obviously didn't register on his brain. "There's a war on."

"Sure, but that's nothing new." Tim was pulling her to her feet.

"Didn't you hear that fellow? He just got it from his office, we're at war with Japan. I thought there was something fishy, all those guys being called away, but I'm damned if I expected this, right now, I mean."

Larraine, against her will and without understanding the need for rush, was hurried along the platform in back of the benches and down the stone ramp. At the foot of the ramp under the El a taxi waited, and Tim shoved her into it. He was intensely excited and wanted only to get to the house to see Devon, divesting himself of Miss Collins en route. When they reached Seventy-third and Park, only a block from where she lived, he stopped the taxi. "I'm terribly sorry, Larraine, to leave you like this, but it's almost time for my appointment anyway. You've been grand." With a sinking feeling he suddenly remembered their dinner date. "I'll—I'll call you later," but Miss Collins had had enough.

"Don't bother," she said with disgust. "If I never see you again, it's too soon. God deliver me," she added fervently, "from any more screwball scientists or married men." The last Tim saw of her was her Siberian-lynx back and little round heels tapping angrily down the street. On the way to the house he felt very strongly that he had behaved like a cad, but he didn't much care.

When he arrived Devon was waiting for him in simple black and pearls, and found she was so happy to hear his voice in the hall greeting Fairweather that her heart sank at the prospect of asking for the divorce. "Tim, how are you, darling?" She met him at the door of the drawing room. "You got here early, I'm so glad," but Tim dispensed with the amenities. He was so full of his knowledge that his slanting eyebrows seemed ready to take wing, and his crew cut sprang upward in vigor.

"Have you heard the news?" he asked as soon as he saw her. "Has it come over the radio yet?"

"What news? I haven't had the radio on all afternoon."

"It's the Japs, baby. They've bombed Pearl Harbor, Manila too, I believe, we're at war."

"Tim! Oh my God . . . you mean the whole country has to fight? Mobilization and everything?"

"That's what it looks like." He went over to the radio and turned the little knob; in a moment came the announcer's voice: ". . . and this dastardly act was a stab in the back, the blackest sort of treachery performed while Japan's diplomats were negotiating with our State Department. Tomorrow morning the President will go before the Congress to ask for a declaration of war between this country and Japan. Stay tuned to this station for further developments." The studio orchestra came up, and Tim lowered the volume. He and Devon stared at each other. "Well," she said, "it's dreadful, of course, but I'm damned if I see what's so treacherous about it. What else did we expect from a race like that? Diagrams? If you're going to attack, the idea is to catch the other party off base, isn't it? I only wish we'd thought of it first."

Tim looked grim. "I'm afraid you're right. When our losses come through, it may turn out that good will comes a little high."

"But how did they get there? What do you suppose our Navy was doing?"

"I imagine a good many citizens would like the answer to that one."

Within the next fifteen minutes they heard the whole shocking, sorry story, or as much of it as was given out at that time. Devon went to telephone to Matthew and Matilda in Williamstown, but was told there was an hour's delay on the line. She left the call in and came back to Tim and the radio, but it was not until something was said about the draft that the war was brought home to her. She turned to her husband in alarm, "Tim, what about you? You've been negotiating with the Army and Navy, haven't you? I suppose now they'll surely take you." Her thoughts flew to Kurt also, but she didn't worry about him. The status of foreigners was vague . . . unless there should be any talk of internment, but that was fantastic . . . her concern was for Tim.

"I only hope to God they will," he said. "The Army or the Navy, I don't care which. As I wrote you, I've been dickering for a commission. There's been about three thousand miles of red tape, but this ought to bring things to a head. I've got to be with Oscar tomorrow, but if I possibly can I'll get down to Washington Tuesday. Oh, by the way, what was it you wanted to talk to me about? I may be stuck there for some time. I don't know how long it will take me to see my man."

"Oh . . . well . . . this rather changes things."

Tim smiled at her. "Why, madam? Surely you and I are close enough to overcome a war."

"Oh, Tim . . . damn those Japs. This couldn't have come at a worse moment."

"That's probably the way they feel at Pearl Harbor too. Come on, out with it."

"Of course if you go in the Army, the whole thing's off, unless . . . well, maybe you'll want it yourself."

Tim's eyes were very level as he looked at her. "Want what myself?"

"I . . . I wanted to talk to you about a divorce."

"Oh . . . I see. Do you want a divorce?" She sat in miserable silence. "*Do* you?"

"Well, Tim, it doesn't seem to me that this kind of an arrangement is going to get us any place——"

"Where do we have to go?"

"I mean it isn't awfully satisfactory. We're neither married nor not married."

"Actually," said Tim slowly, "I've always thought of myself as very much married to you, but I admit you have a point. I started this separation business, and you were damn sweet about it. Your attitude the time I went away meant a lot to me, Devon."

"I wasn't trying to be sweet, Tim," she said honestly. "I know you're independent and awfully determined where your work is concerned. I realized you'd have gone with or without my blessing, so I thought it might as well be with. Besides . . . I wanted you to want to come back to me."

"And you don't any more?"

"Do you want to come home?"

"Darling, my situation hasn't changed much. I'm making progress, but I've still a long way to go on my job. The war makes it even more pressing, and I haven't any more money now than when I left you."

"I suppose you wouldn't consider coming back to the laboratory?"

"No, I'll never do that. I've had to fight too hard to reinstate myself as a serious scientist, and besides, my interest in the lab is dead for good."

"I was afraid of that, but that isn't why I'm talking about divorce, Tim. It isn't out of pique. You believe me, don't you?"

"Good God, Devon, of course I do."

"It's because . . . well, you see, there's someone who wants to marry me."

Tim felt a little cold, as though a draft had blown through the room. He glanced at the windows, but they were closed and an open fire crackled in the chimney. "Is it Fabri?" he said at last.

"Yes."

"Do you want to marry him?"

"I . . . I'm terribly in love with him, Tim. Believe me, it seems to me fantastic to sit here and talk to you this way, but the whole thing is so frightfully mixed up. I don't see how it's possible to love two men at once, but I seem to be doing it. Nothing in the world can ever change what I have for you, what we have together, but I can't pretend to you not to be in love with Kurt." As Tim said nothing, she hurried on, "Darling, please try to understand. Please be my friend."

"You bet," said Tim. "The complacent husband, the understanding pal. . . . Count on me, kid."

"Oh, please, dear——"

He got up and prowled around the room, his broad thin shoulders hunched a little forward, his hands thrust deep in his pockets. "There's one thing you haven't mentioned," he said. "Is this guy in love with you?"

To her embarrassment Devon felt herself blushing. Because deep in her heart she was uncertain of the answer, the question humiliated her. She replied without looking at Tim, "He asked me to marry him."

"Why?"

"Because he finds me attractive, I suppose. Why do men usually ask women? Why did you ask me?"

"Because I was crazy in love with you, because I wanted to spend my life with you, and because, whatever may happen between us, I expect to love you till I die."

She looked at him a little surprised. "For the past year you've been showing your passion in a very strange way, I must say. But what makes you think Kurt isn't as much in love with me as you were? Why else would he want to marry me?"

"Good God, don't be naïve. You're a tremendously wealthy woman, the Europeans' dream, only most of them aren't as lucky as your boy friend. If they get the moneybags, it's generally an old hag who owns them. Here he's got dough and looks and brains all in one bundle, not to mention a possible draft exemption. I don't suppose the man's a moron. Naturally he grabs at the chance."

"You're not fair, Tim. Why should you impute to Kurt the most unattractive motives? Another man might say the same thing about you. I wasn't anything like so rich maybe when we met, but I was doing all right, and I was seven years younger."

Tim turned on her. "Let me ask you something, and I want an honest answer. Did you ever at any time in our life together think for one split second that I was around you for any other reason except that I adored you?"

Devon, remembering how prickly and pigheaded Tim had been about money, how for the first years of their marriage they lived the life he could afford, how even when they moved to the large house he scrupulously paid fifty per cent of the bills up till the time he left the firm, and of how in the beginning he had given up the work he loved and where he was winning respect and advancement to be with her, broke down. "Of course not, you goon. I knew you loved me every instant of the day and night. I knew it in my bones."

"Ah! And what do your bones tell you about Mr. Fabri?"

"I think he loves me very much too. In a different way is all."

"But damn it, he isn't the person for you."

"How do you know that, Tim? You don't know anything about him."

"I know his reputation, Devon. I haven't been spying, but your affair isn't exactly a secret, and I had a natural curiosity as to whom my wife was running around with. The stories I've heard about Herr Fabri aren't reassuring. Besides, he's a very strange foreign mixture, isn't he? How can you be sure where his loyalties lie?"

"Oh, that's a ridiculous suspicion, Tim. You make him sound like agent 8734."

"Well, just the same . . . And if he is a chaser, Devon, that's bad news. Don't delude yourself, if that's the kind of guy he is, even your beautiful eyes aren't going to change him."

Devon longed to refute the charge, but there was enough truth in it to make rebuttal unconvincing. She changed her tack. "Kurt has his points, Tim. He doesn't drink, he isn't pompous, he's good at his job. There's a lot to be said for him."

"Does he make enough to keep himself in cigarettes?"

"He doesn't smoke."

"Don't be flippant."

"Sorry. But as a matter of fact, he's making a pretty good thing of his work. In a small way, of course."

Tim ruminated over this for a while. "Any mind?"

"A very good one," she said loyally, though she had never thought Kurt's mind incisive. "Of course he's no scholar, if that's what you mean, but I scarcely spend my time buried in rare old manuscripts, either."

Tim paced the length of the room and back. "He's Jewish, isn't he?"

"Half."

"You don't mind that?"

"Lord, no, Tim," said Devon impatiently. "I've never had that kind of prejudice, and you know it. One of the things that first attracted me to him was the very fact that he was Jewish. He . . . he was kind of a symbol of all that European wretchedness."

"Well," said Tim slowly, "I suppose that's the right way to feel, but you want to look out for snobbery at the other end of the line too. During the depression the new poor were worse snobs than the new rich had ever been. It sometimes works out that way in the case of the Jew, and basically it does him a gross disservice. What I'm trying to say is, don't be proud of your affection just because he is Jewish, and don't let sympathy for a race carry you away if the individual isn't the right fellow for you."

"I'm not, Tim. I think what you say is sound, but it isn't the case in this instance."

"You'll be faced with certain practical inconveniences, don't forget; clubs and places you can't get into."

Devon smiled. "I suppose that would feel funny, but after all, darling, I've never spent much time at Piping Rock, and the world is such that with my money we'll be welcome pretty much any place we'd want to go. I don't say this is admirable, but I think it's the way it is."

Tim tried another approach. "What does Jasper think about it?"

"I haven't spoken to him yet." Devon had said to Kurt she wanted to tell Jasper they were engaged, but so far she had been busily concocting ingenious excuses to herself for not breaking the news. "Jasper's close to me, certainly," she continued, "but somehow this seemed strictly our thing, yours and mine."

Tim looked at her with a small twinkle. "What's Jennie's opinion?"

"I haven't consulted her." After all, a check was scarcely a consultation. Their subsequent conversations she conveniently forgot.

"Devon, you put me in an awful spot. If you honestly want the divorce, I won't stand in your way, but I think marriage to this man would be fatal. You wouldn't know ten minutes' peace. I can't *not* give it to you, I suppose, but I can't *not* feel like a conspirator either. It—it seems to me I'm deliberately plotting against your happiness."

"Oh come, it isn't as bad as all that. I don't like to be tactless, dear, but Kurt and I often have extremely pleasant times together."

"Yeah, I can imagine when."

"Tim! That's uncalled-for."

"If you ask me, this whole damn situation is uncalled-for. If we both sit tight, we'll be able to work our way into the clear with our own setup. The war, as a matter of fact, may make a big difference to you and me. Through it, this thing I'm working on can come to quicker fruition."

"And then what? What guarantee have we that we can blend happily together again as if nothing had happened? There's been a lot in between, Tim. Besides, how do I know that in another couple of years you won't be wandering off in pursuit of some other damn vitamin?"

"What I'm working on," he said, speaking with great distinctness, "has to do with blood cells and nerves and plasma."

"O.K., so what's the difference? I'm still left flat, aren't I? What kind of an old age is that to look forward to?"

Tim exploded. "Ha! That's a good one! Are you counting on that European stallion as a prop for your declining years?"

"He's not; but, considering the two of you, I agree that it looks like Hobson's choice. If you want my true opinion, I don't think any man is so hot."

"You'll admit, however, you know some very strange men."

"Not at all. I know the usual men, and a pain-making bunch you are."

"Well, I'm sorry, madam. I'm doing the best I know how, but you're a grown woman and you ought to know your own mind. When do you want to start the divorce?"

Devon had not expected such a swift capitulation and was caught off balance. "Well . . . there . . . there's no wild rush; I . . . I'd naturally do it at your convenience, Tim. It seems to me we could wait until you see what your army status is."

"I'd appreciate that."

"After all, we're at war, divorce may not be so easy, judges going into the service, all things like that. . . . I suppose there'll be terrific troop movements . . . I may not be able to get to Reno right away."

"Shall we let it ride till I get back from Washington?"

"Let's."

"You don't mind if I talk to Jasper, do you?"

"Go ahead. Not that it will make any difference. I'll tell him about it in the morning."

"What's that nice family of yours going to think?"

Devon looked unhappy. "Aunt Mom and Uncle Pop. Well . . . I don't suppose they'll like it much. They think you're quite a fellow."

What the Stevenses were likely to think of Kurt, she could guess only too easily. Well, they might never see him. They were darlings, of course, but she couldn't pattern her life according to their tenets.

"In one way," she mused, "I suppose divorce will be easier for us than for other married couples. After all, we have no children; even the dogs I got after you'd gone away, so they won't be upset."

"I don't know about that," said Tim, hackles rising. "When I stayed here in October we got to be very chummy indeed. In fact I may say we had quite a close corporation. That Jot especially—he's my man."

"Really?" said Devon, and her voice was chilly. "He's very nice, of course, but I can't see that he's superior to Tittle and Trinket."

Tim shrugged. "Well, it's like people, I guess; some you like more than others. Matter of chemistry, no doubt."

"No doubt."

"Er . . . do the dogs like their new master?"

"They adore him." The answer was so glib that, though he couldn't tell quite why, it fanned a spark of hope in Tim's heart. It was unlikely, he felt, that anybody could adore anybody else quite that much, even the undiscriminating.

"Where are the boys, by the way? I'd like to see them."

"Of course." Devon rang for Fairweather, who when he appeared also announced that her call to Williamstown had come through. She went to condole with Matilda and Matthew over the outbreak of war, but she couldn't bring herself to tell them of the divorce. After all, she reasoned, why upset them when things were still so indefinite?

Tim stayed long enough for a brief roughhouse with the poodles, who gave flattering yelps of joy at seeing him again, and then took himself off, saying he would call Devon as soon as he got back from Washington, and that he'd have a talk with Jasper too.

But Jasper did not wait upon his coming. The next day he had Tim on the phone. "For God's sake, what is all this? Devon's just been in my office with a lot of eyewash about a divorce. I want to talk to you. Will you meet me in the Ritz bar for a drink this afternoon?"

"Well, Jasper, I'm pretty tied up, I've got to be in the lab all afternoon and——"

"To hell with that," cut in Jasper. "I'm busy too. Be there at six, will you?"

Tim hesitated. "O.K.," he said finally. "See you then."

When he got there Jasper was already seated at a corner table with a highball before him, reading in the *Evening Sun* the censored accounts of Pearl Harbor and the United States' declaration of war on Japan. The two men exchanged greetings, and Jasper remarked that the situation looked pretty grim.

"Yes," said Tim, "I'm afraid we're in for a long pull, but in one way it's a relief; it's certainly an eye-opener for the It Can't Happen Here boys. I bet a lot of mighty fancy explanations are being offered right this minute." Tim's remark was not entirely without malice. Jasper, though certain of America's eventual participation, had leaned slightly towards the Let-George-do-it-as-long-as-possible school, feeling that the interim would give us time to arm. He knew that an amicable dig was implied, but he laughed. "You're too hard on me, Timothy. I always knew we'd be in it, but I still think playing for time was a good idea."

"I can't go along with you, but to hell with it, the ball's been taken away from us, so we can relax and fight. I'm trying to get away to Washington tomorrow afternoon."

Jasper looked at him speculatively. "You going to enlist?"

"If I can get a commission. I want to find out what my status will be. I'm pretty excited about this new treatment Oscar Hogarth and I are working out. It looks good, and if we're able to experiment with some of the war casualties, we may make real strides, double up on our time, so to speak."

"I suppose you'd like to go overseas?"

"You're damn right, that's what I want to talk about in Washington. Explain to them what we have to offer, Oscar and I, and see where they think I'd be the most useful. Oscar of course is too old for active service."

Jasper looked thoughtful. "I see. Who are you going to speak to down there?"

"Dean in the Navy and Oglethorpe in the Army Medical Corps, if I can get to him."

"Oglethorpe's a good man. I don't know anything about Dean, but if you get stuck, let me know, I might be able to do something."

Tim looked at the older man gratefully. "Thanks, Jasper, that's swell of you," and he added hesitantly, "I didn't know how you'd feel about it. I'm glad you think it's a good idea."

"I don't. I don't mean about your being in the war; if you want to do that, more power to you if it's really for war's sake, but if you're joining up by way of deferring to this screwy divorce scheme I think you're making a terrible mistake. This mess of Devon's has me worried."

"You think it doesn't worry me?"

Jasper's gray eyes were perplexed. "Then why do you go away?"

"Listen, pal, don't blame Pearl Harbor on me. If my wife thinks she'd like to be rid of me and Uncle Sam can use me, it may be a handy coincidence, but it's none of my doing."

"I thought you loved her so much."

"I do, but what of it? She apparently wants something else. The little woman can be a very tough dame, Jasper. You ought to know that."

Jasper had a moment of discomfiture. His affair with Devon was water over the dam long since, but he had never been sure whether or not Tim knew of it. The remark might refer to those old times or he might simply be commenting on her business proclivities. But if it was the former, Tim was wrong. When Devon loved she could be very sweet and singularly untough. That he did know, and he still remembered how he had been surprised and touched when he found it out. "I'm not so sure about her toughness," he said gently, by his reminiscent tone possibly bolstering Tim's suspicions, and suddenly a little startled to have done so. Tim looked at him without rancor. Had Jasper and Devon . . . ? Well, not that it mattered now; in the old days he used to think they had been lovers, but that was before he came into the picture. He knew that for years Devon had been completely true to him; that is, until she met this professional two-timer.

"Do you know the guy?" he asked suddenly.

"You mean Fabri?"

"Yes."

"I've met him a few times," said Jasper, and his mouth closed in a thin, uncommunicative line.

"What do you think of him?"

"Son of a bitch."

Tim nodded. "I've never seen him, but I've gathered there's a kind of a fishy aroma about him."

"Crescendo, no doubt," and Jasper's tone betrayed his disgust.

"For Christ's sake," said Tim, and though he kept his voice down, there was a drive behind his words, "will you explain to me what that's all about? I gave Devon hell for that ad when I saw it in Washington, but she said you and Moreley had passed on it."

Jasper shrugged. "Listen, the ad I thought wasn't bad. . . . What the hell, it knocked your eye out, but I fought against it till I saw it."

"How do you mean, till you saw it?"

Jasper looked at him with surprise. "Why, just that. Fabri's by way of being a hot amateur photographer, and Devon wanted to put him on a professional footing, give him his first break. . . . Well, I'm usually against making business a family affair, I opposed it, but when I saw the picture I had to admit it was good."

Tim stiffened. "You mean he took that photograph?"

"Didn't Devon tell you?"

"No. No, she didn't. When I spoke to her about it in Washington she said it was some unknown she wanted to help along."

Jasper's mouth twitched ever so slightly. "Well, of course, strictly speaking, that was true. The man's not untalented, but he's a no-good customer, plus which he's a Jew."

"Half, Devon says."

"What's the difference?"

"If he was a right guy, none of it would make any difference. Except to me," Tim said a little sadly.

"And to me," said Jasper. "You forget, my lad, I've known Devon a long time. She's part of my life too; we're a family, you and she and I. And Mollie," he added hastily, not wishing to give the right impression a second time.

Tim's glance was quizzical. "Can't you talk to her?"

"What do you mean? I talked to her like a Dutch uncle this morning, but I didn't walk out on her last February. Knowing her temperament, what did you expect?"

"Well, what am I supposed to do now? She's apparently set on marrying Fabri, she won't believe he only wants her for her money."

"I told her the same thing," said Jasper, "but that's where we weren't too smart. She let fly with a spiel about had she no feminine attraction and it was only natural for a woman to want a man of her own. I pointed out that with Fabri it would be a fairly communal setup, and then she said I was a rotter, so I shut up."

The two men sipped their highballs in moody silence. Jasper took out his tobacco pouch and lovingly restoked his pipe. As he lighted a match he watched Tim closely over the little flame. "Supposing Devon could be talked out of the divorce, would you go back to her? She loves you, don't forget. I saw her that morning she got the letter you wrote from Louisiana telling her you weren't going to live with her any more, and she was sunk, all right. It isn't easy having the world shot from under you by the person you've always counted on."

Tim looked troubled and unhappy. "But damn it all, Jasper, I didn't intend anything of the kind. I explained it all to her, about the research work, how I'd be at it night and day, and it's turned out just as I said it would, only more so. And I told her how I felt about money. I wasn't going to live in that house and have her support me."

"You realize that the second reason is baloney?" Tim's face tightened with anger. "I mean as far as she's concerned," Jasper said. But Tim was piqued. Really it was a little tough; a man behaves with the greatest integrity, refusing to sponge on his wife, and his best friend announces that his attitude is baloney!

"I must say, Jasper," he said with dignity, "I'd counted on you to understand me."

"I do, my lad, I do. I'm only giving you Devon's angle, which, when you consider her wealth, is a perfectly sound one and doubtless why she brushes off our warnings about Fabri. Even if he is hungry for her money, when it comes to protecting her own financial interests she's alone in her class and she knows it."

"I wish she was as smart about protecting herself from heartache."

Jasper shrugged. "Who has everything?"

Tim moved his empty highball glass back and forth across the table. "It's a funny thing," he said softly. "In another woman that shrewdness about money might seem unattractive, but with Devon it just seems smart and kind of funny. You know, cute."

"I believe," said Jasper, "the general impression in the trade is not quite along those lines."

"I suppose not," Tim agreed, "but——."

Jasper chimed in, "On her, it's becoming."

The two men laughed. "Well, what about going back to her?" asked Jasper as he lightly knocked the bowl of his pipe against the thick rim of the ash tray. "I know she asked for the divorce, but she probably thought there was no alternative anyway. Offer her the choice of getting her husband back or marrying the town lay, and that's a different story."

Tim turned a dark, angry red. "How many people know about this little episode, do you suppose?"

Jasper, who privately thought that it must be obvious to any interested New Yorker, replied that he would be very surprised if anyone outside their immediate circle was aware of it. Tim, however, was slow to mollify. His old suspicion of Jasper surged up again, and as he thought of Fabri he remarked bitterly that his wife seemed to be fairly public property. Jasper was unmoved. He had reached the stage where he no longer considered sex a question of morals but of capability, and he felt that the whole thing, while pleasant, was overrated.

"Don't be that way, Tim," he said, and his gray eyes, while cynical, were not unkind. "Your wife, whom you walked out on of your own accord, has a lover. So what? In all these months have you taken no time off either?"

Tim stirred uncomfortably. "Well . . . it's not the same thing, and there's been damn little even of that. This affair of Devon's is so sort of established!"

"Would you like it better if she were promiscuous and had a whole string of men?"

"No, of course not, but she might have had the decency to mourn me a little. As far as I can gather, it started as soon as I was out of the house."

Jasper, who suspected this was true, tried appeasement. "That was merely the way things fell out. It might have been three months later that Nick Van Alston brought the man to the house. What's the difference?"

"Jesus," said Tim, "your viewpoint is fantastic. I suppose basically

I'm lucky that my wife is two-timing me with some Middle European bastard?"

"I think you are. Just because Devon has had the affair, your chances of getting her back are good. She and Fabri have already struck twelve. Where can they go from there?"

"What about the Affinity of the Spirit?" mocked Tim.

"What's that?"

Tim laughed and capitulated. "O.K., boss, perhaps you're right. We agreed to do nothing till I got back from Washington in any case. Let's relax. My private life will probably be taken out of my hands by the War Department anyhow."

☆   ☆   ☆

Kurt, when Devon told him, with deletions and added coloring, of her talk with Tim, urged her, as Tim suspected he would, to quick action. He had an obstinacy of temperament which drove him to the attainment even of what he didn't want, once he had decided he should have it. And he wanted Devon very much. He was in love with her and had persuaded himself that the advantages of matrimony in this special instance might well outweigh his prejudices.

But still she vacillated. It was next to impossible for her to bring herself to a decision; no matter how much she buried him out of sight, she could not rid herself of the thought of Tim or of her affection for him. He came to be for her a haunting presence entombed in an oubliette, and no matter how gay the music or how bright the light abovestairs, they could not obliterate the beloved prisoner. It was she who was held fast by her captive, but in the end the captive forced the key upon her and guided her to the door. For Tim returned successful from Washington.

He had been gone for about ten days, and when he got back he came to dine with her. It was three days before Christmas, and they sat cozily in the library by the fire, the poodles for once semisomnolent at their feet. Tim glanced at his wife and thought she looked very lovely in the lamplight; she was wearing his favorite gown, the one that was the color of faded violets; her hair was dark again and brushed softly back, showing her small ears and the lovely modeling of her brow. She leaned against her chair, her eyelids lowered, her marvelous lashes brushing her cheeks as she watched the poodles with an amused little smile.

Tim felt a constriction in his throat as he thought of their life together, the happiness they had had, the times gentle and tempestuous which had united them. He loved her then as much as he had loved her in all their seven years, and he wondered at the essential loneliness of man which drives him to fulfill his own destiny even when it was pregnant with danger, even when it was impersonal, as the pursuit of science must always be. It was self-preservation, he supposed, in the profoundest sense, the deep subconscious safeguarding the essence of man despite his own apathy, without his knowledge and without bravado. Nature was marvelously economical; once having produced a thinking creative human being, she was damn well going to see to it that he thought and created, and she generally succeeded unless he was shot to pieces. War was bitter waste, thought Tim, in that it deprived a man of the fruition of his powers; yet, since we all must die, that waste was negated, became in fact an affirmative force when we died fighting to preserve the free spirit.

They said death was silence, but that kind of death was a shout compared to the muted living of those who atrophied spiritually, unaware that their independence was being drained away from them. Trust Nature: if she had to lose her best men, she turned their loss to good effect; and Tim smiled when he thought that Devon should have greater appreciation of the lady, for his wife was Mother Nature's true offspring, abhorring waste. She ran her business efficiently and economically, and Tim had worked with her in that business, if not gladly, at least without coercion, for he loved Devon and he had succumbed willingly to the material security of the Devonshire House laboratories.

But that time was over; the ancient mistress had reasserted herself, and Tim, looking at the secure room and the wife he loved, knew that he would leave them. This then was the end. Without deliberation and without intention, simply through being themselves, with a little enmity perhaps on both sides, born of jealousy but without rancor, with pain and the tough-fibered humor which was an integral part of their relationship, life had brought them to the end of their way.

Tim spoke at last. "You see, my dearest, the rest of what I was telling you at dinner is that the lads in Washington are sold on the idea, and I'm actually going to get what I wanted but was afraid to hope for in a million years."

Devon gave him a companionable wink. "You mean they're willing to overlook your base association with the paint business and are forced to admit you're an excellent research man?"

"Well, that's about the size of it, I guess, but don't forget Oscar, he's the power. His name and my association with him bolstered me no end, so the upshot is I'm to be sent overseas."

There was a pause. "Right away, you mean?"

"Very soon, possibly within ten days. I'm not supposed to tell anybody, but the truth is they haven't told me anything definite yet. The Washington guys are still groggy and kind of gone at the knees, but they're anxious enough to have my kind of work proven on the ground. They want me to go to London first, see what they've been doing with their blitzed cases, compare notes and so on, and then, although this angle I dreamed up myself, I'd like to get to North Africa."

Devon looked at him in amazement. "Africa?"

"The British are there now, aren't they? That's quite a battle zone, and my guess is it may eventually be a hell of a lot more so. You can bet that Churchill and Beaverbrook and the British staff didn't arrive here today just because they wanted the trip. They're sure to discuss future campaigns. I'd like to get attached to a British outfit. Eventually we're bound to join up with them, and anything I will have proven can only help our own men. One of the great things about this treatment of ours, its strength and its weakness too perhaps, is its immediacy. If you can apply it to burns and wounds right off the bat, the chances for complete recovery without scars are upped about seventy per cent."

"But you're no surgeon, Tim. Is it necessary for you to be in the very front line?"

"Baby, it's extremely necessary for me to see how it works on all kinds of cases under all sorts of conditions. This war's the greatest laboratory in the world."

"It's nice to think it's useful for something," she murmured bitterly. "I'm sure the boys will be awfully pleased to know they're dying for science. Easier really than getting guinea pigs."

"Don't, Devon."

"You'll be in uniform, of course?"

"Madam, I think I am right in saying that you are at this moment addressing Major Wainwright. He may not know how to salute, but by God, he's going to have a uniform that will knock your eye out."

"Darling, you got the commission!" Devon's face was alight with enthusiasm. "Why didn't you tell me sooner, you great oaf?"

"It isn't signed, sealed, and delivered yet, but it looks good. I've got to go down to Washington the day after Christmas for the final arrangements."

"And then after that, you'll be going. . . . Oh, Tim!" Devon turned very white and suddenly felt sick in the pit of her stomach. Tim too was shaken, not with the fear that swept her, but with a sense of his loss, the realization of the enormous changes his own life would undergo.

"Well, after all, darling"—he stopped to clear his throat; unexpectedly several frogs seemed to have taken up residence there—"after all, if we act too grim about this, we aren't being very honest, are we? Things had pretty well split for you and me anyway. My leaving ought to make it a lot easier. I . . . we . . . well, we might as well face this divorce business. I told you what I feel about the man, but I know how you feel too, and I can be mistaken, possibly you'll be very right for each other."

"Thank you, dear, I hope so. I can't pretend to feel any wild ecstasy, but I guess once you're past eighteen, wild ecstasy doesn't come easy."

"I guess not," he said, but they both silently thought of the welling happiness they had known together. "How do you feel about a New York divorce, Devon?"

"Awful. I couldn't put either of us through that, Tim."

"The idea is grimy, isn't it? Still, it's quick. The only thing is my sailing date. We'd better call Henry in on this, or have you already spoken to him?"

"No, I haven't. He was in the office yesterday, we were signing some new contracts, but I didn't get around to it. I imagine he'll advise Reno. If the divorce is uncontested, I suppose it can go through even if you're out of the country?"

"Sure. He can cook up a statement for me full of legal jargon whereby I renounce my dower rights or whatever the hell I have to do, and it's in the bag." They smiled at each other, but the smiles were a bit crooked. "Do you mind my saying something, madam?"

"Of course not."

"Well . . . er . . . it's a little delicate, but don't let that son of a bitch get any liens on your money."

"On my money?" There was such shock in Devon's voice that Tim laughed with relief.

"I'm sure you won't, darling, but it's just a friendly warning. You have unpredictable fits of openhandedness, and I didn't want him to catch you unawares someday."

"Good God, Tim, you don't have to worry about that. I might make a little settlement on him, you know, for his pride. Maybe $25,000, certainly no more, and I'd never let him have any stock or anything. He can stick to his leather business. A man ought to have something to do, and I certainly wouldn't want him hanging around the house all day," and she thought to herself, *Nor around women either; he damn well better have a job*. Tim's eyes twinkled. He had an inkling that his successor was not in for a life of un-adulterated tranquillity.

"It's your idea," he asked with interest, "that a substantial financial settlement from his wife is likely to bolster a man's pride?"

Devon moved uncomfortably. "Well, the problem's a very difficult one. He may object, of course; he's quite proud about things you wouldn't suspect. I mean Americans always assume Europeans are going to live off them—they always have—but Kurt likes to hold up his end of things, only he can't very well do it on his present income. There'd have to be a few mild subsidies, but as long as he's a luxury I can afford, I expect to pay for him."

"I see." They looked at each other and smiled, tentatively, politely, like strangers. "Well, we seem to have come to the parting of the ways, Mrs. W., but for my money you're still a winsome wench. By the way, when will you be going to Reno?"

Devon shivered. "I don't know. It's a repellent idea, isn't it? Remember that awful scene in *The Women?* It smelled of female, didn't it? And why do you have to establish a residence for six weeks? That's just the Chamber of Commerce making hay."

"Why don't you make hay too? Why not start a salon?"

Devon looked at him in surprise. "Tim, are you on the level?"

"Why not?"

Her mouth hung open for a moment. "Well, I . . . Well, I don't know but what it isn't a wonderful idea! All those women out there with nothing else to do . . . we could have local advertising . . . 'Don't eat your heart out for these six weeks, take the Devonshire House Concentrated Beauty Course. Makes an old husband sorry he lost you and a new one easy to get.' . . . Tim, it's splendid. You're a genius, baby."

Tim looked modest. "Oh, it's nothing."

"Gee, I wonder if six weeks will be enough."

"With your organizing capacity? It's a pipe."

"I wonder what Jasper will think of it, and Moreley. Maybe I ought to take him out with me; he might get some very good ideas for copy, being on the spot. We probably ought to plug the nourishing cream, I expect Reno's very dry. Deserts."

Tim repressed a smile. "It should be a cinch," he said. "Henry Barlow will be able to draw up the corporation papers along with the divorce decree."

He was teasing Devon, but actually he didn't see why it might not be a sound enough idea, even if the salon failed, it could do her no great financial damage, and organizing it would have helped her through a bad time. "There's only one thing that worries me a bit. I know how you plunge into a new venture; twelve feet over your head. Take it easy, will you, and watch your health a little? You don't have to knock yourself unconscious to make a success, you know."

"I'll be all right, never fear."

A silence fell between them, a new self-consciousness enveloped them both. "Well," said Tim finally, "I guess that's that."

"Look, Tim," and Devon spoke with unaccustomed diffidence. "It's a little difficult because of the things we've just said about it, but if you are short of money, you probably have to get all kinds of equipment; I'd think it terribly unfriendly if you didn't let me help."

Tim hesitated. "You're a grand person, Devon; there's nobody who can equal you, no place, ever. I don't need anything for myself —I'm all right, I promise—but if you'd like to help a great man, someone whose life is an endless fight against poverty, I wish you'd think about Oscar Hogarth. He's working at the Rockefeller Institute, but the salary's not much, and right now he's terribly worried. He's afraid his daughter's got t.b. and they want to get her out of the city. If you're willing to relieve the pressure a little, you'd be doing an awfully worth-while thing."

"If that's what you'd like, Tim, of course I will."

"Oh, that's fine, that's fine, Devon. He wouldn't take it for himself, but he's crazy about his kid; it's two-edged—not only that she's his daughter, but he says she's got an unusual bent for research work, she's got the patience and knowledge and skill. It's breaking his heart to think that her whole life may be wrecked for lack of money. From what he knows himself and from what the doctors tell him, he thinks there's a good chance of a total cure if she can get into the right surroundings and get the right treatments at once."

"I'll make out a check now. Tell me how much."

"No, don't do that, let me talk to him first. He's got great pride, but I think he's devoted to me and I can get around him by telling him it'll be a big load off my mind if I know he's not worrying but concentrating on the old pill factory."

"You're kind as they come, Timothy. You're a toughy all right, but you're pretty sweet."

Tim looked a little embarrassed. He reached into his pocket and pulled out a small package from Cartier wrapped in dark blue Christmas paper. "Darling, this isn't very much, but it's something from me for Christmas morning. And don't tell me I shouldn't have done it," he added quickly as she opened her mouth to speak. "I've gotten in the habit of giving you Christmas presents, and being a selfish man I see no reason for depriving myself of my pleasures. This year, I regret to say, the pleasure is small; I mean that in ratio to the gift, not to my sentiments."

She was deeply touched. "Oh, Tim . . . after all, it's——"

"I know, the thought that counts," he said gravely.

"Where will you be spending Christmas, darling?" She had suggested to Kurt that perhaps she might see Tim Christmas Eve or Christmas night, but his reaction had been so unpleasant that she had not insisted. After all, he was probably right; if she and Tim were going to break, they'd better break; but her heart was heavy.

"Don't worry about me," Tim said, "I'll be run fair ragged with good cheer. I'm going out to Nutley to spend Christmas Eve with Jasper and Mollie and the kids; I'll be there overnight and most of the day, and I'm cadging more turkey from Oscar and his family later on."

"Jasper and Mollie are dining here Christmas night."

"I know."

"I . . . I don't suppose you'd like to come over to the plant for the annual party?"

Every year for the past six years, since they had moved into the big new laboratories on Long Island, Devon had given a party Christmas Eve afternoon for the some five hundred employees in the plant. The girls from the New York salon were always invited and were never able to come, as that day was one of the busiest in the entire year, what with seventy-five per cent of New York buying last-minute and conscience presents. The exquisitely packaged Devonshire House products, the fragile lingerie, the glittering costume jewelry were expensive, but they were gilt-edged, and more than one customer had been heard to murmur venomously that their nearest and dearest could have no beef coming when she opened *that,* for God's sake.

Tim hesitated; the parties were fun as a rule, with a great deal of good cheer and everybody mildly tight, but he finally decided against it. Seeing all the people he had worked with so many years would only make the wrench harder; he and Devon would have to pretend a happiness they once had in such full measure, and besides, as Tim said, "I think it would be easier for David Ullman if I wasn't there. It'll be his first Christmas party and a bit nicer if the old boss isn't around."

"I'm sure he wouldn't feel that, darling, considering he cwes the job to you, but it's up to you to decide, of course." She was wondering whether she would ask Kurt to go with her. If she didn't, he might feel hurt and jealous of the business, but if he went he would be out of place, she would be self-conscious for him, and the whole laboratory would be buzzing with gossip. Love, she decided, between two people who were forever hurting each other's feelings by being themselves, might be passionate and exhilarating; it was also a damn nuisance.

"Tim, if I don't see you before you go, call me from Washington, will you? I'll be terribly anxious to know about the commission and everything."

"You bet. I'll keep the lines open so you can hear them clap me on the shoulder with a sword or whatever they do."

"You have delusions of grandeur, my pet. Changing you into a major is feat enough without trying to make Sir Galahad out of you."

They smiled and were silent again. "I suppose you'll be leaving for Reno soon?"

"I suppose so. Right after the first of the year probably, especially if Jasper likes the new salon idea."

"And I expect Mr. Fabri is anxious to take over."

Devon said nothing. Tim was standing very close to her, the lovely familiar fragrance of Felicity in his nostrils. He sniffed. "I'm glad you wore that tonight; maybe I'll take a bottle with me. Remind me of my married life. . . . Ought to cause quite a sensation in Tobruk if I ever get there. Well . . . I'll be seeing you again before I go, of course, but . . . watch out for yourself in the clinches, will you, madam?"

"Tim, take care of *your*self. Don't go barging into the cannon's mouth or hurling yourself at any tanks. Think how the men depend on you! They'll get all smashed up and they'll need you to be all in one piece with your pills and little bottle of newskin ready to put them together again." The tears were very near now. "Don't get malaria or anything, and above all, don't get brave. Just stay with the Italians, darling."

"Come here." Tim's voice was husky. He caught her in his arms and kissed her with a fierce hurting passion that would obliterate Kurt, the forces that drove them apart, and their separate unknown destinies. When he released her he turned and went quickly away without looking back.

PART SIX

It was shortly after the first of the year when, somewhat to her surprise, Devon found herself consulting Kurt about a business matter. It had nothing to do with policy, but it was important to her, and she considered herself lucky that he was in a position to advise her, or rather to corroborate her own judgment.

Minerva Ritchie, who had managed the salon for her for nine years, was leaving. "She finds it too much for her powers, poor thing," Devon had observed to Kurt. "Those ulcers, I fancy." As Minerva had never had them, that was not the case, but she came from a small town in upper New York state and realized to her amazement that she wanted to go back to it. There she owned the comfortable shabby old house that had been her parents', there she had two brothers, they were both married, and their wives had never heard of the more esoteric muscle oils and believed that the way to clean your face was by washing it with soap and water. On holidays she gave their children presents and was greeted with whoops of joy and was known to half the town as the Ritchie kids' aunt Min, while in New York she lived in a small, tastefully furnished flat where she had a complete dinner set of six of everything, but she had never needed more than four, and generally only one, for there were only a handful of people who didn't call her Miss Ritchie, and when she saw them it was generally in their own houses when they were having a quiet dinner, just the family and an extra woman didn't matter.

One of the few people she would miss and who would miss her was Hedwig Lindstrom, of the Swedish Room at the salon, the authority on health foods. The two women were close friends, and their separation would mean a loss to both of them.

Devon, when Minerva told her she wanted to leave and go back home, had considered her reasoning fantastic and her action disloyal. She thought Minerva was trying to hold her up, and it was quite a time before she could bring herself to accept the facts: that Minerva was not going to either of her rivals, considered that she had been fairly paid all these years, but was lonely, fed to the teeth with the cosmetic industry, and wished to quit it cold.

Devon had been casting around trying to find someone to replace her when manna fell from heaven in the person of the pretty and capable Maria Sellner. Before the war Maria, who was a young Viennese, had been running Bouchère's famous salon in Paris and had been known throughout the trade as an extremely able woman. Devon had at that time made overtures to her, but Maria liked her job at Bouchère's and saw no reason to leave. Besides, though raising the ante on her salary, Devonshire House had not exactly gone overboard.

Maria stayed in Paris for more than a year after the German occupation and had finally had to leave France under particularly grueling circumstances. She was seriously ill at a time when the Nazis discovered that they had twice arrested her father in Vienna for anti-Nazi activities. The first time they had released him, for he was a man of considerable standing, but the second time, while they were waiting to bring him before a firing squad, he had escaped. They had reason to believe he had received help from agents in other countries and that the most effective ones were in France, so that Maria, though too ill at the time to have been of any assistance, was, as his daughter, in a dangerously suspect position. She had been smuggled into Spain and after undergoing tremendous hardship had sailed for America on a small Portuguese freighter. The result of these experiences was a breakdown, and she had been living quietly in the country until a few weeks ago, when she came to New York to look for work. Devon heard of her, and with Minerva leaving she seemed like the perfect solution to her problem. "Besides," as Devon said happily to Kurt, "Arden and Rubinstein will be livid to think I've nabbed her." She was just now on the verge of definitely engaging Maria when she happened to ask him if by any chance he had known her in the old days in Europe.

"But my darling, yes. The Sellners are well known in Vienna. My parents knew her family quite well."

"And what about you young people?" teased Devon, her eyes dark and glinting through her lashes.

Kurt laughed. "No, it is not what you think, I knew her like that, what you call casually. We have dined sometimes together with friends."

"And I daresay ridden in the Prater behind a spanking team done up in Grandpop's famous harnesses, no?"

"That too, perhaps, but there was never anything more," and indeed this was true if you did not consider a spring evening in a small country inn when they were both very young, but that was more spring than love and they had returned to Vienna at two in the morning and retired to the bosoms of their respective families, and since there had been no consequences, it didn't count.

Kurt thought it unnecessary to inform Devon that he had seen Miss Sellner several times since she had been in this country. To be sure, it was more a case of refugees' reunion, and there were always other Europeans around, and even the couple of times there weren't, the friend of his youth had seemed disinclined to dalliance; but why bring it up? It would necessitate wearisome explanations, doubtless he would not be fully believed, and if her suspicions were aroused, Devon might not give Maria the job. He must warn Maria not to say anything, either. Kurt wished Maria well for both their sakes. She needed money, and if she were not able to earn it, he would be a natural person to turn to, and although his business was rolling nicely he could not command a great deal of cash. What he had he wanted to spend on himself and Devon. Her appetite alone was enough to give a man pause. His bride-to-be had certainly never learned to read the menu from the right. Fortunately Devon seemed favorably impressed with Maria and appeared to be counting a good deal on his opinion.

"Shall I take a chance on her, angel?" she asked. She had already made up her mind to do so, but Kurt was behaving like a darling recently, spending every evening with her, and she wanted to make him feel he influenced her.

"I think you should," he said firmly. "You will have relief from the routine work, and anyway what can go wrong when you are there?"

"But my honey love, you forget that I will not be there for at least six weeks. I am heeding the call of the eloquent West."

"Darling, should I come out to Reno, do you think? Perhaps it is not good for your reputation."

Devon's eyes twinkled. "It's a little late to be worrying about my reputation, wouldn't you say? I'd love you to come, baby, but don't if you don't want to. Did I tell you, by the way, Jasper thinks the idea of a Reno salon is a good one, so I will be terribly busy."

"You will go soon, you promise? I am beginning to feel most domestic."

Devon was very happy. She felt Kurt's attitude really was changing. Supposing he wasn't the man Tim was? He was another one, and she loved him. It was foolish to go through life expecting everyone to be just the same. "I'll get your Miss Sellner installed, darling, and as soon as I'm sure she knows the ropes, I'll be off."

A few days after this conversation Devon engaged Maria and introduced her to the salon. The impression was felicitous. Though her manner was gentle, one sensed an air of authority. Also she was extremely pretty, with soft chestnut hair which she parted in the middle and wore in a chignon at the nape of her neck. She had brown eyes and a lovely skin and used Pear Blossom No. 1, the most discreet of the Devonshire House lipsticks.

Jasper was quite smitten and emitted a long, low whistle when she had left the room. "And you tell me she can cook too?" he asked Devon.

She laughed. "She's capable and knows the job, if that's what you mean."

Even Moreley, whose eulogies on women were generally confined to the improbable creatures bedecking his advertisements, was moved to remark in perfect seriousness that "for a weal woman" she was "wemarkably attwactive." The only slightly sour note was struck by Miss Hedwig, who held for Minerva a twisted but stubborn loyalty, and though she knew that her friend had left of her own accord, she nurtured against the successor an obscure resentment.

It seemed, however, that Miss Sellner had revived in Moreley's mind an inspiration which had come to him a few days after Pearl Harbor. "This war," he said to Devon and Jasper, "is going to mean upwooting, upwooting for millions." Devon, thinking of Tim, acknowledged that this was so. "And what happens when people are upwooted? They are homesick." Jasper said gravely that the point was irrefutable. "And when you are far away," continued the psychologist, "what single thing weminds you of home more than anything else? An odor, a fwagwance, am I not wight?"

Devon and Jasper both nodded, and in spite of herself Devon found her nose wrinkling slightly as she thought of the tar roads in Williamstown and the way they smelled hot and clean in the strong spring sunshine. "That being so, what do you think of this idea?" and Moreley's pale eyes gleamed like enthusiastic oysters. "We cweate odors and put them out in small cwushable vials, but instead of being ordinawy flower or synthetic scents, they are homey smells: baking bwead, the scent of tomato plants, pweserves—pweserves would be wonderful for the boys in Iceland and Guadalcanal—or the way a barn smells, warm and milky. Washington is bound to be cwowded soon with hundweds of girl stenogwaphers, all cooped in little wooms; think what it would mean to them to have a homelike atmosphere when their young man comes to call. They just cwush this little vial and for half an hour it's as if they were living in a weal place, not in a suitcase. Burning leaves, that's another good one, or the fine smell of leather pwehaps; lots of people like that," he added, magnanimously tossing a rose on the boss's romance.

Jasper stared at Moreley incredulously and turned to Devon. "What do you think of it?"

Devon, who had been trying to keep a straight face, burst into delighted laughter. "I think it's the damnedest thing I ever heard of, and I think it might be a brilliant idea if we could do it cheaply enough. I can just smell it, six delicious flavors in every kit bag!"

Moreley's face glowed like an extolled cherub. "Can you weally?" he cried. "I hope, I do hope that Ullman will be able to bwing it to pwacticality."

Devon promised she would consult her chemist that very day. "I'm just trying to think what Tim would like, I'm getting together an outfit for him."

"Pipe smoke for lonely wives might be an idea," said Jasper derisively.

"We must send the first vial to Mollie, dear," replied Devon sweetly. "But I'm trying to remember what domestic smells appeal to Tim particularly. The only one I can think of at the moment is fertilizer. There's a special kind he always orders for the asparagus bed at the farm, and he gets an absolutely beatific expression on his face when he spreads it around."

When he departed for the wars, Tim sailed with enough kits, trench coats, and accessories from Abercrombie & Fitch to equip a regiment, but Moreley's homey atmospheres were not among them. Though he was deeply touched by Devon's generosity and flights of imagination, some of the enclosures could only have been conceived by a loving woman, a stranger to life in the field, Tim was obliged to unburden himself of many of them before landing.

Because he sailed with a convoy and the time and place of departure were military secrets, Devon could not see him off, but he telephoned her just before he left for the pier, and as she sobbed her farewell it was brought home to her afresh that joy is fleeting and the only full measure we can count on is rue.

Maria rapidly hit her stride, and when she had been at the salon for two weeks Devon realized that in the orderly and hard-working little Viennese she had indeed found a prize. She went off to Reno, secure in the knowledge that with Maria to keep an eye on the personnel and Jasper pursuing his usual function of dynamo the business would roll smoothly.

She was right as regards New York; there all went well, but in Reno the course of true love hit a corduroy detour, which she recounted with some gusto in a letter to Jennie. She wrote in reply to one from her beautiful friend, in which Jennie told her that her own divorce from Ollie Newcomb was at last under way, Ollie after three years having done the decent thing and allowed himself to be caught in a West Side hotel with a lady referred to as Unknown. "Though of course," said Jennie in her letter, "it was Boo Boo Miles, who's been living with him for the past eight months."

In fact, dear, I might say of Boo Boo and Carla, her predecessor, that never have so few been known so much by so many. Naturally I had already signed the paper guaranteeing Ollie his allowance for the next five years. They call it allowance instead of alimony when the woman pays. Men have delicate sensibilities, don't you think? But at least Dick has finally agreed to holy matrimony when the decree is final, though the poor lamb was in a frightful sweat over the money situation, which he found more embarrassing than ever, due to the complications with Ollie, but we seem to have devised a working plan—I think he'll become a producer. This for some reason sounds richer than scenic designer; I can't think why, considering that producers are forever in need of backing, but I guess backing is grander than being just plain broke. Anyway, my duck, it looks as though we'd be able to plan a double wedding if the unlikely desire should seize us.

JEN DARLING (Devon wrote in reply):
The news about you and Dick is simply grand and I'm elated. Will you do a testimonial saying you hooked him because of your smooth white hands which you keep bridal-soft by using Devonshire House Hand Lotion?

I could spit when I think of that Ollie, in fact when I think of almost any man, especially the ones who are likely to cross our paths, from which fretful comment you will have guessed that Mr. Fabri and I have once more had the merest smitch of a run-in. Poor beast, this time I admit it was not entirely his fault. I had been here about ten days when, sure enough, he arrived, as he said he would. I don't mind saying I was extremely touched and felt quite tearful and tender for a good twenty-four hours, but lovely as it is one has only so much time for moonshine. After that I had to get on with the salon. In fact, they had already put the wrong color paint in the treatment rooms, and they all had to be done over.

Moreley arrives tomorrow with layouts and copy for the local papers, and I believe he has a hideous plan afoot whereby the day the salon opens I am to give facials myself, charge a hundred dollars apiece, and turn the money over to the Red Cross. I would far rather write them a check and be free of it, but Moreley claims the publicity will be invaluable, and he may be right, as fortunately a good many well-known women are currently divorcing: Lillian Carmichael and Mrs. Grant Seton (how she's stood Seton all *these* years, I'll never know), and the people's idol, Julia Manning. When I got my first look at Miss M., my respect for Hollywood cameramen leaped into the upper brackets.

But anyway, darling, as you can see, I've been on a merry-go-round, and Kurt, poor angel, was in a rather dangling position. I like to think I was the epitome of allure and womanly tenderness in the evening, and I think maybe I was, for he stuck it out a week. But then he began to get fractious, and I could see it was dull for him having me up to my ears in work all the time, so I told him he'd better go back to town, which he finally did, though not without a few ill-humored remarks about women in business. It didn't seem tactful to point out that this business would keep him very pleasantly cushioned for what I sincerely hope will be the rest of his life, because I am really mad in love with him.

With Kurt away, the rest is silence, for he is a wretched correspondent, nor do I, to be honest, have much time for writing him, so we have to depend on Mr. Bell. He seems to be on the town every evening, but I am careful not to inquire into it, because I don't want him to feel that the final tail feathers of Personal Freedom are disappearing round the bend. I wish, though, if you feel like it, you and Dick would take him out with you from time to time. I ought to be home in between three and four weeks myself; I suppose we will take the plunge shortly afterwards. God help us both.

I am glad, darling, that *The Mountain Top* is still packing them in. Isn't it nice Dick has a little piece of it! He's practically a producer already. My love to you always.

DEVON.

The day the divorce was granted she sent a cable to Tim:

WE ARE DIVORCED ON PAPER. THE REST OF MY LIFE I SHALL BE A BIGAMIST. FOR YOU ARE MY FIRST AND MY EVERLASTING HUSBAND.

But actually it was nearer six weeks before she was home again, because, though Henry Barlow saw to it that the divorce came through on schedule, complications necessitating a delay in the opening of the salon kept Devon in Reno. She stormed and fretted, but the war involved a shortage of both labor and materials, and in her daily telephone conversations with Jasper he persuaded her that as long as she was on the spot she would be wise to see it through.

She explained to Kurt that the delay in no way reflected on her love for him, and since he now knew that marriage was a certainty he at first accepted the postponement amiably enough. His very acquiescence, however, threw doubt into Devon's mind. Feeling so insecure with him, she at once suspected that he did not want to marry her.

Kurt, on his side thinking matters over, would come to the conclusion that if she loved him as she said she did, it was certainly odd of her to prolong her stay in Reno, salon or no salon. Perhaps it was a trumped-up excuse to delay the wedding, eventually to cancel it altogether. Such conscience as he had would trouble him, and, suddenly uneasy lest he had muffed his chance at the life which had come to seem to him highly desirable, he would telephone Devon and importune her to such an extent that she was for the first time in the delicious position of having him want her more urgently than she wanted him. Though harassed, she savored it to the full.

General relief prevailed among themselves and their friends when she arrived back in New York and they were able to come to a clearer understanding and set a date for the wedding.

They were nearing the middle of March, and Devon and Kurt decided they would be married in early April. "It seems more springlike," said Devon; besides, it gave Kurt time to finish up an order for Georg Jensen, and she could sandwich in a little work at the office. Their plan was to honeymoon in Mexico. She signed a pledge that she would give three days to the salon in Mexico City and the rest of the time would be devoted to being Mrs. Fabri.

Kurt spent considerable time turning this over on his tongue. Lying in bed, he would murmur to imaginary acquaintances crowding around, "Of course, you know my wife, Mrs. Fabri, Mrs. Kurt Fabri," and he would kiss Devon lightly and observe complacently,

"It is sounding very well," and she would smile, "But surely, darling, you must have heard it before. Wasn't that your mother's name?"

"No," he said, "my father's name was Alexander, but I think that has not the same puritan simplicity." And Devon would laugh, for the idea of Kurt as a puritan was piquant.

She had returned to New York on a Wednesday and the following week end took a house party to the country. The men all went back to town Sunday, but as Jennie had not arrived till late Saturday night, having driven out after the theater, and as it was lovely weather, Devon, Estelle, Claire Dangerfield, and she decided they would stay over and only drive back in time for her to get to the theater for the Monday-night performance.

Their gentlemen kidded them unmercifully, saying that as far as New York they would hear the crunching sounds as the ladies bit into the backs of their dearest friends and took their bones apart and that furthermore they would die of ennui. "Most females can resort to bridge," crowed George Lowery, "but you career wenches lead narrow lives, ignorant of vital social activities."

"Poor creatures," said Kent Davies, lugubriously, "they will be reduced to talking to each other." Mr. Davies was the love interest in Claire's life. Their bond was close, but he had not yet been able to sever the equally close ties binding him to a wife acquired some nine years before.

He, Kurt, Dick Hadley, and George drove away making low vaudeville gestures out of the car windows, such as weeping copiously into their handkerchiefs and wringing out the imaginary tears as they thought of the sad plight of their women, but their dire prophecies were not to be fulfilled.

As the ladies sat around the fire after Sunday supper, sipping their coffee and brandy, they looked quite content with life and with each other.

"There is undeniably something to be said for no men in small doses," said Jennie with a contented sigh. She had opened her vanity case and was peering closely at her perfect skin. "M-m-m, I'm badly in need of a good creaming, and tonight's my chance. I shall slather it on."

The unctuous sound of the "slather" alarmed Devon. As an avid businesswoman she was delighted to have Jennie use her products lavishly, as an immaculate housekeeper she feared for her shell-pink linen sheets. "Darling," she said hastily, "I'm so glad you mentioned it. I'll have Louise put those slips over your sheets and pillow cases the way she does on my bed when I smear myself. It's not a very fetching sight, I admit, but there's got to be time out for repairs once in a while during romance or the old allure begins to crack under the strain. By the way, I'm having those slips made up to sell in the salons, don't you think it's a good idea?"

"Swell," said Claire. "They don't happen to be flowered on a striped ground, do they?"

"No, they're just soft toweling in pastel colors, why?"

"I thought not." Claire's tone was gloomy. "My boss, Mary Mann McCormick, is making my life hell because she feels *surely* there must be such a fabric in the wholesale market. I've looked at stripes till I think I'm peering through prison bars, but none of them sprout camellias, which is what the old girl wants. Oh well, if she asks me why I'm not in the shop tomorrow I'll tell her I spent the day hunting. By the way," and Claire turned to Estelle, "how do you get out of showing up at the foundry?"

"Ah ha," Estelle chuckled triumphantly, "I've got a week's holiday coming to me, my lass, and this is it. Now that we're living in Stamford, George says I should take time out in the spring to learn about hot frames and such. He assures me it's my patriotic duty anyway. He feels very strongly about the war even if he is overage and says I should be prepared to take over. He and another chap are training for something mysterious, National Guard, I believe he said—that's the class at the armory he had to get into town for tonight. It was sweet of you, Devon, to let him stay at your house."

"Nonsense," said Devon, "he's more than welcome. I suppose," she added thoughtfully, "as time goes on there's going to be an awful dearth of men. We've already lost two or three boys in our shipping department, and when I got back from Reno Jasper announced the gladsome tiding that our star powder mixer is off to the wars. All I need is to have Ullman walk out."

"Don't beef, baby," said Jennie glumly. "Most of the men in your laboratory are over the draft age, aren't they, and in a pinch you could probably make do with women temporarily. How would you like to be in the good old theater, where you have a very tasty choice of leading men: anything under eighteen or over sixty is yours for the casting."

Claire kicked off her platform soles and stretched her toes toward the fire. "You know," she said, puckering her little monkey face into a grimace, "if this war goes on for long, everybody's world is going to be topsy-turvy. Not just ours."

"What do you mean, ours?" asked Estelle.

"Well, do you realize that none of us is a normal woman?"

Devon raised her eyebrows. "Tootsie, you may be one of Nature's mistakes, but I'll thank you to leave my baser nature out of this. I admit it's active, but it runs in orthodox channels. Great, strong men are what I crave, and old slippers don't interest me."

Claire laughed, but she said impatiently, "That's not what I mean. Here we are four women, and each of us is not only self-supporting but is taking care of somebody else besides. We are breadwinners, kids, and in the case of you and Jennie, Devon, it's ice cream and cake as well."

"Well," said Estelle slowly, "do you think that's so awfully unusual, especially in America?"

"West of the Hudson River it is, until you hit Hollywood, of course, where all the women are richer than the men. But don't you see, that's my point." Claire was warming to her theme. "With the war on, more and more women will be replacing men. They'll be in jobs where they make good, and they'll be earning good salaries."

"And the bosses will kick them right out when the men come back," said Devon.

"Why?" asked Estelle. "If they're competent, that would be grossly unfair."

Claire snorted, "Since when has that made any difference to a man?"

"Would you fire a good worker, Devon, just because she was a woman, even if she were holding a job a man could do?" Estelle's voice held a challenge.

"No, I wouldn't," said Devon flatly. "But I'm shrewder than many businessmen."

"That's true, God knows." Claire's corroboration was heartfelt. "But I can only pray that there are some businessmen smarter than my boss, Madam McCormick, or industry must be a shambles. Personally I think lots of women hope to hang on to their jobs after the war. That pay check is an insidious habit."

"What abaht the love of an 'ome and tiny children?" croaked Jennie tearfully in comic caricature of an old cockney woman.

Estelle laughed. "The old instinct is probably stronger than we think," she agreed. "But just the same, what Claire says is true. Even if George got a fine job tomorrow, I wouldn't want to give up mine; I enjoy it, and even though I adore Cynthia I like to do something else besides sit around and watch her grow. I think it's better for her too to learn self-reliance, within limits of course, than to be tied to my apron strings."

"I agree," said Claire. "All mothers should have interests outside their children. The children have a much better chance of survival. The nation is strangling in silver cords."

Jennie broke in: "If what you say is true, Claire, about average women going to work and becoming financially independent, I wonder how that's going to react on the American male ego. Are they going to like it or are they not?"

"Personally," said Devon, "if I were a man I'd be flattered if my wife were self-supporting and still stayed with me. It would prove that she really loved me. With the present economic setup, a man can never be sure that he isn't just a meal ticket."

"Devon, I said almost the same thing to a fellow once, but do you know what his answer was?" and Claire's expression was one of blank amazement.

"What?"

"He said, 'I certainly wouldn't want my wife to be self-supporting. Do you think I want to feel like a goddamned stallion?'"

Devon stared at her. "I don't get it."

"Well," said Jennie, and she giggled her deep giggle like an underground stream. "You know how men are, frightfully interested in sex but wanting it with no strings attached, yet at the same time they can't bear to think they're not loved and depended on. It's all very complex and illogical, and of course it's hard to make them realize you are dependent when you're making five times the money they are, but you are just the same."

"Of course you are," said Estelle stoutly. "For social life and helping with the children and getting train tickets . . . but then so are they dependent on women, for companionship and such."

"Mostly for the 'such,' dear." Devon spoke with what she considered the voice of authority. "Men really enjoy each other's companionship. They like going on sprees together. You know, fishing trips, conventions, things like that."

"Fishing, maybe," agreed Jennie. "But aren't the conventions liberally sprinkled with Tootsies? Rather like raisins in a pie, I've always understood."

"I believe that's the idea," said Estelle. "It's just their wives they don't want to be with, but they have nothing against women as a sex, you know that, Devon."

Devon had a nebulous feeling that perhaps this snowball concealed a stone, but she let it pass, only remarking that as a case in point men often sat around after dinner parties playing gin rummy or talking to each other while the ladies languished among themselves, and she added, "Women like us at least have business things to talk about which are fun, but what must that be in communities where the conversation runs exclusively to clothes, servants, and babies?"

"Don't worry," said Claire, "you'll probably never crash those circles. But if you ask me," she continued bitterly, "women making their own money have to be mental giants if they're going to find a way to persuade men that they are clinging vines." A glum silence settled over the party.

"Well, it seems to me," and Devon spoke with weary resignation, "that women do their part pretty well in the new economy. It's the men who can't adjust. My bridegroom, I will admit, seems to be taking my money on the chin with fair grace, but Major Wainwright—pardon the lapse of taste—liked the idea so little that he hurled himself at the cannon's mouth."

"It's the same with Dick," muttered Jennie. "Yet the truth is,

I consider him a relief instead of a burden. I've entirely supported Ollie, whom I don't like, for so long that it will be a positive pleasure to help out a man I'm in love with."

"Don't I know!" said Claire disgustedly. "But the trouble is the nice men hate the idea or feel called upon to say that they do."

Estelle, remembering George's behavior when they first came back to America from England, and comparing it with his present attitude, smiled with rueful amusement. "Well, I'll tell you," she said slowly. "Even the good ones, they . . . they slip into it somehow. It seems distasteful at first, but, little by little, they get . . . comfortable."

"And the bad ones don't slip, they plunge." Jennie had Ollie firmly in mind.

Claire laughed. "The truth is, I suppose, this really is the transition period. Historically speaking, it's such a new thing for women to be making money that, in spite of what we say, we resent parting with it. I wonder if we'll ever feel it's normal to support men. Certainly right now we still think they ought to be grateful to us."

"Claire, I don't agree with you." As she spoke, Devon filled Jennie's coffee cup from the silver urn in front of her and passed it back to her. "I know my weakness is liking money, though I can't see what's weak about being practical; it makes life lots more agreeable, and if you earn it, why are you a parasite?—though I guess the Russians would think I am because I don't fill every pot of cream with my own hands, but——" and here she stopped for breath and laughed, and the others did too.

"That's not what——" cut in Claire.

"No, let me finish. . . . *But,* even liking money as I do, it isn't that I'll expect gratitude from Kurt. If a woman's able to earn it, why not share it? I think what Jennie and Estelle are referring to is a sense of appreciation. That's pleasant in any relationship."

"Exactly," said Estelle. "But," she added honestly, "George has appreciation, he's sweet about things, and now that we're in the country he works ten times more than most men do at their desks. Sometimes I worry a little, I'm afraid he's pushing himself too hard, but it gives him satisfaction. He can feel proud again; that's why our marriage works out all right."

"And Ollie could never feel any pride, and that's why ours worked out all wrong," said Jennie. "That and the fact that he was swacked as a mink most of the time and that I never knew who I'd find in my bed when I came home at night."

"Jennie, how dreadful!" Estelle's blue eyes were soft with sympathy.

Jennie shrugged. "To tell you the truth, duck, after the first three damsels I didn't mind so much. As long as he kept rotating them I knew it couldn't be true love that he felt for them, and I thought I still had a chance, but one night I came home from the theater and there was a new one, and she opened a bloodshot eye and asked me would I mind bringing a basin, as she thought she was going to upchuck. Do you know, in a curious way it seemed to reflect on Ollie. I never cared for him much after that."

"Pete Jordan—he was my first husband," said Claire by way of explanation—"before I met any of you, used to drink like a fish too."

"It's odd, isn't it?" remarked Estelle with some puzzlement. "So many American men drink too much. I'm really very lucky with George. He never goes overboard any more. He only had that bad time there for a while when he brought Cynthia and me to this country and business was so awful."

"As a matter of fact, George is a darling," and Claire spoke sincerely. "But sometimes girls who have known drunks go around with men with nothing special to recommend them, they're just rather pleasant nonentities, and people wonder what that bright girl sees in so and so. They don't realize that to her he's a dream boat simply because he's sober."

"On the whole men can do extremely unattractive things," said Jennie. "The ones who have a mania for telling you about the other women they've had affairs with! That's very peculiar, isn't it? Why should they think it's interesting?"

Claire shrugged. "I suppose sometimes they're obscurely afraid they're bad lovers, so they're quick to tell you about other women lest you think they've had no experience."

"But actually that makes them out even dumber, doesn't it?" said Jennie. "If they've had lots of opportunities and still never learned . . . I mean to say!"

As Devon listened, Kurt began to appear in a highly desirable light. He was mute about other women and positively reluctant to take a drink. "You know," she said with gracious detachment, "that is true about American men drinking, especially through the Middle West. That was brought home to me on the last tour I did of the salons. Of course half the populace is bone dry, and that's appalling, but sometimes you can't blame them when you see how the other half behaves. At parties it's kind of a religion with them to get as ossified as possible in the shortest possible time."

"I suppose they're trying to obliterate Kansas," said Claire, who had once been sent there by Mary Mann McCormick to decorate a client's house and had never recovered.

"You should see Detroit," observed Devon. "If I could write I'd do a treatise on sophistication. Half the populace think they're sophisticated because they put on paper hats and get pie-eyed, and the other half are afraid of the word and think it means being cold and hard. It doesn't. It means knowing how to live with grace and taste and imagination. It means knowing how to enjoy things. Teetotalers don't know how to enjoy liquor and neither do drunks."

Estelle chuckled. "I'm frightfully sophisticated, duck. I'd love to enjoy a little more brandy if I may."

Devon smiled and tilted the crystal decanter which stood on the low coffee table in front of her into the frail bubble Estelle held in her hand.

Jennie had been impressed by what she said about George being proud. By doing the work of their small farm he was able to make it pay and was again necessary to her. It could work out that way for herself and Dick, she thought. The chances were she would always make more money, but professionally Dick would be indispensable to her. People might not realize it, but he would be the *more* important of the two: the star-maker. In her zeal Jennie overlooked the fact that she had been a star for years before she ever met Dick Hadley and convinced herself that from now on she would be a broken reed without him. "You know what I think," she cried, her face aglow with inner fire. "I think all this money for women is simply wonderful; it will probably give rise to a great spiritual renaissance."

Estelle and Claire raised skeptical eyebrows, but they looked interested.

"They don't believe you, Jennie," said Devon, "but I know what you mean. This new financial relationship between men and women may mean a whole new appraisal of values. Money won't be the thing any more, I mean who has it won't matter, it'll be love and what you're worth as a person."

"Exactly," cried Jennie. "Of course in one sense that's true now. I mean to say a famous scientist is even more respected than a popular actor, and he hasn't a sou, but the new part"—and she tossed in a hasty "I hope"—"will be that the scientist or inventor, or whatever, will himself realize his worth without being smug about it, so that he can marry the woman he loves, even if she has money, without a lot of inhibitions." Jennie came panting up to the finish line, a bit breathless but with the triumphant air of one who has successfully scrambled through an obstacle race. Claire laughed a little scornfully.

"I never saw anything so pathetic as you rich dames wanting to be loved for yourselves alone, which is the idea at the bottom of all this gab. You two will have to reverse the old fairy story and go out in rags to see which of your subjects really cares about you. What if you are deluded?" she asked, a sudden tartness in her tone, for her patience with the sorrows of the rich was limited. "If the delusion holds, isn't that as good as the real thing?"

"No, it isn't," said Devon quietly. "But you admit that delusion is necessary?"

"Well . . . I . . . yes, I suppose it is, though people ought to have the guts to face things."

"Fundamentally I agree with you." Devon's voice held an unaccustomed note of sadness. "But there comes a time when people weary of the stark facts of their own lives; they have to draw a veil of illusion in order to bear them. It's as though you curtained a window to shut out an ugly view. You know the view is still there, but at least you don't have to look at it twenty-four hours a day. It's the same kind of reasoning that makes perfectly intelligent adults embrace Catholicism when they haven't been bred to it. It is a charming concept; it shadows the harsh outlines of reality and relieves the disciples of responsible thought. They don't read certain books, they eat fish on Friday, and in a magic way they become heirs to the life eternal. In one form or another we all seek refuge in some such dream. For most women it's a man, I suppose. The religious converts are satisfied, or at any rate comforted, by spiritual love which to the earthy seems a poor substitute, but the same impulse drives us all, the need to enhance the spareness of our real existence."

"You'd think that love at least could work out, wouldn't you?" said Jennie despondently.

"How can it," asked Devon, "when human beings have to do the loving?"

"Oh boy, would that be nice!" Claire spoke softly. She was thinking of Mr. Davies, or more specifically, of Mrs. Davies. Why couldn't it work out for Mrs. Davies to fall possessively in love with someone else, thus leaving Mr. Davies free for Claire, who had a deep, haunting conviction that though Kent Davies was a man of parts, taking the bull, or in this case the cow, by the horns was not one of them. Initiative was what he lacked. Here she had thrown over Gil Emery for him, and after having asked Gil to marry her too, and he had accepted, poor lamb, and felt terrible when jilted, and supposing it didn't work out with Kent and she couldn't get Gil back . . . she would be up the creek without a paddle, and Mr. Davies' lack of delicacy would be responsible. "I swear to God," she said irritably, "if it weren't for sex, I don't think men and women would ever talk to each other. They don't seem to have the same ideas at all about life."

"I feel just the opposite, Claire," said Estelle. "In one way sex is the stumbling block. It makes men and women think they're more different from each other than they really are. After all, the same emotions, the same likes and dislikes, the same reactions, they're experienced by both sexes equally."

"I suppose you're right," Devon acknowledged grudgingly. "But the trouble is that the opposite sexes are rarely experiencing the same sentiments at the same time."

"Why, listen to our Middle European friend!" mocked Claire. "Are they rarely indeed, Frau Fabri? When, by the way, is the wedding?"

Devon still experienced a little shock at the thought of actually marrying Kurt. It seemed somehow that she was still married to Tim. It seemed . . . "Probably the ninth or tenth of April," she said. "We're not quite set yet."

"I wish to goodness my decree was final so Dick and I could get married before I go to the coast," said Jennie. "But there's such a feeling against bigamy!" She was closing *The Mountain Top* for the summer and going to Hollywood to make a picture, reopening the play in the fall.

"When is it you leave, Jennie?" asked Estelle.

"The show closes down the first of June. I'll probably go the next day. I think Dick will be out there part of the time, but he can't stay with me the whole three months, he's got a script in preparation for an early fall opening. I'm going to miss him awfully."

"I do think," exclaimed Estelle, "it's very difficult being separated when one is in love."

"It's still more difficult when two are in love." Claire's contribution was evoked by the thought of Mr. Davies and their frequent partings.

"Of course," said Devon, "if you're Pollyanna and hell-bent on a silver lining, I suppose there's something to be said for separation."

"What?" asked Claire coldly.

"Not by me," said Devon hastily, "by philosophers, I mean. In not having long periods together, it's true, your roots don't get a chance to intermingle, which I believe is the accepted theory for a happy marriage; on the other hand, the relationship stays fresh and exciting longer."

"Uh-huh," said Claire. The other two ladies said nothing.

Devon sensed something dank in their silence. "I don't like the idea myself, I was only saying——"

"Personally, I don't believe in long separations," observed Jennie, "but what are you going to do? They're inevitable in war, certainly, and in the theater they're unavoidable."

"I sometimes think that in the theater people have to love each other more than anywhere else," said Estelle. "Maybe it's a good thing Nick's never married. He's forever popping off on tours and flying to foreign parts, no kind of family life at all." That there was perhaps another reason for Nick's not marrying, Estelle was too loyal to mention.

"That's just it!" said Jennie. "Besides, theater people are open to more temptation than most, because it's a business where physical attractiveness is the rule, and when a play is on tour husbands and wives may be separated for long periods. I've always felt it was a mistake to probe too closely into road tours, but I think it's nice to be faithful to each other when you're in the same town."

"That would seem reasonable," murmured Devon.

"Of course when I was younger there were lads here and there, you know how it is in stock companies . . ." Jennie smiled deprecatingly. ". . . I expect, though, it is wrong, promiscuous, I guess. . . . Oh dear."

"I used to worry about that for years," said Claire, "and then I decided I might as well face it. I like to sleep with men; as long as they will sleep with me, I will sleep with them. Oh, poetry!" she added in happy surprise.

"Of course," said Estelle thoughtfully, "there's a lot of difference between loving a man and going to bed with him."

"Of course," agreed Devon. "Still, it's risky. Once you've done that, it's a woman's tendency to sell herself a bill of goods. Even when your intelligence knows better you pretend to think he's all right. But that's a mistake, that's where men are stronger than we are."

"Well, my Lord, what are you going to do?" asked Claire, who was a candid girl and believed in putting the cards on the table. "If a man turns out to be a good lover and is charming and makes you happy, what about that? You're not going to hate him, are you?"

"No," said Estelle, "but you don't have to marry him." Her tone was casual, but her remark was directed at Devon. Estelle rather liked Kurt, but the idea of the approaching marriage depressed her. She did not consider him suitable husband material, not by a long shot.

"No, I suppose you don't have to marry him," Claire sighed, "but you always seem to want to. It's a more enticing reason than compatibility of interests and those other standard come-ons. According to that logic, Dickie Masters and I were made for each other—we're both nuts about beige velvet."

Estelle laughed. "No, even I agree that that would be excessive. Dickie's shortcomings, I'm afraid, outweigh the advantage of mutual business interests."

"Anyway," said Claire peevishly, "there's always so much academic talk about physical attraction or self-interest or is-it-going-to-last-through-the-ages, there are so many red herrings tossed in the path, how do you know whether or not it's love anyhow?"

"There are ways," said Devon.

Jennie observed that she knew one infallible rule. "What?" they asked in chorus.

"You know how curious you can be about who's on the telephone; well, I think it's love when you're in a room with your fellow and the phone rings and you don't give a damn who it is because the most important person in your life is right beside you."

The ladies mulled over this for a bit and finally decided that that was a pretty good test.

"Of course," remarked Estelle, "even when you're with him, if you're waiting to hear about a job or whether or not the bank accepted your offer on the property, that's something else again."

"Of course," said Jennie courteously, "I just meant l'amour."

"It's remarkable the part the telephone plays in modern romance," said Devon, her thoughts on Kurt's nocturnal calls.

"It certainly is," agreed Claire. "A little while back Kent and I busted up forever and he didn't call me for two days. Two days isn't much, I suppose, but it can seem awfully long."

"Long!" echoed Devon. "My Lord, the five minutes between the time you bang down the receiver in a fight and the time he rings you back can seem an eternity!"

"I wonder if anybody will phone us tonight," said Jennie; but it turned out that nobody did.

"One theory I should like to explode," said Estelle, "is that men you can count on are no fun. I don't know who's responsible for the tradition that rotters are so irresistible."

"The rotters, I guess," mused Devon.

"Pleasant, well-behaved, civilized men seem to me to have far more sex appeal than all those charm boys or wolves or whatever they are called, and furthermore I think it's quite true that if men don't like a man, there's something the matter with him."

"Well, not always." Devon was weighing the home talent, as Estelle intended she should, and remembering Tim's and Jasper's reaction. "I think it's annoying, the way when men don't like another man everyone assumes he's no good and that the men know what they are talking about, yet when women dislike another woman people just think they're being catty."

"I suppose that's because women are so worried about each other's morals," said Claire slyly. "We're hard to please. No woman likes any other woman to assume that she has affairs galore; on the other hand she's resentful if the girls think she hasn't the opportunities, and God knows only a bitch would emphasize the virginity of another woman who's past twenty-four or -five."

"I'd call that a liberal allowance," said Estelle, who had married at eighteen. Cynthia was born when she was twenty-two, and two years later her husband died; but Estelle had not let time hang too heavy on her hands while waiting for George to turn up. However, she was essentially domestic and was happy when she could concentrate her energies in double blessedness. Estelle had few moral scruples regarding sex, but she had an orderly mind and was appalled by the inconvenience involved in irregular relationships. That was the only reason she could understand for Devon's marrying Kurt. "I suppose," she had said to George when Devon told her of the decision, "that if she wants to take him with her on those tours, it's easier to say, 'Come in, waiter,' than 'Get in the closet, Kurt,' but it still seems a desperate measure."

Sunday evening, when he left Devon in the country with her guests and drove into town with the other men, Kurt had a dinner engagement with Maria Sellner. He was taking leave of her to be married, and this was in the nature of a farewell.

Shortly after she went to work in the salon, Maria had heard the gossip about him and Devon, but she did not at the time believe

that their marriage was a probability. True, Miss Elliott was in
Reno, divorcing Mr. Wainwright, but that was not a guarantee that
she intended to marry Mr. Fabri, and even if she did? Surely
Maria had some kind of a prior claim. Was he not the friend of her
youth? What harm was there in seeing him occasionally? Kurt had
called her up to congratulate her on getting the job, and Maria,
who was rather lonely in New York and had always held for him
the casual and light affection which had inspired their moment of
romance long ago in Vienna, asked him to come and join her in a
drink by way of celebration. One thing led to another, and two
exiled Europeans revived old memories in each other's arms. They
were both aware of the transitory nature of their relationship, but
it was as if, passing along a road, they had gathered a spray of wild-
flowers, knowing they would have faded by the time they reached
the journey's end.

That the reunion became something other than an intermezzo
known only to themselves was due to one of whom they were
scarcely aware: Miss Hedwig, of the Swedish Room.

Kurt had met her once. On one of the rare occasions when he
went to Devon's office, she had taken him all over the salon and
they had passed through the Swedish Room on their way out and
Devon had introduced him. Having met him in her company,
Hedwig regarded Kurt as the exclusive property of her lady. She
liked and admired Devon, who knew that she was doing a good
job, paid her well and let her alone.

Hedwig had of course encountered Maria frequently, the first
occasion being when she took over Minerva's job and was introduced to the entire staff. Because Maria usurped the place of her
close friend and because she was so pretty, a smoldering resentment
was born in Hedwig's stubborn breast, and she vowed darkly to
avenge the departed Minerva. She had not long to wait before
events played into her hands.

One evening while Devon was in Reno, just as Hedwig was going
home at the end of the day, a taxi had driven up to the green door
of Devonshire House, and Maria, who stood there waiting, ran
across the pavement. The man who stepped out to help her in was
Kurt. Hedwig's thin mouth tightened in her square face as she

watched them drive away. So that was it! Playing fast and loose behind Miss Elliott's back. Foreigners they were and not to be trusted. That she herself was Swedish as smörgåsbord, Hedwig overlooked. She came from the north country where the people were honest, but those Viennese were twisty; besides, that Sellner had lived in Paris, and Kurt, she understood from the girls in the salon, was a strange dark brew. She would bide her time a little, and if her suspicions were confirmed she would act. Miss Elliott should know she was being hoodwinked by the soft little Sellner with ice water flowing through her veins, and she would be fired and then perhaps Minerva could be persuaded to come back. Minerva could make her good salary again, which she had been a fool to give up, and Hedwig would not be lonely any more.

During the weeks that Devon was in Reno, Kurt and Maria met many times, but he did not call for her again at the salon—they both agreed that was too risky; nor did Hedwig see them again till that Sunday night in late March, and then God was good to her.

Hedwig had a married brother who lived in Minnesota, but he had come to New York on business. Strangely enough, he had a passion for Italian cooking, and that night he had taken his sister to one of the best of the small Italian restaurants. It was situated in the East Fifties; the tables were set in little booths, covered with red-and-white-checked cloths and lighted by small lamps. The place was cozy and very quiet, and in the booth next to Hedwig and her brother, and ignorant of their presence, sat Maria and Kurt. The little she overheard told Hedwig what she wanted to know. They were speaking in low tones, but her already excellent hearing was attuned to their softest word, and she realized they were lovers, though the trend of their conversation was a farewell. There was no tragedy; rather they played at parting with a conventional and gentle melancholy and with easy acceptance of its necessity. The subtlety of the emotional equation escaped Hedwig, nor would it have interested her had she understood; she only cared that the conversation armed her with the weapon she needed. She said nothing to her brother, but that night after he left her she lay awake plotting how best to expose and punish the culprits. Hedwig was not of that world where people had casual love affairs and where the inaccurate revelation of the more intimate details was among the lesser glories of a free press, but she knew that channels for tattle existed, for she followed them with scornful interest. Many of the Devonshire House clients popped up in them with noticeable regularity.

If I could get it in those columns! she thought. *Then Miss Elliott would see it and she'd have to fire the Sellner.* So intently was her mind fixed on that one idea that it never occurred to her what the unhappy knowledge might do to Devon.

Hedwig made one or two false starts, but towards the end of the week she reached interested ears. Maria was unknown to the ladies and gentlemen of the press, but her job gave her a certain news value, and Kurt was by way of being a columnists' stand-by. They had at one time or another coupled his name with every unattached girl in the night-club circuit, and when they understood that Devon Elliott was involved, the lid was off. Monday of the following week, led by Mr. Winchell and Ed Sullivan, the gossip columns expatiated upon Hedwig's tip with happy abandon.

It had been a good week for Devon. Kurt was a persistent and charming suitor. The wedding date was definitely set for the ninth of April, and Devon had ordered the dress she would wear. "Scarcely virginal white, my heart," she murmured to Kurt, "but print on a light ground, I think, is permissible—something spotted, like my reputation."

She and Kurt and Nicky Van Alston, who had been with them over Sunday, drove in from the country Monday morning, and Devon smiled to herself as she remembered how much she had suffered on a similar occasion last summer, and how useless it had been, for the story had a happy ending after all. She had been quite wrong in her judgment of Kurt's character. To be sure, he had given her a springboard, but her fertile imagination had attributed to him chicaneries of which he was incapable and infidelities in which he had never indulged. He was a dear, funny, sweet creature, intelligent, a gifted artist, and with a touch that turned her to water. Life was very good.

While waiting for the boss to arrive from the country, the salon whirred with speculation. Hilda and Miss Suzanne and Barbara Horlick, the exercise instructor, whose next client wasn't due for half an hour, were gathered in Devon's office poring over the *News* and the *Mirror*. Barbara's lithe figure in the brief black trunks and sweater she wore to work in was bent like an arc, her hands braced against her ankles as she read the paper spread out on the floor. "Oh boy, oh boy, oh boy, listen to this:

"Does the beauty czarina, Devon Elliott, who was recently Renovated from Major Timothy (research scientist) Wainwright to wed foreign charmer Kurt Fabri, as first printed in this column, know he has been simmering with Maria Sellner, to whom she recently gave a job in her organization?"

Hilda said nothing, but her morale was low. She was fond of Devon and knew how terribly in love she was with Kurt. Hilda had suffered too much this past year from her boss's moods, plunging one minute, soaring the next, and almost always attributable to the behavior of Mr. Fabri, not to realize that the item would throw the entire salon into turmoil. "How in Heaven's name do you suppose Winchell got hold of that?"

"How do you suppose? *Celui-là se cache sous les lits des gens pour savoir ce qu'il veut.*" In her excitement Suzanne's French worked overtime.

"Do you think it's true?" asked Barbara, her face bright with interest.

"Well, whether it is or not, it's a stinking thing," said Hilda heatedly. "Have you seen Sullivan?" and she quoted from the paper she held in her hand. It was the first item under the heading "Men and Maids and Stuff," and the title in reference to her boss pained Hilda:

"The eyeful Maria Sellner of Devonshire House and the oh so popular Kurt Fabri an item. The wedding bells which were supposedly to have chimed for him and Devon Elliott have jingle-jangled out of tune."

"My feminine intuition tells me this is the end of Miss Sellner," sang Barbara with no noticeable regret. As she spoke, the door opened and Jasper's secretary, Miriam Dudley, came in. She held a copy of the *Journal-American*, opened at Dorothy Kilgallen's column, "The Voice of Broadway." She grinned as she saw the other three. "Hullo, vultures. Lapping up the dirt?"

"It's revolting," said Hilda. "I bet it isn't true."

"They all carry it," said Miriam. "They can't all three be crazy."

"It is that they copy each other, so that if one is wrong, all are wrong," said Suzanne hopefully, for she too suspected that the ensuing rumpus would rock the salon to its foundation.

"Has Uncle Jasper seen it?" asked Barbara.

Miriam shook her head in disgust. "I doubt it. He isn't in yet, but he was weaned on the New York *Times,* never knows anything."

"Anybody talked to Sellner this morning?" Barbara believed in tapping the source.

"I didn't talk to her," said Miriam, "except to say hello. We came in at the same time, but I thought she looked a little seedy."

"Well she might," muttered Hilda darkly.

"Maybe the wedding's off?" And Barbara grinned cheerfully. She had nothing against Devon, but a little scandal brightened the day.

"*Ne pas Se Marier?*" Suzanne felt shocked at the very thought. It was lamentable that there should be such gossip in the papers, American journalism was *drôle* and created all sorts of trouble, but after all one did not marry or not marry for such reasons as that. Of course Americans were not practical in these matters as the French were, but even an American woman would not be so unreasonable as to turn down a husband on grounds of infidelity.

"My God," said Miriam, "what a fool Sellner is! New York is full of men. Why does she have to pick the one guy who automatically insures her the loss of her job?"

"If you ask me," and Hilda spoke with loyal anger, "the loss of her job is too good. She ought to be boiled in oil, the little sneak."

"Don't worry, honey," laughed Barbara, "the boss is no frail flower. She'll be able to protect herself; but, kids, what wouldn't I give to overhear the interview with our pal Fabri! There's a boy whose shoes I don't envy."

"It will be difficult for Miss Sellner to find other work, do you not think?" asked Suzanne.

Miriam shrugged. "A story like this spread all through the trade can't do her any good."

"But she is a fine worker," said Suzanne earnestly.

"And don't forget, baby," said Barbara, "it's women she'll have to work for, and they aren't keen to have any body snatchers on the premises."

"I'd still like to know how they got the information," said Hilda with a puzzled frown. As she spoke she glanced at her watch. "Oh-oh, you'd better beat it. Miss Elliott will be in any minute, and there'll be double hell to pay if she thinks we've been talking about it." Hilda meant what she said, but she also wanted to get rid of them for her own sake. The gossip and speculation made her feel disloyal and a little sick and was, she supposed, a sample of what was going on all over town.

Barbara retreated to the gymnasium and Suzanne was just leaving for her treatment room when Devon arrived. She was in excellent spirits and greeted the girls gaily, not even bothering to ask Suzanne why she was off the Sixth floor. The operator slipped away, tossing a backward glance at Hilda and Miriam. It was obvious that the blow had not yet fallen. Devon nodded to Miriam, who hastily folded the newspaper and stuck it behind her back. "Good morning, Miriam. Is Mr. Doolittle in yet?"

"No, he's not, Miss Elliott, but I expect him any minute. Do you want to see him?"

"There's no rush. He'll probably come in here anyway as soon as he arrives." Miriam melted gratefully away.

"Any mail, Hilda?" Devon took off her hat and fluffed her hair in front of the mirror.

"Well, I . . . that is . . . yes, yes, there is, Miss Elliott." Hilda was trying inconspicuously to dispose of the *News* and the *Mirror* in the wastebasket and lay out the mail at the same time. Devon glanced at her questioningly. "What's the matter?" she said with a little laugh. "You seem undecided. Any bad news?"

"Oh, no, no, Miss Elliott, it's fine, I mean the mail. . . ." Hilda had been dreading the boss's arrival because she assumed she would have read the papers, but she found Devon's ignorance even more alarming than her knowledge; the shock still lay ahead. The suspense, however, was not prolonged. Within ten minutes after Devon had arrived in her office, Jennie was on the phone, outraged and stammering. "Darling, the whole thing is probably the most outrageous lie. Just hold tight till you get an explanation. I imagine there's nothing to it, they knew each other in Europe, didn't they, and probably lunched together once or something of the sort. God, I could kill columnists." Her deep voice was rough with anger and worry. Devon didn't know what she was talking about, but there was a funny little catch in her heart when Jennie said "they knew each other in Europe." Europe. That was Kurt, of course, but who else?

"Jennie, wait a minute, hold on. What is all this?"

Jennie stopped short. That she should be the bearer of bad tidings, the well-meaning fool who couldn't wait to hurt someone she loved! "Devon, haven't you seen this morning's *News* and *Mirror?*"

"No, I just got in the office. Why? What do they say?" Hilda's action of a few minutes ago, stuffing something in the wastebasket, suddenly registered on her brain. "Hilda," she said sharply, "was that the *News* and *Mirror* you had there?"

"Yes, Miss Elliott," said the secretary miserably.

"Let me see them."

Hilda retrieved the papers and spread them on Devon's desk. The columns lay face up, and Devon's eyes fell on her own name. She read the paragraphs in silence and for a moment was aware of nothing but a churning nausea in the pit of her stomach.

"Well, have you seen them?" Jennie's voice was subdued at the other end of the wire.

"Yes," she said after a long pause, and her mouth was dry. "Yes, I have."

"It's a lot of disgusting gossip, darling. God knows how they got hold of it, but don't let it get you."

There was another long pause, and Jennie grew uneasy. "Hello, Devon, are you there?"

"Yes, yes, I'm here. Just a minute." Devon turned to dismiss Hilda, who had already slipped from the room. She stared again at the printed matter before her. "Oh, Jennie, what am I going to do?"

"Baby, you don't believe that cheap nonsense?"

"Don't you?"

"Oh, Devon, perhaps we do malign him. Kurt hasn't had a very good reputation, it's true, but he does love you. I think marriage is going to make all the difference in the world. The columnists have always picked on him. Why, if the poor devil has a cup of coffee in Childs', they say he's having an affair with the waitress. You know that's so."

Devon pulled herself together. "Well, I guess it's pretty lousy not to talk to him about it first. I'll call him now and see what he says."

"That's the girl," Jennie spoke with an enthusiasm she did not feel.

"After all," Devon was hauling at her own boot straps, "it's very likely he did see Maria while I was in Reno. Why not? They're old friends, it's perfectly natural, especially now that's she's working here."

"Why, of course," said Jennie. "He probably didn't give it a thought, and if he did, he didn't mention it for the very reason that you might misconstrue it. Cheer up, darling, give yourself a break." The simple friendliness of the beautiful creature at the other end of the wire warmed Devon's heart. The pain in her eyes melted a little.

"I'll call him now, Jennie. I'll let you know what happens."

Devon sat considering what she would say. *It's ridiculous to fly off the handle,* she thought, *and besides these columnists print so many inventions and distortions . . . surely, I have better sense than to let anything they say get under my skin. Where's your sense of proportion, my girl?* She was in the midst of this silent pep talk when there was a disturbance at the door. It was flung open and, greatly to her surprise, Miss Hedwig walked in. It took Devon a moment or two to focus her attention on the presiding genius of the Swedish Room.

"Yes, Hedwig?" she said. "What is it?"

"Please, Miss Elliott, I must speak to you."

"Well . . . Hedwig, won't some other time do as well? I'm very busy this morning. I'm afraid I'll have to ask you to come back later."

Hedwig planted herself, an amazon at bay. "I think, Miss Elliott, it is better I speak now."

"But Hedwig——"

"These stories in the newspaper, I see you are reading them," and she gestured to the papers on Devon's desk. "I put them there. They are true. The little Sellner, she has done those things behind your back with your gentleman. She is sleeping with him. You are always good to me, Miss Elliott, and then you give to someone a job, who is your enemy, but Hedwig shows her up so you can be free of her and get back those whom you can count on."

Devon stared at this flushed, self-righteous woman who in such a fantastic way was toppling her world and shattering her new-found confidence. When she spoke her voice had a funny hoarse quality hard to recognize. In her desperate desire to prove Hedwig wrong, she found she was defending Maria against her detractor. "Hedwig, you don't know what you're saying. You have no right— even if you are foolish or stupid enough to believe such a thing— you have no proof. It is evil, evil, what you've done, putting all this gossip in a cheap newspaper, smearing Miss Sellner and Mr. Fabri with all this vicious slander—like mud."

"Like mud, yes, Miss Elliott," and Hedwig's eyes flashed in her stolid face, "but not gossip. I would not do such a thing if I did not know it to be true."

"But how—how do you know it?"

"One evening I am going home and I see Miss Sellner waiting in the doorway downstairs, and then a taxi comes to the curb, that is what she is waiting for, and in the cab is Mr. Fabri and they go off together."

Devon's relief was so great that she laughed a little hysterically. "Is that all? But Hedwig, why not? They are old friends, they knew each other in Europe. This is shocking, shocking of you to have made such a scandal out of something simple and natural."

"Miss Elliott, please, Hedwig is not a stupid woman. I do not think this is nice, but I still say nothing, but later on I have proof and I know they are lovers. And because they are cheats I put it in the papers so everyone knows about it and they are shamed."

Devon spoke carefully. She felt as though she were very weak and must husband her strength. "What proof have you?"

"In a restaurant I heard them, Miss Elliott. They said such things to each other as people should not say in public. They are talking about when they are in bed and how that must stop now because you and Mr. Fabri are going to be married, and then she said, I heard her, 'This is the end, Kurt,' and then Mr. Fabri said, 'Not necessarily, you are a part of me that will never end,' and then they drank a toast, and afterwards——"

"Stop it!" Devon felt as though a sheet of flame swept over her, leaving her burning with shame. The relentless vulgarity of this woman was like a brand on her mind. She felt as though she had been stripped naked. "Hedwig, I . . . you . . . how dared you do such a thing?"

But Hedwig was defiant, a John Knox gaining fresh strength from every epithet. "Maria Sellner is a whore, so I go to the newspaper offices and I see these people, when they know I come from Devonshire House they are glad to see me, and I tell them these things. Send away this bad person, Miss Elliott, then Minerva comes back, yes, and it will be like old times in the salon."

"Minerva? What has she got to do with this?"

"It is because you send Minerva away that all this trouble comes. If *you* had said to her, 'stay,' she would have stayed." Hedwig's twisted resentment against Devon and against Maria gushed out like a dirty cataract. "Minerva is my good friend; you, the Sellner, rob me of my only friend, this woman who is for me everything. I do not go chasing after men, nor does Minerva, this we would scorn to do." Her breath was coming in hard, tearing sobs. "You engage this whore, she hurts you, yes, it is bad pain for you, yet you think it is nothing, nothing that you have done to Hedwig, but I show you the evil, I protect you. . . ."

Watching her, sick and bewildered, Devon could suddenly bear her presence no longer. "Stop it, stop it!" she shouted. "You're out of your mind. Minerva left of her own free will, and you can follow her. Get out of here, get out of this office. It's you who are fired, you with your shocking, ridiculous, vulgar gossip, smearing my name over every cheap rag in New York. I pray to God I never see you again as long as I live."

Hedwig turned a sickly green. In all her plotting she had never dreamed such a thing could happen to her. She was fighting for her friend Minerva and defending Miss Elliott from the machinations of that trollop she had so ill-advisedly engaged. The injustice of her dismissal was a terrible blow. "But, but my contract," she stammered, "I . . . I don't have to go, I will not go . . . my money——"

"I'm aware of your contract. It has five months to run. You will see Mr. Henshaw in the Accounting Department and he will give you a check for the full amount. Now get out of my sight." Devon, blind with anger and shock, for the first time in her life ignored cost, driven only by her urge to get rid of Hedwig. Hedwig, now thoroughly frightened—perhaps they would throw her into jail—for libel—made her way to the door, her mouth working, her breast seething with emotions so long suppressed and now in turmoil.

Left alone, Devon paced her office until her own wrought-up feelings subsided, leaving only a dull ache in her heart. *Kurt, Kurt, Kurt,* she thought, *oh my darling, how could you?* It was then that she realized that not for one instant had she doubted the rumor. If Kurt had seen much of Maria, he was having an affair with her, and on the eve of his wedding. And even if it were untrue, how sorrowful that he should be the kind of man about whom it was possible to say such things! How cheap it made him, how stripped of all dignity! She sat down, her elbows on her desk, her head in her hands. *O dear God,* she prayed, *how long am I to go on loving him?* Strangely enough, she harbored little resentment against Maria. If it had not been she, it would have been someone else. Maria was merely the agent of his desire, not the object. That was true, she thought, in all Kurt's love affairs. He lacked the ability to focus his emotional forces which was the endowment of quite ordinary men. He thought that through constant change he would find renewed inspiration, the ultimate rapture; but in exercising no restraint he defeated his purpose; because he imposed no discipline of the heart he was cheated of the ecstasy he sought.

She lifted her head wearily and sat staring at the telephone. She

must, she supposed, speak to him. It was unfair to condemn him
unheard. She reached for the instrument and was dialing Kurt's
number as Jasper came in from his own office, the paper in his
hand. "Yes, I know," she said. "I've seen it. I'm calling him now."

"That bastard!" said Jasper, but Devon was uncertain whether
he referred to the columnist or to Kurt, who at that moment answered the phone.

"Hello?"

"Hello, Mr. Fabri." Devon spoke gently enough, but her voice
was not a sound to reassure him. He had picked up a copy of the
News, as was his custom, on his way to the workroom and had no
sooner gotten in the door when Maria called him. She had not seen
him since their dinner a week ago Sunday and had been trying
desperately to reach him since last evening, when she had bought
the papers on her way home from the movies and read the story.
She had had a sleepless night and was half hysterical when she
spoke to Kurt. He was shaken, but he told her to keep calm. If
Devon questioned her she was to deny everything, and he would
too, except to say that they had dined together a couple of times to
celebrate her good luck in getting the job. "After all, Maria, no one
can prove anything, and since you and I know we did nothing
harmful, what does it matter? You are probably making a storm in
the teapot. You do not know Devon. She is very nice and human.
I can handle her, and you will not lose your job," and he had added,
"I think it will look better if you go to her first, she is in her office
now, I have just dropped her at the salon, and make it is like a joke.
She knows we have known each other since years ago. Remember
a couple of dinners, nothing more." But he admitted to himself that
the situation was delicate and required nice handling. Accordingly,
when he heard Devon's voice he spoke warmly and with a genuine
wish to soothe her.

"My darling," he said, "I am this minute reaching for the telephone to call you. Have you seen this absurd unpleasant nonsense
in Sullivan's column?" He sounded so affectionate, so sincerely
annoyed, that Devon's belief in his perfidy wavered.

"It's not only Sullivan," she replied after a pause. "A full dossier
seems to have been sent to the entire New York press."

Maria had told him this too, but Kurt thought it wiser not to know too much of the story. "You mean other papers have it too?" he asked with a very fair semblance of incredulity.

"Yes, they have."

"But my baby, this is the most insane malicious kind of rumor. You do believe me, don't you?"

Devon thought, *This is my chance. If I say I believe him, the marriage will go through, I can have him the rest of my life if I am willing to have him on this basis.* "I . . . I don't know, Kurt," she said slowly.

Kurt, suddenly fearful of the future, spoke angrily: "This is not loving me very much, I think, to believe column gossip, nor do I dream you will be so stupid as to take such a thing seriously."

Devon, with Jasper as witness, had no desire to repeat Hedwig's testimony, so she merely said with such levity as she could muster, "Well, dear, you do rather lay yourself open to these cracks, don't you?"

"No, that is unfair and unkind. I do not know what you mean. I see no reason why I should be subjected to such things; I can have a suit with this paper. Twice I took Maria to dinner while you were in Reno. I did not tell you because you get jealous, and you know how I hate having to account for every little move, but because I love you I do not want you to be miserable. Please will you have luncheon with me and let us make up this unhappy, silly row? We will be sending out a denial too if you wish it."

Devon glanced at her engagement pad. The buyer from Bullocks-Wilshire was in town, and she and Jasper were lunching with him. It was a good excuse to put Kurt off. She knew herself well enough to know she would do better when time, even a few hours, had given her a little perspective. "I am sorry about luncheon, Kurt, but I have an engagement."

"But I will surely see you at dinner?" There was urgency in his voice.

"Yes. I'll be home a little after six." At another time she might have felt some small satisfaction that he for a change should be the one on tenterhooks; just now she was too wretched for gloating.

Kurt, wanting to make good his promise and honestly concerned for her job, spoke of Maria. "Look, Devon, she will be feeling terribly about this. Maria has for you much admiration and gratitude, she will be sick if you are for one minute thinking this is more than casual old friends meeting. You would be very wrong to send her away, and because you are the one with the power, you should make it easy for her."

The audacity of this did more than any amount of denial could have done almost to convince Devon that her suspicions were groundless and that Hedwig was indeed out of her mind. Unfortunately under the circumstances she also regarded Kurt's reminding her of her duty a gesture of unparalleled insolence, so she remarked coldly that Miss Sellner had a curious sense of gratitude, no doubt European, and that she would deal with her as she saw fit. She hung up the receiver, and Mr. Fabri embarked on the most uneasy day of his thirty-eight years.

Jasper looked at Devon from under his eyebrows. "Is there anything to this?" he asked, tapping the paper.

Devon shrugged. "Curiously enough, the gentleman says no, but the evidence is fairly damaging."

"Firing Sellner?"

"I don't know, Jasper. I've got such a headache I can't think. I suppose I've got to see her, it's the conventional move, though I don't know what in God's name we're going to say to each other."

There was a long pause. Jasper, who was sitting on the edge of Devon's desk, in one of his rare demonstrative gestures reached out and caressed her soft dark hair. "My Donna, are you going to marry this bastard?"

"I ought to have my head examined, Jasper. I know that."

"Of course," he said reasonably, "it's foolish to feel any worse about this mess than about any of the others. You know what he is. If you're willing to put up with him, I can't see that one woman more or less makes any difference, and in this instance, I must admit, his taste wasn't bad."

Devon looked at him with a gleam of her old malice. "I'd say his timing was poor, wouldn't you?"

"Look, why don't you postpone the wedding, go away for a while, really think it over?"

"My dear Jasper, I went to Reno for eight weeks. See what happens. Mr. Wainwright went to Louisiana, and the results were unforeseen. No, I think the thing to do is to stay put. Besides, I read once that it was much braver to stay and fight a thing out than to run away. Me, I am the courageous type." Devon pressed the buzzer on her desk. "Want to stick around while I interview Miss Sellner?"

Jasper snapped to his feet. "Thank you, no. I will make myself scarce while you ladies remove each other's scalps."

"It's a mug's game, Jasper." Jasper looked at the small face, at the curving mouth and extraordinary eyes that could hold so much of gaiety and passion and shrewd common sense. Looking out at him from behind those eyes was a woman weary and disillusioned, but mistress of a sardonic humor and grained with an indestructible fiber which would endure despite an inner urge to emotional self-destruction.

When Hilda answered the buzzer, Devon sent her to fetch Maria and, while she waited, carefully powdered her nose and arranged her hair so she might enter the lists with banners flying. Her armor was highly becoming, a tailored black wool suit, a hand-tucked blouse of white batiste, and an immense jewel on her lapel. Maria, after her telephone conversation with Kurt, had gotten control of her nerves, and though very pale, she seemed composed as she entered Devon's office.

"Good morning, Miss Sellner." Devon's gaze was level as it rested on the smooth face of the young woman opposite her.

"Good morning, Miss Elliott." Remembering Kurt's admonition, Maria continued without waiting for her superior's question or accusation: "I am so glad you sent for me. I wanted very much to come to see you. It is disgraceful and shocking, these lies they are printing in the papers. Mr. Fabri I have known when I am very young, a girl in Vienna. I have seen him a couple of times while you are away, and we speak of your great kindness in giving me this job, and that is all, Miss Elliott. It . . . it is so disgusting, these things they say about us."

There was a sincerity and distress in Maria's manner which was very convincing. Again Devon hesitated. Was it possible that Hedwig could have made up the story out of whole cloth? The woman was obviously ridden by her obsession with Minerva and hatred of her successor, yet hers was not an inventive mind. She might be tormented by dark fancies, laboring under strange misapprehensions, but it was scarcely likely she would have done what she did without fairly conclusive evidence. Still, Devon, feeling an outright accusation might be ill-advised, tackled Maria from another angle.

"Didn't you know that Mr. Fabri and I are engaged to be married? That I was in Reno getting a divorce so that I could marry him?"

"No, at first I did not know. Kurt speaks very little of his affairs. . . ." That bit at least was true, thought Devon dryly. "And after all, it is so many years since I have seen him, it is not likely he would tell me of such a private matter."

A glimmer of a smile flickered across Devon's face, and she said with a kind of cold humor, "Come, come, Miss Sellner, even if Mr. Fabri kept his own counsel to the extent you claim, you surely must have heard the gossip here in the shop. Beauty salons are hotbeds of rumor, and Devonshire House is no exception. I may be the owner, but for that very reason I am discussed even more avidly than the clients. You can hardly expect me to believe that no word of this marriage came to your ears."

Maria turned a little paler and moistened her lips ever so slightly. "At first, Miss Elliott, no. I was very busy learning my job. I did not discuss such matters with any of the girls. I would consider that to do so would be disloyal. Later on, I admit I heard different things——"

"What things?"

"That you and Kurt would be married very probably, that——" She stopped.

"That what?"

"Well, that . . . that——"

"That we were having an affair. That's what you heard, isn't it?" Maria looked away. "It was said, yes."

"And it is quite true, Miss Sellner. I am very much in love with Kurt Fabri. Now I appreciate the fact that you and he are friends of old, which is perhaps a little different from being old friends, but I am curious to know why a clever businesswoman, which you are, should voluntarily jeopardize a job which must mean the difference between good living and possibly serious want."

Maria felt a small panic beginning to grow inside her, but she struggled to subdue it and said with dignity, "I would be very greatly distressed were you to send me away, Miss Elliott, because I . . . I think I have done good work for you, but because this is so, and I am innocent, I would be able to get a job elsewhere."

Devon spoke with more impatience than anger: "Why, you poor little fool, even in this business where the competition is cutthroat and fifty per cent of the deals are made out of spite, I could spread such a story about you that my most violent competitor wouldn't engage you, not even for the joy of getting even with me. You must know enough about me to know that I'm no saint, you can't for one minute believe I'd keep in my employ a woman who is having an affair with my lover, the man who will soon be my husband."

Maria's head was swimming, but she held fast to her lie as though she clutched the mast in a storm at sea. "It isn't so, Miss Elliott, that isn't true. When I first came to this country, months and months ago, I got in touch with Kurt, I saw him a few times. It is natural, we refugees seek each other out." She smiled with pretty pathos, but her information was news to Devon. According to Kurt, when Devon first mentioned her to him, they had not seen each other since Maria had been in America. "But then," continued Maria, "I was not well, I had been under a great strain in Europe, so I went to the country for the summer. I stayed on a farm in Jersey near Red Bank."

"Red Bank?" The name sent an echo vibrating through Devon's memory.

"Yes, the country near there is very pretty."

Red Bank, Red Bank, she thought, and suddenly she remembered: the postmark on the blue envelope the day she had picked up Kurt's mail in the workroom and taken it to his apartment. So the letter had been from Maria. Well, it didn't matter now, she supposed. Indeed she would have settled for a letter and been happy if that were all there was to it.

Maria expatiated a little on the beauties of the New Jersey countryside but ran down rather like a dying gramophone record as her employer sat in silence, seeming hardly to notice her.

Uncertain of Hedwig's story, to still her own mental turmoil Devon determined to call Maria's bluff. "You are lying to me, Miss Sellner. You may have called it off for the time being, but I know quite well you and Kurt have been having an affair. You were overheard one night in a restaurant, drinking a toast, I believe, to your current farewell but to a possible future reunion."

"But this is not true," cried Maria.

"It is quite true," said Devon quietly, and seeing Maria's expression, knew that in winning her point she had lost all hope.

Maria, usually intrepid, in the face of this evidence sat silent. The game was up and her job was gone. It was almost comic to think she had lost her livelihood for something which had been completely without importance. Well, since that was the way things were, she might as well tell the truth. A slow flush mounted from her throat and spread over her face as she said slowly, "It was never of any seriousness, Miss Elliot. I have known Kurt all my life, and I know the kind of man he is, but there is something . . ." She stopped. "Something compelling about him. I was rather lonely, and that's how it happened. I have been lying to save my job, but also because I didn't want to hurt you. It is unnecessary to hurt a person when the other two are not even in love. When I said good-by to Kurt that night I meant it. I would never have seen him again—in that way, I mean—nor would he have seen me. Even if he might have said differently, it was a performance, play-acting. It is customary when a love affair ends to say certain things. Kurt is like many of my countrymen—they are, I believe you call it, sticklers for form. They do heartless and irresponsible things, but they do them in a very correct framework."

This was so exactly Devon's own experience that she couldn't be fraud enough to contradict it, nor could she seem to find the energy necessary to build up a case for Kurt and condemn Maria. She had never subscribed to the apple theory of temptation, and over a dappled lifetime had learned that men rarely went to bed with women unless they wanted to or had something to gain. Maria sat quietly, her hands in her lap, staring unseeingly out the window. Devon watched her a long time, mixed but not antagonistic thoughts passing through her mind. At last she said formally, "Very well, Miss Sellner, that will be all. Please go to your own office." Maria's hand went to her throat.

"I . . . I will get my things together."

"I will send for you to make the final arrangements."

When Maria left her Devon sat for a long while tapping the desk with her paper knife. Finally she seemed to make up her mind about something and rose and went swiftly into Jasper's office. Jasper looked at her questioningly, and she nodded. "It's true, all right, they've been having an affair."

"Have you given Sellner the gate?"

"No," Devon said. "No, I haven't, and I don't think I will, Jasper."

Little lights flashed in Jasper's eyes. "Good girl!"

She smiled ironically. "Thanks. I scared the living be-Jesus out of her, though. She's waiting now in her office to hear the verdict, but she thinks she's through." Jasper grinned.

"I suppose you have the right to lay on the torture a little," he said, "but I think you're making a wise decision."

"Well, I haven't much choice. I know Kurt, she didn't have to do any very hot luring to get him, and besides, I feel kind of sorry for her. She's had a hell of a life the last few years. God knows I can recall one or two casual excursions in my own past. It would have been pretty tough if I'd lost my career because of them. Anyhow," and Devon laughed a little because she knew Jasper would be amused, "she's a damn good worker. She's doing admirably the job I engaged her to do."

He tossed her a quizzical glance. "You're not always so scrupulous."

"I am when I profit thereby."

He laughed outright. "I'm proud of you, Donna. You're tough. Most women envy you and wonder why you get on. You get on because you have guts. A woman in business has to have a kind of fairness and discipline most of your sex never dreams of. I've seen you pull some pretty fancy passes, but I'm damned if you've ever shirked the hardest kind of work, and you've always given a break to any other worker—who was on your side," he added in deference to veracity.

"Well, my kind of success comes high, Jasper. I hope it's worth it. In order to get where I am I've had to develop qualities which are scarcely lovable." Her brow darkened as she thought of Kurt. "I'm afraid my feminine appeal is pretty slim."

Jasper cleared his throat. "I don't seem to recall so many long, lonely years."

She made a face. "Oh well, affairs, sure."

"And for seven years a pretty remarkable husband and another one on the threshold. Not the highest quality, perhaps, but if he's what you want . . . And I might also add, my own not inconsiderable affection. Don't forget, my dear, you're pretty strong drink, only a few of us can stand up to you. Believe me, you've done all right, and I will thank you to snap out of this slightly motheaten rendition of the lonely soul in high places."

"You son of a bitch," she said with affectionate good humor, and Jasper grinned. He had succeeded in pulling her from the doldrums.

☆   ☆   ☆

"So you couldn't be true to me even while I was in Reno getting my divorce?" There was a note almost of amusement in Devon's voice. They were in her fabulous dressing room, and she was changing for dinner. As she slipped into a gray chiffon negligee and fastened on her softly gleaming clip of diamonds and moonstones she reminded Kurt of a misty evening, but he was in no mood to tell her so. He had at first hotly denied her accusation, but when Devon wearily told him that Maria had admitted the truth he had been forced to capitulate. Now that the cards were on the table he was making an honest attempt at self-analysis which was somewhat impeded by a feeling of resentment that he had been found out and placed in a position where he was obliged to exonerate himself.

"But you see, my darling," he said, "I cannot feel as you do that sex is evil."

Devon looked at him without anger, but her eyes were very clear. "Oh Kurt, how can you be so specious?"

"I do not see that I have in any way wronged you, Devon. I do not love Maria."

"I see. Only had you been sincere, would it have been wrong?"

"Now you are deliberately trying to——"

"The hell with it. Do you love me?"

"I do. Women will never believe that a man can have an affair and it means little or nothing to him, yet this is so." Devon thought of Tim and their lusty discussion that night in Washington. The funny, sad thing was that what both men said was true. Depending on the point of view of one's parents, one was brought up to believe that the act of love was either sacred or not quite nice. One approached it fearfully or tremulous with hope, but one certainly anticipated a little soul-shaking. It was a pleasant surprise to discover it could be fun and anticlimactic to realize that for both men and women it could become—of all things—casual. Somewhere along the line somebody had slipped up, the information was askew. "Well, I'll tell you something," as she spoke Devon drew on a gossamer thin stocking. "As a matter of fact I do believe you, because the same thing holds true for women. We've surrounded the most vital and commonplace human function with a vast morass of taboos, convention, hypocrisy, and plain claptrap. But as regards you and me, I'm only interested in one thing. We do have this tremendous physical bond between us, that you'll admit?"

"From the first night I saw you."

"Then why are you constantly untrue to me? To every woman? What is it in you, Kurt, that makes you this way?"

He answered slowly and with complete honesty. "Because I am afraid of missing something, I want to live fully."

"But countless piddling little affairs, what kind of full living is that? That sort of thing is for people who have nothing better or for the inexperienced, those who haven't yet learned how to satisfy themselves. You should know that by nibbling a piece of cake here, a bit of plum there, you only blunt the edge of your appetite. You cheat yourself, Kurt, out of the good full meal of life through lack of concentration. You don't take hold with both hands, my lad, you don't get value received." There was a pause. "I don't think I'm wrong," she continued gently, "because you have just said that Maria meant nothing to you—or isn't that so? Perhaps you do find as much happiness in her arms as you do in mine?"

This kind of conversation Kurt found acutely embarrassing; it required a detached attitude, and he had never disciplined his mind to this manner of thinking. He moved uneasily about the luxurious room, and Devon followed his reflection in the mirrors as she put on her other stocking and fragile slippers.

"You see, these are not nice things to talk about, Devon. Either you love or you do not love, and all this conversation about it is silly."

"I don't see why, I think it has great clinical interest. If I am going to marry you I wish to understand you. It may be impossible to love you after a while, so I wish to give you what I can. You at least will be one man who will be able to say that his wife does understand him."

Kurt's mind was not a sensitive plate, but it did receive the impression that he had hurt Devon badly. So badly that he stood a very good chance of losing her and, along with her, the pleasant companionship and the easy life he so desired. Besides, her remark cut him deeply; her love for him soothed and warmed him, that she might not care for him any more made him genuinely unhappy.

"I do not know what to say so you will believe me," he said at last, "because I have done a thing which makes you think it is not so, but I do love you with all my heart. The very fact that I denied the affair should prove that to you. If I did not care, I would have said quite frankly, 'Yes, I have been with another woman, what of it?'"

"But you see," she said, and her voice was suspiciously husky, "why I mind this affair more than any of the others you have had since we have been lovers is that you had really convinced me, or I had convinced myself, that things were going to be different. They say there's no prude like a reformed rake, so in order for them to know that, some rake someplace must have reformed, and I thought perhaps you were he."

"Oh darling." Kurt knelt beside the low slipper chair in which she sat and put his arms around her. "You are so sweet. I *have* reformed, I *am* different. When we are married we will be very happy." Wisdom cautioned to let it go at that, but his pride demanded a passing blow, so he continued: "Just the same it is a shock to me that you are so intolerant. I would not have expected you to be narrow-minded."

She drew out of his arms and looked at him with contempt. "You consider a woman narrow-minded who objects to her husband servicing the entire community?"

Kurt's Oriental features assumed that impassive stubborn look she knew so well. "You have devoted so much time to business, you are so enmeshed in artificial values and codes," he said coldly, "that you cannot understand a man without hypocrisy, one whose conduct is absolutely natural."

"My dear Kurt, it would be absolutely natural to relieve oneself on the drawing-room floor, but the civilized amenities are against it. Just because a thing is bestial doesn't make it attractive."

Kurt got to his feet. "I am sorry my manners are not up to your exalted standards," he said stiffly.

"Your manners are very charming. You may be interested to know that Maria and I agreed on that. You click your heels and kiss the ladies' hands and you send imaginative and pretty gifts, but the trouble with you is, Kurt, you haven't any guts. You want all the gaiety and excitement of a love affair, all the froth and none of the responsibility. Forgive my drawing your attention to the bromide, but privilege and responsibility do go hand in hand, and love may bring all sorts of unglamorous appendages in its wake: fidelity, perhaps, and illness and debts and children and sacrifice, and in these days, blood and death; but the adult people and the lusty ones seem able to cope with it. It's only the frivolous and the cowardly who have no stamina and run away."

"You are crazy," he said angrily. "My responsibilities I am never shirking, but I must have my personal freedom."

"I appreciate that, dear, and if I could feel it was a genuine basic need, I'd be very sympathetic, but I think you delude yourself with that alibi because you don't want to admit that you're too backward to conform to group living. That's what all civilization is based on, but apparently it's too complex for your primitive mind to cope with."

In most fights the pattern and weight vary. There are the moments when the bitter cutting thrusts are given and received, when heartbreak and hatred and black anger are interchanged in grim and lethal swordplay, but there are other times when the insults are exhilarating, when both sides play at fighting, as it were; they adopt an attitude towards it. The combat takes on the flavor of an Irish brawl, the battle assumes a certain good-humored lusty spirit. Devon was feeling this way now. She was brandishing her shillelagh, and though she meant every resounding whack and thump, the blows were delivered without venom. She was, if the truth were known, momentarily enjoying herself and felt a sense of irritation that Kurt could not reply in kind. It was this which caused her to remark crisply after a brief pause, and with, as far as he could see, no provocation, "You're very pedestrian, Kurt."

As Kurt privately considered himself anything but plodding, he quite naturally resented the epithet. He was angry and bewildered and had to think very hard why marriage to this virago had ever seemed desirable, but his native stubbornness did not desert him. "You seem to find nothing but unpleasant things to say to me," he began, and unexpectedly his humor flashed upon his own predicament. "I do not doubt that I am very stupid, because I still want to marry you, but God knows you are not the easiest person in the world to be married to."

"There must be an echo in this place," murmured Devon, thinking of what Jasper had said that morning.

"What do you say?"

"Never mind, go on."

"You do not like to admit it, but you are always wanting to tie a man down, Devon."

"That isn't so," she cried, for this time the poisoned sword tip went home. "And it's terribly unkind of you to say it. I would never want a man to be tied down. I only want him to be domestic and to love me with all his heart and to be kind and true."

"You are wanting a hundred-per-cent perfection. That is what I say: you are intolerant of real human nature."

"Well, if I were you, I wouldn't put myself up as an example of a human being. I don't say that I haven't perhaps exaggerated, even invented, misdeeds which you've never committed, but you deliberately do things to make me jealous. Some faculty in you is underdeveloped, for you get a certain enjoyment out of the suffering of others. You remind me of a shallow and depraved little tart who lived in Williamstown when I was very young, she was pretty and several of the boys fell for her—one kid in particular was desperately hard hit. She knew it and used deliberately to flaunt her affairs under his nose to cause him agonies of jealousy. It was as cheap and ugly as anything I've ever seen, and your behavior is uncomfortably close to it."

Kurt's clear hazel eyes grew nearly black, and he struck her a hard glancing blow across the mouth. She tottered but steadied herself against a chair. The blow was a shock, but it did not outrage her. Uncontrollable anger she could understand. She gave a breathless little laugh. "In China it's considered disgraceful to be the first to strike, it means you've run out of invective."

"And what about yourself?" Kurt shouted. "You are always thinking you are so perfect. Is it or is it not true that you are spoiled? Everything must be your own way. Your first husband, whom you are always quoting as such a saint, couldn't stand it and walked out on you."

"Leave Tim out of this." Devon's voice was low, but it flashed through Kurt's mind that if a snake had spoken it would have sounded just like that; he swerved from the topic of Mr. Wainwright.

"You are wrong, Devon," he said more quietly. "I do not like to see you unhappy, but apparently the only way for you to be happy is for me to be completely different, yet I do not seek to change you. I am quite satisfied."

Devon bowed ironically. "You have a magnanimous temperament."

Kurt, his anger quickly spent, grinned mischievously. "I am different from you."

"Yes, you are," she said soberly. "And somehow I feel it would be a mistake for two people to marry who are so dissimilar." There, it was said. To her own surprise she had spoken her inner thoughts, and they were what Kurt had feared to hear ever since he emerged from the fury which had swept over him when Devon told him Hedwig's story. That a woman whom he did not know should have the audacity and power to interfere with his plans outraged him; he would marry Devon now if only for revenge. He would show that monstrous Hedwig that she could not affect his intended course. His determination made him crafty, and he brought his most winning qualities to bear.

"Darling," he said gently, "I realize that from your point of view, perhaps from the point of view of most people, I have done a bad thing, but I can only say to you that I will change so that I may please you. If you will help me, I promise to use all my power to make you happy. I love you, I love no other woman, and to have you as my wife is what I dream of."

Devon shook her head. "Kurt, I would be destroying myself. I can't say to you I don't love you, it wouldn't be true, but I've got to force myself to get over you, that's all. If you behave this way now, if we have these terrible rows while love is supposedly young and fresh, can you visualize what our future would be? My God, dear, we'd kill each other."

"I do not agree. By living together we may come to understand each other better. We will become satisfied."

"I would never be satisfied with a lot of other women in your life, and you would never be satisfied that I was not."

"Then perhaps we would become like other married people who cease to care."

"Thanks. I would just as soon live in a dead volcano." There was silence between them for a little while. It was with an effort that Devon broke it: "You see, Kurt, I feel that, in love, gallantry is necessary. Even when the first wild desire is gone, especially then, there is an inherent need for good manners and consideration, for the putting forth of effort. Two courteous and civilized human beings out of the loneliness of their souls owe that to each other."

"Devon," he said sadly, and this time he was sincere, "what I am not understanding is why you ever cared for me at all, but you have cared. I am no different from what I ever was, except I had thought

I was more the way you want me. Why do you cease now to love me?"

"I'm tired of being lied to, Kurt."

"But I do not lie, that is just it. This was the only time. Or dinarily perhaps I do not say what I do, but I do not lie."

"I want to be lied to."

"Ach, you are very difficult."

"Yes." She was draped sidewise across the chair, her neck bent, her head resting on the back like a boneless creature in a fairy tale. Kurt felt a great longing to shake her, but he supposed it would do no good.

"You are my little silly thing. But it is good that we should be married. I will help you to grow sensible, you will see."

But she shook her head. "No, Kurt, I do not think I will marry you." She spoke in a curious monotone, almost as though she were in a trance. "I am surprised to hear myself say this really, and in another mood I expect I shall temporarily regret it, but I have got to save myself. You are like a drug to me. You are like a virus that gets into my blood and I become ill. It is not the drug's fault that people take it and get ill, but if they want to live, after a time they stop taking it. The struggle is very hard, I know that, but it must be gone through. Just now I feel numb, so I do not suffer . . . the bad time is coming . . . but you and I are through. You want personal freedom, so do I. You really don't give a damn about anyone else—that is part of your lighthearted charm; but I can only feel free if I am securely held in love. Tim and I had that for a while. We lived in a wonderful country."

"But Tim has gone away."

"Yes, so he has. I am alone now." Suddenly the color came back into her voice, and her eyes glinted through her lashes. "You should try going away, Kurt. You should go to the wars. You could fight for the fifth freedom, the personal one," and she smiled with light and not unfriendly mockery.

"I am perfectly willing to go to war," he said with dignity, "whenever I am called."

"That's nice of you, darling."

He took her hands and pulled her up from her chair. "Devon,

stop this joking, you do not mean that you will not marry me." He spoke forcefully; if he spoke with enough force he would be able to change this ridiculous decision. She had said it in such a dreamy way, she did not realize . . .

"It's funny, Kurt, a year ago I would have given my immortal soul to hear you say that. This morning, even, this morning I was thinking of myself as already your wife . . . that seemed kind of funny too, but awfully nice . . . and now . . . it's all over. I don't think it makes a great deal of sense, but that's the way it is. The last straw, I guess."

Kurt turned a strange, dirty gray. He had allowed his imagination free play of late. Not only was he losing the only woman who had ever touched his heart, giving him a glimpse of a vernal world he had never before known, but countless little schemes and plans had begun to form in his mind about a new way of life. How he would expand his business, how he might be able to get some of his relatives out of Europe, the pleasant existence which would be his, relieved of financial worry. After the war, the trips to Europe they would take so that Devon might learn of his background. He had a deep-buried, unacknowledged desire to prove to her that he was a man of substance, something other than a footless refugee. His understanding could not accept the fact that this . . . this . . . this nothing at all with Maria, who was already fading from his consciousness, had destroyed his chance of entering into a sweet and secure world. Why, the thing was ridiculous. Even as he stood there holding tight to Devon's hands and saying to himself, *If this woman is so trivial, so stupid as to let this absurd deflection swerve her from happiness, I do not want to marry her,* his heart cried out that she was what he wanted. "You really mean that we are through? That you will not marry me?" he asked, and there was such a lost sound in his voice that she was touched and could only nod. He stared at her for a long time. "Well," he said at last, and he drew a deep breath and made a rather pitiable effort at jocosity, "even if this is so, we are not people having nothing in common. We could perhaps meet sometimes, discuss the weather, I could keep you abreast of developments in the leather business. We . . . we would broaden our scope."

"No, Kurt, no. Perhaps my unhappiness with you is largely my own fault, but it takes too much out of me. If I married you, every time we met a new pretty girl I'd say to myself, *There he goes again.* Every time you blandly announced that you had an engagement for the evening and went no further, I should be resentful of what seems to me insolence and lack of consideration. I don't doubt that I have habits that irritate you, but when I ceased to care about your comings and goings or your little affairs, it would mean that I had ceased to care about you, and therefore why be married anyhow?"

"I never thought our end would come like this," he said heavily.

"Nor I. Please go quickly, Kurt, and know that I shall remember the lovely bits as long as I live."

Kurt released the hard, tight grip he had kept on her wrists, clicked his heels, bowed over her hand as he had done the first evening he met her, and turned and left the room. He never even saw Fairweather who held the front door open for him when he went out.

When Devon said that the bad time was coming, she knew whereof she spoke. In that last meeting with Kurt she passed through a mood of suspended reaction, when it seemed that nothing in any way touched her, either to interest or to hurt her, but she knew from past experience that this emotional numbness was only transitory. When she sent Kurt away she did it without pain, almost as though she were under anesthesia. Besides, shadowy in the back of her mind was the thought that perhaps, perhaps the impossible would happen and Tim would return. Of Kurt she expected little, but Tim was a man of quality in the ancient sense of the word, and the quality endured. Hadn't he said that he loved her and would love her always? Surely, then, he would come back. She had been so busy, she had for so long unthinkingly accepted the proposition that love was the strongest force in the world, that it was with a sense of slow awakening that she was coming to realize that it was far outdistanced by dearer concerns: patriotism, money, pride, ambition, and the instinct of self-preservation. These

were among the more immediate competitors, but the slow pressure
of space and time as well as custom also played their relentless parts
in the obliteration of love. Even she and Tim, and they had been
exultant lovers, were finally separated by other concerns, and in the
case of Kurt, her instinct of self-preservation spoke louder than any
endearment. Yet in the past year the ecstasy and the unhappiness
he had caused her had made him so much a part of her that in up-
rooting him from her life she suffered the retrospective agony of an
amputated limb.

The mood of indifference wore off, to be replaced by the slow
mounting pain of loss. She crammed her days and evenings with
work and entertainment and for the first time in her life knew what
it was to be lonely. She hated cocktail parties, but remembering that
Kurt had said they were the market places, the stock exchange, for
sex and romance, she went to every one to which she was invited,
thinking perhaps she would meet someone who would distract her
mind. She served on every kind of war committee, seeking diversion
from boredom, because her very suffering bored her. The reason for
it seemed unbearably trivial. It was like the threadbare French plays
of a few years back when the French stage had but one plot exclusively, infidelity among the well-to-do. How shabby and frivolous
they seemed, those rickety little props of a toy theater, gone down
in the dust and ruins of a vanished world!

But the cocktail parties with their heat and crowds and over-
stimulation were distasteful to her, and though she stuck them for a
time because the cause was urgent, the war committees, with their
jealousies and antagonistic factions and stuffed-chemise members
secretly regarding the holocaust as a titillating and glorified bridge
club, disgusted her and she finally withdrew, salving her conscience
by large and outright cash donations to the Red Cross, the China
Relief, and any other likely endeavor, ranging from personally sub-
sidized mobile canteens to false teeth for anti-fascists.

One afternoon after a surfeit of committees and cocktail parties
she stepped into her car and told Owens to drive to the laboratory
on Long Island. It was very late, and the chauffeur looked at her in
surprise, but she was lonely and bored and needed to feel solid
ground under her feet. She did not go often to the laboratory these

days; Tim had chosen well for her, and David Ullman was doing a masterly job. Besides, the laboratory had been Tim's bailiwick and was too full of old memories, but tonight she needed them for comfort.

They were repairing the street directly in front of the plant, so Owens drew up to the opposite curb. Devon stepped out of the car and stood looking across the road at the impressive mass looming in the spring twilight. She thought what a beautiful building it was, compact and functional, pure in line and mellow in color. A solid testimonial to her achievement and a strong prop to her currently shaky ego. She smiled as she looked at the long, low extension housing the delivery trucks. How proud she had been of the very first truck, one of the sage of Dearborn's minor efforts, but representing for her the bottom rung of the ladder.

She crossed the road and entered the small door leading directly into the shipping room. Old William, the night watchman, sat in his little cage reading the evening paper. He looked up when she entered, and though he seemed pleased to see her he did not evince much surprise at her unexpected visit.

"Pretty near everyone's all gone, Mrs. Wainwright," he said mildly. William had been Tim's buddy, so though everyone else in the plant called Devon Miss Elliott, he always addressed her by her married name.

"I expect they have, William. I certainly hope so. I don't want to see anyone. I've done enough talking for today."

He peered at her over his spectacles. "Them committee meetings, I'll bet."

Devon was surprised. "Why, William, how did you know about them?"

William chuckled. "The papers even get 'way out here, Mrs. Wainwright, you're in 'em a lot recently." Devon flinched slightly. He held up the *Journal-American* he was reading, where she was pictured in a group of women organizing a ball for the United Nations.

"And it's my last one, believe me," she said grimly.

"Yes, ma'am. Can I do anything for you?"

"No, thank you, William, I'm just looking." This was all right with William. The boss was a little screwy, but she was a nice woman. A fool to let Mr. Wainwright get away from her, but women never did know when they had a good thing. Ought not to get mixed up in them columns though, looked cheap.

Devon wandered through her building. She had stood for a few minutes looking into the shadowy gloom of the huge shipping department, where the preparations were packed in great cartons and sent all over the United States, Canada, Mexico, and South America. They had never shipped to Europe because the preparations for England and the Continent were manufactured over there, and Devon's eyes clouded as she thought of the French plant and the formulas in the hands of the Nazis.

She went upstairs and passed slowly through the big airy rooms with their high studio windows. They were deserted now by the workers, but she looked around contentedly. The machinery and paraphernalia still had the power to fascinate her; the machine with the pistonlike shaft, a super cookie cutter where two men stood slipping out the wafers of dry rouge and powder which went into the compacts. The great shining copper vats with enormous wooden paddles where they stirred the creams, twelve hundred pounds to a vat. She still thought it ingenious, the way the heavy cream flowed from the tubs through a labyrinth of pipes and tubes to the floor below, where girls sitting at long benches caught the smooth stream in porcelain jars. In another part of that room a conveyor belt carried the jars to be labeled. They lay on their sides, and the girls had only to twist them, synchronizing them to an automatic machine which stuck the labels on. The labels alternated in the machine: the label on the front, twist, the label on the back, and the next jar was under their hands.

She walked into the kitchen where the lipsticks were made. Everything about the lipsticks was fun, the big saucepans in which the luscious colors were heated and stirred, incarnadined pools of crimson and vermilion and scarlet and warm blood-red, the steam that kept the mixture at the correct temperature while it was poured into the bullet-shaped molds, and the enormous iceboxes that a hotel kitchen might envy where the molds were set to cool, and the way they acquired the glaze, by being passed swiftly through a flame. She crossed the hall and went into the small room where the electrometer was housed, the costly and delicate precision instrument which tested the finished products to define the alkaline and acid content. She unlocked the cool storeroom where lay a fortune in oils and concentrates, pomades and crystals, which were the base of all their perfumes. There stood the essence of jasmine and there, felt-wrapped with their wax seals, lay the flat canteens holding the attar of roses. Devon found them a source of infinite satisfaction. She felt like a contented housewife gazing upon her stores. In season there would be long tables laden with strawberries and cucumbers and water lilies, crushed for their juices that went into the lotions and creams.

She left the vault, carefully locking the door behind her, and on her way down to the office passed through the powder room that was like a flour mill with a coating of colored scented dust over everything. A man couldn't work too long a time in the powder room, the particles got into his lungs. The great barrels of unmixed colors stood in rows, dark brown, brick red, raw ocher. Devon liked the powder in this state. It stimulated her to think that these strong, violent colors were the coarse peasant parents from which flowered the fragile Spring Primroses, Chiffon Softs, and Sunset Glows. The powders were mixed and sifted through infinitely fine silk strainers and packaged into the gay boxes from which millions of women drew their daily quota of beauty.

As Devon had known it would, the round of the factory refreshed her. Loveliness might be ephemeral, but the business of creating it was substantial, drawing upon man's skill, upon the fruits of the earth and the oil of animals. The ingredients themselves were more worthy of respect than the dithering women who used them and with whom she had been associating. She paused at the door of the room that had been Tim's office. Ullman worked there now, but he had left things pretty much as they were. She felt sentimental about the place, but her native honesty of thought caused her to dispel the mood. *It's the one place Tim never wants to see again,* she thought, *why should I shed a tear over the prison cell?* She went in, straightened the chair in front of the desk, looked at some orders and memoranda that Ullman had left ready for tomorrow, and her glance fell on the battered files in which Tim had never been able to find anything, but which he stubbornly refused to have put in order. There was something rakish and friendly about the scarred old chest; it had a permanent air, and without knowing quite why, Devon felt comforted. She closed the office door softly and went on her way.

She heard from Tim off and on. He had succeeded in getting himself attached to a British unit and was in North Africa, and he wrote fairly frequently. Sometimes his letters were aglow with enthusiasm, sometimes raging against bureaucracy, red tape, and the dunderheadedness of a command which kept him in the front-line dressing stations when his own idea, as far as she could gather, was to advance ahead of the troops. But always his letters had vitality. "The salve," he wrote, "is more wonderful than Oscar and I dared dream, but its potency lies in the immediacy of its application. If no time at all elapses, even the most grievous burns seem to respond miraculously well." He ended his letters "Love, Tim," but he didn't speak of coming home, and in the turmoil of battle he seemed to find a curious peace and satisfaction. The destruction did not appall him as Devon had feared it might; it only gave him limitless material on which to work his own constructive efforts. She felt profoundly envious of him, for he had come to grips with reality and found he could face it, self-sufficient. He was a whole human being; she was not. Her engrossing business, her fortune, her list of acquaintances limited only by her own energies and wishes, still left her incomplete.

She so crowded her days that when she went to bed at night she fell at once into a deep sleep, but she would awaken at four or five in the morning, and then the slow tears would seep from under her eyelids as she thought of Tim and tried to thread her way back through the maze of her life to the place where she had taken the wrong turning. She never tried to exonerate herself, but at last it came to seem to her that, given their two selves, the end they reached was inevitable. And this was sadder than a preventable error would have been for the very reason that there was no remedy. They were powerless to alter their own natures. She had no truck with a superimposed fate, for she believed passionately in free will and in man's power to form his own destiny; but he was impotent to the extent that his limitation was his character. Beyond that he could not go; outside of that he could not climb.

Of course life did not exist in a vacuum, and ideas and events and forces molded characters, but the quality of the clay which took the imprint had been selected long ago. Since there was no equality of spirit, all the more reason for equality of opportunity; for what man could say who would triumph and who would not?

From the standpoint of education and background, Kurt should have developed into an adult and responsible human being, yet he couldn't help it if he didn't care that he was not. Had he been able to care, he would have helped it, therefore he would not be the way he was.

The weeks stretched into months, and she and Kurt did not see each other. The countless small and charming gifts he had bestowed upon her had no power to evoke him, but sometimes she would see his name in the paper or come across a snapshot of him she had taken in the country, and then, though she thought she was gradually recuperating, an overwhelming longing for him would sweep over her. While the mood lasted she would cling fast to her resolution, reiterating to herself over and over again, *This will pass, this will end, it cannot go on much longer now,* but it seemed to be going on longer than she believed possible.

She reorganized her life, she went to Williamstown to visit Matthew and Matilda Stevens, whom she had always thought of as her family, and formally adopted them as parents. In drawing up the papers, Henry Barlow found himself in the highly embarrassing position of a lawyer without a precedent to lean on, and was obliged to use his mind, a nasty jar to his equanimity. "It's the parents who adopt the children, Devon," he fumed. "I never heard of it the other way around." But his client was adamant, and papers were duly drawn up whereby the Stevenses legally became her parents, and she made a generous settlement on them at the time, and left them a large slice of her fortune should she predecease them. "You've got a pretty good chance of collecting, too," she told them candidly. "You know my family, nobody lives very long." Matthew and Matilda were entertained and touched by these tactics, but also

a little uncertain, being none too sure that at their age they cared
to change their way of life. Devon finally agreed that they should
live on in Williamstown if they wanted to, but she firmly attached
one string: they were definitely to come to New York for four
months in the winter and spend at least three weeks at the farm in
the summer.

That year they came to spend August with her, but were saddened by the divorce, for they loved Tim dearly. Devon told
them little about Kurt. They knew there was a man she had thought
seriously of marrying, but she said only that she had thought better
of it and changed her mind.

They felt that she was looking well, and her unmistakable delight
in having them with her warmed their hearts, but Matthew was
worried. "It's as though she were hollow, Matilda," he kept saying,
"a fine pretty shell, doing everything it's supposed to do but hollow
inside. Even if that fellow she broke off with wasn't altogether
right, maybe he'd be better than nothing," but they could find out
very little about him, because none of Devon's friends who came
out to the country seemed to feel that Kurt's was a personality the
Stevenses would be interested in discussing, and Devon herself,
after a few meager references, ignored the subject.

She was in her office one late afternoon winding up a few loose
ends before leaving for the country—since Matthew and Matilda
had come she commuted almost daily—when Hilda came scurrying
in, her eyes almost popping from her head. "Miss Elliott," she said
breathlessly, "there's something very peculiar going on in the hall—
a little parade of men with presents, I think they are, anyway all
sorts of things, and they insist on seeing you personally. They say
they're a confidential messenger service."

"What sort of things, Hilda?"

"Well, just . . . just *things*. Shall I let them in?" Devon thought
Hilda had taken leave of her senses, but she told her to open the
door. Hilda did, admitting a small procession of five men. They
were quite ordinary-looking citizens, but what riveted the attention
was the extraordinary burdens they carried.

The first one bore a large green branch with small objects
dangling from it, which on closer inspection turned out to be olives

that had been wired on. The second held a wicker cage of doves, who would presumably coo when the novelty of their surroundings had worn off; the third carried a long, antique Dutch pipe, the fourth a reproduction of Millet's "Angelus" and a small toy train with an envelope sticking out of it, and the fifth held before him a banner of purest white rayon which he bore as proudly as if "Excelsior" had been embossed thereon. Devon stared at them as though they were a row of ghosts. "What . . . what is this?" she stammered. "Where do you come from? Who sent you?" For one wild moment her heart leaped. Had Tim . . .

"I'm to say it's all explained in this here note, lady." The train-bearer stepped forward and set the toy train with the envelope on her desk. He seemed to be the leader, for he turned to the men and spoke with the tone of authority: "O.K., youse can put the other stuff down." There was an awkward silence as the men, having deposited their burdens, stood stolidly waiting further orders, and the chief shifted uncomfortably. "Well, that's all, I guess," he said finally. "Get goin'."

Devon jumped up. "But wait a minute, what is all this?"

"I got orders to say nuttin' but that it's in the envelope, miss. Well . . . so long." And the poor man's Roxy ushers shuffled off.

Hilda stood spellbound. "Who on earth . . ." she began, but Devon had guessed.

"Don't you know, Hilda?"

"Oh, Miss Elliott, could it be . . . do you think . . ."

"Yes, I think." Devon looked at the display. "I'll call when I want you," she said, and Hilda slipped from the room. Devon's heart was pounding so hard she felt suffocated and her knees were shaking; it would be impossible for her to read Kurt's letter with anyone else in the room. She sat down and drew the letter from the little train and held it in her hand for a long moment before opening it. Finally she slit the envelope and unfolded the sheet of paper it contained. She read:

My DARLING:

I have stood our separation as long as possible, and as I am a logical man who can no longer endure this war of attrition—for since you are all that I want, without you that is what my life has become—I am begging for an Armistice. Since the two most notable ones of our day seem to have been concluded in a railroad train, I send you a replica in the hope that the atmosphere will put you in the right frame of mind, that it will inspire you to mercy. The other offerings are symbols of peace. If I had been able to think of any more I would have sent them. We said cold things to each other, but the months of loneliness have wiped them out for me, and I pray for you, also.

Perhaps I have no chance at all, perhaps you are already in love with someone else, but I must try and I must hope or never any more know happiness. Please will you not see me? I will call you tomorrow for your answer. I love you very, very much.

KURT.

Devon sat for a long time, her eyes resting unseeingly on the white flag of truce. She was trying to read her own heart. That Kurt was capable of changing, she no longer believed. The question was, did she still love him, and if so was her love strong enough to surmount his infidelities and accept him as he was? Presumably he still possessed the qualities which had originally drawn her to him; she never completely vilified a man she had once loved, her pride was too great, but hadn't their love been so desperately wounded that it would never be whole and strong again? Only . . . Devon was lonely; Kurt lacked stature as a human being, but he had certain attributes which charmed her and a capacity for outstripping discouragement which she admired. Whether he would have wanted to marry her had she been poor was an academic question, although she thought wryly that, with the way the war and taxation was going, she might soon know the answer to that one too. She pondered for a long time, but when Kurt phoned the next day she agreed to dine with him the following evening and specified a restaurant, being none too sure that were they alone in the still, fragrant gloom of the drawing room, with the river slipping by outside, Kurt might not resort to a means of persuasion more potent than the intellectual.

But the next morning a letter arrived from Tim, and the whole world changed. Tim was coming home, and Devon experienced a jubilation she had forgotten was possible. It was as though he had intervened a second time to save her. She remembered his letter from Louisiana, when she had been hovering on the brink of Kurt. She rushed into Jasper's office, aflame with excitement. "Jasper, Jasper, the famine is over! They're crowding in from all sides, yesterday Kurt and today Tim! Never one star but a galaxy. Look, look, here's his letter," and she thrust it towards him. "He's been wounded, but he's all right. No, maybe it's secret only to me," and she snatched it back, but then she changed her mind again. "Oh heavens, no, it's for you too, he'd want you to see it."

Jasper dove for the letter, which was fluttering like a wild bird over his desk, and scanned it hastily. Tim had been wounded, it seemed, in the chest, but was on the mend and would be invalided out of service and sent back to America. He wrote:

It's a little embarrassing, but I believe I have been awarded a medal. Think nothing of it, however, I require no special consideration and will be quite satisfied if you walk ten paces behind me. And speaking of promenades, I hope, dearest madam, that you will walk and talk with me when I do get back. I have done a lot of thinking in the past six weeks, that being about the only form of exercise not sternly proscribed by the authorities, and there have been moments when I feel I have behaved like the rear end of an entire troop of cavalry. I appreciate the fact, but my belief is that you and I might work out some kind of communal life if you are agreeable to the idea. I seem to have found out about myself in a way that has given me a certainty I lacked before. The things that seemed confusing are now quite clear. I know what I must do, but I know it quietly without the feeling of revolt which has permeated the last couple of years. I want so much to be near you. I would never have mentioned it had you not written that there had been a change in your plans, and indeed perhaps my offering is too little and comes too late, but it is desperately sincere. If you will turn your agile mind upon this matter, a man's mind, I have heard say, though you are a feminist and I know how it irritates you, perhaps you will regard the proposition from a man's angle. If it is from this man's angle, you can not but fall in with the plan. God bless you, my darling. Within two weeks I hope to be out of this hole, which must remain a mystery until I see you. Once I am dismissed from the hospital, there may be a brief waiting spell, but I will, if not jugged on grounds of comforting the enemy, try to send a cable giving you an approximate arrival date. All my love.

                                                            Tim.

Jasper and Devon looked at each other for a long, happy moment. "It's wonderful, isn't it?" she said, and her eyes shone like stars.

"I guess it's the happy ending, all right," said Jasper, and all his grayness seemed to take on a silvery glow.

They talked for a time about Tim and how he had come to be wounded, and Devon decided he must have committed deeds of derring-do to shame the Commandos, and she thought it glorious justice that he should have invented the salve which doubtless saved his own life. "When he comes home, whatever he wants, Jasper, any way at all that he wants to work and live, will be wonderful with me. I will never interfere, you'll see. If he has to work outside of New York for long periods even, I won't complain. I'll never mention the business to him. We'll be *so* happy."

If Jasper privately doubted the appearance of the stigmata upon the newly invested saint who stood before him, he said nothing, injecting only one practical note into the roseate dream. "What about Kurt?"

"Oh . . . oh, him . . ." She had shown Jasper Kurt's peace offerings, but his reaction had been sour. "Mr. Fabri does not impress me," was all he said. "I'm dining with him tonight, you know, Jasper."

"And?"

"There's only one answer, of course. Tim. I still can't pretend that I don't care something for Kurt, it's not as if he never happened, you know, but I do feel in a curious way that my life is being saved. I've been given a second chance, Jasper; that happens to so few people ever, and it's happened to me. I don't intend to muff it."

"Good girl," said Jasper. "I shall lift that medal right off Tim and pin it on you."

"Can you imagine the brave darling . . . probably hurled himself under the wheels of a tank to save his companions."

"Tanks have treads." Jasper himself was feeling rather like an escaped balloon and needed a few common-sense staples with which to peg himself to the ground.

At dinner that night Devon was very honest and told Kurt about Tim's letter and how happy she was that he was coming home.

"I see," said Kurt. "Then you never really loved me at all."

"Oh, my dear. I have adored you, Kurt. In some ways you were more profoundly a part of me than any man I have ever known. That's one thing that has always seemed to me very strange about love, its inequality. One would think that a violent passion would call forth an equal response, but it doesn't. I wanted so much for us, really good things. I wanted us to have bread, but you only wanted stone. At first I thought it was humiliating that I should care so much and you so little, but now I don't know. When I look at such a situation objectively, as if it were two other people, I realize that the one who is satisfied with the stone is mistaken. A self-induced pauper."

"You are always assuming that only you know how to love," he said with a teasing smile.

"No, darling, only that I know more than you." The remark was half-laughing, half-sad.

Kurt felt very strange. He was stubborn and proud, and it had cost him an effort to be the first to capitulate, but when he became convinced that Devon would never seek him out he determined on one last gamble to win her. He had made a joke of the peace offerings because he was afraid to seem heavy, but he was just the same desperately in earnest. He who was rarely moved by anything was moved to complete reversal of the philosophy of a lifetime by a kind of emotional cupidity. And ironically, it was too late. "Tell me something, Devon," he said. "If you had not heard from your husband, would you have come back to me? Would you have married me?"

"I don't know," she said slowly. "That's why I agreed to see you tonight. It was an experiment in a way, a dare I made myself take. I didn't know whether all my feeling would be dead, whether it would blaze up again the instant I saw you, or whether we could start gently as friends. . . . I . . . I honestly didn't know."

She had given him an idea. "Well, it may be many weeks yet before Tim gets back. Would you like to see me in that time? Perhaps when you are seeing him again you will not have the same feelings any more either. You cannot be sure."

"Oh yes," she said simply, "I can be sure about Tim."

Kurt, in pursuing women, did not have great patience, because his interest was seldom keen enough. If a woman capitulated within a few days or a few weeks, he was delighted; if she prolonged the suit, he lost interest and turned to easier prey; but in the case of Devon he had possessed her, she was a famous personality, and he had unexpectedly fallen in love. To have lost her was humiliating, to get her back a point of pride. Besides, though he wanted her for all the material security she represented, there was something more: something he had not anticipated: an emptiness, an aching that confused him. "It is so hard for me to believe you do not want us even to be friends," he said, and he seemed to be searching for something. "You think badly of me, darling, but I do not change so much as you. I am still in love with you, you know."

"I'm desperately sorry, Kurt, believe me I am. I don't suppose I shall ever quite get over you. If we had been otherwise, our lives might have worked out differently. God knows there was a time when I wanted them to, but that time has gone by."

He understood her words, but they alone would not have convinced him. It was the expression in her face when she spoke of Tim that spelled his defeat. Kurt knew then, even allowing for the feminine trick of building up the absent swain at the expense of the present incumbent, that her whole spirit was turned towards Tim, and he didn't have a chance. His laugh was twisted, but a certain sardonic humor about himself forced him to laugh at his own discomfiture. They parted in friendly fashion, yet in the end with a curious indifference. A repeat farewell performance loses in intensity.

From then on Devon's days built and focused around Tim's homecoming. Jasper, the State Department, and the Red Cross were goaded, harried, browbeaten and exasperated by her efforts to get him out of Africa and safely back. "It can't be done, Devon," Jasper remarked at last with some irritation. "They're doing everything they can, but they can't make any extraordinary exception in Tim's case even if you do happen to love him. Now relax and keep calm. It may be a month or so yet, but he'll get here. Even if it could be done, you don't want him to travel before he's able, do you?"

This alarmed her, and she said meekly, "No, no, of course not," and set about completely redecorating his room as a surprise.

She and Claire Dangerfield came into the salon one day laden down with curtain and wallpaper samples. Somewhat to the surprise of his friends, Dickie Masters, who had done the house originally, had enlisted in the American Field Service, so Devon had pressed Claire into use. Claire was delighted as they all were by the news of Tim's return, but she did mutter that she wished Devon could stabilize her affairs. "I run my legs off to the knees every time you switch your love life. For God's sake, this time, light, will you?" and Devon replied that when they were all eighty she would invite Claire for tea and they should sip it in those identical surroundings.

As they entered the office Hilda handed Devon a telegram which had been delivered ten minutes before. "Oh good," she said, "I'll bet it's from the St. Louis salon and high time. They seem to have been doing a little jujitsu out there with the accounts. I told them to send me the daily statement by telegram." She tore open the envelope and glanced at the enclosure, but even before she unfolded it her face turned gray. Claire sprang forward. "Devon, what is it?" A sort of paralysis had settled in Devon's fingers, and she clawed at the paper before she got it fully spread open. The words seared through her eyeballs onto her brain:

THE WAR DEPARTMENT REGRETS TO INFORM YOU THAT ON AUGUST 28, 1942, MAJOR TIMOTHY WAINWRIGHT DIED OF WOUNDS RECEIVED IN ACTION SOMEWHERE IN NORTH AFRICA.

Twenty-five words. Devon as a rule was a rapid reader, but it seemed to take her a long, long time to assimilate the meaning of that sentence. Claire took the telegram from her and led her to a chair. "Get Mr. Doolittle," she said briefly to Hilda, who, white and shaking, hurried from the room. She returned in a moment with Jasper. As he looked at Devon he received a terrible shock. Her tall, slender figure was slumped forward in her chair, her eyes were sunken in her head, she looked gaunt and desperately ill. Jasper thought she had had a stroke. "Devon, good God, child, what's the matter?" She moved her lips, but no sound came out. Claire handed him the telegram in silence. Jasper read it, and it seemed as if he too could not take in the meaning. He and Devon stared at each other, and their eyes were blank. He turned to Hilda. "Go into my office," he said dully, "and ask Miriam to give you some whisky. It's in the closet back of the desk." When Hilda returned with the bottle Jasper poured it into the glass that stood on Devon's desk, added water from the small silver thermos jug and, going around beside her chair, held it to her lips while she drank. As a little color came back to her face, the dreadful gray look faded and Claire breathed easier. At least Devon didn't look as though she were going to die. She spoke at last. "The happy ending, Jasper," she said. Hilda and Claire didn't know what she was talking about, but Jasper remembered his own words when Tim's letter had arrived, saying he was coming home.

Claire wanted to help, but she realized that the kindest thing would be to leave them alone. Her piquant little face was miserable. "I'll go now, Devon," she said, "but let me know if there's anything on earth I can do. Do you want me to send Jennie around? I can phone her."

Devon replied with an effort: "No, thank you, Claire, I'll speak to her later." There was a pause; her eyes fell on the big envelope of stuffs and wallpaper she and Claire had brought in. "You'd better take back the samples," she said tonelessly. "I don't need them now." Claire picked them up and walked out quickly, trying to stifle her sobs.

Left alone, Devon looked at Jasper with haggard eyes. "But I . . . I don't understand. . . . In his letter, the way he spoke, the wound didn't seem so much . . . it was nearly cured, I thought. What about his formula, his miraculous preparation?"

"It was a different kind of wound, Devon. It probably had nothing to do with burns or flayed skin. It must have been something deep. We'll be able to learn later on. . . . Later on, they'll tell us."

She rose and moved painfully about the room as if her agony were too great to bear. Movement, a changed position, might bring a little surcease. "He wanted to come home . . . he wanted to come back to me, it's my fault; as soon as I had the letter I should have gone at once. I could have taken the Clipper——"

"Dear, dearest Devon, they would never have let you go."

"I could have made them, I could have bought my way. Sweet

God in heaven, what good is all this money if it can't buy . . . if it can't buy . . ."

She was getting hysterical, and the tears were beginning to come. Jasper did not try to stop her; he knew that anything would be better than this dry-eyed anguish. "Maybe he didn't get my cable, Jasper, maybe he died not knowing I love him, that I was blessed because he wanted to come back. Maybe he thought I didn't care, maybe he thought I didn't care. . . ." For the first time in many years Jasper gathered her close in his arms and held her against him while the sobs tore through her body. He caressed her soft dark hair. "Never fear that, my Donna. Never fear. No matter what, Tim knew always that he was the greatest thing in your life."

The news of Tim's death had brought on a nervous collapse, and for weeks Devon was in wretched health, overcome by a lassitude from which she found it impossible to rouse herself. For the first time that anybody there could remember, she was not at Devonshire House nor could she make her customary fall tour of the salons. She spent her days lying on the terrace in the country, watching the men cutting down the hay fields and looking at the white sails drifting by in the autumn sunshine. She lay for long hours gazing at the elm trees on the ridge, silhouetted against the hazy sky and absorbing the memory of Tim so deep into her bones that he became forever a part of her own ego. When the weather grew colder she was moved into town and spent most of her time by the fire, or a little later, warmly muffled, walked up and down the small garden at the river's edge, watching the squat tugs or the PT boats or occasionally, and with a curious electric shock, the passage of a British submarine.

During this time of her illness Kurt showed remarkable tact. He felt no grief at Tim's death, nor did he pretend to, but whatever he might have thought of his own chances under the circumstances he was careful not to indicate. He sent flowers and once in a while a thoughtful little gift, and he came occasionally to sit with Devon, but always in the role of an interested but not intimate friend. He

In Bed We Cry

was discreet in his outside amatory pursuits, and when he took any of his ladies to the fall openings, he would tell Devon he had been invited by friends, implying a party, and he would relate with considerable skill the plot of the play and the caliber of the actors' performances. He would relay the latest gossip of the night clubs, and his quips were almost as funny as Nicky's. He sometimes spoke to her of his business and asked her advice in small matters that did not involve consideration of intricate or previous business transactions. He was in short understanding, affable, and kind, and he was not around too much.

The Stevenses grew rather fond of him, for with Devon's breakdown they had prolonged their visit and in mid-November were just preparing to leave. She was beginning to regain her strength and starting to kick over the traces in her eagerness to get back to work. Matthew was not as smitten as Matilda, who was quite captivated by Kurt's charming manners, for Matthew suspected that very little of importance went on in his head and heart, but so long as Devon was pleased, Matthew was ready to concede a certain worth.

One afternoon in November after she had been back at work for about a week Devon came into the salon, having just put the Stevenses on the train for Williamstown.

She went into Jasper's office to tell him they were safely on their way, for he had seen a good deal of the old couple and had fallen in love with them. Jasper was studying charts; they were one of his few passions, and Devon always said he got the same pleasure looking at broken angular lines and sharp peaks that other men experienced in observing luscious curves. He remarked with some heat that he appreciated the curves too, but that his taste was more catholic than most. He glanced up as Devon came in. "Uncle Pop and Aunt Mom get off all right?"

She threw her handbag, an enormous squashed suède affair, onto Jasper's desk and collapsed into an easy chair. "Yes, they did, God love them. They are the sweetest people who ever lived. I'm a little worried about Uncle Pop, though. It seems to me he's failing a bit, more than would seem normal at his age."

"I don't know as I think that," said Jasper thoughtfully, "but you've got to remember they live at another tempo. While you were ill that was one thing, but your normal existence is a very different proposition. You've uprooted them from the life they're used to."

Jasper's tone implied criticism, and Devon was nettled.

"Nonsense, they had a fine time. The theater, restaurants, they loved it."

"O.K., O.K.," said Jasper. "I was merely pointing out that you're up to your old tricks of changing people's lives again. I don't say that your ideas may not be better than theirs, but they don't like them."

"I don't agree with you, Jasper. I don't try to change people's lives or their natures, I only want to help them develop."

Jasper laughed. "In the case of the Stevenses, who must be darn near seventy, I'd say you were a little late. Besides, it never works, really."

"Thinking of Tim?"

Jasper stirred uncomfortably. "No, dear, no," he said hastily, "I just . . ."

"Never mind, Jasper. It's all right to talk about him. You and I can talk about him often. All the dreadful, bitter feeling has been washed away. I can't pretend I no longer have a sense of loss, I imagine I'll have it till I die, but I'm not actually unhappy. I know that other scientists might consider the years Tim spent here in the business as wasted, and perhaps they were professionally, but humanly speaking, I think he gained something. I mean during the days that were so radiant, and even in our last months when we'd lost the magic, he found the strength to do what he had to, to fulfill himself. Oscar Hogarth said that to me too when he came to see me after Tim's death. He said, 'Your Timothy was a great soul, Mrs. Wainwright, and with every experience of his life he grew in stature.'"

"That's right too," said Jasper. "But Timothy was tough, just as tough as you are, Miss E., and that was the great thing about him. If you'd ever succeeded in twisting him around your little finger, it would have been tragic, because you'd have ceased to love him."

Devon laughed a little ruefully. "I guess you're right, but Tim was an extraordinary person. Damn it all, I don't see why the ordinary run-of-the-mill people should never be asked to change, why they should go on forever being selfish and unkind and thoughtless and say smugly, 'This is my nature. I shouldn't be expected to alter it.'"

A silence fell between them. "Have you seen him lately?" asked Jasper. "Fabri, I mean."

"I know who you mean. He was at the house a few times, but always very correct and platonic. I haven't seen him now in about three weeks. I believe Nicky sees him occasionally. Oh, I didn't tell you, I've had a proposal of marriage."

Jasper looked surprised. "Not from Van Alston, surely?" Devon nodded. "Isn't he a nance?"

"Jasper, you're awful. Of course he's not, he's an absolute darling. Not frightfully virile perhaps, but in no sense a pansy. Lots of Englishmen are like that."

"Look, kid, you've got troubles enough. If this fellow isn't frightfully virile, lay off, and if he is, the advice goes double. You've been passion's slave long enough."

"Don't worry, I'm not planning to wed Mr. Van Alston, though a person might do a lot worse. He's kind and entertaining and well educated and he has a lot of amusing friends. He's just a little bit . . . neutral, that's all," and Devon made a small, fluttering gesture indicating Nicky's neutrality. "He's upset about Kurt because he first brought him to the house. Poor lamb, I think he proposed to me by way of apology, a sort of consolation prize."

"For God's sake, Devon, you're hopeless."

Devon shrugged. "A lady must consider matrimony, Mr. Doolittle. After all, I'm thirty-two."

"You're thirty-six."

"Well, there you are," she said amiably. "What are you doing this evening?"

Jasper glanced at his desk calendar. "Er . . . surprisingly enough I seem to be dining with Mollie and my in-laws, we're going to the theater. Why?"

"Your plans for the evening are moderately pleasant. I have none at all. See?"

"That's ridiculous," said Jasper a little impatiently. "With your

money and beautiful houses and a certain personal appeal to which
I am not blind," and he bowed, "you could be the most renowned
hostess in New York, surrounded by crowds, dated up to the eyebrows."

"It sounds terribly gay," she said coldly.

Jasper sighed. "If you're hell-bent on matrimony, though Lord
knows what there is in it you find so interesting, maybe Van Alston
isn't such an awful idea, but have you ever thought what your life
would be like if you married Kurt?"

"For very nearly two years, mine friend, I have thought of nothing else."

"But he's a son of a bitch, Devon, a no-good bastard. Why do
you want to embroil yourself in a situation like that?"

"I can't explain it, Jasper. I don't like Kurt very much, but deep
inside me I guess I still want him, and in a highly individualistic
way I think he loves me. He resents me, but he can't let me alone."

"Just tell him you've lost all your money," Jasper said jeeringly.
"He'd be able to drop you. The Sahara Desert would look like a
baseball crowd compared to the solitude you'd enjoy."

"No, Jasper. I know it will sound to you as though I were kidding
myself, but I don't honestly think that's so. If he were a fortune
hunter he'd have given up the extramural activities long ago when
they threatened the pot of gold."

"Oh, for God's sake, don't turn his skulduggeries into virtues.
You know Kurt is a chippy chaser, but you never call him for it.
The fellow thinks he can get away with murder, and he damn near
can."

"I don't think that's fair. The only time I had real proof, which
was with Maria, I tossed him overboard, didn't I? And what's more,
my instinct about Maria was right. Look at the fine job she did
while I was ill."

"That's beside the point. My objection is that the first time Kurt
goes pixie on you and runs up the white flag, you fall into his arms."

"I haven't been in his arms in a longer time than is any of your
business."

"Then maybe that's what's the matter with you. Go ahead, take
him as a lover if he's what you want, but I implore you not to marry

him. You ought to have some kind of dignity in your life, Devon. My God, after a man like Tim, how could you?"

"I'll always have Tim," she said quietly. "He was the most wonderful thing that ever happened to me. I wish I had a child of his, but I haven't, and Tim is dead and I'm alive. After all, Kurt isn't a monster."

"He'll do in a pinch."

Suddenly she laughed. "Shall I tell you, Jasper, what my life with him would be like?"

"Shoot, Scheherazade."

"He'd be very nice about the money at first, I think. I had thought something of making a settlement on him, you know——"

"Not if you want to keep him, you dope."

"Well, I had, just the same. He could expand his business; that's one thing you've got to hand him, he has a real flair for his own work. I believe that in the beginning he'd be punctilious, he might even want to pay me back——"

"Dream on, sleeping beauty," said Jasper coldly.

"Now wait, I'm coming to the part you'll enjoy . . . but later on he'll want to start new enterprises or after the war he'll want to go to Europe and have me put bathrooms all over his old man's feudal estates, which I will first be supposed to buy back from the Government, but I will balk at these suggestions and we will have dreadful rows about money."

"What about his getting into the war, by the way?" Jasper asked sharply.

"Oh, he's very nice about that. He says he'll go any time they want him."

"Oh, he does! I notice Tim didn't wait to be asked."

"The two men are very different, dear. And it is, after all, undeniable that Tim is dead and Kurt is alive and well." There was the most exquisite and icy irony in her voice. "He flourishes. He is already bald and a little inclined to heaviness, though he is, I must say, the most immaculate human being I have ever met, but he will probably get fat as he gets older and grossly self-indulgent in the matter of food. Still, he doesn't drink, he doesn't gamble and he's not lazy. That is a great deal in his favor. In the meantime, of course, he will have countless affairs. We will hope that he will not take up with any hard-eyed trollops who will want to put the squeeze on him, figuring that if he won't pay up, his wealthy wife will, to avoid scandal. I say we will hope, for of course there is no guarantee that this won't happen. At first, though my eyes are already open, every infidelity, every selfish act will make me very unhappy. If I meet enough new men, probably I too will have affairs, out of spite and defiance and boredom. . . . And then, little by little, I shall cease to care. The day my love completely flickers out will be a great day, for I shall be free of Kurt."

There was a silence. Jasper felt sick at heart. Devon was his friend and his comrade and the darling thing in his life, and he was deeply sad. "And when did you chart this idyll for yourself?" he asked dully.

"In my bed at night."

"But I don't see how, feeling that way . . . how is it possible that you should in your wildest dreams consider marrying him?"

"Sometimes I get afraid that he won't want to marry me any more and he begins to seem quite desirable. Also I am lonely. Also, as I am already completely disillusioned, I have no place to go but up. I would be the lucky bride with no disappointments in store."

Jasper had risen and was prowling around the office. "Devon, Devon, I hope to Christ you don't marry this man."

"Oh ho, I hope so too," she said feelingly, and her eyes twinkled.

He wheeled and faced her. "That's the trouble with you, damn it. Never for one minute serious about your own affairs. If it isn't business, it's a big joke."

She smiled at him. It was one of her good days, and she looked very pretty. Still too thin from her illness, he thought, but those hollows in her cheeks gave her a rather touching appeal. "I'm very serious, Jasper darling. There are times through the night . . . Oh, by the way, I nearly forgot, I've thought of a swell new name for a perfume."

Jasper laughed. Like the mythological bird that fed on its own flesh, even Devon's broken heart in some way nourished the business. "What now?" he asked.

"Well, you know how Moreley's always wanting to have an odor remind you of something, the barnyard or your lover or your grand-mother's workbasket?"

"You've thought of a way to combine the three?"

"No, you goon, but what would really make him happy would be to have a perfume taste like something too. This new one might be made to do the trick."

"Ah?"

"Yes, it would have a rather salty flavor, should be used for universal seasoning."

"What's its name?"

Devon's soft red mouth curved in gentle raillery; in the shadow of her wide hatbrim, her eyes, a little sad, a little mocking, glowed like dark jewels. "Midnight Tears," she said.